Alphonso A. (Alphonso Alva) Hopkins

The Life of Clinton Bowen Fisk

Alphonso A. (Alphonso Alva) Hopkins

The Life of Clinton Bowen Fisk

ISBN/EAN: 9783337055417

Printed in Europe, USA, Canada, Australia, Japan

Cover: Foto ©Raphael Reischuk / pixelio.de

More available books at **www.hansebooks.com**

OF

CLINTON BOWEN FISK.

WITH A BRIEF SKETCH

OF

JOHN A. BROOKS.

BY

ALPHONSO A. HOPKINS.

NEW YORK:
FUNK & WAGNALLS,
18 AND 20 ASTOR PLACE.
1888.

To

MRS. JEANNETTE CRIPPEN FISK

— AND —

MRS. MARY FISK PARK,

THE

Worthy Wife and Daughter

OF

CLINTON B. FISK,

WHO HAVE SO TENDERLY AND LOYALLY HELPED HIM TO
HELP MANKIND

I Dedicate

THE SIMPLE STORY OF A LIFE THEY LOVE.

To

MRS. JEANNETTE CRIPPEN FISK

— AND —

MRS. MARY FISK PARK,

THE

Worthy Wife and Daughter

OF

CLINTON B. FISK,

Who have so Tenderly and Loyally Helped him to Help Mankind

I Dedicate

THE SIMPLE STORY OF A LIFE THEY LOVE.

Love cradled in a cabin of the West,
  The babe to boyhood's hunger quickly grew,
  And hungered, thirsted, for the things they knew
Who passed with men as wise; and in his breast
There throbbed a longing, always unexpressed,
  To stand some day upon the world's far blue
  Horizon, 'mid the great, the strong, the true
The world might honor, as an honored guest.
The boy to manhood built his stature well,—
  Of truth and courage, purity and grace;
The mother's love clung round him like a spell,
  And calm-eyed Duty gave him lofty place,
Till fame's fair garland on his forehead fell,
  And gladly great, and strong, and true, did greet his face.

PREFACE.

WRITING the life of a living man has its embarrassments. I realized this fact when the publishers asked me to prepare a biography of General Fisk ; I realize it yet more keenly as now I send these final though first pages to press. Yet, if my task has been rather a difficult and embarrassing one, it has been at the same time agreeable—to the biographer ; and its ample compensation has come through the nearer acquaintance made with a ripe character, the satisfaction found in close study of manly motives and unselfish acts, and the reward of a strong friendship, grown to full stature through these months of more intimate contact and more perfect trust.

I have not sought in the following chapters to be rhetorical, analytical, philosophical, or elaborate. My one purpose has been to tell, in simple, unadorned fashion, the story of a typical American career, reaching from the log-house of a pioneer to high places of honor, from the struggles of a boyhood unblest by helpful surroundings to the rounded successes of a manhood richly helpful to Church and State. It should be a source of inspiration to all men, that lives like this are possible in our country ; and all men may learn a lesson from the fact that this life has its true sources of nobleness and power in humble Christian faith, in devoted consecration to good works, and in sincere loyalty to the principles of right, and temperance, and truth.

While seeking to avoid the tone of extravagant praise, I have not cared to assume the air of an impartial narrator. History is one thing, biography is another ; and though they may be close akin, their qualities differ. I suspect that the biographer should always have sympathetic partiality for his subject, in order to the best results.

It has been thought fit and timely to include within these covers, also, a sketch of the Rev. Dr. John A. Brooks. That it is so comparatively brief and incomplete may be accredited to the fact that mainly this volume was not proposed for campaign uses, but as one of a standard series for permanent sale.

A. A. H.

Rochester, N. Y., July, 1888.

CONTENTS.

PAGE

SONNET...................................... xi

CLINTON BOWEN FISK.

CHAPTER I.

ANTECEDENTS AND BIRTHPLACE........................... 1

CHAPTER II.

PARENTAGE AND EARLY SURROUNDINGS.................... 9

CHAPTER III.

EARLY BOYHOOD IN MICHIGAN 24

CHAPTER IV.

AT THE DEACON'S AND AFTERWARD....................... 31

CHAPTER V.

BEARING THE BIRNEY FLAG.......................... ... 28

CHAPTER VI.

STRUGGLES FOR AN EDUCATION. 34

CHAPTER VII.

MARRIAGE AND BUSINESS AT COLDWATER.................. 41

CHAPTER VIII.

DOLLAR FOR DOLLAR.............................. 48

CHAPTER IX.

PAGE

A Private Soldier... 55

CHAPTER X.

A Commander of Men 61

CHAPTER XI.

Some Army Incidents 68

CHAPTER XII.

Administration Among Guerillas........................ 75

CHAPTER XIII.

Protecting the Capital................................. 82

CHAPTER XIV.

An Army Story and the Sequel......................... 89

CHAPTER XV.

Reconstructing Society................... 94

CHAPTER XVI.

The Freedman's Friend........... 101

CHAPTER XVII.

Aiding Colored Education...... 108

CHAPTER XVIII.

The Story of the Singers.............................. 114

CHAPTER XIX.

Fisk University..................... 120

CHAPTER XX.

As a Railroad Financier 126

CHAPTER XXI.
PAGE

PRESIDENT OF THE INDIAN COMMISSION 134

CHAPTER XXII.

SOME TROUBLED DAYS 142

CHAPTER XXIII.

CHURCH ACTIVITIES 147

CHAPTER XXIV.

CENTENNIAL SPEECH UPON MISSIONS 159

CHAPTER XXV.

PARTY AND PROHIBITION 169

CHAPTER XXVI.

HIS NEW JERSEY CAMPAIGN 181

CHAPTER XXVII.

CAMPAIGN SPEECHES AND CALUMNY 189

CHAPTER XXVIII.

THE NATURAL RESULTS 198

CHAPTER XXIX.

MICHIGAN'S AMENDMENT CAMPAIGN 208

CHAPTER XXX.

INEVITABLE LEADERSHIP 218

CHAPTER XXXI.

NOMINATED FOR THE PRESIDENCY. 227

CHAPTER XXXII.

AT HIS SEABRIGHT HOME 238

CHAPTER XXXIII.   PAGE

WORDS OF PATRIOTISM 249

LETTER OF ACCEPTANCE 260

JOHN ANDERSON BROOKS.

CHAPTER I.

BOYHOOD AND YOUTH 269

CHAPTER II.

PASTOR AND COLLEGE PRESIDENT 276

CHAPTER III.

MASTER WORKMAN AND PROHIBITION LEADER 283

CHAPTER IV.

NOMINATED FOR THE VICE-PRESIDENCY 292

CLINTON BOWEN FISK.

CHAPTER I.

ANTECEDENTS AND BIRTHPLACE.

In the town of Killingly, Conn., about the beginning
of the last decade of the last century, the beloved wife
of Ephraim Fisk gave birth to four babes. There were
two boys and two girls, and all lived, but the mother
paid for such uncommon maternity the tribute of her
life.

To these four thriving orphans gossip lent four indica-
tive names — Wonderful, Marvellous, Miraculous,
Strange. Other cognomen came in due time—Samuel,
David, Deborah, Miriam — more biblical, because
Ephraim Fisk was a deacon of the church and a lover of
the Book ; but people yet lived in Killingly, not many
years ago, who could recall the quadruple birth which
proved a neighborhood wonder, and the appellations
which that simple-hearted community bestowed.

With four such infants to care for, and two other
motherless children who needed care, the father had
ample reason to seek another wife. Character and circumstances commending him, he found her, and brought
her duly to his home. She bore ten children, giving
him, all told, the paternity of sixteen. The youngest of

her brood was Benjamin Bigford, named partly after herself, who, grown to manhood, married Lydia Aldrich, and became the father of six sons.

There were two strains of the Fisk family in New England three generations back—the Connecticut Fisks and the Massachusetts Fisks. Some branches spelled the name as here written, and others added a final e. All were of Lincolnshire ancestry, and all dated their record back to about the year 1700.

In the county of Lincoln, on the east coast of England, one of the mightiest movements in all church history had its genesis ; and Lincolnshire has been spoken of as the remote parent of our own Republic. From that royal habitat of conscience, conviction, and courage in the Mother Land, New England drew much of her finest Christian fibre, her undying manly spirit. It was natural that John Fiske, father of Ephraim, should take up the sword, and wield it so well as to become a major-general. It was not less natural, perhaps, that Ephraim, dying at fourscore, should be mourned by those about him as a peacemaker and a gentle man of God. Nor was it strange that Wilbur Fisk, another of John's descendants and first cousin of Benjamin B., should leave strong impress upon later generations as a profound theologian and President of the Wesleyan University at Middletown. Ecclesiastical and military tastes appear to have blended quite harmoniously in the Fisk blood, even until now.

John Fiske, born in old Salem, Mass., April 10th, 1744, who rose to the rank of major-general in 1792, was a naval officer during the Revolution, and commanded the first vessel commissioned by Massachusetts, the " Tyrannicide." He took part in many combats, and was placed in command of the State ship " Massachusetts " December 10th, 1777. Afterward he engaged in commerce, became wealthy, and wielded wide influence. But while his early life was of the sanguinary sort, his father was a clergyman—Rev. Samuel Fiske—and his son Ephraim, as has been intimated, had the fervent spirit of simple Christian faith, and devoted himself to promoting neighborly fellowship and establishing neighborhood peace. The name of Fisk, indeed, has been long and closely identified with church work and religious effort, though often found in the annals of war. Dr. Ezra Fisk was a conspicuous Presbyterian divine ; Pliny Fisk went as a missionary of that church to Syria, and died there ; Nathan Fisk was a Congregational minister of high repute ; Nathan Welby Fisk, his son, became a theological teacher at Andover ; and a younger Samuel Fisk, better known by his *nom de plume* " Dunn Brown," left the pulpit for a soldier's work during our late war, and in that service gave his life. In the line of letters, too, the Fisks have been eminent, giving to literature Dr. Willard Fiske, and Professor John Fiske, and Helen Hunt Jackson, daughter of Professor Nathan Welby Fisk.

Early branches of the family in this country seem to have been well off in worldly goods, as likewise well endowed with educational and religious tendencies. Ephraim and his brother Isaac were graduates of Brown University, and therefore had advantages which at that time only the wealthier class enjoyed. Wilbur, son of Isaac—born in Brattleborough, Vt., 1792—had opportunities equal to those given his father and uncle, and gifts evidently superior to theirs, or ambition greater. But Benjamin B. was less fortunate. Perhaps those sixteen children consumed unduly of his father's substance ; it may have melted away in bad business ventures, or losses by fire and flood. There was not much money, at any rate, in the household where Benjamin B. grew up, and no college course awaited him outside. His chief inheritance was that so common among Americans—hard work, and strength and will to do it. Largely he must make his own future, with little help of the schools, and unhelped by paternal hands. His education was barely sufficient for the common need of a mechanic's career, on which he early set out.

Killingly was and is a township of Windham County, twenty-eight miles northeast of Norwich, and not farther from Providence. It borders on the Rhode Island line, and forms a part of some rather sterile country not remarkable for wealth-making possibilities. It is not now agriculturally productive in high degree; and though manufacturing interests have changed that region much since the first decades of our century, it may be, even yet, as then it surely was, less fruitful of material fortune than of genuine manhood. To Rhode Island many went who craved religious liberty, when elsewhere it did not so much abound, and who saw in the pure democratic government of that miniature State our true American idea realized; and with like feeling and spirit many located in Eastern Connecticut, where Rhode Island impulses were dominant, and for topographical, religious, and patriotic reasons made Providence their central rallying-point. But as years passed, and population multiplied, the region held less of promise for each young man and woman within it, and the eyes of some turned wistfully to the West.

Benjamin Fisk, through boyhood and youth inured to labor, had learned the trade of a blacksmith, and wanted to ply it on some more lucrative field. Lydia Aldrich, grown from girlhood to the same narrow chances which in Killingly were his, and having linked her life with his own, was willing with him to seek the wider field of his desire. Killingly born and bred, she came of Welsh descent, and in her veins yet flowed somewhat of the sturdy faith, the heroic courage, and the unfailing will which her ancestors knew. Her nature was deep, womanly, tender. Certain gifts of poetic insight must have been hers, allied with superior practical traits. Giving heart and hand to the young and ambitious artisan who won both, she therewith gave to him a companion-ship of the best womanly type, and to his children a motherhood sweet, uplifting, beneficent, with a disposi-tion wherein native paternal severity was mellowed by maternal tenderness.

Hopeful and eager, ardent of belief in the better op-portunities which a new country would afford, in the fall of 1822 Benjamin and Lydia, with Cyrus B. and Leander, their baby boys, left Killingly for Livingston County, N. Y. Other of Ephraim's children had settled in the northern part of that State ; kinsfolk of Lydia had preceded them to the same locality whither they went ; it was not an untried thing for people to migrate ; yet this journey of the young Puritans might well enough have appeared momentous. It was surely a great journey for those times. Eastern Connecticut was then as far from Western New York as Alaska from Maine to-day. Western New York was " on the frontier." Railroads were undreamed of. The Erie Canal did not exist. Livingston County was but the recent haunt of Red Stocking and his dusky race. It was all " the Genesee country," in popular parlance, west of the river Gene-see, until Niagara's foaming border line. Men came to it as settlers, lured by the beauties of a region rich in Indian romance, agriculturally fertile, and full of promise. But to steady-going, home-staying New Englanders it seemed the edge of the world.

You will search far to find a more lovely valley than that of the upper Genesee, across which Geneseo, from the eastern slope, looks westward with serene content. There lived the elder Wadsworth, like some feudal lord, who held in fee vast areas round about, his broad estate comprising part of the original Phelps and Gorham Purchase from Massachusetts, obtained when that section of New England had right to sell a portion of New York. There lives to-day a Wadsworth of the third generation, still holding much of the old family manor intact. In that fair domain, before any Wadsworth came to title-ship, the Six Nations had their Council House, and across the upper Genesee their favorite trails were made. There dwelt Mary Jemison, "the white woman," on lands conferred by the natives with whom she cast her lot. It was an inviting locality to which migrated Benjamin Fisk and Lydia, and in which they established themselves. The valley's breadth was beautiful then as now—its flat bottoms thickly wooded where the river wound along, its rolling uplands lifting gently above them and adding to the landscape a varied charm—while farther south its narrower sweep grew yet more picturesque, until at Portage Falls heroic grandeur wore consummate grace, and wed itself to legend and to song.

Where the valley is broadest, counting bottoms and uplands both, in the midst of rare pastoral loveliness and surrounded by uncommon wealth of historic association, stood and stands a little hamlet known then as Clapp's Corners, called Greigsville now. Its first settler was Ellis Clapp, who married an aunt of Lydia Fisk, and whose son, Amos Clapp, was long time Government Printer at Washington. Three miles above York, from which the township takes its name, and five miles below Genesco, Livingston's county-seat, it was the natural centre of quite a territory contiguous, and offered to one of Benjamin Fisk's avocation steady employment and fair pay. There he located, and there he led a busy life of varied, vigorous activities. He was blacksmith, wagon-builder, and general mechanic for the country round. Muscular and willing, equipped with a fine physique, he did not shrink from hard toil. His shops became the source of mechanical supply for farmers all up and down the valley, and their proprietor soon acquired local repute as a man of intelligence, enterprise, and character. He took rank as captain in the militia, and was deferred to as a leading spirit in town affairs. A contract, still in existence, which he drew, and which, with others, as a trustee, he executed, for building a school-house in the town of York, shows that he could put language on paper with precision, and that he possessed good business sense. The fact that his colleagues appointed him to draw such an instrument shows that they had confidence in his ability and good judgment.

The hamlet did not grow; there was no special reason why it should. It is, indeed, no larger now than fifty years ago; and the marvel, when one sees it, is how anything can be so very small of its age. But the Fisk household increased, and household requirements multiplied. Two more boys, Welcome V. and Horace A., made glad the father's heart and kept active the mother's hands. The name of one bespoke the reception of each, yet both added burdens of care and need. Mistress Lydia bore her part in providing for family wants. She washed wool and spun yarn and wove cloth. She did whatever she could. She was the helpmeet essential, amid surroundings like theirs.

Then Captain Fisk was called on, it is said, for some
service in connection with the Erie Canal—contempt-
nously alluded to often, in those days, as " Clinton's
Ditch." What that service was cannot be verified, and
whether any service was rendered is open to doubt, for
the Erie Canal ran full thirty miles from Clapp's Corners,
and Captain Fisk's labors were confined there ; but if
he had no part in the making of that water-way, as is
the probable fact, he somehow made the acquaintance of
Governor DeWitt Clinton, or grew to know much about
and greatly to admire him, perhaps to think him their
friend. So when a fifth boy came to the Fisk domicile,
in witness of regard for the governor, and borrowing
from the mother's family tree, they called him Clinton
Bowen.

CHAPTER II.

CLINTON BOWEN FISK was born December 8th, 1825. Clapp's Corners had not a dozen houses, and none of them was pretentious. The home in which Clinton first saw light was not the birthplace of his youngest brothers. Two streets, forming a country cross-roads, comprised the hamlet ; and the Fisks originally located on the road running north and south—the same which, continued three fourths of a mile farther up the valley, toward Geneseo, in like manner formed and still forms part of another small settlement, known as Greigsville then, called now South Greigsville. Before Clinton's advent they changed to a lot on the road running east and west, about forty rods west of the four corners.

The site they chose there was very charming. It was on the north side of the street, facing the upper Genesee's blue southern boundary line, some twenty odd miles away. The river itself cannot be seen from this point, since it is two miles distant, and hidden by a rise in the upland on the east ; but wide reaches of intervale stretch magnificently southward, and end in a lofty range of hills belting the southern sky from west to east. Half a mile farther west, up the valley's gentle western slope, the view sweeps unobstructed over this depression in the upland, over the ridge beyond, over the fertile Genesee flats, and traverses not less than forty miles of eastern horizon dotted with farm buildings and village groups.

Half a mile eastward, on the upland ridge, one commands the same far-reaching prospect, with a western background, if he turn to note it, only less captivating, where sleep the twin hamlets of Greigsville in a minor valley of their own, and covet nothing more.

The house to which Benjamin Fisk removed Lydia and their four boys, and which was hallowed soon with the sacredness of a new maternity, was built for unhallowed purposes. Before the Fisks converted it into a domicile it was a distillery—one of those modest manufactories of liquid death so common in our country sixty years gone by. Its conversion to better uses can be credited to no spirit of local reform, for there were few temperance reformers then, and Benjamin Fisk was not one of those few. Perhaps the distillery did not pay. Larger affairs may have rendered its product unprofitable. As a distillery it must have been small ; as a residence it was not large. Eighteen by twenty-two feet at the most, and but one story high, it could not have contained more than three or four rooms, and small ones at that. It is standing yet, in habitable preservation, and belongs to the Delaware and Lackawanna Railroad Company, whose thoroughfare cuts clean across the original five-acre lot on which the house was built. Its batten sidings have never seen paint, and look weatherworn, though they are not the same which covered the frame at first. It has grown half a story in height since Mistress Lydia made it homelike, and a small wing has been added on the west end.

On a summer's day in 1884 General Fisk went to see it. He had never been back to his birthplace since carried away in his mother's arms. The discovery of salt-fields in that neighborhood, and a certainty that the whole region was underlaid by salt beds, had set speculation rampant.   Sharp bargainers were going about leasing or buying, under various pretences, all the land thought available for salt-producing purposes.   With a friend the general sought out old residenters, whose recollections might run farthest back.   Two sisters were cited—maiden ladies by the name of Tuttle, living alone ; and he called upon them.   But when General Fisk began his neighborhood inquiries, explaining that here was his birthplace, the elder sister interrupted him.

"You needn't come around making believe any such thing," with quick asperity she said.   "I know all you salt speculators, and what you're after.   You'd like to get our land, but you can't have it.   We won't sell it or lease it to you at any price, and you might just as well go along."

General Fisk's keen sense of the ludicrous was excited, and he greatly enjoyed her remarks.   Her harsh and suspicious mood melted soon, however, as he went on to establish his identity and prove his errand, and she said at last :

"Yes, I remember the morning you were born.   I remember rocking the cradle, with you in it, months afterward, when your mother went out to weave some full-cloth at a neighbor's on the hill.   You had a good mother.   Step to the door with me, and I will show you the very house where she lived."

It was duly pointed out, not far up the street, and then they sat down again to inquiry and reminiscence. Presently, and picking up a church journal lying on the centre-table, the lady asked :

"Are you the General Fisk this paper tells about ?— the one who is so much of a temperance man ?"

The general recognized his own denominational organ, and answered :

"Yes, I suppose I am."

"Well," she went on, giving a little chuckle characteristic of her, " I don't know as I ought to tell you, but the truth is, your father wasn't just the sort of man you are."

"Do you mean that he did not believe in temperance ?" asked the general.

"Not exactly that," was her hesitating reply ; "but he wasn't just like you ;" and she chuckled again. "He would drink sometimes."

"Didn't have a monopoly of that sort of thing, did he ?" the general inquired.

"Oh, no, not a bit of it !" she made haste to say, punctuating with a chuckle as she ran on. "'Most everybody drank then, and your father was in the military, you know ; and on training days and Fourth of July he drank. But he was a good man and a first-class mechanic, and a man of influence."

She has borne similar testimony since, with more freedom of expression, perhaps, than in the general's presence she could feel ; and she tells, with some pride, how he called to see her, and what she said. She insists that Benjamin Fisk was not a church-going or religious man ; that he seldom or never heard preaching while at that place save at a funeral, with one droll exception. And she chuckles and shakes her plump form more than ever when she recounts that.

A minister came along one day, so her story goes, who wanted his horse shod. He was a Baptist minister, and he lived at York. His church was the nearest house of worship, if at that time, as is declared, their only place of religious meeting, at South Greigsville, was a school-house. He drew up beside the shops of Captain Fisk and asked what would be the charge for shoeing his horse all round.

"Preach me a sermon, right there on that horse-block," the blacksmith said, "and I'll do the job and not charge you a cent."

It may be that Captain Fisk was more religious than the old lady admits ; it is possible that he craved the preacher's service, even at considerable cost, when close to hand. Or he may have possessed that swift sense of humor for which his son is noted, and may have seized upon the idea of a wayside sermon as offering some elements of sport. He shod the horse, and then demanded his pay. The preacher, nothing loth, mounted the horse-block, and solemnly, deliberately, set about the task of compensation. He chose a text, announced a theme, divided and subdivided it, and went through with his exegesis, argument, and application, as thoroughly as if facing his congregation from the pulpit. And so far as known that one auditor never repented his bargain. He sat the sermon through. And if there was any joke in the transaction, it may not have been all against the preacher.

Whether religious and church-going or not, Benjamin Fisk had a creed. He was a Universalist. He believed that all men will be saved. He had not held to the orthodox faith of his fathers, to which his good wife still clung. Of a virile, unyielding, rather severe nature, masterful and combative, he could more easily step outside the narrow lines of individual trust than walk within them. His temperament, of the more heroic, assertive order, grew rebellious against meek personal submission to the personal requirements of orthodox faith. His dominant characteristics may have come from his grandfather, who fought so bravely on the quarter-deck, as the dominant characteristics of his son, Clinton B., must have come from *his* grandfather, the gentle-souled peacemaker of Killingly, or from the maternal side.

CHAPTER III.

AFTER eight years of close economy and hard work at Clapp's Corners, Captain Fisk concluded to go farther West. He was not rapidly getting ahead, and there were the five lads to think of and provide for. Better chances could be found, he felt certain; and in May, 1830, he sought them in the new territory of Michigan.

That was a long way from "the Genesee Country," but, as compared with their former removal, an easy way. They went to Buffalo with teams; from there the journey was by steamboat to Detroit. Taking passage on "the staunch, low-pressure 'William Peacock,'" as described in the handbills then, they encountered one of the gales for which Lake Erie is famous, and were blown back into port. It was a stormy passage throughout, and occupied nine days. Clinton's older brothers remember it well, and speak of it in tones which imply less lively enjoyment than might have been expected. One of them, Welcome V., came near drowning in the river at Detroit, after they reached there. Leaving the wharf, to see a bear-show opposite, he slipped off a log and sank. As he was disappearing the third time, a sailor caught him with a boat-hook and drew him out. Life was apparently gone, and the word went round that a boy was drowned. But resuscitation followed, and just as Mrs. Fisk was counting her children, to see if the reported loss was hers, the dripping lad was brought to her arms still more dead than alive.   Thus for the wife and mother Michigan's first greeting had in it trouble and pain, with an outcome of great joy.

Lenawee County, in southeastern Michigan, was at that time alluring many settlers.   The river Raisin traversed it, upon the banks of which occurred the bloody massacre of 1813.   It was all a wilderness nearly, with wet, swampy bottoms, rich, wooded uplands, and Potawatamie Indians in plenty.   These latter yet hung about the neighborhood, always friendly and inoffensive, but often a nuisance.   Daniel Porter had gone there from York a year earlier and built a log-house two and a half miles north of Clinton, which was five miles north of the then small village of Tecumseh.   Clinton had been started and named in 1828 by Alpheus Kies, who there and then opened a log hotel.   When Captain Fisk went to it, the place had two hotels and a blacksmith shop, and little else but its name.   It has been said that this was given by Clinton's father in equal recognition of the boy, Clinton Fisk, and the governor, DeWitt Clinton ; but such statement is in part erroneous.   Kies gave the name in honor of New York's governor before Captain Fisk applied it to his boy.   It was a mere coincidence that Clinton Fisk's boyhood should be spent in the town whose name he bore.

The Fisks at first moved into Daniel Porter's house, and lived there six weeks.   Then they bought out the Clinton blacksmith, one Mordy, locally known as " the bell-maker," because he made so many bells for cattle to wear.   His log shop stood on an acre lot upon the east side of the north and south road, only two lots removed from the present home of Welcome V. Fisk, and near the present centre of Clinton.   Captain Fisk had spent about all his ready money in the transfer of family and effects, and reached Clinton with but one dollar and fifty cents left. They must therefore make shift for awhile as best they could, and cheerfully they did it. To the shop they added a log and slab attachment, small and rude, and there for two years they lived, the ringing anvil near at hand, the smoking forge equally close, the wheezy bellows puffing half the time by day, and from the wide-mouthed chimney scattering a frequent shower of sparks by night. The first recollection which abides with General Fisk is of seeing his father stampede the Indians, who often crowded into the shop and annoyed him, by swinging a white-hot iron bar from the forge to the anvil, so that the blistering scales flew from it in profusion and stung their naked legs. It was his accidental way of clearing out the Potawatamies when they became too friendly and familiar. And it never failed.

Captain Fisk got on here more encouragingly than hitherto. The country was fast settling up. Several men followed him to Clinton from the township he had left, and the place bid fair to thrive. He worked early and late, ambitious to secure home and fortune for Lydia and their six growing lads, another boy having been added to the number since they came. He managed to buy eighty acres of wild land two miles away and to pay for it, with the help of some cloth which Lydia wove before their removal and brought with her, and which proved valuable as an article of exchange ; he also built a small frame house near the shop, into which they gladly and proudly went. Then the strong man sickened within six months after that better home was his, and when all their prospects began to brighten and give them gladder hope. Smitten with typhus-fever, the result of malarious conditions, no doubt, he mastered the first attack and was getting well, when slight exposure caused a relapse that carried him off. This was in 1832, and his remains were the first which found sepulture in the graveyard at Clinton. A Methodist minister, Elder Bangs, preached the funeral sermon.

With her six boys—one but a mere babe—her quarter section of wild land, her shop and her encumbered new home, Mrs. Fisk faced rather a sombre future. The home was given up, and the land sold for three hundred dollars. This money she expended in erecting a frame cottage upon another lot, and there she bravely struggled to keep her family together. How busy and brave she must have been! She kept boarders, and did laundry work, and bound hats ; and still she found time to care for the neighborhood sick. All who knew her then and are living now speak warmly of the unselfishness she exhibited, the unfailing courage and noble womanliness that were hers. She was loving and true and strong.

When his father died, Clinton B. was a chubby little fellow less than four years old. From his mother he inherited a sunny disposition, which quickly won him friends. Sportive, fun-loving, and frank, he grew to be the village favorite. An eager thirst for knowledge early possessed him, and almost before any one knew it he had learned to read. In like self-helpful way he learned to write. On a dry-goods box one day, in front of the village store, he saw painted in compact, back-hand Italic script the address of

Knox, Smith & Townsend.

CLINTON, Mich.,

Lenawee Co.

He was captivated by the neat style of lettering, which some expert shipping clerk had achieved, in the remote city of New York. With impetuous desire, Clinton sought the merchants named, and asked if they would sell him that box. They would, but the small price put upon it was quite beyond his reach. Disappointed and sorrowful, he turned about to leave, but then an alternative suggested itself. Would they not sell him the one board on which that pretty writing was? Liking the boy, the merchants said they would do that, and that he might have it for so much, or so little.

"And will you take pay in eggs?" he further asked.

Yes, they would accept eggs in payment.

"And will you trust me?" was his final inquiry.

They would even do that. And after the bargain was thus closed he took the coveted board and ran homeward, big with elation, to sit down and calculate how long before he could finish paying his debt with the eggs given him as a premium for careful watching of the nests and gathering of their contents. Having patiently figured out this problem, he set himself to patient imitation of the backhand letters, finding in them more than half the alphabet. The broad, smooth hearthstone before the ample fireplace was all the slate he had, and lying there, close to the roaring flames as he could bear, he practised writing, as days and nights wore on, until he mastered the style, and wrote it easily and well. In the same position he studied Daboll's "Arithmetic," and on the same stone surface he set down and wrought out the simpler problems Daboll gave. To the heat of that fireplace and another, so long directed upon his young head while prostrate he wrote and ciphered, his early baldness was unquestionably due.

One by one the four boys older than Clinton were put out to live with farmers and mechanics in the vicinity, and thus maternal burdens grew less. Cyrus, Leander,

and Horace had comfortable homes, and fairly enjoyed
them ; Welcome fell into the hands of a fiery, brutal
Irishman, and finally ran away in self-defence, and
much to his advantage, though he did not go far or stay
long. Their mother hoped that Clinton might be kept
with her, but it seemed wiser, at last, that he, too,
should be making his own way. Across the river and
the river flats, beyond where Indian bands had often
camped since the village began, in a small log-house
containing a big chimney, lived Deacon Elijah Wright.
It was barely a mile from the cottage of his mother, and
there it was decided Clinton should go.

He pleaded for the chance himself. But nine years
old though he was, the hunger for an education had
seized him and would not be satisfied. Somewhere and
somehow he must have the school opportunities which
his hard-working mother could not afford. And though
he missed no offer of a penny for errands he could do,
and saved each coin paid him toward the purpose he had
formed, there was little prospect of success unless he
should accept the proposition made. He heard it, in his
mother's kitchen, his heart beating one tattoo within his
breast and his heels beating another upon the washtub
whereon he sat. By the terms proposed he was to live
with and work for Deacon Wright until twenty-one
years old, was to have three months of "schooling"
each year for at least four years, and when "of age"
he should be paid two hundred dollars in cash and given
a horse, saddle, and bridle and two suits of clothes. It
seemed a magnificent opportunity, and much as he loved
the good mother and hated to leave her, he was in a
tremor of fear lest she might pass it by.

"O my !" he ejaculated, "such a chance as that !
I'll go, mother ! I'll go !"

And so he settled it. Go he did next day. There was a wide, wide world of knowledge outreaching before him, and he could explore it, or so he fancied, from those paths near by which focused at the deacon's farm. So glad and grand a thing it seemed, this chance of his, and so glad and elate was he as he kissed his mother good-by at the door, that looking back he wondered why her face grew swiftly sad, and why she put her apron often to her eyes till he was out of sight.

CHAPTER IV.

It was but an ordinary pioneer home to which this hungry lad so gladly went. In it and about it there was enough to busy a chore-boy from year's end to year's end. He was not allowed much leisure, nor did he have a harder time than has or had the average farmer's son. But he lacked the advantages which to-day the average boy enjoys. Books were few in the neighborhood, and his craving for them was constant, insatiable. His three months yearly at the log school-house but served to whet an almost abnormal appetite for knowledge, and render him more passionately eager for that which was denied. His chief opportunities for study were not in school, but at the fireplace, as in the home he had left ; and there, stretched flat upon the hearthstone, he lay long evenings through, conning the lessons to be learned, devouring every printed page that he could capture. When tired of study he would turn upon his back and count the stars that crossed his field of vision through the yawning chimney's throat.

The first literary possession he could call his own was a mutilated copy of Shakespeare. He happened to see it one day in the hands of a neighbor, who was wiping his razor upon its leaves, tearing off one at a time as needed for that purpose. This vandalism had gone on so long that two or three plays were missing already, but

still he begged to buy it.   The farmer consented to sell,
and Clinton paid him by hoeing corn two days.   He felt
a sturdy pride in his purchase, damaged though it was ;
and what remained of Shakespeare he read as best
he could, catching even then, we may believe, some
glimmer of the great poet's finest meanings and grandest
thoughts.   Beginning with this one volume, he established a genuine circulating library, a shoe-box for his
bookcase, of which the emasculated Shakespeare, an
entire " Robinson Crusoe," a worn " Pilgrim's Progress," a " Paradise Lost," and a " Columbian Orator,"
formed the largest part.   If these were not all entertain-
ing books for so young a lad, one of them, at least, had
fascination in it, and they were such as neighborhood
resources would permit.

Clinton was bright, quick-witted, ambitious.   He had
an exceptional memory.   He thought much about what
he read, and talked of it freely with those around him.
The man he served had fair intelligence, and a sensible
appreciation of the superiority knowledge gave.   Perhaps as much encouragement was given the boy by those
he daily met as prudence could justify.   He worked
faithfully, often hard, but all his spare moments were
given to reading.   His thirst for knowledge grew daily
more intense.   Like many another lad, he dreamed of
broad endeavor and splendid achievement, and felt in
eager haste for manhood's royal morrow.

It was in front of Deacon Wright's fireplace that his
earliest anti-slavery convictions took root.   The deacon
was an abolitionist of the original type—tenacious, ardent ;
and so was his wife.   They held long and animated con-
versations over slavery, and all the innate hatred of
Clinton's boyish heart quickened and grew strong against
it.   Yet that he should ever have such part as came to

him in caring for slavery's effects, no prophetic aspirations might foretell.

The year after he went to live at Deacon Wright's, a
veteran Baptist missionary, Rev. Robert Powell, held
revival meetings in a school-house two miles west. He
attended these, and became interested. Young as he
was, he had more mental maturity than many older
youth ; and back of him was a religious lineage unusual, from which he had inherited unusually strong religious tendencies. His temperament was responsive to
the touch of divine things. He had read so much, too,
that he was well grounded in the fundamentals of Christian faith.

One night the preacher's text read : " Come unto me
all ye that labor and are heavy laden, and I will give
you rest " (*Matthew* 11 : 28). A weary working boy,
tired with the labors of the day, Clinton had trudged
over to the meeting. That Scripture touched him very
deeply. He listened with a new tenderness to the sermon which followed, and afterward went forward with
others for prayers, while the congregation sang, " Alas !
and did my Saviour bleed ?" Across his soul there
rolled a burden of conscious guilt unknown till that
hour. He thirsted for the personal comfort of Christ.
Then came the hymned confession and covenant of those
about him, sweet and pulsing with recognition and
avowal—

" But drops of grief can ne'er repay
    The debt of love I owe ;
Here, Lord, I give myself away,
    'Tis all that I can do."

Upon the wings of faith and song his burden lifted.
" I adopted the statement and pledge as mine," he testified later, " and was born into the kingdom." A happy

walk across the fields homeward finished the day for him, and in his life it formed a way-mark memorable above all others.

He was baptized a little later, on a Sunday afternoon, in the river Raisin, by Elder Powell, and joined the Baptist Church. A sturdy little Baptist he remained, too, for some time afterward, as affirmed by one of his playmates still living in Clinton ; an earnest believer in and advocate of immersion, and quite well read in the *pros and cons* thereof. Best of all, as this gentleman testifies, he was an active, working Christian, solicitous for human souls. He talked often with the boys who worked and played with him about religious things, and prayed with them as well ; and though he did not cease to be a boy himself, alive, alert, with genuine boyish pranks and innocent mischief, they knew that he was devoted and sincere.

His lips were clean. Only twice does he remember to have soiled them with an oath. On the first occasion he was burning brush in a back lot half a mile away from every one but God. He had heard much profanity, as in those days every boy did hear it. Young tongues and pure could easily echo oaths. They seemed to many youth the manly form of emphasis. Vexed and fretted by some obstacle his hands encountered, Clinton voiced a mild expletive, which did not violate the third commandment. It shocked him, however, coming from himself. It violated his integrity of Christian speech. Conscience began at once to goad him and give him punishment. He could neither be happy nor work on until, kneeling by a stump near by, he had acknowledged his fault and sin, and implored God's forgiveness. And of his second slip he repented in similar swift fashion, never to err that way again.

As Clinton read and studied on before the fireplace in the farmer's home, or, often, with book in hand, about his duties as chore-boy, there grew within him a desire for wider things. This chance that had appeared at first so fine did not develop as he supposed it would, or in the ratio of his developing aspirations. At best he could count upon two or three years only, in the aggregate, of school advantages, before he should come " of age " and command his time ; and he daily hungered for more, and of a better sort. At length hesitation yielded to hope, and he laid the case before Deacon Wright. But the deacon failed to see any way of satisfaction. Then Western, his younger brother—so named because of the Western fever which brought Captain Fisk to Michigan—fell ill and died. The older boys were scattered, as has been said. Their mother was left entirely alone. She missed her baby, and grew more lonesome and unhappy week by week. She coveted Clinton, and sought to secure his return. Between her and Deacon Wright there were many interviews and seasons of consideration, with the subject of them all a deeply interested listener or participant. It grew to be a grave question, in his mind, whether the terms his master proposed, as conditioning his release, could be met ; and he spent anxious hours with the deacon in discussing them. At last concessions were made which Mrs. Fisk accepted, and after two years and a little more of farm life Clinton found himself back with his mother, sharing cheerfully the poverty she bore, because free to work out, with her consent and help, the better things of which ambitiously he dreamed.

He did not find the doors of opportunity wide open even now. It was not easy for the boy of eleven to overcome such difficulties as hedged him in. But he was at home, and his mother's counsels were wise, her love was great. There must come brighter days farther on. He should be her brave and cheerful helper. Somehow they should get along. He might go to school, when school there was ; the way would grow kinder by and by.

Blessed is the lad who has a royal mother-heart to comfort him in such sweet and blessed wise ! Blessed is the man who can look back upon a boyhood ennobled and inspired by such a mother-heart !

Whatever he could do Clinton did to help the mother who so helped him. All sorts of odd jobs were thrown into his hands by neighbors and clerks, each of whom liked the lad and wanted to see him succeed. He ran errands, he carried packages, he watered horses, he drove cows ; he took such pay as came. Often his compensation was in some printed form or other—a stray magazine, or an old newspaper, or a well-thumbed book which none coveted but he. In this manner he acquired and read " The Pickwick Papers," then running as a serial in a Philadelphia journal, and reverting from the regular subscriber to himself. His taste did not discriminate against anything in the shape of print that fortune threw in his way. He read omnivorously, with varying interest, to be sure, but always interested. Whatever treated of the Revolution or slavery, or was adapted to declamation, he caught at quickest. The native instincts of an orator were his, and he soon committed to memory every page in the old " Columbian " collection, reciting favorite pieces often to an imaginary audience, and thrilling with the effort thus made.

It must have been just after his return from life on the deacon's farm that he first publicly appeared in an oratorical capacity. With some other active lads he planned a Fourth of July celebration, and was designated to deliver the address. With all possible care he wrote it out ; Schoolmaster Tidd corrected it and perhaps a little improved it ; and then he carefully memorized the production. It glowed with revolutionary spirit and patriotism. It was radical with anti slavery sentiment. Its delivery, in a grove by the riverside, before a real audience numbering about all the people in that neigh-borhood, brought the climax of exultation and exaltation to Clinton B. Some grown-up patriots had taken the affair partly in hand and given it more general char-acter, and it surprised the town. Having organized a little company of cadets, Clinton marched them about the village, some hint of his military qualifications thus early manifest, and halted them in front of the Eagle Hotel. The landlord, one Parks, invited them in to drink. But that was a cold-water company, made so through the influence of a cold-water captain. The company hesitated, and the landlord urged.

" Can we have anything to drink we want ?" inquired young Captain Fisk.

The landlord said they could.

" Then we'll all come in and take some lemonade," said the captain ; and in they went.

The result was a speedy dearth of lemons and sugar in that hotel, and widespread enjoyment of the landlord's discomfiture.

CHAPTER V.

THE Presidential campaign of 1840, with its " log-cabin and hard cider " features, is well remembered by the middle-aged men of to-day. Especial interest was felt in it throughout southeastern Michigan, because two of the candidates had figured actively in a fiercer and bloodier campaign on that same soil a generation previous. General Harrison's Indian warfare along the Maumee and up and down the Raisin had not yet become ancient history ; and in that wilder campaigning Major Richard M. Johnson, of Kentucky, had taken conspicuous part. Now Harrison was the Whig nominee for President, and Johnson had been nominated for Vice-President by the Democrats. The name of each was familiar, from local association, in all that range of country round about Detroit, on both sides the Canadian line.

Johnson came to Lenawee County, and spoke in Clinton. He had been a gallant soldier in his early manhood ; he was a brilliant orator now, with the dash and fervor characteristic of Southern speakers. The boy Clinton went to hear him, though not a Democrat.

For it should be recorded that while all the other lads in his neighborhood were Democrats or Whigs, Clinton Fisk went with an unpopular cause, and shouted for liberty. His party was the Liberty Party. Descended from ancestors who ever held strong moral and political convictions, he was born to hate that great prophetic fact in our national life which begat abolitionism and inspired political organization to put the fact away. Quickly and faithfully he identified himself with that organization, and felt a sturdy pride in his alliance which could not be repressed. And while his mates were growing up to walk in the partisan way of their fathers, and his well-grown brothers would soon vote the Democratic ticket, he stood out with boyish boldness for the little party scorned and sneered at on every side. His faith in it never faltered. With brave and resolute heart he could hold alone by what he thought was right, and feel no sense of shame.

Those were exciting days when vast crowds gathered to shout and sing for "Tippecanoe and Tyler too." Hard cider flowed abundantly at every assemblage of the Whigs, and it may be true, as has been said, that many a drunkard in after years could trace his downward course to "log-cabin" gatherings during the summer and fall of 1840. There were processions and barbecues and banners everywhere. The very air grew heavy with political feeling and party strife. Even youngest lads were eager in party demonstration, and vied with each other, and excited men, in the heated clamor of the times.

It humiliated Clinton Fisk to see the little Whigs and Democrats bearing their neat banners and flags about, gay with color and glorious with possible victory, while no cheers went up and no flag was lifted for the candidates of his choice. He wanted a banner, too, and determined to have it. By selling molasses candy he earned a little cash, and with it purchased three fourths of a yard of cotton sheeting. Some axle grease served him for paint, and with that he inscribed, in crude black letters upon the white cloth, the ticket which had few friends :

BIRNEY AND LEMOYNE.

Having a banner, he needed but a staff to bear it as proudly as his mates were bearing theirs. The need was urgent, and his resources were meagre. He must take part in the processions, large and small, and his flag must be held aloft. So he justified, to himself, the appropriation of his mother's broom-handle, after sawing off the brush, and on it he nailed the banner " with that strange device," and bore it to victory. To victory, because he had to fight for the privilege of carrying it at all, and won his first actual battle in life upon that issue of reform. The other boys made a vigorous attack upon him when he appeared with it in their midst, and he made still more vigorous defence. It was a lively *mêlée* which followed, and in it flags, staffs, boys, and a broomstick were sadly mixed up, if not much demoralized ; but the Birney banner triumphed, and Clinton bore it exultantly and unmolested from that time. It may be his exultation was a bit discounted, however, when his mother spanked him for spoiling her broom. Whether she often punished him that way he does not testify, though he often refers with a sigh to " those *palmy* days."

He went to the Democratic meeting at which Johnson spoke, and with his banner perched himself just front of the platform, in the grove where a crowd was gathered. Ossian E. Dodge, a then popular minstrel, sat there, with other singers forming a quartette—the first Clinton had ever heard. The Birney flag caught the minstrel's eye, and to the Birney boy he said :

" See here, boy, go away with your dirty rag !"

Then the Birney boy was led indignantly to prophesy.

"This dirty rag will one day swallow up all other political banners!" he declared, his shrill tones quivering with a consciousness of insult.

It may not be amiss to add just here that in 1860, speaking for the Republican candidates at another town in Michigan, General Fisk met Ossian E. Dodge again, singing for party success, and publicly reminded him of the incident above given, and of that prophecy uttered twenty years before.

Colonel Johnson's oratory captivated Clinton, and made him wish to hear more of it. Next day the brilliant Kentuckian was to speak at Tecumseh, and the boy grew crazy to be there. What matter if it was not a gathering of *his* party ?—*his* party had not yet come to the mass-meeting estate—all the same he was eager to see the crowd, and hear the music, and catch its inspiration. The martial spirit of his father and of certain forefathers rose and thrilled within him at thought of the splendid assemblage, the sharp vigor of fife and drum, perhaps the glitter of military parade, and the sure glow of impassioned speech. Then the glamour of heroism and romance hung about the orator's personality, for he it was, as campaign stories ran, who with his own hand slew the great Tecumseh upon the bank of the Thames. What boy with a soldier's future waiting even far ahead could not feel the strong allurement of such a candidate, with oratorical power such as his !

His brother Welcome and another young man drove to the Tecumseh meeting in a buggy. When over half way there Welcome saw something sticking out from under the buggy-seat behind. It was a boy's foot. It belonged to a boy. The boy was Clinton B. He had smuggled himself on board, and curled up in this painful fashion was bound for the place of his desire. He might easier have walked the five miles, possibly, but it would not have been so much fun. And he loved fun dearly always.

A year after this wonderful campaign an important event occurred. Mrs. Fisk married again. William Smith, a wealthy farmer living at Spring Arbor, twelve miles from Jackson, having somehow heard of her worth and work, sought her acquaintance, and persuaded her to abandon widowhood. The little home was given up, the struggles of a lonely life terminated, and with Clinton, in the fall of 1841, she went to easier conditions and an apparently assured future for her boy. He won the warm affection of his stepfather at once ; and Mr. Smith, thinking so highly of education that he soon planned the establishment of a college, was willing and anxious to give his bright stepson a chance.

But for a time Spring Arbor advantages were limited. The district school was two miles and a half away, and Clinton walked that distance daily to and fro when any school there was. Sometimes he went to the schoolhouse for other than school reasons. Mr. Smith was an abolitionist, like Deacon Wright, and under his arrangement abolition meetings were occasionally held there, for which Clinton built the fires, and in which his young convictions grew steadily stronger and more mature. He breathed now an intenser radical atmosphere than ever, in point of fact, for the Smith homestead was a station on the Underground Railroad, and boy as he was, Clinton became a sub-conductor of that famous thoroughfare. Many a time within the next three or four years was he called up at night and despatched with some dusky passenger toward the Detroit River and Freedom. He could drive to the next station and get back by daylight generally, with no one the wiser for his going or returning ; but some suspicion existed in the minds of pro-slavery neighbors, after all, and it found expression vaguely now and then.

He was nearing home one morning a little later than it should have been after such an errand, and rather tired and sleepy from his all-night's trip. Jogging along without much care or concern as to who saw him, he met a stern religionist of the town, who was also sternly opposed to abolition ideas, and who believed slavery a divine institution. He, too, was a deacon, but not of Elijah Wright's kind. Looking sharply at the tired horse and the sleepy driver, and suspecting both of unholy uses—perhaps imagining Clinton to have been out on some midnight lark of quite another sort—this deacon said :

" Young man, I know where you're going !"

Pulling up short, the young man simply asked :

" Where ?"

And slowly and with solemn emphasis the deacon answered :

" You're going to hell !"

Then as slowly and solemnly the young man made response :

" No, sir ! You are mistaken. I'm going home to breakfast."

And the look of horror and surprise upon that deacon's face as the young man drove on is not forgotten by the young man yet.

CHAPTER VI

Two years were spent by Clinton in the Smith family without interruption. He was rarely idle. When not in school he worked upon the farm. A very comfortable home was his, with some luxuries, including more books than he had known ; but it does not appear that he had quite all he craved.

His effort to obtain one special text-book was tinged with pathos. He was then fifteen years old, rather tall and slim and slight. Whoever looked at him must fancy that he was less fitted for hard knocks than for the quiet of a student's life. Yet he could devote much physical energy to give the student in him a chance. He caught a coon—no strange thing for a boy where coons abounded, but he caught this one for an unusual purpose. Then with singular patience he taught the coon more tricks than were ever dreamed of before in a coon's tricky philosophy. Of course he came to love the sly, sleek, serene yet semi-humorous animal, and to feel a certain pride in him as well. He would gladly have kept him, after all his patient application, followed by the reward of such expertness. But resolutely he put love and desire one side, and as resolutely walked twelve miles to Jackson, sold his coon as a trick wonder to a circus exhibiting there, bought Anthon's " Latin Lessons," and walked the long way home again, sorrowful over the loss of his pet, but glad in possession of the book he had coveted so keenly.

It was not easy to study Latin alone unaided, now that the Latin grammar was his. But at night, in front of the fireplace, and by day while afield, he plodded on through nouns and verbs, declensions and conjugations. With the help of written slips prepared for such use the night before, he conned his Latin exercises many a daylight hour behind the plough, or driving the cattle to pasture, or following the drag. The genitive diphthong troubled him more than all else. Was its pronunciation determined by the *a* or the *e ?* Not a serious question, the average youth might have said ; and Clinton might have thought so, only he was not the average youth. His ambition said constantly to him, " Be right. " Nobody near him knew a Latin word, but he learned, by chance, of another boy studying the language who was to be at a camp-meeting ten miles distant. To meet that boy he walked the twenty miles of that round trip, and he fairly hugged himself the whole returning distance because of his success in pumping the boy dry of Latin information without telling how little he really knew himself.

His liking for declamation did not cease. He memorized about every bit of stirring prose or verse which came under his eye, and never tired of repeating it. Stepfather Smith had an old bay horse known as Jerry which Clinton rode regularly to the post-office, two and a half miles away, on mail days, and Jerry became his patient audience. The boy's voice, it is said, could often be heard a full half mile as, standing in the saddle, he made some writer's eloquence his own, while Jerry wondered, possibly, what it all meant, yet seldom answered neigh.

Deacon Smith—for, if not actually a deacon, they called him so—was a very pious man, and besides being a Christian and an abolitionist, he was a "Millerite." He looked for the end of the world. With a few of like faith he had ciphered out the problem of Christ's reappearance, and the final ascension of the saints. And more than once Clinton was called up in the night or bidden be ready by day to mount heavenward. With so good and strong a man as his stepfather believing implicitly in the near finis, a summons like this could not be other than impressive and awesome, even though the boy doubted much and did very little dread.

In the fall of 1843 Clinton went to Albion Seminary for the preliminary course of study that should fit him for college. Not so much from necessity, it may be assumed, as from independent choice, he rather roughed it there. With a Miss Benedict, a Miss Depew, a brother of the former and some others, he organized a students' club, and they boarded themselves at an average weekly cost of sixty cents each. By the kindness of Rev. Loren Grant, Clinton slept in a loft over that gentleman's woodshed. His previous self-teaching had served so well that he took front rank promptly in all classes, and was able to hold his own throughout the winter term with ease.

In the spring of 1844 he went back to Spring Arbor to resume work on the farm. Not yet were the plans for his thorough education fully made, but they took shape during the next few months. With other men of means and influence, William Smith that summer founded Michigan Central College, in the little town near which he lived, and here Clinton Fisk was to go forward and graduate. Daniel M. Graham became its first principal, and with Andrew Jackson Graham, Clinton began the

study of Greek that fall.   He was happy in the though:
of unbroken educational opportunity till a college
diploma should be his, and after that he had no:
clearly made up his mind.   Sixteen, sunny of heart,
swift to learn, the adopted favorite of a man whom
every one respected and whom he had come to love, the
future seemed bright before him, and hope was literally
bounding in his breast.

Then suddenly, for William Smith alone, the world's
end came.   He died almost without any warning, on
Christmas Day.   And again for Clinton Fisk, as for his
twice-widowed mother, all things were changed.   On
May 5th, 1845, they left the Smith homestead for Albion,
where Mr. Isaac N. Swayne, son-in-law of Mr. Smith,
provided for them a little home which together they occupied until autumn, when the mother went back to
Clinton for permanent residence, and later once more
remarried there.   Her third husband was the minister by
whom Clinton was baptized, Rev. Robert Powell, and
with him she had many years of peaceful companionship
on a farm two miles from Clinton, free from burdensome
cares and in an atmosphere of comforting Christian trust.

Clinton's college purposes were not abandoned.   Part
of the years 1845 and 1846 he pursued his preliminary
course, leading each class he was in.   He had some
bright classmates, too.   One of them was Wirt W.
Dexter, now of Chicago ; another, J. Stirling Martin, of
the same city ; a third was his partial namesake and
perhaps very distant relative, L. R. Fisk, now President
of Albion College.   Like all students, these had their
merry times, their practical jokes.   One of the latter
came near to tragedy, and grew almost too serious for
sport.   Boxes of food were sent sometimes to Clinton
from the mother's kitchen, and were welcomed, of

course. Another youth, named Stewart, thought it no
sin to slip into Clinton's room occasionally while Clinton
was out and fill himself with pie and cake. Willing to
punish him a bit, and missing half a pie which he
had placed conspicuously, and which Stewart had
made way with, Clinton said soberly, but in anxious
tones :

"Stewart, you didn't eat *that* pie ?"

A little frightened, the victim allowed he did. Heaving a troubled sigh, and looking much concerned, his
tormentor said :

"Well, I hope it won't kill you !"

"Why—why—what was the matter with it ?" inquired Stewart, now much alarmed.

"You didn't know it was fixed there on purpose to
kill rats ?" insinuated Clinton.

"How should I know it ?" the young man asked,
frightened yet more terribly. "What shall I do ? Am
I poisoned ? Do you think I'll die ?"

Then Clinton's chum, Martin, came forward and offered
to fix him some medicine that might ward off death. It
was prepared, and taken with almost fatal effect. In a
few hours Stewart grew so weak and used up that he
looked like a hospital patient near his end, and all the
time the young man's alarm became more terrible. At
last his sister, Miss Mollie Stewart, suspected the secret
of his illness, and laid her suspicions before the principal. Young Martin and Fisk were arraigned in his presence, and manfully confessed the joke. He reprimanded
them severely, but his keen eyes twinkled as he did so,
and they saw him laughing silently as they left his room.
The joke got out, and for some time afterward the door
of these two young men bore upon it this sign, placed
there by appreciative hands :

FISK & MARTIN,

BOTANIC PHYSICIANS.

Refer to W. W. S

General Fisk may well, as he does, give credit to those school terms at Albion for the larger part of his life's worth and work ; for he won there more and better things than an insight into Greek participles and a knowledge of Cæsar's "Commentaries." He learned by heart, as never in solitary field studies could he have done, the Latin verb *amo*. Among his fellow-students was a round-faced, rosy-cheeked, black-eyed girl of fourteen, from Coldwater, Mich.—Jeannette A. Crippen. He saw her first in June, 1845, and the school-days were brighter for him every month afterward. By and by he won her heart, as altogether she won his, and with it he won, for a near and a long future, all the better things implied above—helpful companionship, loyal devotion, unyielding confidence, and the sweet, fearless, faithful strength of a character fine-fibred, close-knit, self-reliant in superlative degree.

During a part of 1846 he taught school in the township of Bridgewater, near where his mother had gone to live ; but this only as a makeshift. He had set his face toward Ann Arbor, and the University of Michigan there. He was ready indeed to enter Sophomore year at that institution, when Providence ordered otherwise. Hard study by night, and the intense heat of fire-light by which he had read and studied much, bore fruit in disease of the eyes so acute and continued that further close application became impossible ; and with keen, lasting regret he gave up his long-cherished hope, put away the books he loved so well, turned his back on teachers and teaching, and began as best he might to work out a business career. His bitter disappointment can be understood only by those who have hungered with desire like his for all that books and schools can yield, have tasted a little time the sweets of their satisfaction, and then have been thrust suddenly away where famine is.

During six months of 1847 he served as clerk in the store of John Keyes, at Manchester, Mich., and through the spring and summer of 1848 he was a clerk at Albion for M. Hannahs & Son. His genial good-nature, his native politeness, and his active ways made friends for him and for his employers, and he speedily developed business gifts and adaptiveness of a superior, even a surprising order. He was quick, discriminating, ready. He gave to the poorest patron equal courtesy accorded the rich. He had unyielding convictions, but they were covered as with velvet. His tact made contact with him agreeable for all. By some swift instinct he started at once on the sure road to business popularity that in general means business success; which accounts largely, if not altogether, for the fact that he went to Coldwater in September, 1848, and formed a business alliance with Crippen & Kellogg in that place. It was another way-mark, the going there.

CHAPTER VII.

Miss Jeannette Crippen had a brother, J. B. Crippen, who at Albion formed for Clinton B. a warm attachment, and it was ostensibly to visit him that Clinton sought Coldwater at first. He may have confessed also a wish to see Miss Jeannette herself. The young lady's father, Mr. L. D. Crippen, was the leading business man in Coldwater at that time, with large capital and varied interests, comprising mills, a store, farm lands, etc. The place numbered from two to three thousand population, and was a recognized commercial centre of Southern Michigan. Round about it were fertile reaches of country being rapidly brought into cultivation and requiring large cash advances for development. It was a wide, rich field for sagacious business operations.

By advantageous arrangement with the Crippens, Clinton became associated at once with the firm as it stood then, J. B. Crippen and himself having part therein without name. It remained Crippen & Kellogg two years longer, and grew yet more successful. Having put away entirely his higher educational ambitions, and possessing acquirements ample for a commercial life, our young friend was ambitious along these lines of alternative effort, and set his heart on success. His self-confidence grew strong. It was not undue assurance, but a fair measure of his own powers, that gave him faith and lent firmness of purpose. He had rare incentive, too, to work and win. A home and fortune were one day to be his. He was trusted, and given a chance. He had lost much, but prodigal things were yet in store. No wonder that he gave himself so freely and with such prosperous results. He was spendthrift of good-nature, cheerful courtesy, willing zeal. He shrank from nothing that was honorable and profitable. He became a necessity in the various departments of business carried on. Alert, adept, adaptable, he could not be spared.

In 1850 Mr. Kellogg retired, and the firm was made L. D. Crippen & Son, with Clinton Fisk a still silent but very active partner. On February 20th of that year he married Miss Crippen, and thus established a dual partnership, which compensated him for loss of college honors. The young couple began domestic life together under favorable auspices in a modest cottage on Chicago Street, the chief avenue of Coldwater. The parents of Mrs. Fisk furnished and fitted up this home for them, and in it the sweetest ambitions of Clinton B. were realized.

In business too he prospered far beyond his dreams. The same year Crippen's Exchange Bank was started by Crippen & Fisk, and with good capital its operations extended widely in a short time. Mr. Fisk managed bank affairs chiefly from the day it opened, and here, as in the more miscellaneous business activities, he showed exceptional sagacity, the instinct of success. His unfailing good-fellowship, his consummate skill in dealing with men, insured patronage and commanded friends. He took part or led in every enterprise for the town's welfare. He was active and zealous in all the community's good works. Among other things which helped his popularity with the younger generation, he organized the first band Coldwater knew, and himself played in it for some time, taking the E flat tuba. He proved himself accessible, many-sided, clear-headed, with executive talents remarkable and diverse.

Perhaps in token of past remembrances, in 1853 he bought a farm. It lay just outside and adjoining the corporation, northeast, and could not be surpassed for beauty and fertility in all that fertile region. Upon it he erected fine buildings and conducted practical experiments. He made it the premium farm of that county, and Mrs. Fisk yet has a set of silver plate awarded him by the committee who pronounced it so. It boasted the best stock known, and became, with its equipment, an object of local pride. It advertised the owner as a man of exquisite rural taste allied with practical sense as an agriculturist. If he did not make money off his well-kept acres, he made a better rural sentiment around them and lifted higher the standard of neighboring rural life.

It was not until 1854 that the distinctively Christian quality of his manhood became dominant. He had never let clean go of God, as do so many youth between fifteen and twenty-five, but his church relations for a time were rather nominal. Of composite religious antecedents and of Baptist conversion, he came while at Albion into Methodist communion and faith, but not then into full Methodistic activity. The need of prayer seemed less pressing than the call for work during those busy years before and after marriage. Almost without realizing it he had drifted religiously into that indifferent, careless, well-nigh prayerless condition of mind common to energetic, overworked business men.

At home one night, after supper was over, his little three-year-old daughter Mary came and knelt by him to say her evening prayer. The mother was occupied un-

usually, and for once her sweetest maternal duty she dele-
gated to him.   White-robed and pure as the white-robed
ones above, the tiny figure bowed its head upon his knee
and prayed.   It was a new experience to this busy young
man.   He listened, with heart beating swifter, to her
simple formula, and to the special plea of "God bless
papa, God bless mamma," at the close.   And when the
child rose up her question smote him like a blow :

"Papa, why don't *you* pray ?"

He made some hasty answer, and kissed her haunting
lips good-night.   Then he went down street and into the
bank, and tried to labor there.   But his mind would not
fix itself on matters of finance.   Between him and credit
balances, bills of exchange, discounts, and the like came
persistently that little form in white ; over and over he
heard again the prayer breathed softly at his knee, and
echoing in his ears, with sweet and strange persistence
that would not be put aside, her question repeated itself :

"Papa, why don't *you* pray ?"

At last he yielded to the influences which he could not
control, thrust business considerations quite away, and
did the soberest thinking he had done for many a month.
And in the midst of commercial success, facing what
promised to be a widely prosperous future, he resolved
hereafter to be as active for God as for Clinton Fisk, and
to leaven all his business life with prayer.

Bolting his safes and turning the key of his bank door,
he walked homeward.   Reaching there, he sat down near
his wife and said :

"Did you hear the question Mary asked me, Jeannette ?"

"Yes, Clinton, I heard it," answered Mrs. Fisk.

"Well, Jenny, I've been thinking it all over, and
I've made up my mind that, with God's help, we'll have

all the praying there ought to be in this household hereafter. If you'll hand me the Bible, we'll begin now."

So there and then, with the Book in hand and a new
resolve in his heart, they set up a family altar which
neither time nor care nor disaster has torn down. And
often since that night the question of little Mary has come
to him with talismanic charm and sent him to the surest
source of help and comfort. When burdens have pressed
heavily upon him, or grief has overwhelmed, or great
sacrifices have made him sore, or great losses have made
him well-nigh bankrupt of all but faith—in the stress of
business, in the shock of battle, in the darkness of
national conflict—sweet and clear and with another emphasis his ears and heart have heard it again and again—

" Papa, why don't you *pray ?*"

Following this almost new conversion, Mr. Fisk gave
himself as actively to church as to other interests.

" He was the best Sunday-school superintendent we
ever had!" not long since testified one of the oldest
members of the Coldwater Methodist Church.

His readiness of speech, his retentive memory, his old
habit of declamation, helped him in every department of
public effort. His Christian spirit, moreover, was so
catholic that he quickly won men to the Master's work.

Writing to a friend years later, he said :

" My early association with different branches of the
living church of Christ has through all my subsequent life
given me freedom from sectarian bias. I am at home
with all believers everywhere."

About this time his public temperance activities began.
He seems to have been born with a twin hatred for
slavery and the liquor traffic, if so severe a term be compatible with so mild a nature. As a boy in Clinton we
have seen how he stood for total abstinence, and how his

influence was exerted upon those within its range. To the mother-side of him, no doubt, this trend of life was due. True throughout those years of youth to the principle of personal prohibition, with man's responsibility he must espouse and advocate Prohibition for the State as well. He could see no other consistent course.

The first great tidal wave of Prohibition reform had swept across our country from Maine to Iowa. It was the logical sequence of Washingtonianism. No earnest, widespread work of moral suasion ever was or ever will be conducted but that closely in its wake you shall see the sweep of statutes and legal force. State after State had adopted " the Maine law," as commonly termed, and among them Michigan. And even so early as 1855 it was clear to many that a law fares best in the hands of its friends—that a State policy, formulated in law, will be upheld and established in State government only by executors of the law who believe in the policy. It happened, therefore—no, it was inevitable—that there should be " Maine law tickets " nominated by the Maine Law Party in some States and many places. Not that there was a party bearing that name in every or any State having the Maine law. But parties may be and be nameless. A party is only one of the parts into which the people are divided on some question of public concern, and always upon the question of temperance people are divided. There is always, then, a temperance party, and there must be so long as the liquor traffic exists. It may not always assert itself in the way of political nominations, but while law requires enforcement, and enforcement must come through officials, temperance conviction and purpose will quite likely manifest itself through party action at the polls.

There were " Maine law tickets " in Michigan. There

was one at Coldwater.   With such a name that place could not well avoid having such a ticket.   Liking that name, believing in the idea it symbolized, earnest for the success of a law which embodied the idea, Clinton B. Fisk could not refuse that ticket the strength of his name.   And thus he became a candidate for Justice of the Peace.   He was not elected, for still he was on the unpopular side, but his own popularity almost carried the day.   And he had the satisfaction of standing for truth and right, though he missed the glory of victory.

The same year or the next he went back to his boyhood home for another Fourth of July celebration, taking the Coldwater Band with him.   Of course Clinton people turned out *en masse* to see and hear the boy Clinton Fisk, grown to a manhood of which they could feel proud.   His address is well remembered by those now living who were there.   It dealt a good deal in reminiscence, and the speaker evoked laughter and tears at his will.   It was wonderful to many ; what must it have been to the mother whose love never failed him, and whose faith in him was finding ample realization ?

CHAPTER VIII.

CRIPPEN's EXCHANGE BANK finally occupied the corner of a brick block north side of the main street which Mr. Crippen erected in 1854 and in which the First National Bank of Coldwater now has quarters as its lineal descendant. When this block was built the bank had large deposits and made larger loans. Its capital and its credit were widely spread out in mortgages throughout Southern Michigan and Northern Indiana. Those were the days of ten per cent and big discounts. The farmers must have money, and could afford, or thought they could, the heavy interest exacted. They bought land at low prices on time, and they raised large crops. They prospered in appearance if not in fact ; and many of them, as is well known, paid comfortably out of debt.

The financial crash of 1857 found bankers everywhere with a host of debtors and comparatively small piles of cash. Like other extensive business men, Crippen & Fisk had reached out widely in many directions. They had their country stores, including one managed by Welcome V. Fisk in Clinton ; their saw- and grist-mills ; their Western lands ; their farms, and blocks and other rental property. They had loaned money on every side. They were assisting a railroad down on the Eel River in Indiana. So fortunate had they been throughout several years of extensive financiering that they gave less heed than perhaps they should have given to signs of business distress

Then came the great panic. One by one heaviest banking houses went down. Speculation had started an avalanche which would not be stayed. At all the great money centres credit nearly ceased. Business suffered as by a paralytic stroke. Confidence fled everywhere. The bank that did not fail was an exception. It was considered no discredit to suspend. Assignments were too common almost for record.

In the midst of his prosperity Mr. Fisk saw the cyclone close at hand, and marvelled what the end would be. But he did not murmur when wreck impended. With stronger manliness than some accredited to so sunny, suave a temperament, he faced the storm. It swept over him as over all. Creditors wanted their cash, but borrowers could not pay. The mortgages on property round about were good security, but not current for bank bills. He was advised to assign and save utter ruin. He risked the ruin, but would not assign. Temporarily his bank suspended, because temporarily it could not command the current funds wherewith to meet presented claims ; but no assignment was made, no creditors brought suit, no judgment decrees were entered up.

A little shock to the community followed Crippen & Fisk's suspension, but no serious general results. Their depositors were well protected, and a universal feeling prevailed that Mr. Fisk would come out all right, give him fair chance. With cheerful energy and unselfish purpose he set about mastering misfortune and meeting their obligations. He labored as never before. By day and night he bent every energy of body and brain to the task. He spent himself with a prodigality unmatched in all his endeavors hitherto. Having refused the advice of well-meaning associates, he must prove his policy the better one at any physical cost.

And so he proved it. He paid in full every valid claim, according to the testimony of business men now in Coldwater who were familiar with the facts ; moreover, he paid full interest.

" His record is as clean as any man's on earth," said one leading merchant of the town long afterward.

And he did not wholly impoverish himself, except in strength of nerve and brain. His handsome farm was left, and something besides, when months of unremitting care and perplexity were over and the final settlements all made. It mattered more, perhaps, that health was gone than the larger share of fortune ; it mattered most that no man suffered loss which he could prevent, though he lost all.

The bank was given up, and the banking business. The firm of L. D. Crippen & Son and of Crippen & Fisk was dissolved. For the junior partner there remained nothing immediate but to restore a shattered nervous system by regaining wasted physical strength. For a year ensuing he gave himself to that achievement. The farm helped him. A sound constitution assisted. Clean habits of life were in his favor. Hopefulness and good-will toward men, and the good-will *of* men, were co-ordinate agents. He was not born to despond. With manhood left, and Christian faith, and returning health, there were surely more good times ahead. As God might will, he should come to them.

In the fall of 1858 the Ætna Insurance Company of Hartford, Conn., proposed that Mr. Fisk should become their Western financial agent, with headquarters at St. Louis. It was a timely proposition, because it offered activities to his taste which he now felt physically able to undertake, with sufficient travel to aid in the complete restoration of health. They paid his expenses to go and

look over the field. Hitherto he had been too busy
with local affairs for rambling much abroad, and what
he saw was like a revelation. He enjoyed the Western
dash and spirit. His quick business instinct recognized
the immense commercial possibilites of that wide new
West. He decided for St. Louis and a new future.

During the next year or two he travelled much up and
down the Mississippi Valley and across the States contiguous. He saw the South—the South of cotton-grow-
ing Arkansas and Mississippi and Louisiana—the South
of cotton and of slaves. Abolitionist as from boyhood,
he insured the lives of many a slave band shipped southward from St. Louis, and went upon many a plantation
where slavery exhibited its worst and its more humane
qualities. Some of those old Mississippi planters might
not have greeted him so cordially had they known of his
early Underground Railroad connection at Spring Arbor.
He enjoyed his work, despite some associations which re-
pelled, and his wide contact with men. He formed
friendships both North and South that were cherished.

Some weeks of one winter he spent as a lobbyist about
the Illinois Legislature, at Springfield. His mission was
to prevent insurance legislation that should keep his
company from pushing business in that State. It was
then that his acquaintance with Abraham Lincoln began.
Bishop Simpson at that time resided in Springfield, or
was often there, and Governor Evans, of Colorado, was
a legislator in the body which there met. With these
two gentlemen Mr. Fisk often spent an evening at Mr.
Lincoln's house, and listened to the great man's quaint
stories and homely talk. Lincoln was not then widely
thought of for the Presidency, but throughout Illinois
he had been long a popular idol. Between him and
Bishop Simpson there existed a strong attachment of

which the country learned something a few years later on. And the bishop had even then come to know Clinton B. Fisk as a wide-awake, level-headed, warm-hearted Methodist layman of great power in Sunday-school work and great promise in other ways.

On one visit to Mississippi Mr. Fisk was entertained at a village boarding-house for a little time, and saw come in and take seat at another table a tall, sallow, bent, black-haired young man, with the look of a student so positive in his face as to excite curiosity. He made inquiry and learned the young man's name. It was Professor L. Q. C. Lamar, now Justice of the Supreme Court.

St. Louis was the metropolis of a slave State, the northwestern *entrepôt* of the whole region dominated by slavery. It lay in that debatable land known then as "the border," and life there between 1858 and 1861 was in a growing ferment. Mr. Fisk felt and heard the mutterings of a political earthquake long before they shook our Northern country. He was one in whom both sides put confidence. He antagonized no one. He won the regard of all. He knew the spirit of the North ; he had grown familiar with the feeling and views of the South. He feared a bloody contest some time before it came. Yet how little he dreamed of having responsible. part in it himself ! How unconscious he was that often he met right there, in the city of his home, the man who was to be military chieftain in the end ! Ulysses S. Grant lived then in St. Louis, and gave no token of the greatness in him. Mr. Fisk knew him well, and had dealings with him often. But it was not then the Grant of the war and the White House.

His business prospered, his health came back, and Mr. Fisk had no reason to be apprehensive on his own ac-

count. But as the days wore on he grew deeply concerned about public affairs. In politics he was a Republican, having helped to organize that party in 1856, and
he voted for Abraham Lincoln, of course. He was politically ardent. He believed intensely in the abolition of
slavery. Despite its financial power, its constitutional
grip, its church domination and its partisan tyranny, he
was certain it must and would be smitten and put away.
But he knew how slavery would fight to live, and how
the States Rights idea was fixed in the bed-rock of
Southern political faith. He might well dread the issue.
He did dread it. But with sure forecast he helped to
shape conditions for righteous success when it should
come.

For months before the outbreak in 1861 bodies of men
were practising secret military drill in St. Louis. Both
sides had organized thus quietly for what they felt inevitable. So sharply was public sentiment divided that
there grew up general distrust and doubt. Only by
secret oath did any one feel sure of even his neighbor.
Yet spite of much Union sentiment it appeared natural
that St. Louis' location and interests should throw her
final choice with the South, if time of choosing came.

In the ranks of those who secretly drilled for liberty
and union, and among the earliest there, was Clinton
B. Fisk. He asked no place of honor. With some
hundreds of well-known business men—merchants, bankers, lawyers, and the like—he regularly shouldered a
musket, and was taught the manual of arms. They
met in a disused and somewhat remote warehouse, going
to it singly and from different points of approach, and
were admitted only after giving the countersign. All
through that winter of 1860–61 their secret preparations
were making for later open acts.

When Sumter was fired on, as if by magic there sprang into active organization a well-drilled body of Missouri Home Guards for loyal service in defence of the Stars and Stripes.   In the Third Regiment, as a private, stood Clinton B. Fisk, and his name was one of the first upon the muster-roll of Company C.

CHAPTER IX.

THE Missouri Home Guards were enlisted for ninety days only, and saw little exciting service. They were mainly a check against local eruptions of disloyal sympathy. They did one day march out to a Confederate camp on the edge of town and capture it. It looked like the beginning of open war. Governor Jackson was a secessionist, and the whole State officiary were with him for carrying Missouri out of the Union. By his act State arms had been supplied to disloyal citizens of St. Louis, drilling with disloyal intent, and they were sworn into State service. Under command of one Frost, commissioned a brigadier-general by Jackson for that purpose, they formed a militia camp in the suburbs, and, that their true character might not be known, kept flying over it the American flag. Their purpose was to seize the United States Arsenal, with all its valuable stores, and master the really dominant Union majority with one blow.

The arsenal was in command of Captain Nathaniel Lyon, and guarded by 500 regular troops. By Presidential order the loyal citizens were also enrolled under him, forming the Home Guards, and these were quartered at the arsenal and on ground near by. They formed part of the Union force which, commanded by Captain Lyon and Colonel Frank Blair, early on the afternoon of May 9th swept round the secession Camp

Jackson, with its 1200 men, and demanded immediate surrender. The movement was not quite a surprise, but Frost had no time for defensive preparation, and attempted no defence. An armed mob of secessionists from the city rushed out to assist their friends, but they came too late. There was rioting on the streets, and some firing resulted whereby the crowd and the soldiery suffered ; but it could not rank as a battle, though it might have been a bloody one.

Among those whom Mr. Fisk saw as his regiment marched out that day was W. T. Sherman. He was not then a general nor a private, only an interested civilian. He stood in a field near by, holding by the hand a little boy, and watching curiously this initial military movement in the State where he lived.

Great excitement followed in St. Louis several days and nights afterward, and the Home Guards were on duty as an armed police much of the time throughout the balance of their three months' term. There was bloodshed in the city but twice ; there was promise or probability of it through riotous demonstration almost every day. Perhaps nowhere else save at Baltimore did there seem such insecurity and hourly pending revolution. The status of Missouri was more peculiar than that of any other State. East, west, and north it was bounded by loyalty, and its metropolis was counted a Union city ; but the Legislature, sitting at Jefferson, favored disunion, and would support Governor Jackson in any secession course he might pursue ; and the financial influences of St. Louis were largely wielded to the same end. There was actual if not open defiance of the National Government by State authority ; and as a condition vital to pacification, Governor Jackson demanded immediate disbanding of the Home Guards. To this Lyon, now made a brigadier-general, would not listen, and on June 12th the governor inaugurated civil war. His proclamation called into service 50,000 State militia, "for the purpose of repelling invasion, and for the protection of the lives, liberty, and property of the citizens." The possible neutrality of Missouri became impossible.

Quite a year after being mustered out of the Home Guards, Mr. Fisk busied himself in many ways for the public behoof, while still endeavoring, as best he could under conditions growing steadily more adverse, to promote the business interests grown very extensive in his charge. He was a recognized leader among the Union men of St. Louis, and his counsels were sought and regarded with growing respect. He went to Washington, as soon as discharged from the ranks, and reached there when the first battle of the war impended at Bull Run. Like scores besides, he called upon President Lincoln, and, like some of these, he urged a speedy forward movement "on to Richmond." He had assisted slightly in capturing a camp of Confederates ; he believed the Confederate capital could be taken if prompt movement were made. The President heard him as a friend and answered little, though complaining that he had rather more advice than he knew what to do with. He even smiled with some questioning irony when Mr. Fisk told of his purpose to join the army and go forward to Richmond himself.

" I've ordered my mail sent there," this Presidential visitor remarked as he took leave, " and am going after it."

With thousands more civilians, Mr. Fisk did join, or follow, the Federal Army as it marched from Arlington Heights to cross Bull Run. With them, and with, or preceding, thousands of undrilled soldiers, their smart

uniforms all draggled and soiled, their spirits broken
and their faith temporarily gone, he came back to Washington.   It was his first retreat, and he laughs yet to
think of the plight he and so many others fell into.   His
hope for a speedy termination of the war vanished as he
sought the capital again.

Hour after hour the retreating crowds poured in.   Members of Congress, citizens, visitors from every Northern
State, and the disheartened soldiery, afoot, on horseback,
by carriage, returned to the excited town.   Singly, or in
squads and shattered companies, the soldiers came, grimy
with powder and dust, exhausted from lack of food.

Standing in front of Willard's, Mr. Fisk saw some
stragglers from a Michigan regiment passing wearily by.
Love for his old State and pity for those who wore the
blue prompted an act of sympathy, and uniting with two
or three other Michigan gentlemen, he invited the boys in
to a square meal.   They had eaten nothing in twenty-four
to thirty-six hours, and were about famished.   Having
satisfied those, Mr. Fisk and his friends told them to send
every regimental comrade there who might come in for
like hospitality.   Their story was that the regiment had
all been cut up and nearly every man killed.   To the
amazement of their entertainers, the survivors kept reporting and being fed until several hundreds were filled
up ; and the bill for their entertainment proved a standing joke against those by whom it was paid.

Mr. Fisk called on the President as he was about to
return home.   With a touch of mild sarcasm in his voice,
Mr. Lincoln asked :

" Did you order your mail forwarded from Richmond ?"

And then, his sad face lighting with a smile, he remarked : " You may not get it unless you did."

Shaking Mr. Fisk's hand as he took leave, the President slowly said :

" You must all have patience, my friend. I am bound to do my best. This will be a mighty struggle. God only knows how it will end. But tell all your friends to be patient—very patient."

Sectional feeling ran so deep, and the wall of partisan partition grew so high, in St. Louis, that religious and business associations were moulded chiefly thereby.

A Union Methodist Church was formed, in the organization of which Mr. Fisk had conspicuously leading part. He was first superintendent of its Sabbath-school, and aided much in making both school and church the positive power which they became.

The Union Merchants' Exchange owed its organization to him. In the old Exchange, which long had been the city's commercial right arm, there were two bodies corresponding to the upper and lower houses of Congress. The upper branch controlled, officially, and that was thoroughly disloyal. As a result, the Exchange threw all its mighty organic influence against Union and on the side of Jackson and the Confederacy. An effort was put forth in January, 1862, to elect a Union ticket and change this hostile attitude, but it failed. Then Mr. Fisk mounted a table in the lower hall and made a speech to the Union members. It rang so true and strong, and the Union sentiment of the lower house was so pronounced, that immediate general secession followed, and the formation of a new Exchange was resolved upon. Mr. Fisk drew up the articles of association, personally hired quarters for it in a new building owned by a secessionist of another type than himself, and in twenty-four hours the Union Merchants' Exchange was fully organized, with a membership of hundreds, with financial support unlimited, and comfortably housed in a central location, where it flung out the Stars and Stripes and compelled instant respect. It sapped the vital resources of the old Exchange, and soon took head place as the exponent of St. Louis' business capital, while it stood loyally for freedom and the Union. Mr. Fisk was its secretary and active spirit. To it he gave his best energies, believing that so he could well serve the country's need.

In July of the same year President Lincoln requested him to raise a regiment of volunteers. It was to be one of eight that Missouri's quota required under national call for 300,000 more troops. The President asked that behind this one, at least, the Union Merchants' Exchange should stand, with influence to secure it and means to see it equipped. Mr. Fisk laid the matter before his associates of the Exchange directory. It was clear to all by this time that more men and more money must be forthcoming if the Union were saved. The loyal merchants, through their officials represented, agreed to meet the demand. Mr. Fisk was bidden go ahead, with ample assurance from his colleagues of cooperation and support. His own loyal devotion emphasized the command.

Receiving proper authority July 26th, 1862, he donned the blue, opened an office, flung out his flag, and had forty men recruited before sunset. His promptness was ever a conspicuous quality. Deciding on a given course, he would move forward without delay and with despatch. The times now were imperious for haste.

In six weeks the Thirty-third Regiment of Missouri Volunteers stood complete. On September 5th Clinton B. Fisk was commissioned its colonel and the regiment mustered in.

CHAPTER X

COLONEL FISK's recognized character helped on the celerity shown. The fathers who knew him were willing to trust him with their sons. His Christian influence made steadily for the good of all.

While the regiment was forming, Colonel Fisk held regimental religious services every Sunday afternoon in the great amphitheatre of the Fair Grounds, occupied then by troops, and known as Benton Barracks, close by town. Thousands of citizens attended them. The city pastors preached in turn. None will ever forget the effect of those meetings who had part in them. They were wonderfully impressive.

One of the sermons was by Rev. Dr. Nelson, and before its close he made a personal appeal of great power. It was a sober, solemn time, for the Thirty-third was to march next day, and in its welfare all the State felt special interest. Cautioning the men against various sins which army life might induce, Dr. Nelson spoke of the sin of profanity. After dwelling upon it a little, he told of a certain commodore who made a contract with every midshipman that he, the commodore, should do all the swearing for the ship ; and in substance he said : " Now, I want all of you to agree that Colonel Fisk shall do all the swearing for the Thirty-third Regiment. As many of you as will enter into this contract stand up !"

Instantly the whole regiment rose to their feet, and in

solemn silence the covenant was made.   And all knew
what it meant, for they had a praying colonel, and at
his headquarters, conspicuously visible upon the wall, this
placard they had read :

SWEAR NOT AT ALL.

*Attention is called to the Third Commandment and the
Third Article of War.*

And six hundred of the regiment were praying men.

On September 15th Colonel Fisk's regiment was
ordered to report at Rolla, which place it entered one
week later.   So successful had his recruiting service been,
that he was soon returned to St. Louis with instructions
to recruit other regiments and form a brigade.   By order
of Major-General Curtis, then commanding the department of Missouri, he was (October 28th) assigned to
duty for that purpose at that officer's headquarters,
where he remained nearly two months.   On November
24th he was notified by Secretary Stanton of his appointment as brigadier-general, and as such was reassigned
to headquarters at St. Louis by General Curtis, December 1st.

Having completed the organization of his brigade, in
which labor he still had the co-operation of those who,
by their substantial help, had made its initial organization
known as the " Merchants' Regiment," on December
24th General Fisk was ordered by General Curtis to
Helena, Ark., with his command, " reporting *en route*
to Brigadier-General Davies, commanding post, Columbus, Ky., for temporary duty as commander of all forces
sent to General Davies from this department."

Columbus, base of supplies for all the Federal troops
in Mississippi, was threatened by Van Dorn and Frost,

the former of whom had just captured Holly Springs, with a large quantity of stores that General Grant had left there, and was supposed to be sweeping northward. General Fisk reported to General Davies on the 26th, and joined with him in defence of that post until January 8th, 1863, remaining there twelve days. Then the threatened danger being no longer imminent, General Fisk transferred his brigade to Helena, where he reported for duty on the 11th to General Gorman, commanding the district of Eastern Arkansas.

General Grant was then actively pushing military operations through all that region tributary to the Mississippi between Memphis and Vicksburg. The latter was his objective point. If he could capture that and remove the Confederate blockade there established, immense gains must accrue. His approaches to and investments of the place were attempted from every direction. With patience characteristic of himself, he sought out various lines of attack on both sides of the Mississippi, and hesitated at no obstacle in his path. The story of that campaign is one long record of hardship, loss, and disappointment, extending over many weeks before the tide of success was turned. Much depended, for Grant and for the nation, upon what he should do and what results might soon follow.

One of the movements preliminary to his more important ones was the White River expedition, which General Fisk was immediately ordered to join on reaching Helena. It proceeded up the White River to Duvall's Bluff, where a lively engagement took place, and then returned, occupying ten days. Back at Helena January 22d, General Fisk was there assigned to the command of the Second Infantry Division of the Army of East Arkansas, and had placed his forces upon transports, for embarking them to Milliken's Bend, when the order was countermanded by his superior, and they went into camp at Helena.

They remained there about three weeks. Meanwhile, Grant was hoping and striving to reach Vicksburg from the northeast, via the Yazoo River. It appeared to him the easiest and safest route. Nearly opposite Helena is Yazoo Pass, a crooked bayou reaching from the Coldwater to the Mississippi, which two rivers are at this point but ten miles apart. In former times the pass was navigable for ordinary steamboats; and the regular route for them between Memphis and Yazoo City was through that to the Coldwater and down that to the Tallahatchie, which, uniting with the Yallabusha and other streams, finally swells to the Yazoo, and finds the Father of Waters near Vicksburg. Before the war a levee had been thrown across the pass on the Mississippi's east bank, and Grant's idea now was to cut this, let the current once more along the old water-way, and float his army down to the Yazoo River's mouth.

The levee was cut February 3d by Colonel Wilson of Grant's staff, who exploded a mine under it, and whom General Gorman, in command still at Helena, was ordered to assist as needed. Four days later a gunboat entered the pass and found plenty of water in it, also an excess of trees. Confederates had felled the latter across it and across the narrow Coldwater in great numbers to render each watercourse impassable.

On February 15th General Gorman was ordered to send Ross's division through the pass and along the Coldwater, the Tallahatchie, and the Yazoo rivers, to see if they would permit the passage of a large force, and thence up the Yallabusha, to cut the enemy's railway connections at Grenada. Ross's division was the Thirteenth of the Third Army Corps, and of it General Fisk's brigade formed part. It was now ordered upon the most important expedition yet attempted during the Mississippi campaign, and on its effort hinged mighty interests. If successful, it might lead to the opening of the whole Mississippi Valley and a complete severance of the Confederacy. To carry it forward, Admiral Porter sent several light-draught gunboats, two ironclads, and one ram, to protect the transports and destroy anything which the Confederates might set afloat.

It took several days for the fleet to make its way through the impedimenta placed in the pass and reach the Coldwater, but this was accomplished March 2d. Without waiting longer, and acting on advices from Wilson, which said the combined water-ways were open, General Grant planned to throw McPherson's whole corps of five divisions down them and crowd Pemberton and Johnston to the wall. The advance body moved on as rapidly as possible, and for a time with encouraging success. No opposing force was encountered until half the distance to Vicksburg had been traversed, but then the fleet could no farther go.

Confederate General Loring, ordered to defend the Yazoo, had erected a line of works on a peninsula five miles below the Yallabusha's mouth, where the Yazoo and the Tallahatchie are but five hundred yards apart. These works he christened Fort Pemberton, and by them he expected to bar all passage down the Tallahatchie and the Yazoo. March 11th the Union fleet arrived at this unlooked-for obstruction. It had come thus far with exceeding difficulty and much hardship, covering but few miles a day, and earning by hard toil every foot of the course. None of McPherson's corps had yet come through the pass, for lack of boats. The whole fighting force consisted of General Fisk's command and a few more of Ross' division, numbering only 4000 all told—besides the gunboats. Wide overflows prevented the landing of troops, and attack could be made by the boats alone. They opened fire and bombarded Fort Pemberton all that day, but with no special harm to it. Next day a Federal battery was constructed on a bit of raised and dry land half a mile from the fort, and all through the 13th bombardment was continued, but without success. The Confederates were masters of the Yazoo situation, and of this fact no one could have a doubt who possessed familiarity with the river bottoms of Mississippi and knew the spot chosen by Loring for his blockade.

The Yazoo expedition was a failure, as earlier attempts against Vicksburg had been and as more would be. In a few days the fleet started back up the river, but soon met Quinby with one brigade of his division, which had penetrated thus far. He had met the same obstacles which impeded the vessels ahead of him, and could not earlier push through. Re-enforced by Quinby, who now assumed command, Ross and Fisk turned about and once more assaulted Fort Pemberton, but without avail. Quinby's hope was to find a landing-place for his troops while he sent the transports back after the main body, but there was no ground suitable for that purpose. Then he formed a plan to swing round the fort, cross the Yallabusha above it on pontoons, cut off Loring's base of supplies, and so compel surrender, and he despatched a boat to Helena for bridge equipment, but it was met by another boat bearing Grant's order to abandon the expedition and return at once. On April 5th General Fisk's command was withdrawn from Fort Pemberton and borne back to Helena. Grant had decided that not enough light-draught boats could be had for transporting so many men down the Yazoo, and gave up this expedition before he learned of the special difficulties which were in its way. The civilian wonders why he did not reach this vital conclusion previous to so much cost of time and means, but wonders more why an expedition of such difficulty was attempted, its success possible only as a surprise, when surprise itself was impossible, and when, not being surprised, a small force of the enemy could block the advance of a whole Federal corps and hem it in completely.

On his return to Helena, General Fisk went into camp there with his brigade, and had much to do in holding the Mississippi open for transportation of supplies. The weeks which followed were not peaceful, as rebel forces occupied the country in rear of them, under Marmaduke, Shelby, and Dobbins, and frequent skirmishes were engaged in, also some considerable battles. The whole spring and early summer were indeed full of active military work.

CHAPTER XI.

IT was while General Fisk's command lay at Helena, after their return from the Yazoo expedition, and one evening as he sat on a bluff of the Mississippi, looking across its muddy current and still muddier bottoms, that he heard some superlative swearing not far below. It was about the worst to which he had ever listened, and it grieved him to think, indeed at first he would not believe, that it could come from one of his own men. Walking out to the edge of the bluff, and looking over, he saw a teamster of the Thirty-third, who had been to the landing with a wagon and six mules, and, coming back up the river, had snagged on a stump and broken the wagon-pole. And, according to this teamster's profane declarations, everything conceivable and inconceivable, in the Confederacy and out of it, was in the way just at that particular time, and to blame for his mishap. He blamed everything, too, and everybody, in language exuberant with curses, till the miasmatic air seemed blue.

General Fisk walked back and sat down. By and by, soberly leading his six mules, along came the teamster. Saluting him kindly, the general said :

"John, didn't I hear some one swearing dreadfully over there a little while ago?"

"Oh, yes," the man answered, "I reckon you did."

"Who was it?" asked the general.

"That was me, sir," he replied.

"But," said General Fisk, "don't you remember the covenant made up at the Benton Barracks, between you and me and the others of the regiment, that I was to do all the swearing for the Thirty-third Missouri during the war?"

"Oh, yes," the man answered, promptly, "I remember that; but you were not there to do it, and *it had to be done then.*"

General Fisk enjoyed the humor of this reply, as much as he had been pained by the occasion for it, and gave it over to his staff. It gained wide currency, and afterward, through all the Mississippi region, whenever a teamster was heard cursing some one would suggest that he wait till General Fisk came along and let him have the job.

Shut away from all mail communication, during the six weeks that the Yazoo expedition lasted, when General Fisk returned to Helena all his men were eager for home news, and besieged the post-office tent at once.

After receiving his own postal budget, with its precious letters from wife and children, and pastor and Sunday-school, General Fisk sat down on a log near his headquarters tent to peruse them. He had undergone toil and privation forty-five days, but the sorest privation of all was to miss these messages of love. Now came his compensation, and he lingeringly read them through. He was not in uniform which denoted rank, and an old soldier sitting by accosted him familiarly.

"I say, old fellow," said this man, "I want you to read my letter for me."

General Fisk turned and looked at him, and then reached out his hand, into which the letter was placed.

In a straggling, downhill fashion, it was addressed to " John Shearer, Helena, Ark."

" But can't you read it yourself, John ?" the general asked.

" No," the man answered, half ashamed.

" Then I will, of course," said the general ; " but why don't you know how to read ?"

Briefly the man explained. He was an Iowa soldier, but born and raised in a slave State, amid great ignorance, and without school opportunities.

The letter was from his wife, and General Fisk read it through, slowly, aloud. It spoke of the crops, and the harvest, and all the little affairs of home—" mentioning even Susy's new dress, the new boots for Johnny, and the cunningest wee bits of socks for the baby"—as the general later said, and then it went on with a bit of wholesome reminder like this :

" It was quarterly meeting last Sunday, John, and the presiding elder stopped at our house. He told me that a great many men who go into the army Christians come back very wicked ; that they learn to swear, and gamble, and drink. Now, John, I want you to remember the promise you made, as you were leaving me and the children, that you would be a good man."

And as the general read on, big tears began to run down John's cheeks, until finally he raised the sleeve of his blue blouse and wiped them away, and out of a soldier's heart, and in the soldier's vernacular, he said :

" Bully for her !"

" Well, John," asked the general, finally, " have you been the good man you promised to be ?"

Then with more tears came a sad story of drunkenness, and gambling, and sinful speech, until the general's heart ached. Disclosing his identity at last, somewhat to the

man's confusion, General Fisk talked with him as a
brother, and won his pledge of renewed consecration and
a better life.

John Shearer came to all the brigade prayer-meetings
after that, a changed man. But one day the general
missed him, and sought him out. The swamps and
bottoms bred disease and begat death on every hand.
The Army of the Mississippi was under tribute every
hour to malaria, fever, and the grave. Hundreds of
brave men in General Fisk's own command closed their
eyes wearily and sank to sleep—

> "Waiting the dawn of the judgment day."

Low with fever, John lay in a hospital tent breathing
his last. But he was dying in the faith. And after receiving his final messages for wife and children, General
Fisk said a word of prayer by the dying man, and then
sang :

> "Jesus can make a dying bed
> Feel soft as downy pillows are,
> While on His breast I lean my head,
> And breathe my life out sweetly there."

So one of the homesick went home.

Before the war ended, more than twenty-five thousand
Bibles and Testaments were given out to soldiers and
sailors from the headquarters of General Fisk. And it
was at Helena that a pleasing incident occurred in Bible
distribution.

Advices from the War Department, at Washington,
had announced a new edition of "Casey's Army Tactics," and copies were looked for eagerly at the front.
While still expected, General Fisk one morning received
a thousand bright New Testaments from the American
Bible Society. They were unpacked and put up at
headquarters in a neat case, and, with their gilt-lettered

backs, made quite a show. Within an hour or two in came Colonel Samuel Rice, of Iowa, and glancing casually at the volumes he said :

" So the Tactics have come ! I am glad of it. "

" Yes, colonel," was the general's answer, " the Tactics have come."

" Can I make my requisition for them this morning ?" Colonel Rice inquired, still giving to them no closer scrutiny.

" Certainly," he was told.

" Have you read these Tactics, general ?" he further asked.

" Yes, colonel," was the prompt answer ; " I have studied them, and I mean to study them morning and evening till mustered out."

Colonel Rice's requisition for " forty-two Casey's Tactics " came soon through the adjutant-general, and General Fisk made up a package of forty-two New Testaments and sent it to Colonel Rice. The officers gathered round him to receive each a copy, and watched their colonel while he opened the package and handed out the books.

Astonishment followed, of course. It was not the kind of joke common in army circles, but they took it kindly. For a long time Colonel Rice had been thinking soberly on religious things. He began now to study *the* Tactics, and gave himself prayerfully to the warfare therein taught. For others of that group, also, these Tactics had special message and blessing.

Always while at the front, with the armies of the Mississippi and the Tennessee, General Fisk felt that he must care as well for the souls as for the bodies of those under him. He maintained prayer-meetings, and regular divine service, whenever practicable, and was equally

chaplain and commander the whole time.   His Christian
Commission antedated the military commission given
him by Government.

There was a broader Christian Commission than his
own.   It grew in the thought of Christian men like himself, and its work among the soldiers was a blessed benef-
icence.   For the dying it did much ; for the living
vastly more.   It went up and down upon the battlefields with ministering presence ; it illumined the hos-
pitals and mellowed stony hearts.   It was the divine
inspiration of a Christian humanity.

"The *majority* of the men came out of the army
better than they went in," afterward testified General
Fisk, " and all owing to the Christian Commission."

He believed in it from the first.   He gave it everywhere " God-speed."   He gave it, moreover, the largest
material aid in his power ; and, as if by his own heart-
throbs, he gave it loving, loyal service in the person of
his wife.   Mrs. Fisk was often under fire while doing
Commission work, and the service that she rendered
showed her fitness to be the companion of such a man.

General Fisk was one of the earliest to aid in the
Christian Commission's organized effort to be and to do,
and stood faithfully its friend till the close.

" Thank God," he said once at a reunion, long after
peace came, " thank God that it ever entered into the
heart of George H. Stuart—God bless him !—to hang
the banner of the Cross in every camp on the Potomac,
on the Cumberland, on the Mississippi, that through him
the throbbing heart of the Christian Church strengthened
the palsied arm of the Union."

In the spirit of this Christian Commission he did the
military duty assigned him, wherever and whatever it
was.   But he was common-sensible about it.   He

believed religious effort should bide its proper time, and
he had sympathy for that man whose arm was shot off,
and to whom an over-zealous and not very practical chaplain said :

" John, do you love Jesus ?"

" You take your handkerchief," said John, " and
tie up my arm, and then talk to me about my soul."

Physical helps are often the very best preliminary to
spiritual ; indeed, they are often the only ones that will
avail.   If the body bleed to death how shall the soul be
saved ?

CHAPTER XII.

By Special Orders No. 183 from the War Department at Washington, dated April 22d, 1863, General Fisk was relieved from further duty in the Army of the Tennessee, and commanded to report at once to General Curtis in St. Louis. Affairs in Missouri were unsettled and anomalous to an alarming degree. Two State governments existed, one Union and the other Disunion. "Knights of the Golden Circle" were numerous. Bushwhackers and guerillas abounded. Life and property were everywhere unsafe. The State was as if on a volcano of revolution every hour. Wisdom in military administration could be nowhere more essential. So the supreme authorities, recognizing General Fisk's rare administrative characteristics, transferred him to service calling not less for these than for the more common qualities of a military commander.

There was delay in transmission of the War Department's order, and it did not reach General Fisk till June 12th. He reported to General Curtis as soon as possible, and a few days afterward was ordered by him to relieve General J. W. Davidson in command of the District of Southeast Missouri, with headquarters at Pilot Knob.

He remained commander of that district until November 30th, when, by order of Major-General Schofield, now commanding the Department of Missouri, it was consolidated with, and made part of, the District of St. Louis, and General Fisk was ordered to relieve Colonel R. R. Livingston in command of the same.

On March 25th, 1864, he was relieved by General Thomas Ewing, and ordered to relieve General Guitar, of the State Militia, in command of the District of North Missouri. This was his most important command, and was longest held, covering more than a year. His headquarters were generally at St. Joseph, though part of the time afield. While thus engaged he was appointed Major General of the Missouri Militia, by Governor Fletcher, though still holding United States commission as Brigadier-General in command of Volunteer Troops.

Through the whole period of nearly two years, during which General Fisk was a district commander, his chief duties were of the bureau order. Detachments under him were often fighting small bands of the enemy in Southern Missouri and Northern Arkansas, while he remained at Pilot Knob, and his forces there captured Jeff Thompson and broke up all serious inroads upon that territory for a long time; but later, save through the summer and fall of 1864, or a part of both summer and fall, he was the administrator of peace rather than the prosecutor of war.

Northwestern Missouri was a very hotbed of lawlessness during the most lawless times. In it border-ruffianism had long been rampant; marauders seemed more numerous there than peaceful citizens. Before the war opened its counties were exceptional for wealth, and their fine plantations were famous for beauty and fertility. As soon as hostilities began the worst spirit of secessionism seized upon many of the people, especially the younger men, and one long reign of disorder was inaugurated and maintained. To stop it, and to restore a wholesome social and political condition, General Fisk was sent there.

His tact at managing men, his peculiar diplomatic gifts as a peacemaker, and his firmness, often unsuspected, under a gentle exterior, were well known to those in power above him, even to President Lincoln himself. In the long Fremont *vs.* Blair controversy, which so embittered the two Unionist factions of the State, General Fisk had retained the regard of both sides and the respect of all, and had written the President about it in such terms as to call forth this reply from his own hand :

EXECUTIVE MANSION, October 25, 1863.

GENERAL CLINTON B. FISK.

MY DEAR FRIEND : I have received and read your letter of the 20th. It is so full of charity and good-will that I wish I had time to more than thank you for it.

Cordially yours,

ABRAHAM LINCOLN.

It was believed that if any one could re-establish peace and prosperity to a once prosperous region General Fisk might and would. He knew Missouri, and much of Missouri knew him. He could be both suave and severe.

For a time matters grew steadily more aggravating after General Fisk took command at St. Joseph. The fact was that a secret, insidious, and very far-sighted movement had been begun by the Confederate authorities, in co-operation with General Sterling Price, to overcome the dominant loyal power in Missouri, to revolutionize that State and Kansas, and to hold both in hand at the next election in November, so as, in conjunction with disloyal parties at the North, to prevent the lega choice of a President and perhaps revolutionize the whole nation. Something of this plan became known to the Federal authorities as early as the sending of General Fisk to this difficult district, and an invasion of Missouri by Price was anticipated if the whole scheme were to be carried out.

Indeed, such invasion was planned as the climax of it and to determine its final success. Preliminary thereto must come a new and assertive cohesion of the rebellious elements wherever existing, and a development of disunion sentiment which would justify Confederate authorities in furnishing Price the invading force he asked. Hence there were spies and secret agents constantly operating ; the secession " Order of American Knights," or " Knights of the Golden Circle," grew in membership by some invisible means ; and through this oath-bound organization the entire disloyal portion of Northern Missouri was pledged to disorder, bushwhacking, and bloody deeds. Its hidden influences were felt in every walk of social, political, and military life. Their ultimate end was not less political than military, and socially they had frequent manifestation in dark and mysterious ways. Outrages were committed that now would make decency blush to narrate. Wrongs were common that manhood should everywhere have condemned.

Early in June, Platte County, adjoining Buchanan—of which latter St. Joseph was the business centre—saw a genuine insurrection, the open result of secret endeavor many weeks put forth. From that time on, through much of the summer, General Fisk's entire available force was kept busy scouring the brush in pursuit of hostile bands. It was a guerilla warfare of the most vicious kind. And not all his own men could be relied upon, it soon appeared, for two or three militia regiments developed untrustworthiness. Desertions from them grew numerous, and indicated systematic action and achievement on the enemy's part. An orderly-sergeant's returns would often run like this : " 37 Company G absent ; supposed to have tuck to the brush." Nothing seemed altogether reliable where so much was demonstrated uncertain, where sinister hints were heard on every hand, and when, as gathering rumors rendered week by week more clear, an unknown power was making ready for some effective and startling manifestation.

In his prompt, yet persuasive, fashion, General Fisk sought to uncover the secret resources of wrong, as well as to punish its active agents, within his jurisdiction. He knew of the prospective invasion by Price ; he was aware of the purposes involved in all this mysterious business so persistently carried on ; he comprehended the shrewd political intent under so much of semi-military marauding and actual violence of arms. And he realized that the possible climax of an armed invasion could be averted only by finding who were the most influential ambassadors of it and through whom their mission was being wrought out.

It grew plain that certain daring young men, representing the best families in certain counties, were the direct inspiration of this widespread mischief, or the efficient tools of bold mischief-brewers outside, and that the grip of a strong hand upon them and their fathers would conduce to the general good. He arrested several at once, and put them in prison. Immediate consternation ensued. One leader, not knowing how much had been actually revealed, grew frightened and told all to the general himself, whose happy knack of asking questions captured him. When others in the prison heard that Coon Thornton had peached, their grit failed them, and they were ripe for swift repentance and good works.

From Thornton General Fisk obtained the names of twenty-five planters, living in Platte and other near-by counties, who, it was said, could stop disorder and insure peace. Some of them the general knew. All were men of great local influence and of eminent respectability. A few were not suspected of disloyal things. To each of these twenty-five men and one or two more known Unionists General Fisk wrote a personal request for an interview at his headquarters on a set day. It was not like a notice of arrest, but it was mandatory. It implied the necessity of compliance. It insured the same.

Every man came. They all assembled at the Patee House, his headquarters, on the evening of the day named. Then the general made them a genial, sunny, sensible talk. In kindly terms he put before them the purpose of his administration, and showed them how he desired the best welfare of all. With mild firmness he declared that what could be must be, and that these men could and must bring lawlessness, marauding, and murder to an end in that entire region, that he should hold them responsible thereafter for any continuance of the bush-whacking, bulldozing, and bloodshed so long prevalent.

The men were nonplussed. They admitted themselves rebels, and frankly testified to the good Union character of those additional men invited merely to serve as "a blind." They as frankly stated the case from their standpoint, and rather justified their conduct, or sought to ; but they accepted the situation, and gave those guarantees which were exacted. Henceforth they would do all in their power to restore quiet and enforce law. And they kept their word.

But the Price invasion was not averted. So much appeared to hinge on the revolution desired by Confederate leaders in Missouri and Kansas, and on the wresting of these States from radical Union control, and so greatly had the real rebel sentiment of Missouri and the developments of it been magnified—so necessary did it become, in short, for the South to achieve some great diversion in its favor before and at the Presidential election then impending, that Price's plan went forward, and Missouri saw an anxious, bloody autumn.

It might have been much worse but for the wisdom in administration and the strategy in arms of General Fisk. To him was due the failure of Price to command large numbers of recruits to his standard when he came, and his further failure to capture Missouri's capital, the objective point of Price's campaign. With the capital lost to our side at that time, after results might have been vastly changed. What would have come to that State and Kansas, who can tell ? And with these both smitten off our Union column in the fall of 1864, with the political unrest that was increasing day by day, with Fremont a candidate for the Presidency and winning some followers from Lincoln, with the Peace Party of the North more and more assertive, and the national situation more and more doubtful to human eyes—with all this, as was part of it, potentially a fact, who shall calculate what might have been the end ?

CHAPTER XIII

On September 24th, 1864, General Price's army entered Missouri 20,000 strong. With him were Marmaduke and Shelby, his chosen chiefs for the splendid expedition he had contemplated so long. Their forces were flushed with hope and promise of successful achievement. Price expected 20,000 State recruits to join him when he crossed the border of Arkansas and that his onward march would be one growing momentum of victory. And, according to the subsequent report of General Rosecrans, then commanding at St. Louis, " rebel agents, amnesty oath-takers, recruits, sympathizers, and traitors of every hue and stripe had warmed into life at the approach of the great invasion." But these do not seem to have accomplished much or to have given the help or encouragement anticipated. The farther northward and westward Price went, the less of support did he receive and the more difficulties did he meet.

St. Louis was threatened and Jefferson City, the capital, was directly aimed at. While Rosecrans made all possible haste and effort to protect the former, he ordered General Fisk to Jefferson City with all his available force, and all possible speed, to defend the capital as best he could. St. Louis was in a greater ferment than ever before ; and all Missouri bubbled with military and political excitement like a full caldron over the flames. The hour of destiny was at hand.

General Fisk reached Jefferson City on the 28th and there took command over General Brown. He had but a handful of men, for his own force at St. Joseph was originally small, and had been depleted by militia deser- tions. The men he had were chiefly militia and raw recruits. With these and the help of willing towns- people, he proceeded to throw up such defences as would convey an impression of large numbers and much strength. Then he brigaded his 2500 infantry into sev- eral brigades, as if they were 25,000, and issued orders to them of a purely fictitious character, which were pur- posely let fall into the enemy's hands, at the proper time, through an avowed deserter who bore them.

On October 6th, after nine days of active preparation by General Fisk, he was re-enforced by Generals McNeil and Sanborn, with their cavalry commands of about 4000, and waited Price's appearance. The latter had fought with Ewing, at Pilot Knob, who made a gallant defence and then retreated to St. Louis, but had swung round that city and was moving forward upon the cap- ital. The danger of its capture grew hourly more im- minent. So far the invasion was aggressive, and though Ewing's blow against it had been severely felt, victory was with the invaders.

As reported later, by Rosecrans, "it was decided by General Fisk, the other generals concurring, to oppose a moderate resistance to the enemy's advance across the Moreau, a small stream with muddy banks and bad bottom, four or five miles east of the city, and then to retire and receive his attack at the defensive line, which with industry and good judgment had been prepared by the entire laboring force, civil and military, at Jefferson City."

This plan was efficiently carried out. Price's army

crossed the Osage and burned the bridge behind it the same day General Fisk was re-enforced. On the 7th Price moved across the Moreau, after sharp fighting there with the Union cavalry force, and, as his resistance fell back within the defensive line, advanced upon the town. He was surprised to find an enveloping system of earthworks, which, by their extent and apparent strength, implied a large garrison and ample equipment. He was misled, too, by the fictitious orders that had been brought to him from General Fisk. Not to assail the place meant abandonment of his errand, in large part, and to make assault might mean utter destruction. Price had got a taste of fighting earthworks at Pilot Knob, and was not eager for more. These were formidable beyond all previous hint, and apparently so well manned that capture was out of the question. So, after developing a line of battle three or four miles long, east, south, and west of the place, and after making a careful reconnoissance that did not encourage him, Price swung round Jefferson City, as he had swung round St. Louis, though nearer, without attacking, and after massing again upon the west, as if still unwilling to give up his game, he retired, leaving the town unharmed. It was a momentous victory for the Union side, and, so far, nearly bloodless.

On the 8th Price's movement became a retreat westward, with the Union cavalry force of McNeill and Sanborn following him. A retreat it continued most of the ensuing four weeks, and the range of it traversed pretty much all Western Missouri. On the 25th Pleasanton's cavalry division, provisionally formed for the pursuit, forced Price to a stand, and in the engagement which followed Generals Marmaduke and Cabell, five colonels, and over 1000 prisoners were taken, and what remained

of Price's command was sent flying, shattered and demoralized, into Western Arkansas. The great invasion
had come to an inglorious end ; its military and its
political purposes were in no degree achieved.

Concluding his report of it, made some weeks later,
General Rosecrans spoke warmly of the work Missouri
troops had done, and said they had " blasted all the political schemes of the rebels and traitors who concerted
with Price to revolutionize Missouri, destroy Kansas,
and turn the State and Presidential elections against the
cause." He added, further, that their service, with the
Union triumph at the polls, had " given to gallant and
suffering Missouri the fairest prospect she had ever yet
seen of future freedom, peace, and prosperity." And
after generally thanking all the soldiers who took part,
General Rosecrans especially thanked " General Fisk for
the prompt and cheerful discharge of very trying administrative duties and for his energy and good sense in
preparing the defence of Jefferson City, as in the subsequent repairs of Lamine Bridge."

This latter mention refers to the service rendered by
General Fisk's infantry after the cavalry force began
pursuit of Price.

Efficient as were his military services, thus hastily
sketched, and without any attempt to enlarge upon them,
the administrative work done by General Fisk subsequent to Price's invasion and prior to the election in
November may have been quite as effective and far-
reaching. Missouri gave 40,000 majority for Lincoln's
re-election, but how did this result come about ? Not
altogether, we may believe, through the defeat of Price.
Less extensive and less powerful, perhaps, than he had
supposed, there were yet disloyal agencies in the State,
and their efforts could be insidiously kept up ; they

might even make a secret and surprising show of strength at the polls. It became a grave question, indeed, who at the polls were to have rights and recognition, and to share in the assertion of popular power.

General Orders No. 195, Department of Missouri, had said : '' The general commanding expects the united assistance of true men of all parties in his efforts to secure a full and fair opportunity for all who are entitled to vote at the approaching elections in the State of Missouri, and in excluding from the polls those who, by alienage, treason, guerillaism, and other crimes or disabilities, have no just right to vote.'' This language would seem fairly plain, but its interpretation was open to divers opinions ; and on returning to his headquarters at St. Joseph, November 6th, after several weeks of service at and around Jefferson City, General Fisk found many communications waiting him from leading citizens, including several who had been appointed judges of election, seeking more specific information as to the qualifications of voters, and judges, and clerks of election, the duties of judges and clerks, the right of military interference at the polls, etc. In reply to these he issued, on the following day, a circular addressed '' To the citizens of the district, and especially to the judges of election.'' It condensed the various interrogatories to five, and gave as many clear, positive answers.

According to General Fisk's decisions, which carried with them the final determination of this whole matter within the bounds of his authority, none but legal voters were eligible as judges and clerks of election, none but loyal men were legal voters, and to insure these full ballot rights, and to prohibit the disloyal from enjoying such, military interference was justifiable and would be exercised. He further declared :

" The judges of election are the authority chosen to decide upon the qualifications of voters, and I conceive that the commanding general had this fact in view when he forbid the appointment of the specified class as officers of election, to the end that there should be no treason-able sympathies as incentives to the reception of illegal votes to the ballot-box ; and it is apparent that the chief source of illegal voting, in the opinion of the command-ing general, was likely to come from that class who, by treason and complicity of treason, had destroyed their right to the privilege of the elective franchise."

" In my opinion," said General Fisk, " all persons who in August and September, A.D. 1862, voluntarily enrolled themselves as disloyal, or as sympathizers with the rebellion, have no just right to vote." This opinion he based on the fact that the Convention ordinance, de-fining qualifications of voters, had been adopted on June 10th previous to such voluntary disloyal enrolment ; and that, according to the provisions of said ordinance, widely published, every citizen, before voting at any elec-tion, must be required to make oath that he would bear " true faith, loyalty, and allegiance to the United States, and not directly or indirectly give aid and comfort or countenance to the enemies or opposers thereof."

" It is clearly the duty," General Fisk declared, " of judges of election and all good citizens to see that the purity of the elective franchise is preserved, by prohibit-ing that class of persons "—those disloyally enrolled and rebelliously engaged—" from touching the sacred ark of our liberties with their bloody and unsanctified hands. Judges," he said, " should follow their convictions of duty to an honest conscience, to the country and their God. They are only answerable to the civil law for a corrupt disregard of their oath. If they are satisfied in

their own minds that ' known rebels and sympathizers '
have given aid and comfort to the enemy, it is clearly
their duty as honest patriots and conscientious judges to
reject their votes. Knights of the Golden Circle, or
O. A. K.'s," he specifically said, " should not only be prohibited from voting, but should be lodged in the nearest
military prison for trial as bushwhackers;" and he
charged upon judges the duty of compelling all appli-
cants at the polls, who might be suspected of membership
therein, to meet such suspicion under solemn oath.

Concluding this important administrative document,
General Fisk deliberately announced :

" The judges of election in this district will be sustained by all the power confided to my hands in the
honest and fearless discharge of their duty. Election
should be free from all violence and intimidation. The
purity of the election is equally essential. Traitors must
be repressed ; loyal men must be protected. . . . And
few but traitors will complain of an administration of
law and an enforcement of orders that exclude rebels
from the privilege of the elective franchise."

The salutary effect of the above utterances was so
marked, that on January 11th ensuing this resolution
was unanimously adopted by the Missouri House of
Representatives :

" *Resolved*, That the thanks of the loyal people of this State are
eminently due, and are hereby tendered, to Brigadier-General Clinton B. Fisk, commanding the District of North Missouri, for the
bold, just, and manly circular issued by him prior to the late election, in reference to the qualification of voters, and that said circular
be spread upon the journal of this House."

CHAPTER XIV

So faithful had been General Fisk's devotion to his trusts, as a military officer, that when called upon by Adjutant-General Thomas, with others, in February, 1864, to make report of furloughs and the like, he could say :

"I have never had a leave of absence ; have never been off duty an hour."

The months following of that year, as has been seen, were too busy for him to change this praiseworthy habit of incessant service. When came January of 1865, and every one felt that the Rebellion drew near its close, he was invited on to Washington, for some part in the anniversary of the Christian Commission. But he declined to leave his post, and not until he was ordered there by the Secretary of War did General Fisk respond and seek the national capital. He believed, as not all officers of high rank did, in scrupulous attention to duty, where that duty lay, and had no wish to wait about Government departments courting Executive favor.

It was a memorable occasion, that Christian Commission's anniversary-time, the last Sunday night of January, 1865. General Fisk himself gave a charming account of it fifteen years afterward, when the first Christian Commission Reunion took place, at Chautauqua. He said :

"It was held in the great Congressional Chamber just after its completion. It had been made ready for occupancy but a few days, and therefore we helped dedicate it. It was a wonderful assemblage of people. The sacred day on which we met, the cause for which we convened, and the remarkable character of the audience made it so. Long before nightfall the avenues of Washington leading toward the Capitol were crowded with a multitude of people intent upon not being among the thousands who could not find standing room in the hall an hour afterward. And when, at seven o'clock, the venerable Secretary of State took a chair, the scene was striking and impressive beyond description. The President and Vice-President of the United States, the members of the Cabinet, the judges of the Supreme Court, and a majority of the Senators and Representatives, distinguished men and no less distinguished women, representatives of the highest social culture of the country, from the chief centres of the Republic, adorned and graced the occasion. The galleries shone in blue and gold, with the uniform of the officers of the army and navy. The soldier with his fatigue suit was chinked in all around to fill up ; and fringed all about us were the bright, happy, and shining faces of the freed people. It was a mighty crowd."

And after going on to describe in happy detail some of the great men composing part of it, General Fisk resumed :

" Along toward midnight I was put on the platform to weary for a little time this great throng. I saw the President there hobnobbing with Mrs. Fisk, who was his partner, at one of the desks of the members. The speaker preceding me had told us what an easy thing it was to be good. I knew he was mistaken about it, because I had tried it. It is a hard thing to be good under the best of circumstances, and I told them so ; that it might be easy for those who were at home, living on fat contracts, but down on the picket-line, half-starving, walking our beat in the stormiest night, it was rather a difficult thing sometimes to be real pious. And then I told them a story about a soldier of mine."

The story was of that swearing teamster, narrated on a previous page. It pleased Mr. Lincoln very much, and he laughed over it in hearty fashion, his long form swaying back and forth above the desk before him. The whole speech of General Fisk sparkled with pleasant allusion, and the mellow humor so characteristic of his

platform efforts, while it was also tender even unto tears.
Late as was the hour, and much as the crowded audience
had heard, they all sat willing listeners till the end.
The Missouri general, as some designated him, had
brought the grand occasion to its climax.

Next day, or evening, there was a similar anniversary
at Philadelphia, which General Fisk attended, and on
his return to Washington, he said : " I will go and bid
Mr. Lincoln good-by before I go back to my command." What followed can be told best in the general's
own words, from that same Chautauqua speech already
cited :

" I went to the White House on Tuesday morning and passed into
the great room where the throng met on those days who wanted to
see the President, and there sat foreign ministers, and senators, and
members of Congress, and contractors, and judges, all waiting for an
audience. No one could get in. Mr. O'Leary, who used to attend
the door, and get some of you in for ten dollars apiece, came out and
said that no one could see Mr. Lincoln that morning. Among the
disappointed ones I saw a little old man, and I had met him there
two or three evenings before, trying to seek an audience with the
President. This old man staggered away and sat down on the win-
dow-sill, the very picture of despair. I said, 'You seem to be in
great sorrow ; what is the matter?' He raised his eyes, and
said, 'Oh, I am in such trouble, sir.' I said, 'What is it?'
and he said, 'Look at that package of papers ;' and I looked at
them and saw they were worn, torn, and greasy, and had passed
through ever so many headquarters, and were covered with en-
dorsements ; and I found that when the war broke out he lived
in East Tennessee ; that he had two boys, sixteen and eighteen,
and that they both went into the Federal army. That one at Straw-
berry Plains had been wounded and taken to the hospital, and
his younger brother detailed to nurse him. The older boy died, and
the younger one, homesick and lonesome, had deserted and gone
home to see his mother in East Tennessee. It was at the time when
death was the penalty for desertion, and no one could mitigate the
sentence except the President ; but this old man had been to see
that greatest of soldiers, who never made a mistake or lost a battle,
General George H. Thomas, the Commander of the Army of the Cum-

berland. He had been to him and told him his sorrowful story, and General Thomas had written a letter to the President, begging him to interfere and save the boy. And he said, ' It is Tuesday, and my boy is going to be shot next Friday. What shall I do ?'

" It was one of those sad stories, one of a hundred stories, that had made my heart sore, and I went into the President's private secretary's room. I knew him very well, and I said, ' John, I want to see the President.' And he said, ' You cannot see him.' And I said, ' Why ?' And he said, ' Let me tell you, but don't breathe it in Washington. We are going to start for Annapolis in twenty minutes. The engine has been ordered. Stevens, Cameron, and Hunter are waiting for us at Fortress Monroe, and we are going to have peace ; no more war.'

" I said, ' You don't say so ?' Then I added, ' Mr. Lincoln must not go down there until he has seen this old man.' I said, ' I will write him a letter,' and I wrote a letter as follows, and he took it in :

" ' MY DEAR PRESIDENT : There is an old man out here. He has a sorrowful story, and I know you will hear it. Will you hear him a moment and oblige me ?' and signed my name.

" I sent it in, and in less time than I can tell it there came a message from Lincoln to let this old man in, and he turned his back on plenipotentiaries, and senators, and judges and walked into the presence of Mr. Lincoln. I said to myself, ' I will see how this thing comes out,' and I pried the door open just about an inch. It would have been curiosity in a woman, but in a man it was simply a spirit of inquiry, you know.

" There stood the great President, pale and sad, his great hand spread out on the table, and this old man got very close to him before he saw him, and he said,

" ' Are you them an that General Fisk sent in here ?' and he said, ' I don't know who sent me, some one did ;' and the President said, ' Now tell me the story very quickly ;' and he told him the story, and Mr. Lincoln took the paper, and said, ' I will send it to Judge Holt, and you come to-night and see what the answer is.'

" And then the old man's heart sank within him, and he threw himself on the breast of the President, with his hand on his shoulder, and said, ' My God, Mr. President, this must be attended to now ; my boy is going to be shot next Friday.'

" How well I remember the wonderful look of the President—the wonderful look of sadness which mellowed away at once into such perfect humor, as he said, ' That reminds me of General Fisk's

swearing story ; let me tell it to you.' And he set the old man down
there by the table, and he told him the story in as much detail as I
have told it to you, making him laugh as heartily as possible, taking
three times as long to tell the story as it would have required to have
read the papers all through, and then he took an old quill pen, that
I would give a hundred dollars for this minute, and wrote across that
paper, ' Let this boy be pardoned. A. LINCOLN.' "

Back with his command, and having no solicitude
about promotion or other honors, at a time when loyal
Missouri would gladly have accorded him every recognition in its gift, General Fisk was appointed Major-
General of the Missouri Militia, by Governor Fletcher
(February 27th), and a few weeks later (May 13th) was
made Brevet Major-General of United States Volunteers,
by Andrew Johnson, " for faithful and meritorious services during the war.''   But prior to this last recognition
he had resigned as Brigadier-General of the United States
Army, and his resignation was pending at the War Department when President Lincoln's assassination occurred.
Acceptance of it was declined, and on May 18th, 1865, by
War Department Special Orders No. 238, he was assigned
to duty as Assistant Commissioner of the Bureau of Refugees, Freedmen, and Abandoned Lands, for the States
of Kentucky and Tennessee, and was relieved by General Dodge that this new and still more important trust
might be assumed.

CHAPTER XV.

THE Freedmen's Bureau, commonly so called, was established by act of Congress early in the year 1865, for the purpose of protecting freedmen and refugees in their rights and returning property to legitimate owners. In this twofold purpose was involved the complete readjustment of social and business relations at the South —the restoration of society to its new and better conditions.

It was the wish of President Lincoln that General Fisk should become the Bureau's permanent head, with headquarters at Washington and the rank of colonel in the regular army, but the general would not consent. War had cost him all the financial accumulations and all the opportunities open to his hand since the panic of '57. He would not use any advantage of place to recoup the loss, while he had spent freely of his Government pay in meeting Government needs. He felt that when peace came he could and should devote himself to commercial profit-seeking. Therefore his acceptance of a place as one of General Howard's assistants was but temporary.

Kentucky and Tennessee were assigned to him at the special request of Andrew Johnson, who had succeeded to the Presidential chair.

"Fisk ain't a fool," he said, in his blunt speech ; "he won't hang everybody."

Which remark implied that some army officers were

not wise, and that Bureau commissioners, each of the eleven being an officer of high rank, were given great authority. The latter, no doubt, was true. As Assistant Commissioner of Freedmen, Refugees, and Abandoned Lands, General Fisk had almost dictatorial powers. In him rested practical title to half the lands within his juris-diction—which soon extended to Northern Alabama and Mississippi, and part of Arkansas as well—and to a vast deal of church and other property forsaken by or wrested from its rightful possessors during the contest now closed. Upon him devolved the serious task of setting once more in motion a labor system become utterly demoralized and chaotic, wanting intelligence to know its own best good, utterly useless without direction and control, lacking all confidence in the men who once had controlled it, and pitifully expectant of great things as the immediate re-sult of freedom and citizenship. There has never been, and there can never be, a social and political situation, so extensive as this, more fraught with dangers and diffi-culties than was that of the Southern States directly fol-lowing Lee's capitulation.

General Fisk's headquarters were established at Nash-ville, and continued there, but he spent much time in personal visitation on the territory he commanded. For he was, in a large sense, military governor of those two States named ; he was a commissioner *plus*. And the *plus* meant much toward the welfare and good order of both white and black. His initial endeavors were directed chiefly to the re-establishment of kindly feeling and mutual good faith between the ex-slave and the ex-master.

Everywhere poverty ruled. Plantations were not worked. Summer drew near, and the crops were not in, over wide areas of land that should be yielding plethoric

harvest by and by. Freed industry could and must re-
habilitate the South, but freedmen distrusted their
former owners, and were alike indolent and afraid. It
was vital that labor be at once inspired with confidence
in capital, and be guaranteed full protection. It was
imperative that such labor, amid such conditions, should
have steady employment, and, for its own sake, and the
sake of all, should be put promptly afield.

Among the first acts of General Fisk was to gather
large assemblies of white and colored people in the open
air, and there address them. His addresses at these, as
testified by gentlemen who often heard him, were wonderfully effective. Writing of his work at this time, in
an article published in the *Ladies' Repository* for April,
1866, Major Lawrence, of General Fisk's staff, thus
remarked :

" He is very happy in his addresses to the freedmen.
It is really refreshing to hear them exclaiming, when he
goes out into a new place, where the gospel of freedom
has never been heard except as it has been thundered
forth by loud-mouthed cannon, ' O bress God ! Gineral
Fisk has come ! That's him !' ' We'll hear de truf
now.' ' He'll tell us what to do.' And he does tell
them, and while he speaks in his kindly way they devour
every word, and their large, liquid eyes are never for a
moment removed from him. I have seen four or five
thousand of these ' wards of the nation ' crowded around
the general's stand in a compact mass and listening to
his words, and a more interesting and, in some respects,
affecting spectacle, I have never witnessed."

The same gentleman, now well known as Judge Lawrence, of Nashville—where he has been in legal practice
since his Bureau association with General Fisk—in a recent private letter recalls one great meeting, held at

Spring Hill, Tenn., in a beautiful grove. "People of both colors flocked together," he says, "to hear what the head of the Bureau in this section had to say. The general, on reaching Spring Hill, was entertained at the home of a wealthy ex-rebel. The whole question of the relation of the races was discussed with such fairness, solid sense, and eloquence, and such evident sincerity, as to carry his entire audience with him. The substance of his advice to the former master was—'Employ your former slaves, treat them fairly, and pay them reasonably for their work.' To the freedmen he said : ' Be honest, industrious, and faithful, and make of yourselves good citizens.' He told them that freedom meant more earnest work than slavery and greater responsibilities ; not idleness and vice. Every day the freedmen who had flocked into the cities were urged to return to their old homes and make contracts for labor or rent lands."

One of those immense " mixed " meetings, to which came such crowds of white and black, was near Huntsville, Ala., under great spreading oaks, where had gathered a memorable concourse. It numbered thousands, of all shades, and ages, and kinds. At the general's request a white-haired and patriarchal planter acted as chairman, and was invited to tell first what his race and people wanted ; and then an aged negro, with woolly white hair and wrinkled ebony face, was singled out by General Fisk's quick tact and nice discrimination, and bidden speak for the blacks. He was a genuine Uncle Tom, and with that character's native dignity and simple pathos, the old slave said :

" Massa Gin'ral, all my people wants is jist a fa'r chance."

Then the commissioner talked to them with that unmatched candor and in that homelike, sunny-hearted

style which neither black nor white can long resist, and
ended by appointing the venerable uncle and the patriarchal chairman a committee to draw up some basis of
agreement which both sides could accept, to govern
future labor relations. They did their work together,
amicably, and reported to the multitude, which ratified
it with hearty demonstrations. And to this day General
Fisk is remembered with warm appreciation by the survivors of that scene.

Next to, or simultaneously with, the establishment of
goodfellowship between white and black, came the restoration of property. There were no such prejudices
here to encounter as made the first task often delicate,
and much of this work was speedily, easily done ; but
some people had wild notions of justice and equity, and
made extravagant calls upon the commissioner for aid.
His duties, it may be said, formed a perfect university
for the study of human nature. Writes a friend familiar
with them :

" General Fisk, as you know, bubbled over with
humor, and the stirring incidents which occurred while
he was here would enrich a volume. He could put him‐
self *en rapport* with the humblest and the wisest, and
while courteous to all he never lost sight of his work—the
reconstruction of society on a sound and healthy basis."

As an extreme sample of one type with which General
Fisk had to deal, we may mention an Alabama woman,
a mountain refugee, who came into headquarters as if
they would contaminate her, and fairly demanded her
rights. She had, as she informed him, " ben two year
in Injianny," and her business now was " to git transportation back to Alabam'. We uns hearn tell," she
said, " that you uns was goin' to give the refugees the
farms of the old secesh, and we uns wants 'em." The

general told her no, that could not be done ; and as he
said it, and while her disappointment was getting ready
to voice itself, a neatly-dressed colored woman came in,
and begged a hearing.   It was accorded her as politely
as if she had been white and dressed in satin.   She was
neater and more ladylike than the Alabama refugee.
Her story was infinitely more sad.   Her daughter had
been spirited away from Nashville, after being freed by
act of Congress, and sold in Georgia.   It was an unusual and unusually aggravating case, and it touched the
commissioner's great tender heart at once.   Her petition
for aid to bring back the stolen young woman was
granted as soon as made, and the petitioner went gratefully away.   Then this Alabama woman grew wrathy.

"Gineral Fisk," she asked, her sallow face yet more
unlovely than before, " *be* you a abolitionist ?"

"Yes, madam," he frankly answered, " *I be.*"

"Wall, now, gineral," she went on, "you don't
believe in nigger equality, do you ?   I'm sure you ain't
so bad as that ?"

The general's patience did not fail him, but his sense
of justice asserted itself.   With less suavity than usual,
he replied :

"Madam, I do not think you need have the least
uneasiness in the world on the question of equality, for
you will have to learn a great deal more than you now
know, and will have to conduct yourself in a much better
manner, before *you* become the equal of that good
colored woman who just left."

And with a sniff of her snuffy nose, and vigorously
condemning " the nigger bureau," this lady from Alabama took her leave.

A very fashionably-dressed woman came to him, one
day, with a verbal request for the restoration of her

property. Her haughty airs and her manifest consciousness of superiority—the unladylike manner of condescension which marked her—rather amused General Fisk, and he politely requested her to write out her claim. She confessed, with some sudden embarrassment, that she could not write ! And then, a fine stroke of sarcasm under it all, he ordered a young colored man, employed at headquarters—a private soldier of the Ninth Heavy Artillery detailed for office duty—to write out the claim and her petition concerning it, much to her disgust.

The same sense of humorous appreciation, tinged with gentle sarcasm, perhaps, led General Fisk once, when drafting the constitution for a colored benevolent organization which applied to him for such help, to declare that its object was " to provide for the poor *without any distinction of color.*"

It made no difference to the general if the humor of a situation told against himself. At Edgefield one day, near Nashville, he spoke to the colored people in a new schoolhouse just built to replace one burned down by the enemies of colored education. An old Baptist preacher was present, past fourscore, and became overflowingly happy. At the close he came forward and grasped the general's hand, and said, with great pride :

" ' Gin'al, you is a Baptist, I knows you is a Baptist, for no man can talk like dat, *'cept he been washed all over in de Jordan.'* And, becoming confidential, the old man whispered, ' De Methodists, gin'al, are a low set. *You* know they are. They came from Wesley, and he was a outcast, and you may look de Bible clar through and not find Wesley *once* in it, but you find Baptist, John de Baptist ; and all de Baptists come from him ! Yes, gin'al'—with another squeeze of the hand—' *dese Methodists are a low set !*'

CHAPTER XVI.

It was through the uniform kindness and wise judgment of General Fisk, exercised in the recognition of
property rights and the righteous adjustment of personal wrongs, that he so won the confidence of those
under his administration. He sought always to temper
justice with mercy and to soften hard feelings of alienation in the hearts of men. Like his good grandfather,
Ephraim Fisk, of New England memory, his mission
was that of a peacemaker, in this New South where had
grown such pathetic need of peace. And well and
wisely he performed it. Writing of his peculiar service,
a resident of Nashville lately said :

"Some men came South after the war, or remained
here, to thrive in politics and to use the recently enfranchised people to further their ambitious purposes.
General Fisk, from the day he opened his headquarters
here, seemed to be working in faith and hope for the
glorious results which the people in this section, white
and colored, are now enjoying. He had faith in man,
as man, and he certainly contributed greatly to the good
order, peace, and thrift, educational and religious, of
society here."

When General Fisk went there, religious thrift was at
the discount of conditions which had discounted everything. Church worship in many cases had long been in-
terfered with. Valuable church properties were under

alienation from societies long engaged, before war smote them, in their development and prosperous use. These, like all the plantations of men who fought against the flag, were in General Fisk's hands. And nothing gave him more pleasure, we may believe, in his varied acts of humanity, than the restoration of such to proper owner-ship.

The McKendree Church was one of these. In the heart of Nashville, it had known wide influence as the leading Methodist church organization of that whole region. But war's changes had scattered its member-ship and brought to unsanctified uses the honored edi-fice. On a beautiful Sunday of early summer, that year of 1865, McKendree Church was reoccupied by those who loved it. In gladness and gratitude they came to their own again. Sad and sorrowful times had been seen, during those months and years of separation, and wonderful changes had occurred, which gave a tender pathos to the day. The deepest solemnity marked that service of rededication. General Fisk attended it, with his entire staff, in full uniform, and occupied seats at the front. Tears of a hallowed joy flowed down hundreds of cheeks before the benediction came. And the sym-pathetic words of General Fisk, spoken in his abiding spirit of Christian brotherhood, were not least eloquent and thrilling.

The rights of the freedman before the law became at once matter of grave concern. A slave, he had never been allowed to testify in courts of justice against the whites. Freed, and a citizen, the State laws concerning him were in this respect unchanged. He was a cipher in his own defence, as all those years gone by. General Fisk saw the immediate necessity of fixing a different legal status for the blacks, and organized the first court wherein a negro had equal rights of testimony with white men. This was done under an act of Congress whereby special courts were made possible, in which were to be tried all causes, civil, criminal, and equitable, involving the rights of colored people. These courts, established wherever deemed necessary, were the occasion of some alarm in certain quarters, as a matter of course, and at first provoked unfavorable comment. It could not be otherwise. "The old order changes," but its changes, though swift enough when God ordains, do not so swiftly change men. Slavery had gone forever, but its old prejudices remained. White superiority could not at once brook the claim of colored equality in all places. Inward disgust and outward demonstration of it were but natural. The marvel is, when we come to ponder it all over, that such a degree of considerate acceptance obtained among the master race with regard to many things at feud with ancient custom and established social creeds.

These freedmen's courts were absolutely essential under the new dispensation of citizenship and the old code of State laws. But it required clear, solid judgment and the sternest sense of justice to run them fairly. General Fisk was equal to the emergency. He not only saw the courts promptly organized, but he saw them jealously maintained, and great numbers of causes adjudicated by them in a manner which gave satisfaction to all classes. But while these courts were firmly supported and their judgments and decrees enforced, he was using all his influence with the legislatures to induce them to enact laws giving to colored men the right to testify in all the courts ; and he constantly assured legislative assemblies that the freedmen's courts would be abolished as soon as such laws were made. He kept his

promise faithfully.   The civil rights of the ex-slave came
into fair legal recognition sooner than our country had
reasonable ground to expect.

Perhaps the first book ever issued for the practical
behoof of colored men was a little manual compiled by
General Fisk, and entitled "Rules for the Government
of the Freedmen's Courts." Certainly the first volume
ever published specially *for* colored men came from him,
about the same time—"Plain Counsels for Freedmen."
This latter was published in large numbers, by the
Boston Tract Society, and was sold cheaply or given
away.   It contained about eighty pages, and was greatly
prized by those for whom it had been prepared.   A book
written and printed *for them* had rare interest and peculiar merit in their eyes.   They regarded it with great
favor, and took its counsels quickly to heart.   Its very
dedication appealed to them persuasively.   It ran :

TO THE

FREEDMEN OF THE UNITED STATES,

Now happily released from the house of bondage, and fairly set forward in the path of progress, these Plain Counsels are respectfully
and affectionately dedicated by one who has marched with them
through the Red Sea of strife, sympathized with them in all their
sufferings, labored incessantly for their well-being, rejoiced in their
prosperity, and who believes that, guided by the pillar of cloud by
day, and of fire by night, they will reach the Promised Land.

CLINTON B. FISK,

*Brevet Major-General United States Volunteers, and Assistant Commis-
sioner in the Freedman's Bureau.*

NASHVILLE, TENN., March 1, 1866.

Its opening words, " On Freedom," were simple
and to the point :

" Every man is born into the world with the right to his own life,
to personal liberty, and to inherit, earn, own, and hold property.
These rights are given to him by the great God ; not because he is a
white man, a red man, or a black man, but because he is A MAN."

What followed " About your Old Master " was in recognition of the real facts :

" He has had a hard time of it, during the war, as well as your-selves. His wealth has melted away like wax before the fire. His near relatives, and in many cases his sons, have died on the field of battle or have been crippled for life, and the Government will grant no pensions in their cases, because they fought not under its flag. . . . You must think of these things, and think kindly of your old master. You have grown up with him, it may be, on the same plantation. Do not fall out now, but join your interests if you can and live and die together."

Speaking " About White Folks," General Fisk said :

" White people have old, strong prejudices, and you should avoid everything you can which will inflame those prejudices. You know how easy it is to hurt a sore toe. Prejudices are like tender toes. Do not step on them, when it is possible to avoid it.

" White men are very much influenced by a man's success in mak-ing a good living, and if you are thrifty and get on well in the world, they cannot help respecting you."

The chapter " About Yourself " had several para-graphs of wise advice as to personal habits, as well adapted for white men as for black. One of them de-clared :

" *You cannot afford to drink any kind of spirituous or malt liquors.* To say nothing of their bad effects on your health and morals, you cannot, in justice to yourself, pay what they will cost. Three glasses of beer a day would be thirty cents—two dollars and ten cents per week—nine dollars and ten cents per month—one hundred and nine dollars and twenty cents per year ! But if you drink at all, you will want something stronger than beer and more costly, and you will waste your time at drinking saloons, fall into bad company, and, ten chances to one, become a miserable, bloated, wheezing, blear-eyed drunkard. No, you cannot afford to drink. Do not go into a liquor saloon. Let no man see you there. Go straight by without turning your head. God says : ' Wine is a mocker, strong drink is raging, and whosoever is deceived thereby is not wise.' ' Look not upon the wine when it is red, when it giveth its color in the cup, when it moveth itself aright ; at the last it biteth like a serpent and stingeth like an adder.' If you want a clear head and a strong arm, self-respect, and money in your pocket, swear, and keep the oath, that you will never take a dram."

Following some general advice " To Young Men," was this :

" *Avoid the company of bad men and women.* Do not go with a man who does not care for the virtue of a woman. Keep away from gamblers. Never be found in the company of a woman who cares nothing about a good name. Lewd women will lead you down quick into hell."

" To Young Women " brave and beneficent words were said :

" There is no being on earth for whom I have a higher regard than a true woman ; and if there is one thing I desire above another it is that the freed-women of this country, so long degraded and made merchandise of, may rise to the dignity and glory of true womanhood.

" Let it be your first aim to make of yourself a true woman. Allow no man, under any pretence, to despoil you of your virtue. The brand of shame rests upon the brow of the unchaste woman. She is hated, even by those who are as bad as she is. No man can ever love her. Her parents mourn the day of her birth ; her brothers hang their heads in very shame when she is named, and her sisters blush to own her. If in your slave-life you have been careless of your morals, now that you are free, live as becomes a free Christian woman. Stamp a lie upon the common remark that colored women are all bad.

" A true, honest, wise woman is the best work of God. She is man's strength, the charm of the household, the attraction of the social circle, the light of the Church, and the brightest jewel in the Saviour's crown."

How needful such true, strong utterances, at that time and since, all know who have had close observation of the class addressed. " To Married Folks " these counsels followed :

" When you were slaves you ' took up ' with each other, and were not taught what a bad thing it was to break God's law of marriage. But now you can only be sorry for the past, and begin life anew, and on a pure foundation.

" You who have been and are now living together as husband and wife, and have had children born to you, should be married according to law, as soon as possible. This will give you the civil rights of married persons, and will make your children the legal heirs to your property."

These little extracts will serve to show how faithful were the teachings of this freedman's friend, and how true he was to the need of that period in negro experience. There were pages also about Work, Free Labor, Contracts, Dishonesty, Receipts and Expenditures, Homes, Crime and Religion, which had in them the worth of gold ; and several well-drawn illustrations added force to the counsels given and attractiveness to the book. General Fisk knew how swiftly the negro's eyes are won by picture-prints when even he cannot read. There was tact, as well as wisdom, in this modest volume, for the colored people's own good. It gave them a new consciousness of value. A man in whom they trusted and believed had thought them worthy to be advised in a real book, printed for them alone. They must be coming up in the world ! And were they not ?

Slowly, to be sure—slowly before that, slowly then. For them the printed pages were beginning to multiply, and the school-rooms opening freely here and there, and the teachers giving up ease and social caste to see them taught. But it was only as the flushing dawn of a better day. The twilight of ignorance, and of educational deprivation, was not yet dissipating, for these long oppressed. There should be sunrise by and by, though, please God !

CHAPTER XVII

THE sunrise came !—came through the prayers of a struggling people crying out after light and knowledge ; through the generous gifts of devout patriots, who saw that these millions, freed and enfranchised, must be educationally and religiously cared for ; through the sacrifice of brave souls who endured more, under obloquy and ostracism, than suffering thousands on the battlefields. Colored need and helplessness at the South, when freedom was made a fact, stirred the great sympathetic heart of the North as even slavery had never done. It was profoundly felt that by intellectual and religious culture alone could the blacks be fitted for their new sphere, and become safe constituent elements of the Republic. Before emancipation, indeed, this patriotic and Christian impulse moved to benevolent things. It opened the original school for freedmen, at Fortress Monroe, in the fall of 1861. It started the first colored school at Nashville in October of 1863. It had duplicated these in many other places before 1865.

Chief among its agencies, as afterward testified to, in a speech at Fisk University, by General Fisk, " and earliest on the ground with educational facilities, was the American Missionary Association, which for almost a third of a century has been in the front rank of mission work, especially devoted to the uplifting of the lowliest of the earth on both continents and on the sea. Patiently and faithfully, through good and evil report, has this association marched on in the plain path of duty, courting no antagonisms, but winning the favor of all classes, lifting up the lowly, educating the poor, and saving the souls of men by the power of the Gospel preached and taught by their faithful ministers and teachers."

With all his old intense hunger for knowledge fresh in recollection, and inspiring him with sympathy, General Fisk craved school opportunities for these grown-up children in his charge. From the outset his thoughtful attention was directed to the matter of colored education. More and more he saw the imperative demand for it, and realized how all efforts for the freedman must fail largely of success which did not include educational means. He tried to interest the churches along this line, but organically they did not move so promptly as could be wished. There were individual members of the Methodist Episcopal Church, South, however, who aided him much, and to whom he has paid loving tribute. In that same address above referred to the general said :

" Did Christian character ever shine in greater completeness before men than was revealed in the beautiful and blameless life of Dr A. L. P. Green ? Did ever better heart throb in human bosom than that which grew still in his breast ? During the period of my service here, Dr. Green was my constant adviser and wise counsellor. His intimate knowledge of all parties in the South, and his earnest desire to promote peace and goodly fellowship, rendered him invaluable to me in the discharge of the delicate duties to which I had been called. Dr. Green was the first man in the nation to place in my hands any considerable sum of money for the education of the freedman. This noble Southern man was among the pioneers in this good work. I can hold him up before this vast throng of young men who listen to my words this day as a worthy example. Stand to-day with your face to the stars and say, ' I will be a man ; a Christian man in all generosity and earnestness. I will follow the pathway which shall make me loved while I live, and which will make me honored when I fill my grave.' ''

The dominant spirit in which General Fisk was met by Southern men, and which made easier than they might else have been his often difficult tasks, was thus recorded by himself at the dedication of Jubilee Hall :

" When, in 1865, the rainbow of peace spanned the country's horizon, to myself was assigned the duty, in this and adjoining States, of aiding, to the extent of my ability as an officer of the army, in the re-establishment of the supremacy of the civil law, in the restoration of prostrate industries, and of doing whatever else should promote the welfare of a people whose fields, in many sections, had then no fresh furrows save those which had been turned by the red-hot ploughshare of war, and to whom had come, through the arbitrament of the sword, a revolution upheaving the great social and industrial system which had grown with the growth and strengthened with the strength of centuries. In the discharge of the important duties assigned to me, from no source did I receive more cordial and help-ful aid than from those who had been chief spirits in the great con-flict, and who, with sword and pen, had served the ' lost cause ' with all possible devotion and earnestness ; but having returned to the old paths they with equal ardor hammered swords into ploughshares, and thus forgetting the things which were behind, the great aim was to follow those which made for peace. We struck hands of fellow-ship and said : ' How best can we, shoulder to shoulder, " the blue and the gray," uplift the prostrate communities ? ' The years it was permitted me to serve in that capacity are among the most satisfac-tory of my life. From far and near came up the busy hum of resur-rected industry. Churches and college buildings were restored to their original purposes, and the Christian pastor and teacher, the Scriptures and spelling-book, resumed the places from which they had been driven by the stern behests of war."

The Scriptures and the spelling-book !—he was a believer in both. Out of his belief, in large part, grew the institution of learning that has been referred to, bearing his name. It had small beginnings, but around those a large horizon of far-seeing purpose.

Fisk School for Freedmen was opened January 9th, 1866, in some Government buildings west of the Chattanooga depot, known at that time as the Railroad Hospital. These buildings had sheltered the Federal soldiers, and were now, at General Fisk's wise discretion, transformed into an educational centre for the emancipated children of bondage. In August of the year previous the American Missionary Association had sent two of its officers to " prospect " for a school in Nashville. These two men were Rev. E. P. Smith, then recent Secretary of the Christian Commission, and Rev. E. M. Cravath, and ex-army chaplain, who had entered upon service with the association named. And, as told by Mr. Smith at the dedication of Jubilee Hall, they searched Nashville through to find a building or a hall which could be rented for school uses.

" There were vacant buildings, but none for a colored school. We found an army barrack structure belonging to the Government which could be made to insure the purpose for which we were sent—the establishment of a primary school—but it stood upon private ground, whose owner, though in need of money, was not, as he said, ' so low down ' as to sell or rent property for that kind of business. At last, in our search, we came upon the group of hospital buildings near the Chattanooga depot. The ground upon which they stood could be purchased—if it was only known for what purpose—for $16,000, one fourth cash. Professor Ogden joined us, and together, by using all we had and borrrowing all we could, we raised the cash payment and gave our paper and a mortgage for the balance, and the infant Fisk, though not yet named, had a cradle.' '

To these preliminary efforts General Fisk lent all possible aid, and later his purse and credit were often at the school's command in time of need. It took his name, in fitting recognition of the labors whereby he had made its establishment possible, and of the practical interest which from the first he manifested in its establishment and growth. For grow it did. The individual debt incurred to start it was discharged, and in 1869 the American Missionary Association became full possessors of it.

Meanwhile, in 1867, it was duly chartered as Fisk University.

The wildest dreams of colored education did not at first, perhaps, include the university idea. That was but a natural development. The brightness and progress of many pupils came to demand instruction of a higher grade. The adoption, throughout many Southern States, of a colored common-school system spread wide the higher educational desire, and made less needful the low-grade special schools for freedmen heretofore supported by Northern contributions. So generosity was left a chance to rear the higher institutions of learning, and to lift the blacks to a yet loftier level of knowledge. A boarding hall and a dormitory were essential at Nashville, and these were provided. Steadily the needs of Fisk University were met, that in turn it might meet the crying want all about it. But year by year its needs grew more exigent, until 1871.

Then the old buildings, though often repaired, could not, it was clear enough, be much longer saved from decay. A new set of edifices must be erected, and for these it was vital that a new site be had. The American Missionary Association lacked resources, and could do nothing. What could any one do? Speaking of this emergency, when Jubilee Hall was dedicated, General Fisk said:

" The immediate friends and promoters of this institution, though poor in worldly goods and beset with discouragements without limit, were, nevertheless, rich in faith, and never faltered from their original purpose to build here a college, or, at least, make the beginning, trusting to the blessings of God upon those who might come after them to carry forward the enterprise to complete success. Year by year, after the undertaking of ten years since, grew upon us the perplexing problem of obtaining the means to purchase a new site and erect the permanent initial building of Fisk University. When through decay cf the old buildings and the urgent demands for increased facilities the necessity for a solution of the problem became imperative, there was found one man equal to the emergency."

That one man, "a most faithful staff-officer in my own military family," as General Fisk speaks of him, was George L. White. What he did, and how he did it, and what came of the doing, form a wonderful chapter in the record of earnest effort for God and humanity which men and women have made—the story of the Fisk Jubilee Singers. They have borne General Fisk's name across two continents and over many lands. Their story belongs right here, and shall be told partly in the language of General Fisk himself.

CHAPTER XVIII.

JUBILEE HALL, the "initial permanent building of Fisk University," to which reference has been had, was dedicated January 1st, 1876. A great throng of white and colored people crowded into it, and made the occasion memorable. General Fisk presided as President of the Board of Trustees, and gave one of his winsome addresses, which has been liberally quoted from already in these pages, and may be yet further appropriated. After his handsome recognition of Mr. George L. White, the president said :

> " ' There's music ever in the kindly soul ;
> For every deed of goodness done is like
> A chord set in the heart, and joy doth strike
> Upon it oft as memory doth unroll
> The immortal page whereon good deeds are writ.'

" There was music in the soul of our Brother White. He gathered around him the children of the freedmen, and with them

> " ' Sung the old song.'

He conceived the idea of coining the slave melodies of the old plantation and the camp-meeting into gold and silver, wherewith to purchase this commanding site, and upon it erect Jubilee Hall. George L. White was eminently a man of faith, and when he went before God on his knees and asked His blessing upon his efforts, he believed that God was going to help him. His was the prophetic soul. He saw the

> ' Glorious coming years,
> This prophet saw them far upon the way ;
> With timbrel and with song,
> Before the doubting throng,
> *He* bore the standard of the coming day.'

"How well do I remember when this good brother wrote me at my home in St. Louis, and asked me to loan him $300 to take his singers north of the Ohio River. I wrote an answer and told him not to think of such a thing ; that he would bring disgrace upon us all, and told him to stay at home and do his work. He wrote back that he trusted in God and not in General Fisk. [Laughter.] Next we see him marching onward with his little band. Reaching the city of Cincinnati destitute, he went down to our old friend Halstead, of the *Commercial* and said to him, 'You are a friend of General Fisk ; I have some students of his who are going to sing Sunday morning at such a church. I have no money to pay for the advertisement, so will you please say in your paper that they are here ?' This was on Friday and they were to sing on Sunday. Judge of Mr. White's surprise to see announced in Saturday morning's paper that General Fisk's negro minstrels from Tennessee [laughter] were in the city, and would sing in such a church the next morning at 10.30 o'clock, and advising everybody to go. Everybody did go, as it was something really wonderful to witness a negro minstrel performance in a church on Sunday. [Laughter.] It was a grand triumph for the negro minstrels ; it was the foundation of their success.

"The story of the Jubilee Singers fills a volume. The little poorly clad company of emancipated slaves who, four years ago, left Nashville on their mission of song, have, since that day, written their names indelibly on the hearts of millions in our own country and Great Britain. They went forth weeping, bearing precious seed ; they came again rejoicing, bringing their sheaves with them.

"We should fail in the discharge of our grateful duty on this occasion did we not speak of the faithful and persevering labors of Rev. G. D. Pike, who, as business manager for the Jubilee Singers, made their great achievements possible by his unremitting toil in properly presenting them before the public.

"In America they conquered social prejudices, and by their modest, Christian demeanor, which they have so happily retained, commanded the respect and generous patronage of the best and highest in the land. Beyond the sea they have twice received hearty welcome and God-speed from the noblest and best of England, Scotland, and Ireland. We this day record with a becoming spirit of gratitude our obligations to the Earl of Shaftesbury, whose great heart throbs generously for all humanity and its every good cause, for royal welcomes to England by his lordship extended ; to her Majesty, Britain's most noble Queen, and the royal family, for their kindly benediction upon the Singers ; to her Prime Minister, Mr. Gladstone, to Hon.

John Bright, to Rev. Newman Hall, Spurgeon, Parker, and Dr. Allon, and to hosts of others in the United Kingdom, who have smoothed the pathway of the Jubilee Singers, and caused their treasury to ring with the clink of British gold, therein cast for the furtherance of our cause. We can express for them all no better wish than that, in the great day of final rewards, they and we may be gathered into the common citizenship of that better and heavenly country, where

> " ' Unfailing palms we'll bear aloft,
> Unfailing songs we'll sing ;
> Unceasing jubilee we'll keep,
> In presence of our King.' "

The actual sum earned by the Fisk Jubilee Singers, and the way in which their work and the work of the university was regarded by the noblest class of Southern men, found statement in the speech of Rev. John B. McFerrin, D.D., as follows :

" There's not recorded such an instance in history that a few men and women, like the Jubilee Singers, have, within the space of a very few years, raised $100,000 for the education of their race. But the beautiful point in it is this, that I had some hand in that. Now, you ask me, ' How do you account for that?' and I tell you that it is owing entirely to camp-meeting songs. I helped to teach the colored people the camp-meeting songs which lie at the foundation of Jubilee Hall. I have heard those songs sung during my ministry of fifty years. I thank God that, after delivering hundreds and hundreds of discourses to colored people, I have lingered around to hear these beautiful songs, which were sung until the break of day. If the teachers here will teach them to send up songs and shouts of praise to Jesus, I simply say AMEN. I want you, General Fisk, and all others, to understand that the Southern people, as far as my information extends—that is, the intelligent, patriotic, and Christian people of the South, with, perhaps, a few exceptions—rejoice in the education and elevation of the colored people, and fully appreciate the grand work you are doing for them. [Loud applause.] I stand on my native soil and bear this testimony. It meets the hearty co-operation and sincere approbation of all Christian people."

How and whence came the pathetic sweetness of those Jubilee songs, that have so moved the high and the lowly on both hemispheres, and what are represented in

the edifice their service reared, were briefly stated by
the Rev. G. D. Pike :

" We are about to dedicate a building unmatched, in its origin, in
the annals of the world ; for this magnificent edifice expresses more
than the renowned and praiseworthy efforts of the Jubilee Singers—
more than the tact and skill of every one who has given thought and
labor for its construction, because it was only made possible by experiences earlier than emancipation. The price thereof came from
stricken souls who, in times of grievous sorrow, burst forth

" ' O Lord, O my good Lord, keep me from sinking down.'

" It was built with the coin of those who, in their seas of trouble,
breathed in whispered accents :

" ' Steal away, steal away, steal away to Jesus.'

" And it shall ever stand a monument to those who, glorified with
hope, blazing heavenward, midst trials and afflictions, exultingly
sang,

" ' Didn't my Lord deliver Daniel,
'liver Daniel, and why not every man ? '

" ' Oh ! stand the storm, it won't be long,
We'll anchor by and by.'

" This building represents history and ideas. It stands on the
boundary line betwixt two civilizations. On these grounds a fort
was once erected for defence, but this edifice is more than a fort, it
is a lighthouse ; yea, it is more than that, it is a university, in which
may be taught the principles that will shape the destiny of nations.
What we say here will not largely add to what has been done. We
can do little indeed to consecrate, for God baptized this enterprise
long ago. It is rather for us, while we stand here, to dedicate ourselves to the unfinished task of placing the civilization this building
represents beyond peradventure. It is for us to take on new devotion with every triumph won for exact justice and a reign of elevated
industries and Christian intelligence. It is for us here to resolve
that, God helping us, our nation shall be redeemed and made typical
for many nations yet unborn."

On the evening of this very happy New Year's day
for Fisk University, a supper was served in the large
dining hall to over three hundred invited guests, where
General Fisk presided again, with his never-failing

geniality, and where the story of the Jubilees was still further told in the following poem by Professor A. K. Spence :

" Songs from the sunny South land,
    Songs from over the sea,
Songs from the house of bondage,
    Songs of the glad and free,
They sang, those children of sorrow,
    Those children of dusky hue ;
Strange and wild were their accents,
    But their hearts were warm and true.

" Echoes from unknown ages,
    From Afric's distant strand,
Down through the generations,
    To wake in a captive land,
They brought like the summer breezes
    Blown from a land of flowers,
Like the voice of whispering angels
    From a fairer land than ours.

" They caught the sweet inspiration
    When lulled on their mothers' breast,
As at evening they sang of heaven,
    Where the weary are at rest :
And they saw sweet angels coming
    To carry them away,
And the chariot swinging lower
    Through the gates of opening day.

" Sometimes their songs were wailings
    Of the anguish-smitten soul
In the land of dark perdition,
    Where fiery billows roll,
And their strains grew wild and wilder,
    As before their eyes entranced
Things that no tongue may utter
    In fearful visions danced.

" And men in rapture listened,
    And strong men wept to see
These children of the bondmen,
    These children of the free,

And they opened up their coffers,
   And they poured their treasure forth
From the ocean to the river,
   From the South land to the North.

" And afar o'er the restless billow,
   Where castles are gray and old,
And many a bard of sweetness
   Has sung to a harp of gold,
Entranced by the song they listened
   To these children of the sun,
And many a tear-drop glistened,
   And many a heart was won.

" And prayers and benedictions
   Were theirs from many a breast ;
They sang so sweet and mildly,
   So sad, as when oppressed ;
And they stood among the great men
   In the palaces of earth—
They from the house of bondage,
   They of servile birth.

" And aloud they sang in triumph,
   They sang of the Jubilee,
When broken is every fetter,
   And the sons of men go free ;
In the age of peace so golden,
   That the prophets have seen so plain,
When men shall be friends and brothers,
   And Christ Himself shall reign.

" O Africa, land of shadow,
   O Africa, land of song,
Land of long night's oppression,
   Land of sorrow and wrong,
Thy echoes return unto thee,
   Bearing on golden wing
The tidings of earth's salvation,
   The song that the angels sing.''

CHAPTER XIX.

BECAUSE of the deep interest that will always attach to Fisk University, on account of its noble purpose and the marvellous effort of song to win for it world-wide sympathy, and because the later half of General Fisk's life is so closely linked therewith as to be inseparable therefrom, some further words about it may be admissible here.

Its location is fortunate—one mile northwest of Nashville, and overlooking that Southern "city of schools." It stands on a sloping plateau, from whence unobstructed views may be had in all directions. The prospects commanded by it are everywhere pleasing. In war times Fort Gillem occupied the same site—named after General Gillem, of Modoc fame, who lived near Nashville subsequent to his Modoc campaign, and died there. The fort was well equipped, but never saw fighting. When its ramparts were at length levelled, to receive a building earned by the songs of freedmen, no memory of blood or of battle stained the spot.

It is in a neighborhood becoming classic. Another institution of high culture for the colored race lies on beyond—Roger Williams University, of Baptist maintenance ; and near both is the magnificently endowed Vanderbilt University, for whites, with its great and fine structures marking a new epoch in Southern educational progress. And scattered around these, or across the space between them and the city's denser population, are hundreds of neat homes, built since war grew to be a memory, of a class which renders Nashville conspicuous for modest yet elegant home-life.

Jubilee Hall occupies one end of the plateau, Livingstone Hall the other, and future edifices will extend along the space between. The main angle of the main building points almost directly to the capitol, while the city of Nashville, sloping on all sides from that central edifice, is in more or less distinct view from both of the principal fronts of Jubilee Hall. The city view from the hall is fine, but the distant as well as near scenery on the other sides is even more pleasant. Indeed, there is no window in Jubilee Hall that does not command an exceedingly beautiful outlook, and the whole campus, of twenty-five acres, is admirably adapted for outlook, for drainage, for airiness and cheer.

Ground was broken for Jubilee Hall January 1st, 1873, and its corner-stone was laid October 1st of the same year. It is large, English in style, and of massive proportions. Architecturally it is an L, with an east front of 145 feet and a south front of 128 feet. Including basement and cellar, it is six stories high, and has all the conveniences of water, steam, and gas for its 120 rooms. Its ultimate use will be as the ladies' hall of Fisk University, but as yet it does dormitory and chapel duty as well, besides furnishing an office, assembly room, recitation rooms, reception rooms, library, kitchens, laundry, and dining hall, each of ample dimensions.

Its dormitory department deserves especial mention. There are forty rooms, each arranged for two students, with separate and complete appointments for both. Every room has two closets. The furniture is made of solid black walnut. Forty of the sets were obtained by

Mrs. Clinton B. Fisk, and forty others were given by friends in Great Britain. Each bed has a straw mattress and a heavy cotton pad upon it. The three upper stories are *fac-similes* one of the other. All are divided into bedchambers and all furnished exactly alike. Each floor has bath rooms, with hot and cold water, water-closets and wash-closets. Three tanks in the attic, holding thirty barrels each, supply the entire water convenience, and they are in turn supplied from five cisterns in the cellar, holding 25,000 barrels of water.

The large chapel is bright and inviting, with a broad platform whereon the Jubilee Singers have often made plaintive music, and where the Mozart Society now discourses in a more ambitious musical way. The attendance always crowds the capacity and accommodations, and is characterized by an air of earnestness and prayerful purpose which impresses every visitor. Founded in prayer, built with the proceeds of great faith, maintained for the elevation of a race more universally religious than any other on earth, Jubilee Hall breathes ever an atmosphere of devout and aspiring trust. The real dedication of it began a day earlier than New Year's of 1876. Students and teachers held a watch-night service in it as 1875 went out. It is an immemorial custom of the colored people thus to observe the last night of every year. Of that meeting a teacher wrote :

" The special burden of prayer seemed to be that God, who had so surely been with the school in the old home, might take possession of this, might so fill it with His presence that it should be as the temple of old, when the glory of the Lord descended and abode upon it and in it ; that it might be the birthplace of souls for many generations to come. A student prayed, ' O Lord, Thou knowest we hated to leave the old home, which was so dear and so sacred to us, and we do not want to stay in this spacious building unless *Thou* art here.' Mention was made of Moses, when he pleaded with God, ' If thy presence go not with us, carry us not up hence,' and very sweetly came to our hearts the promise given to God's servant, ' My presence shall go with thee, and I will give thee rest.' Just at twelve o'clock, when 1875 was numbered with the past and the untried new year was opening upon us, we all knelt in silent prayer, that God would hide us beneath His wing, safely sheltering us during all the passing years, whether they brought to us trial and sorrow or joy and rejoicing, in the great work that He has given us to do."

A like spirit of prayer and praise possessed the heart of General Fisk when he opened the formal exercises of dedication, and, after inviting all to sing

"Praise God, from whom all blessings flow,"

delivered his address. His first words breathed it, and those which immediately followed were permeated by ardent Christian patriotism. He said :

"With devout thankfulness to the Giver of all good ; with songs of praise on our lips and the spirit of consecration in our hearts, we would this day gather in Jubilee Hall to dedicate it to the good cause of Christian culture. It is a glad day for all ; for those who have planned and labored through much discouragement—who have prayed and watched through the darkness and the sunshine for the coming of this hour. It is a day of joy for those in whose behalf this good work has been accomplished. We hail you with a ' Happy New Year.'

" We listen to the silent footfalls of the Old Year, which has just passed out into eternity laden with its joys and sorrows. We step over the threshold of a glad new year, and hail each other and all with hearty greetings and best wishes and prayers that ' your lives may be long upon the land which the Lord thy God giveth thee.' And was there ever land more beautiful ? Was there ever a more goodly heritage than yours, ye men and women of Tennessee? Did lines ever fall to any people in more pleasant places than in this grand old commonwealth ? From its magnificent rivers to its boundary lines it is fitly described, as was Canaan of old, by the mouth of the deliverer, lawgiver, and prophet, as ' a good land, a land of brooks of water, of fountains and depths, that spring out of valleys and hills ; a land of wheat and barley ; a land wherein thou shalt eat bread without scarceness, thou shalt not lack anything in it ; a land whose stones are iron, and out of whose hills thou mayest dig brass.'

" At the capital of the State, near to the dust of the iron man who sleeps at the hermitage—here, within the encircling arms of the majestic river which flows at our feet, where Nashville sits as Queen of the Cumberland—Jubilee Hall this day throws its doors wide open, and bids you enter in and seek wisdom in her pleasant ways and peaceful paths. How could we better do our part in the ushering in of 1876? How better celebrate the centennial year of the nation's birth than by the recognition of our grateful duty to our God and country? How magnificent the outgrowth of the century of our national existence! Time will not permit us to tell you ; every schoolboy knows it. We will not here undertake to portray the marvellous development of this great country. One hundred years ago the Atlantic coast was fringed with sparsely populated communities. To-day how magnificent the growth from sea to sea, and from the silvery lakes of the North to the Southern gulf !

" One hundred years ago this morning Washington was at Cambridge, planning his attack upon Boston ; Lee was in Connecticut, marching on New York. General Greene, in a New Year's communication to his friend Ward, a delegate in the General Congress from Rhode Island, said : ' The interests of mankind hang upon that body of which you are a member. You stand a representative not of America only, but of the friends of liberty and the supporters of the rights of human nature in the whole world. Permit me, from the sincerity of my heart, ready at all times to bleed in my country's cause, to recommend a declaration of independence, and call upon the whole world, and the great God who governs it, to witness the necessity, propriety, and rectitude thereof. America must raise an empire of permanent duration, supported upon the grand pillars of truth, freedom, and religion.' "

And after adding much in similar spirit of appreciation and faith—a part of which has previously been quoted—General Fisk concluded his address with this wise advice and apostolic injunction :

" ' Wisdom is the principal thing, therefore get wisdom.'

" But, above all else, may they who herein enter be made ' wise unto salvation through faith which is in Christ Jesus,' who by the mouth of the prophet hath said, ' Wisdom and knowledge shall be the stability of thy times, and strength of salvation.'

"Lift up your eyes and behold the outstretching, whitening harvest, which invites you who will go forth from this institution with
the Divine benediction upon you to teach and preach among the
millions of our land who stretch out their hands appealing for
knowledge, and the unnumbered millions more who, from the heart
of Africa, are inviting the means of religious renovation of that mysterious land from which—thanks be to God—the pall of barbarism is
being lifted. Let it be the aim of Fisk University to fashion those
who shall be sufficient for these things. And upon all, the teachers
and the taught, and upon our friends everywhere, may there this
day come, and forever upon them remain, the blessing of the Father
who hath loved us, the Son who hath died for us, and the Holy
Spirit which quickeneth and sanctifieth. Amen."

CHAPTER XX

GENERAL FISK remained with and was a large part of the Freedmen's Bureau till August 18th, 1866, when he was mustered out of the United States military service, to take effect September 1st ensuing. He had then devoted over four years to this Government's needs, with a single and unswerving purpose to help insure national peace on a sure basis, and the fruits of peace to all whom war involved. For the welfare of both races in the South he had labored with patient energy more than fifteen months, spending freely of heart and brain that high and humble might have every right. It had been a service of patriotic love. He never regretted a day of it. In a certain and holy sense it had been the Master's work, and done as for Him. Its droll experiences had been many, its glimpses of the grotesque frequent; its tearful pathos often lent a touch of soberness to daily cares, and offered sharp contrast with the humor so abundant.

He had seen great and essential changes in the legal status of black men. He had made it possible and common for such men to claim and secure recognition in the courts. He had compiled for them a code of laws, and had seen the same in general operation. He had witnessed the adoption of land and labor contracts, under which colored laborers had become self-supporting and were able to command homes of their own. He had restored vast aggregations of property to hands that by right should hold it. He had given healthy and hopeful impetus to industries that meant real prosperity by and by. He had been one of God's instruments in the providing of educational resources for the oppressed, and in the safe assimilation into the body politic of a new citizenship previously unfitted for the sphere assigned, and of doubtful, even of dangerous possibilities, without such fitness and faithful attention as now could be conferred.

So much, indeed, had been accomplished, or set in motion for accomplishment, that he saw an open door out of duties onerous while not lucrative, and felt at liberty to leave them for larger personal opportunities. Yet he forsook the Bureau with real sadness. Its field of useful effort had grown dear to him. The freedman had become his grateful friend, as he long had been the friend of freedmen. He half regretted, at times, that he was not to remain permanently in service for them and for the Southern whites, whose confidence he had won. He has ever since regarded that service as the most satisfying of all his life and productive of the most good, and has held a warm place in his heart for those men, representing more than a hundred millions of capital, who petitioned President Johnson to detain him at his post of duty in Tennessee till reconstruction efforts were no longer needed.

Returning to St. Louis, to which place and whose people he had become deeply attached, General Fisk cast about for some opening wherein he could retrieve the losses occasioned through his patriotic course. The domain of politics was before him, but not alluring. With superlative politic insight, peculiar powers of tact, and a native genius for managing men carefully developed by wide experience, he might have entered on a political career of exceptional popularity, and used its advantages to his own great material gain. But he would not. His tastes ran along other lines. He knew, too, how much the politician must sacrifice of fine moral fibre and of devoted Christian effort if he win and keep a front place. He loved his church, his manhood, and his God better than the gains of a doubtful success or the applause of men.

He did accept an appointment, tendered him by Governor Fletcher, as State Commissioner of the Southwest Pacific Railroad. Its functions were purely administrative and non-political. It gave him no party grip ; he wanted none. It opened, however, some broad business possibilities. Railroading then in the West was experimental and uncertain. Oftener than otherwise it proved unprofitable. The through trunk lines were barely projected, save one. The States were eager for railroad development, but not in condition to aid it save by the grant of lands. And immigration had not yet set in with such a flood-tide westward as was later seen.

The old Missouri Pacific organization had been helped by the State, under certain stipulations, to build branches and part of its line. A land grant of 1,000,000 acres had been conferred upon it, on terms which the company did not meet. Trouble followed, and in 1866 ninety miles of this road were surrendered to the State. This the State sold to General Fremont and others, who agreed to complete the road within a given time, or, failing so to do, to forfeit all interests therein. They failed, and under the agreement, and a law authorizing such action, the State seized upon the road and became full possessor. Then General Fisk was sent as the State's agent to General Fremont to see if that gentleman would take and run the road, but he declined. Scandal had grown out of its management, and Fremont preferred not to assume any liabilities, or appear to derive personal benefits from the changes which had taken place.

At the request of Governor Fletcher, General Fisk assumed full direction of the road, and ran it for the State. He gave to it better system, close economy, live enterprise, and success. He made it pay. He made it a valuable property. But this arrangement could not last. Missouri was not a railway corporation. The State did not wish permanently to engage in railway management. Some different plans must soon be set in motion. So General Fisk enlisted other gentlemen with him, and the road became theirs under conditions guaranteeing the State against loss, and insuring completion of the enterprise. Fifteen men put $100,000 each into the State treasury, as an earnest of good faith, to be drawn out as the work progressed, and the State, in return, gave to them the road and its original grant of 1,000,000 acres of land. Newly chartered as the South Pacific, this road of so many changes and doubts became a fixed fact, and its individual promoters realized handsomely therefrom. General Fisk was vice-president and land commissioner of it, and gave it his best managerial abilities.

He remained in this connection till the early summer of 1877, but removed to New York in 1872. The ten years of his railroad activities were wonderfully busy and fairly profitable years. Sagacious as a financier, methodical, and everywhere commanding confidence, he gave the firm tone of integrity to his enterprise, and liberal results followed. His removal to New York, though not considered permanent, seemed essential to business interest, and threw him actively in association with vast monetary resources. He won speedy recognition as a man of clear brain, strong character, quick but cool judgment, and unflagging zeal.

His aid came to be sought on every side. His name was wanted in the directory of great insurance companies, banking corporations, and similar concerns. Church and other philanthropies called upon him for service and counsel. Colleges insisted upon making him a trustee. The Government appointed him to a responsible place of trust as a known philanthropist and the Indian's friend. The cause of temperance claimed his constant sympathy and frequent help. He was desired as the guardian of great estates. At army reunions and other banquets his voice was invited for the happy cheer it could give and the inspiration it lent. Vast gatherings of various religious bodies were not complete till General Fisk came. Night and day, seven days out of the week, his brain toiled and his heart beat for busy humanity round about him. Nothing but steady habits from boyhood up, and blood pure from any taint of poisonous excesses, kept him from speedily breaking down.

The wonder to family and friends was how he could stand such an incessant strain. Equable temper and serene philosophy carried him through a long time. Amid fires of excitement which would send the pulses of most men far above blood-heat, he could be cool and calm. Business was always put away for the prayer-meeting, and amusement waited on duty ; and with faith in the heart and coolness in the head he would not let worry kill when work might not.

But suddenly, in 1877, a break came. His fine nervous system gave way. The time had come to halt. He resigned all railroad connection, threw business cares all one side, and in three days, at the command of physicians, started for Europe. His companion was Mr. Oliver Hoyt, of Stamford, Conn.

They spent all that season abroad. Putting care quite away, General Fisk sought recreation, and the new vigor it should bring. He revelled in history, scenery, and romance. Not seeking human contact, he yet came to meet many whom the world calls great. Among these was the Emperor William I., with whom a very pleasing interview was enjoyed. The Jubilee Singers had made General Fisk's name familiar throughout Great Britain and over the Continent, and he found himself, through them and their songs, inseparably identified, among lovers of liberty, with the cause of freedom in America. A hearty welcome waited him in England and Germany, and his receptions and greetings were almost embarrassing in both countries.

He was in London during the anniversary of the British Freedmen's Aid Society, and its President, the Earl of Shaftesbury, invited him to deliver an address. No other occasion, perhaps, could have induced him then to make a public effort ; but this appealed swiftly and powerfully to his deepest sympathies, on its own account, and because the Jubilee Singers were present to make music for the great throng. From reports in a London paper it would appear that General Fisk enraptured the earl and those five thousand shouting Englishmen beside to whom he spoke. Their applause was electric, and grew more frequent to the end. After thanking them for their reception of the Jubilee Singers on a former visit, and for material aid rendered Fisk University through them, he said :

" England and America, partners in olden times in planting and maintaining slavery on the shores of the new continent, in later days unite in saying that no slave can breathe on any soil over which floats the Union Jack or the Stars and Stripes. England through peaceable measures broke the shackles of her bondsmen ; America, through a long and bloody war, which cost millions of treasure and thousands upon thousands of our best sons, who sleep to-day in soldiers' graves.

> " ' On Fame's eternal camping-ground
>   Their silent tents are spread,
>   While Glory guards with solemn round
>   The bivouac of the dead.'

With you we share the glory incident to the extinction of slavery ; with you lift up our songs of deliverance to the music of the breaking of the fetters of human bondage, ringing over the hills and plains and across the seas, heralding the Jubilee of our millions of freed people. ' It was the Lord's doings, and it was marvellous in our eyes.'

> " ' Speed on Thy work, Lord God of Hosts,
>   And now the bondsman chain is riven,
>   And swells from all our guilty coasts
>   The anthem of the free to heaven.

> " ' O not to those whom thou hast led,
>   As with Thy cloud and fire before,
>   But unto Thee, in fear and dread,
>   Be praise and glory evermore !' "

General Fisk's references to the inception of Fisk University, and the work it had undertaken to do, and to Jubilee Hall, which their contributions had helped erect, were followed by this tribute to one whom all men honor and all Englishmen love :

" And now, working by faith we have begun a new building, to be specially devoted to the preparation of missionaries for Africa. At its baptism a few weeks since we gave it a name loved and honored in every Christian household throughout the wide, wide world, as also in the abodes of the heathen, to whom he gave the best years of his great life—that true son of science, that hero of heroes, that humble and earnest missionary of the Cross of Christ, David Livingstone. England did him honor, and honored herself, when she assigned him to resting place with the great

> " ' In the great minster transept,
>   Where lights like glories fall,
>   And the sweet choir sings
>   And the organ rings
>   Along its emblazoned wall.

" He sleeps by the side of the best and bravest—heroes, statesmen, and poets—men of art, men of letters, men of philanthropy—but amid the rich memorials of greatness there is

" ' No storied urn or animated bust '

which tells of a nobler life than that of David Livingstone. It is our purpose to give him honor by the erection of Livingstone Mission Hall, from which we trust there shall, as the years roll on, go forth a multitude who will do honorable service for the Master in regions opened to the world through the long weary years of his explorations. We would have all Christian lands, all Christians, unite with us in this great work."

The reports then go on to state that upon the platform with General Fisk was the Rev. Dr. Moffat, father-in-law of David Livingstone, and that he followed the general in a fervent speech in behalf of the culture of the colored people of America.

CHAPTER XXI

THE same abiding sympathy, and enduring sense of justice, that made General Fisk the protector and guardian of freedmen, made him the sure ally and friend of the Indian. Alive to current events, and well posted in the history of Indian affairs, he knew how gravely our Government had fallen short of right and duty in its treatment of the aboriginal tribes. He felt the shame of its base betrayals and repeated acts of unfaith. He again and again spoke freely his mind about it all, and demanded, in the name of civilization and humanity, the better and nobler policies possible. His heart and mind were actively reaching out to the plains and mountains where wrong too often dominated, and misery was the ever-growing result. His interest in the Indian's welfare steadily increased.

In 1874 General Grant sent for him. As President, Grant was better informed on Indian matters than perhaps any other executive had been. He was also serving his second term, and his original knowledge of aboriginal things had grown much. He desired the most liberal, faithful, and far-sighted Indian policy, and wanted the Board of Indian Commissioners to be of the broadest Christian and humanitarian type. They had known each other, he and General Fisk, since 1858. During the war they had seldom met, though General Fisk was some time, as foregoing pages have shown, in Grant's

army besieging Vicksburg.   General Fisk had a call from
him at Helena, it is true, and remembered well Grant's
plain demeanor at that time, also his strong mental grasp
of the situation.   Since the war they had come often
together, and the qualities of General Fisk were well
known to Grant, and greatly admired by him.   He sent
for General Fisk because he knew him so well.

" I want you at the Indian Commission's head," was
the declaration of President Grant.

To take this place involved additional burdens for an
already overburdened man, but he acquiesced.   When
has he ever failed to respond where duty's call was
heard ?   Appointed commissioner, he was elected President of the Commission by his colleagues, and has held
that responsible yet unsalaried place ever since.   For
fourteen years now, without reward or hope of reward,
he has given freely of his time, his energy, his means,
to carry forward that broad, sagacious, philanthropic
policy which looks to the ultimate end of all Indian
troubles and cost through the full, intelligent, responsible citizenship of every Indian within our national
domain.

Of the important work which this board has done little
seems generally known, though its annual reports to the
Secretary of the Interior have furnished ample information, and its frequent meetings and annual conferences
have been well reported in our public prints.   The annual reports contain a vast array of interesting facts
about tribal conditions, school experiments, etc., and
some of them embody full records of the Lake Mohonk
annual conference, held every autumn at the residence
of Commissioner Smiley.   At the third annual thus
held, when General Fisk was a third time chosen President of the Conference, in accepting the place he said :

"There is some progress in Indian affairs—not great, but we may say there is progress. General Grant in his first message used about this language : ' The treatment of the original owners of this country has been such from the beginning as to lead to continual murder and robbery and all sorts of affliction.' He added that his own knowledge of matters on the frontier, his own experience as a soldier, led him to believe that the rulers of this country had pursued a course, or that national legislation had been such, from the beginning, as to be most harmful to the Indian. He then said : ' I have adopted a new policy, which is working well and from which I hope the best results.' The new policy was the legislation which provided for the appointment of the Board of Indian Commissioners, and such other, in the spring of 1809, as led to a better understanding of Indian affairs. From that time—from the time when a certain delegation, one of the members of which is in this room, visited President Grant, when he said his knowledge as President and his knowledge as an old soldier should be thrown in the right direction for the Indian—progress has been marked. At midnight on March 3d, 1871, Congress made that remarkable declaration that thenceforth no treaty should be made with an Indian tribe. They reached that decision after having made four hundred treaties, which had been frequently broken, with nearly one hundred tribes. Congress said, We will put a stop to this wrong ; we will not regard any tribe as a nation. From that time we have been visiting nearly all the larger tribes and making certain agreements with them that are working for better things. Many of us are beginning to believe that the Indian has made all the progress he can under the conditions which have obtained in the past.

"At the first interview I had with General Grant after coming into this Board of Commissioners, he said, ' The trouble is, we regard the Indians as nations, when they are simply our wards.' General Grant went out on the skirmish line. Said he, ' We must make the Indian believe us ; we must treat him as a ward. We should work especially to throw down every barrier in this country, so as to have no foot of land on which any American may not go.' This, of course, meant the doing away with all reservations, and pointed to the ultimate citizenship of the Indian ; to his absorption, for which we have been working for more than a hundred years. We owe the Indian a great deal—land, homes, law, and, above all, patience and care. With such help coming to him, and in confiding in those who deal with him, it will not be difficult in the future to settle this problem. It was more than a score of years ago that I met Bishop

Whipple, at Washington, pleading for the Sioux. Mr. Stanton said, 'What does Bishop Whipple want? If he wants to tell us that we have done wrong, we know it. The remedy is not at this end of the avenue ; it is at the other end. When you convince people, when you make the right sentiment that shall lead Congressmen to believe they had better give attention to this matter, then I shall believe the time is not far distant when there will be no Indians who are not American citizens. It is astonishing that nearly sixty millions of people cannot manage these few.' "

On November 10th, 1885, with a committee from the Mohonk conference, General Fisk called upon President Cleveland, to interest him still further in the Indian reform. After that committee's interview with the Executive, and at his request, the general addressed him a formal letter of suggestions, which so thoroughly covers the ground of the proposed reform, and so well sets forth the conclusions of those who have made Indian affairs a careful study, that much of it shall be given here :

" The Indian question is partly administrative, partly legislative. In so far as it is administrative we have nothing to urge except expedition in every measure which promises to secure permanent tenure of land in severalty to those Indians already entitled to it, rapidity in issuing patents where they have been provided for by law, and the greatest care in securing and retaining, both as agents and superintendents of education, men who are fitted by nature and as far as possible by experience for the very difficult task intrusted to them.

" We strongly and heartily second the purpose indicated by Mr. Oberly at the Lake Mohonk conference to require certificates of competence of all candidates for appointment as teachers, and his plan briefly outlined for a convention of Indian school superintendents to discuss the problem of Indian education.

" The legislative question presents greater theoretical difficulties. But certain things appear to us clear and of both immediate and pressing importance.

" Congress has already provided by treaty a law for the survey in sections and quarter-sections of twelve reservations. The list of these reservations, with reference to the laws, is appended. We would

earnestly urge the immediate appropriation by Congress of the necessary funds to carry out the provisions of these laws already enacted,
and thus prepare the way to give land in severalty to the Indians
who occupy these reservations and to throw open the unallotted land
in them to settlement.

" We earnestly recommend the adoption by Congress of a law con-
ferring upon the President power, in his discretion, to cause surveys
of other reservations and the allotment of land in severalty to the
tribes occupying them as rapidly as their consent can be obtained,
the purchase by the Government at a fair valuation of all the unallotted land in such reservations, the cash value thereof to be appropriated for the industrial and educational advantages of the tribe,
and the opening by this method to settlement of the reservations so
allotted and purchased.   A measure embodying these principles has
already twice passed the Senate at the last session, if not on both
occasions unanimously, and has also received the official approval of
the Committee on Indian Affairs in the House ; and we trust that it
will only require the endorsement of the Executive to secure its final
passage by the Forty-ninth Congress.

" Of course all Indian titles should be made inalienable for a term
of years ; all Indians taking land in severalty should receive the full
protection accorded by the law to other citizens, and as soon as any
tribe is fairly equipped in individual homes and made competent for
self-support, all annuities should cease.

" In addition to these measures, which we think might properly
be urged upon the immediate attention of Congress with a reasonable
expectation that they would be promptly and with substantial una-
nimity passed, we respectfully submit to your consideration a third,
which is the result of a considerable degree of consideration and
discussion on our part.

" We are thoroughly convinced that with comparatively few excep-
tions the Indians can be prepared for land in severalty and the perils
and protection of citizenship as rapidly as the Government can well
provide the necessary surveys and allotments of land ; that, as a rule,
it is safe to throw upon their resources and the protection of the local
community, with the added safeguards of the United States courts,
any tribe of Indians who are ready and willing to accept the boon
and the burdens of civilization.

" We therefore unite in recommending that Congress be asked to
provide for the creation of an executive commission, to be appointed
by the President, to open negotiations with the various tribes, as rapidly as, in the judgment of the President, is compatible with the safety

and well-being both of the Indians and their white neighbors, in
order to secure their consent to the abrogation of the reservation, to
land in severalty, to the cessation of annuities, and to the citizenship
of the emancipated Indians.

"We believe that the time is fully ripe for the inauguration of
such a policy. This is no sudden conclusion ; we have come to it
gradually, as the result of study and deliberation. And it is our profound conviction that this Administration can render no greater service to the nation than by inaugurating, and if possible carrying
through to its consummation, a policy which shall solve the Indian
problem by emancipating the Indian from his present condition of
pupilage and pauperism, and his white neighbors from their alternate
experiences of terror and of wrath."

Under the Indian Commission's wise policy it has
effected the organization of several industrial schools—
one at Hampton, Va.; one at Carlisle, Pa.; one at Lawrence, Kan.; one at Chilocco, in the Indian Territory ;
one at Genoa, Neb.; and one at Salem, Ore. In these
are being trained and taught over two thousand Indian
children, and fitted for civilized home-life when they
go back to their reservations. To visit some of these
schools has been a duty General Fisk enjoyed, and also
to visit several of the reservations.

It was his happy tact and strong good sense which
gave peace to the Creek nation in 1883. He and
others were appointed, by the Indian authorities at
Washington, a special commission to visit the Creeks
and adjust, if possible, the serious difficulties which had
long disturbed them. Himself and the Secretary of the
Board of Indian Commissioners, General E. Whittlesey,
were the only ones to reach Muscogee, Ind. Terr.,
for the duty assigned. They went there in August, and
met, in several daily sessions, the hostile Creek factions.
So strained were the relations between these, and so
fierce the individual hatred which had grown up between
their leaders, that division of the Creek country was

urgently demanded by some, and the overthrow of the
well-organized Creek government appeared likely to
many.   But General Fisk plainly told them that the
Creek government must stand and the Creek lands remain undivided ; and then he brought both sides
together, heard their respective statements, advised a
committee to harmonize differences, and, with that good
nature and good sense which even savages could not resist, he brought them soon to terms.

Their concurrent agreement was read in triplicate,
finally, at the Methodist Church in Muscogee, before the
reunited Creeks.   It was then signed by the leading men
of each faction, and some " talks " followed which were
full of General Fisk's own spirit of kindly Christian
good-will.   These remarks, among others, were made
by Chief Checote, head of the nation :

"It will be well for all the Creek people if they will hereafter
endeavor, on all occasions, under all circumstances, to have their
affections placed upon each other's good.   That alone will bring
happiness and prosperity.

" These good men, these commissioners sent to help us, have not
only used their own judgment ; more than that, they look up to the
Giver of all things ; they invoke His blessing upon you, upon all of
us, in bringing about this great good, so that we should hereafter
remember this meeting.   We should never forget the lesson learned
here, but remember what we have done on this occasion in bringing
about the peace desired.   We have once more made a great agreement.   We have agreed to be united.   We have united.   Now let us
be united in all the future.

" My friends, we should advise all our people at home to look well
to their farms and herds of cattle, to be industrious, to be good
farmers, and attend well to their business ; then alone can they expect
happiness and prosperity.   Above all, advise all the people to look
well to the welfare of your children ; send them to school ; keep
them there ; use your best efforts to have them educated ; and when
we have passed away they will take our places and care for the
necessities of our people."

After Isparhechee, leader of the revolt against Checote, had, at General Fisk's request, said "Amen" to all Checote's words, the general dismissed them with this admirable advice :

"Peace is so much better than war. I had rather see regiments of corn growing in the fields than to see regiments of men ready for a fight ; and instead of columns of men standing in line of battle with uplifted guns and painted faces, I should prefer to see the cornstalks lift their spears to the sun and shake their tassels in the winds that play over the plains of the Muscogees. We hope to hear that you are all in your homes with restored industries and doing that that will bring prosperity to your nation. Let us forget the things of the past, and look forward with hope. Let us not talk so much about how loyal a man was to the United States Government twenty years ago, but how loyal each man can be to the Creek Government —to his own nation. Let the school-houses be erected and the children placed therein, and it will bring you greater joy, greater prosperity than if you were in camps concocting schemes against each other. And now, in bidding you good-by, I can express for you no better wish than that, after serving as the best citizens in this country, you may all have citizenship in that better country which is an heavenly one."

The Rev. T. W. Perryman led in a closing prayer, the doxology was sung, and Chief Checote pronounced the benediction ; after which there was an informal but almost general interchange of friendly greeting between the late opponents, and the assembly broke up in universal rejoicing and mutual congratulation. Peace had indeed come to the Creeks.

CHAPTER XXII.

DURING the years 1878, 1879, and 1880, much grief and trouble came to General Fisk. His mother died in the spring of 1878. In 1874 he had built a house for his brother Horace two miles northeast of Clinton, Mich., and on a farm neighbor to that owned by Elder Powell, their stepfather, who died about that time. Once more a widow, and at an advanced age, Mrs. Powell's one desire was to spend her remaining days with those nearest her heart. In the new home of his brother, Horace A., Clinton B. fitted up a suite of rooms for their mother with every comfort, and lacking naught to make glad and peaceful her Indian summer of life.

And there she " fell on sleep." She sat knitting one day, and was suddenly paralyzed. She could barely speak, but she recognized her sons. When Clinton came she was rejoiced, and willing then to go. He sat down beside her, and she signalled him to sing. Her favorite hymns were " Rock of Ages" and " Jesus, Lover of My Soul." He sang them both through, his voice trembling with the sorrow of her speedy loss. Then he prayed that her end might be gentleness and peace. And almost while he prayed the fluttering spirit fled ; the mother to whom, under God, he owed all, had grown immortal.

Her funeral services were held at the Congregational Church in Clinton, that being the largest audience room in the village, near the little home where she and the boy Clinton had seen such early struggles together. From miles around the people assembled there to pay their last and loving tribute to one whom all respected, whose long life of more than fourscore years had been help-ful, hopeful, and faithfully devout. Her truest monu-ment she left in their tender memory, and in the Chris-tian manliness of her surviving sons.

The two years following were prolific of speculation. The capitalists of New York grew wild with mining fever, and formed companies for Western operations with a reckless unconcern of consequences that now can-not be understood. Within a few months over forty million dollars of New York capital found investment in the West. Many companies were often organized in a day. Mining stocks became the craze. The best and most prudent business men of the metropolis caught at them eagerly, and clung to them as profitable beyond peradventure. Some of the mines were "wildcat," doubtless ; many were "salted ;" a few existed on paper alone ; and the most, it is probable, lacked only money, experience, and fair mining equipment to be made pay-ing properties. In the aggregate they were one huge rat-hole, into which money was poured like water and never pumped out.

With others, gentlemen of the highest commercial honor and Christian integrity, General Fisk engaged in mining ventures, and lost. They had actual mines, in Arizona and elsewhere, and should have coined wealth from them, according to all mining theories ; but those theories oftener fail than win. The veins cost unduly to develop ; or water is remote and must be had at any outlay ; or machinery eats up all the output ; or the superintendent proves inexperienced, if not a thief—

something can be cited to show why fair prospects do not materialize. It is the law of mining enterprises, and can be relied upon. General Fisk learned all about it in due time, but the schooling came dear. However, he did not sorely complain. He was not bankrupt, even by the loss of a large fortune. He had a home yet in St. Louis, and a more alluring one, recently acquired, down in New Jersey, and a competence besides. His health had been restored, and he could make another fortune if need be.

One effort to that end, however, only occasioned further loss, and yet further and more aggravating litigation. It was connected, in some degree, with the mining matters referred to. As concise an account of it, probably, as could be given, appeared in the *Seabright* (N. J.) *Sentinel*, a Republican paper, in the summer of 1886, when General Fisk was making his campaign as Prohibition candidate for Governor of New Jersey. It ran thus :

"Every newspaper in the State has heretofore published full details of the inception and growth of the conspiracy to blackmail General Fisk, and of his triumphs over the villains who made the attack. The press without exception commended the general's course, and congratulated him on his victory. From the reports of the cases, on file in every newspaper office, may be learned that in 1879 General Fisk aided two young men to go into the business of banking and brokerage in the city of New York. The general furnished all of the capital. Neither of the young men had a dollar in money. One held a seat in the New York Stock Exchange, but encumbered by an indebtedness that the general furnished funds to liquidate. The firm began business under the name of Clinton B. Fisk & Co.

"In 1880 the general discovered irregularities on the part of his partners that led him to give notice that the firm must be dissolved at the close of the year. The young men could not bear prosperity. The saloon had obtained mastery over one, and was rapidly destroying the other. By means of fictitious and fraudulent entries on the books of the firm, they made it appear that General Fisk was indebted to them, and brought suit for recovery of a falsely claimed balance. During the progress of the suit an expert accountant discovered and revealed their rascally methods. They then interested an associate conspirator, a former customer of the house, by representing that he had been fraudulently dealt with by the firm, and led him into an attack on General Fisk in the courts, and, as afterward confessed by one of them, they thought the general would rather submit to blackmail than have his name mixed up with such litigations.. General Fisk would not be blackmailed, but vigorously defended their suits.

"The Supreme Court of the State of New York gave the general a verdict against the conspiring partners.

" The Supreme Court found that these said partners had filled the books of the firm with fiction and fraud, falsely charging to General Fisk the sum of $104,985.86, and each partner falsely placing to his own credit $45,160. The court found there was due General Fisk $26,062.63, and that in addition thereto the partners had carried off $3000 in bonds, the personal property of the general. The New York *Tribune* reported the court's decision in detail, and in commenting upon the case said :

" ' This case has an important bearing on the suit for damages against General Fisk, based on some mining transactions. In the suit Plaintiff made wild and reckless charges against General Fisk, and procured an order for his arrest in his absence. General Fisk hastened back to the city when he heard of it, and gave a clear and convincing explanation of the whole matter. Plaintiff has admitted that his suit was inspired by the conspiring partners, who, having a poor case themselves, tried to annoy General Fisk, and give him all the trouble possible.'

" The press throughout the country made similar reports. After General Fisk obtained judgment against the wicked, ungrateful partners whom he had placed in business, one of them confessed the entire iniquity, begged pardon and indulgence, and subsequently paid to General Fisk the sum due from him. The other followed his saloon instincts, and has paid nothing. Their associate conspirator, who at their instigation had brought suit against General Fisk, finding himself without evidence other than the statements of the confessed falsifiers and fraudulent bookkeepers, made oath that he could not go on with the case unless, upon an examination of General Fisk before trial, he might learn something that would relieve him from the charge of malicious prosecution. The Supreme Court of the United States unanimously decided in favor of General Fisk on that point, and since that decision no word has been heard from any of the conspiring blackmailers."

Put forth by a political opponent when party feeling ran highest, and embodying a quotation from another paper also (and bitterly) opposed, the foregoing may be accepted as not partial to General Fisk beyond the inevitable tendency of truth to make it so. He was in Detroit, attending to the care of a large trust estate, when the order for his arrest appeared. The New York *Herald* wired him at once for his statement of the case, because much exciting comment had been made, and printed the same in full, as entire truth. He promptly returned to New York. The court saw fit subsequently to hold him in *constructive* contempt, for refusing to answer certain questions in the interest of his prosecutor, but dared and did no further go. General Fisk's counsel (Senator Evarts and another) forbade the answers sought, and reminded the court that there were such things as suits for malicious prosecution, and damages for false imprisonment. It was to avoid these that the plaintiff, by whom the order of arrest was obtained, ceased his further annoying work, and that the court refused to proceed so far as he had insisted the court should.

CHAPTER XXIII

THE church activities of General Fisk, as a Christian worker, and as a leader in denominational affairs, have been constant ever since the war's interruption of them, and constantly growing. No single layman beside, it is probable, has ever served the Methodist Church in such diverse and responsible positions, and for so long a time, as has he. His wider official relation to that great body began in 1876, when he was made one of its Book Committee.

The now great business headquarters of Methodism in this country, known as the Book Concern, began in New York in 1789, upon a capital of six hundred dollars, borrowed money. It has grown to marvellous extent and power, and on July 1st, 1887, its total assets were $1,653,-197.66. The Book Committee has care of this vast material interest, and is made up of one member from each of the thirteen denominational districts, with three in Cincinnati and three also in New York. This important committee is divided into an Eastern Section and a Western Section, with locations respectively at New York and Cincinnati ; and the Eastern Section is charged with supervision of the New York publishing house, and all properties there. A burdensome responsibility thus rests upon it, borne more especially by the Local Committee of Three, of whom General Fisk has long been one.

With Mr. John B. Cornell and Mr. Wm. Hoyt, who succeeded Mr. Taft, General Fisk has given unremitting attention to the Concern's business management, and to him is due much of its magnificent growth. It testifies of rare unselfishness when such men spend so freely of time and thought to push forward an enterprise that yields them no dividends, and yet causes great care.

Mr. Cornell, who died at Lakewood, N. J., October 26th, 1887, was the general's closest church friend and business adviser, and labored with him in loving unity of effort many years. Mr. Cornell, too, had come up from a poor boyhood to large wealth, and their sympathies were at one upon many lines. "An apprentice at forge and anvil," as General Fisk said of him in a committee report after his death, Mr. Cornell had become the largest manufacturer in his line of business in the world ; and yet he could and did serve the church of his heart with faithful devotion. But he leaned much on General Fisk. And together, and with their colleague, they applied careful business methods to the Book Concern ; they placed it on the firm foundations of business success.

That success is now being crowned by the erection of a new building on Fifth Avenue, concerning which General Fisk lately reported as follows :

"We trust the entire structure will be ready for occupancy in the year 1889, that we may by its dedication celebrate the centennial of the inauguration of the Methodist Book Concern in 1789. It is a cause for devout thanksgiving to God that he has made the Methodist Episcopal Church instrumental through its matchless publishing interests in circulating a pure and wholesome literature throughout the world, thereby supplementing the preached Word in its mission of spreading scriptural holiness over all lands."

In various honorary capacities, temporarily more distinguished, and not arduous, General Fisk has represented Methodism and the broad cause of religion in this country and abroad.

The Second International Sunday-School Convention was held in Atlanta, Ga., beginning April 17th, 1878. The mayor of the city, and His Excellency Alfred H. Colquitt, Governor of the State, made addresses of welcome, and General Fisk gave to their greetings fit response for the delegations from the United States, after Rev. John Potts had answered for Canada. It was an occasion of peculiar good-fellowship in Christian faith, and the general grew peculiarly felicitous of utterance as he spoke on. After some introductory sentences, he said :

"The well-chosen words of my Canadian brother have expressed so well all that can be uttered by way of grateful response, I am inclined to adopt them as my own in behalf of the United States. Yet he will admit that this grand country of ours speaks so well for itself that there is need of but few words from any one in her behalf. These brothers of ours astonish us with their warm hearts. But then, you know, Canada is simply an annex to this country! [Laughter.] And we must remember that as our Annex Memorial Art building at the Centennial contained many of the choicest gems of the great Exposition, so Canada, as the brilliantly appointed annex of the United States, contains many of our most splendid specimens of English-speaking people. And Dr. Potts would make us believe that their excellent virtues, splendid thrift and advanced civilization are the result of government by that most noble woman, the Queen of England. [Applause.] I, too, am governed by a woman, and so are you [laughter and applause], and whatever is beautiful in our homes and country is largely due to the queenly powers of woman, clothed in her majesty of virtue and Christian graces. And in another sense are we all thus governed. Is there on the face of the earth a woman who rules with more grace and dignity than she who presides in the Executive Mansion in Washington? [Prolonged applause.] Much of the good there is in our noble President—and there is a great deal in him—I doubt not is the result of alliance with one who was faithful as Sunday-school scholar, and teacher, and worker in whatever promotes the Master's cause. [Continued applause.] The Ohio delegation doubtless remember with special pride that she hails from their great State. I have the honor, Mr. President, to bear to you and to this convention, cordial greetings from the President and Mrs. Hayes. They commissioned me to bear them specially to you, and I now deliver them. [Applause long con. tinued.]

"One of my most intimate travelling companions *en route* from New York to Atlanta—and I had a host of most pleasant associates in the pilgrimage—was that to me the chiefest of the minor prophets, Zechariah. He was a most wonderful character, a rare combination, from which you can construct a junior Isaiah, and Jeremiah, too. It is profitable to linger among the prophetic visions and utterances, to go backward in thought to the time and place when and where the 'sure word of prophecy' was born; to listen to the song of the seer, as he dwells upon his ever-ultimate theme—the kingdom of our Lord and His Christ. The radiance, the fulness, the power of the whole of prophecy centre in the one grand idea—the reign of God over the world in the glorious coming years—

> " ' The glorious coming years, the glad millennial years—
>   Our prophet saw them far upon the way,
>   With timbrel and with song,
>   Before the doubting throng,
>   He bore the standard of the coming day.'

"Looking across the gulf of centuries, he saw the incarnation, the suffering, and the glory of the Messiah; he saw the developments, the growth, the beauty and the triumph of evangelical truth. With my meditations upon the visions there mingled many thoughts of the approaching meeting at Atlanta. I saw this host of workers in the Master's vineyard thronging toward the Mount of Love—as in the prophetic vision, flowing 'together to the mountain of the Lord's house.' I said, certainly we are living amid the fulfilment of prophecies. I am sure that were I to ask my brother Parsons about it, he would tell me the truth about it, and say that we were. From Zechariah I read these words: 'And the Word of the Lord of hosts came unto me, saying, Thus saith the Lord of hosts: The fast of the fourth month shall be to the house of Judah joy and gladness and cheerful feasts; therefore, love the truth and peace.' And I said, May we not fancy, at least, that Georgia is Judah, and Atlanta its Jerusalem? Is not this blossoming, leafy month of April our fourth month? and is not this feast one of joy and gladness to the house of Judah? The very breezes which bear to us the fragrance of field, forest, and garden, sing sweetly of joy. Every utterance of welcome, every hearty 'God bless you,' thrills our hearts and yours with gladness. And the 'cheerful feasts,' surely they are to follow, in the coming hours and days of this International Sunday-school Convention. What feasts more cheerful than those of the communion of saints? They are the genuine love-feasts about which the governor and myself know something, and you are all to be made as cheerful and happy as the atmosphere of an old-fashioned Methodist love-feast, and that is as happy as you can be here below. I expect to see you all go away from here not knowing exactly where you belong! Why, I even look to see Dr. John Hall go back to New York and shout 'Glory to God!' in his pulpit! [Great laughter.] Well, it is the little child that is leading us, and with his little hands he is beating down the partition walls of sects and creeds. As we here plan for the salvation of the children of the nations, why should we not shout and go away forgetful almost of the names that mark our different church relations?

"Then Zechariah said to me, in the very next verse, 'Thus saith the Lord of hosts, it shall yet come to pass that there shall come people and the inhabitants of many cities, and the inhabitants of one city shall go to another, saying, Let us go speedily to pray before the Lord, and to seek the Lord of hosts. I will go also.' And hither have come the people and the inhabitants of many cities, who, I trust, have said one to another, 'Let us go to pray before the Lord at Atlanta.' From how many of the fairest cities in our land have these inhabitants come? From Augusta, Albany, and Atlanta; from Boston, Bangor, Brooklyn, Baltimore, and Buffalo; from Chicago, Cincinnati, Cleveland, Columbus, and Charleston; Detroit and Denver; Indianapolis and Louisville; Montreal, that beautiful mount of vision, Mobile, Memphis, Milwaukee, and Minneapolis; New York, New Orleans, Nashville, and Newark; Philadelphia, Pittsburg, Providence and Portland; Quebec, Richmond, and Rochester; Savannah, St. Louis, San Francisco, Sacramento, and St. Paul; Toronto and Toledo; Wilmington, Wheeling, and Washington; all these 'inhabitants' of many earthly cities are, we trust, with faith looking as did Abraham, for 'a city which hath foundations, whose maker and builder is God.'

"And right after that this prophet said: 'Yea, many people and strong nations shall come to seek the Lord of hosts in Jerusalem, and to pray before the Lord.' And here within your Jerusalem, praying before the Lord, are, indeed, the representatives of strong nations— the strongest of all nations in the earth; strong, because of their adherence to liberty and truth [applause]—these representatives of the two great Protestant peoples, here stand shoulder to shoulder for the truth as it is in Jesus. [Applause.] England, without a peer among the nations of the earth, God bless her ! ' With all her faults,' we love to hail her as the Mother Land [great applause], and toss our hats in the air at the sight of her banner, which ' for a thousand years has braved the battle and the breeze.' May the Union Jack and the Stars and Stripes in loving embrace lead in the march of Christian civilization the wide world over. Heaven forbid that they should ever be borne against each other in the smoke and flame of conflict. [Cries of Never ! Never !] May God's perpetual bow of peace, which spans the boiling floods of Niagara, a radiant arch of glory resting on the shores of the two lands, symbolize our international harmony and peace, until the kingdoms of this world shall be merged in that better country, that is an heavenly one. [Yea ! Yea !]

> " ' Thicker than water in one rill,
> Through centuries of story,
> Our Saxon blood has flowed, and still
> We share with you the good and ill,
> The shadow and the glory.'

" God bless our own, our native land, stretching from the east by the sea to the sea by the west. ' God give it the glory of Lebanon, and the excellency of Carmel and Sharon, and may all the inhabitants thereof see the glory of the Lord and the excellency of our God. [Amen, and Amen !] Be this

> . . . " ' Our glad refrain :
> From the snows of wild Nevada
> To the sounding woods of Maine ;
> Where the Mississippi wanders,
> Where the Alabama rests,
> Where the thunder shakes his turban
> Over Alleghany's crest.

> " ' Where the mountains of New England
> Mock Atlantic's stormy main ;
> Where God's palm imprints the prairie
> With the type of heaven again ;
> Where the mirrored morn is dawning,
> Link to link our lakes along,
> And California's golden gate
> Swings open to the song.'

" We often sing

> " ' Up with our banner bright,
> Sprinkled with starry light,'

but to-day we lift our eyes far above to another and a better ensign —the blessed banner of the cross—

> " ' Its hues are all of heaven,
> Its red the sunset's dye,
> The whiteness of the moonlit cloud,
> The blue of morning sky.'

It is red with the blood of the Crucified One. It is striped with the
fingers of God's love for our healing—the bright blue of Bethlehem's
glorious morning is upon it—with its guiding, shining star. Under
it we will follow the great Captain of our salvation to certain victory.
[Applause.]

"And the bard still continued to sing, and finally uttered to me
this wonderful prediction : ' Thus saith the Lord of hosts, in these
days it shall come to pass that ten men shall take hold out of all
languages of the nations, even shall take hold of the skirt of him
that is a Jew, saying, We will go with you, for we have heard that
God is with you.' Ten men taking hold out of all languages of the
nations—venturing once more to interpret—I said surely these are
our international lesson committee [applause], the ten brethren
named at Indianapolis, who, with their co-workers in the great
Sunday-school cause, have, by the blessing of God, inaugurated a
uniform lesson system which now girts the world. They have indeed taken hold of many languages. The Sabbath sun sets not in
any Christian nation or mission field where their leaves for the healing of the nations are not scattered. Ethiopia's dark people have
stretched out their hands for them. China, with her teeming millions ; vast, gloomy, and gorgeous India, and populous Japan, and the
islands of the sea, listened with you and me on Sabbath last, as the
golden text was reannounced by the Master, ' Search the Scriptures :
. . . they are they which testify of Me.' It was the inspiring consciousness of a great cause, wide as the world, and stretching through
all cycles, which enabled these brethren, under God, to record this
grand achievement. [Applause.]

"And then the prophet closed his theme by saying : ' We will go
with you, for we have heard that God is with you.' ' The best of all
is, God is with us,' said Wesley, as he brushed the dew on Jordan's
bank, and in retrospection saw what God had wrought. And so may
we say, from this happy beginning of our convention until the last
benediction and good-by words shall be spoken, ' The best of all is,
God is with us.' "

In 1881 the Ecumenical Council was held in London,
to which General Fisk went as a delegate. His attendance there was appropriate in singular degree, for it was

at his headquarters in Nashville, fifteen years earlier, that the project of such a council was first discussed. His presence gave cheer and charm to the unique gathering, and his words there, as elsewhere, were glowing with that diffusive charity which is characteristic of all his public and private speech.

It was in 1874 that he was made a Fraternal Delegate to the Methodist Episcopal Church, South, whose General Conference assembled that year in Louisville, when for the first time in thirty years Northern and Southern Methodism exchanged fraternal tokens of recognition. And the initial efforts to secure this fraternity were set in motion at General Fisk's own home in St. Louis. So to him were due a renewal of brotherly spirit between sectionalities long divided in ecclesiastical life, and the preliminary steps toward entire Church brotherhood.

A dozen years later, he exchanged fraternal greetings with Southern Methodist Episcopal brethren at Richmond, where their General Conference gathered in the Centenary Church. It was in May, 1886. With his own family, and Mr. Cornell and family, he was proceeding northward from a trip farther South, and they all stopped over a day or two to look in upon the great assemblage there. The regular fraternal delegates from the North were Rev. Dr. Miley, of Drew Seminary, and Governor J. B. Foraker, of Ohio, but Governor Foraker did not report for duty. An immense audience assembled, and after Dr. Miley's address General Fisk was called out from the crowd. They knew him, those delegates from the field of his efficient reconstruction labors. They remembered how he had restored their churches to them after war's work was done. They recalled his earnest efforts to bring again the sweet blessings of peace. They received him with the most tempestuous appiause, as if he had been of their own elect. Over a hundred old Confederate soldiers and chaplains were among the delegates, and they welcomed the Northern general with a welcome he can never forget. His impromptu speech warmed their enthusiastic good feeling to high fever heat, and made the evening memorable. Near the outset he jocosely recalled a bit of his own experience, heretofore related, by saying :

"I am greatly pleased that I have finally reached Richmond. It is nearly twenty-five years since I set out for this magnificent capital city of the Old Dominion. It was on a bright July day in 1861, on which, with several other travellers, I left Washington for this city. The Richmond Committee on Fraternal Relations met me far out upon the way. Indeed, they came more than half way. With banner and band and the booming of artillery they gave us a warm reception. Indeed, it was a hot welcome—so hot that I retired on Washington and countermanded my order to forward mail to Richmond. I am more fortunate in this later marching on Richmond. Declining capture then, I now find myself a willing captive in your hands, with not the slightest wish to escape."

Then he proceeded as follows to recognize their individual conference hospitalities :

"Immediately upon entering the conference room yesterday a unanimous vote of the Kentucky brethren seated me with the Blue-Grass delegation. Dr. Haygood secured for me like honors with the Georgians. Brother Magruder swung wide open the doors to the Baltimore sittings. Brother Scruggs claimed me for St. Louis, and the heartiness of a Missouri welcome made me at home with the friends and neighbors of the olden time. Meeting my young friend, Dr. M'Ferrin, he advised me that I was a delegate-at-large from the Tennessee Conference, and thus for a second time in your General Conference, Mr. President, I am the victim of 'disintegration and absorption.' Candidates for office will please take note of the number of votes I shall be entitled to cast when the elections come on, and have me interviewed accordingly."

A little further on, he said :

" Mr. President, my eyes grew dim, and my heart swelled with emotions of deep joy as you so graphically brought to mind that glad day at Louisville, a dozen years ago, when for the first time in thirty years we struck glad hands of fraternal fellowship. It seems but yesterday that you and your associate bishops gave to my co-delegates and myself that sincere and hearty greeting. Alas, how busy since then death has been in our respective Episcopal boards ! All of yours as then constituted have ' climbed the steeps of light,' excepting Bishop Keener and yourself, and from our board a larger number have ceased from labor and entered into the rest eternal. Paine and Morris, Kavanaugh and Scott, Wightman and Ames, Simpson and Pierce, Marvin and Wiley, are in the shining city.

" Their united petitions invoking God's blessing upon the good work then begun have been answered. The seeds of fraternity took root and have had a fair growth. There have been some impatient friends on both sides who would, like children who play at gardening, dig up the seed occasionally, to see why they did not sprout more promptly. And then there are those—and neither side has a monopoly in such—who ' go mourning all their days ' at the very thought of fraternity. They wander about in a very small circle with downcast eyes, never looking upward and outward upon the bright and beautiful things of this world.

" They remind me of a story told me by our lamented Dr. Green, whose genial, happy soul brought joy to every circle he entered. When on duty at Nashville at the close of the war, in the work of reconstruction, restoration, and rebuilding, Dr. M'Ferrin was my chief of staff, and Dr. Green my senior *aide-de-camp*, in many a time of doubt as to the best methods of establishing peace, harmonious relations, industry, and good order in certain sections of my large district, and in which territory these honored brethren had large acquaintance. On one occasion I had been written to by a man prominent in his neighborhood, who kindly, yet emphatically, criticised my administration. He was fearful I was not sufficiently radical in my views, and cautioned me against receiving advice from any one of the sort of M'Ferrin and Green. I assured my well-meaning adviser that I would exercise great care in the discharge of my official duties, but should endeavor to follow after the things that would make for peace. Subsequently, at an interview with Dr. Green, I inquired of him touching the writing adviser, and the doctor said he would illustrate by telling me a story, as follows : He said that a friend of his, a tanner by trade, who ground his tan-bark in a mill run by horse-power, had a faithful old mule that year after year had made the continual round and round in furnishing power for the bark-mill. The kindly-disposed owner at last thought it a duty to emancipate the aged mule from future active service. He turned him out into a large royal pasture where he could graze upon timothy and clover over the wide range of the extensive field. The old mule surveyed the situation, discussed the new order of things with himself, and unanimously resolved to continue to abide within the narrow limits of an old-time tan-bark circle he established around a stump, and there ended his days going round and round as of old, nipping away at the short grass, utterly refusing to enjoy the better things provided for him.

"There are men, so-called statesmen, politicians, and others, who will wander about in small circles, utterly oblivious to the mighty sweep of events around them. Let us lift up our eyes, and behold the outstretching, widening opportunities for obedience to the command of our divine Leader to carry the Gospel of peace and reconciliation to all mankind ; forgetting the things that are behind, let us press forward.

"My esteemed friend and brother, J. B. Cornell, who had never seen an old battle-field with its immense earthworks such as surrounded this fair city a score and more years ago, accompanied me out along some of the old lines, but how little evidence of war he found left ! The snows of twenty winters and the rains of twenty summers had blotted out the tracks of fire and sword. Where once boomed the cannon's thunderous roar we heard the tender notes of life and gladness ; the blue-bird was singing sweetly, and a torrent of melody bubbled from the overflowing throat of the mocking-bird There, where strong men strove and brave hearts bled, were bud and blossom, spangle and bloom, and busy bee.

> " ' And daily on the slope's green breast,
>   The tribes of blossoming things increase,
> But dearer far than all the rest,
>   The fair white flower whose name is Peace ;

> " ' Whose gracious leaves to heal the ills
>   Which sapped the nation's life are sent,
> Whose fragrance blesses all the hills,
>   Whose fruits are Plenty and Content.'

"Shall not all of us take a lesson from forgiving nature, whose maternal, loving soul levels the earthworks of war and strews them with the flowers of peace ?"

Concluding, General Fisk gave this comprehensive benediction :

" And now, Mr. President, may our two Methodisms—no, our ONE *Methodism* in two communions—march on waving the barner of the cross over all lands, and so adjusting our work at home and abroad as to prevent all waste of men and means, and moving toward each other as we move toward God, we shall command His blessing, and the world will say : ' Surely, they are one in spirit, one in purpose, one in fellowship.'   God bless our united country !   May peace and prosperity be within all our borders.

> " ' Lord of the universe, shield us and guide us,
>   Trusting Thee alway through shadow and sun,
>   Thou hast united us—who shall divide us ?
>   Keep us, O keep us, the many in one.'

> " ' Then up with our banner bright, sprinkled with starry light,
>   Spread its fair emblems from mountain to shore,
>   While through the sounding sky loud rings the nation's cry :
>   ' Union and liberty, one evermore ! ' ' "

CLINTON B. FISK, Brevet Major General.

BISHOP HURST and CLINTON B. FISK,

CHAPTER XXIV.

SIXTEEN months before the occasion last referred to, there was a greater Methodist assemblage at Baltimore —in December, 1884—the Centennial Methodist Conference. It also abounded in fraternity of spirit. Delegates came from the entire continent, and met in the exuberance of denominational joy. The Address on Missions was delivered by General Fisk, and so thoroughly did it exemplify his religious ardor and his church zeal, that it is here reproduced in full :

"In the great procession of events, in the mighty march of time, the centennial birth year of Episcopal Methodism wheels into line. We the people called Methodists coming from every quarter of the continent here strike glad hands of fellowship and lift our voices with one accord to heaven in grateful benisons to the great Disposer of events as we gather around the cradle in which was rocked our infant church. The century plant of Wesleyan American Methodism is bursting into magnificent blossom, filling all the land with its light and fragrance in this Christmastide of 1884.

"Not only in this goodly city of Baltimore, rich in its possession of Lovely Lane, is this glad day remembered with devout thanksgiving and joy, but in nearly every city, town, village, and hamlet on the continent, our brethren are rejoicing with us. In the lonely and remote places where the woodman swings his axe in wintry forests, down where the miner rends the rocks that stand as sentinels over the precious veins, out on the boundless prairies, kissed by the golden sunset, where the herdsmen round up for the night, on the ocean wave, where the ships bear our people ' over the sea,' this day will have recognition. London will rejoice with Baltimore as it remembers the precious dust at City Road and retrospects the century— under the shadow of St. Peter's and the Vatican—among the ruins

which proclaim and prolong the majesty of ancient Rome—on the
dark continent from which the pall of barbarism is lifting—in the
land of the midnight sun, amid Alpine passes—on the banks of the
Danube and the Rhine—on India's coral strand—in the empire
whose high thick walls could not keep out the itinerant—in the
nation born in a day—in the halls of the Montezumas, and along the
great rivers of our Southern continent, there are devout and happy
Methodists who have part and place with us in this jubilee of our
history, and who with us, believing in Christ's all-embracing empire,
take up the song, echoing the wide world around :

> " ' Jesus shall reign where'er the sun
> Does his successive journeys run,
> His kingdom spread from shore to shore,
> 'Till moons shall wax and wane no more.'

It is, indeed, befitting that at the threshold of this feast of the century, we devote an hour to the consideration of missions, the supreme
cause of the church.

" It was a glad day for the world when American Methodism took
its place in the system of universal evangelization as an independent
church.   It was in its organization essentially a missionary scheme.
That marvellous man who stood godfather at the baptism of the
Methodist Episcopal Church was the founder of missions, and of and
about Thomas Coke we might talk out this centennial year.   His
memoirs should this month be read aloud in the presence of father,
mother, and children in every Methodist family on the continent.
In travel and preaching he became as indefatigable as Wesley or
Whitfield.   The historian aptly gives him the title of the ' Foreign
Minister ' of Methodism.   He crossed the Atlantic eighteen times on
slowly-sailing vessels, on Gospel errands.   Of affluent fortune, he
cast it all into the treasury of the Lord, for the upbuilding of the
cause of Christ.   At threescore and ten he died and was buried in
the great sea on the bosom of which he was sailing to found a mission
in India.   The sea washing all shores is his monument.   This great
missionary, with his companions Vasey and Whatcoat, upon all of
whose heads had rested the hand of John Wesley in consecration,
had been duly equipped, set apart and dismissed from the shores of
England for the great embassy of organizing Methodism on an independent basis in America.   They found Francis Asbury and his fourscore associate Methodist preachers were all missionaries, and all
eager for the upbuilding of a church through whose agency the
Gospel of our Lord Jesus Christ should keep pace with the growth
of the young Republic.   The last British sentry in the war of the

Revolution had left his post, and gone home, the Stars and Stripes of American Independence floated where had waved the imperial standard of England. National America had taken the place of Colonial America. Washington was the builder of the new Republic. Asbury, contemporaneously, under the blessing of God, laid broad and deep the foundations of the Methodist Episcopal Church in the United States. The temptation to linger amid the attractions of those new days for the church and nation is almost irresistible ; to review the toils and triumphs of the fathers ; to tramp with the happy itinerant as he made the ' grand rounds ' along the picket lines and vanguard of the march of civilization, over the mountains into the great and terrible wilderness where the wild beasts disputed occupancy with the wilder tribes of savage man. Anywhere and everywhere the Methodist preacher, in cheerful obedience to the call of duty, and the demands of the church he loved, went shouting and singing as through forest and field he rode the illimitable circuit :

> " ' O, for a trumpet voice,
>   On all the world to call,
>   To bid them all rejoice
>   In Him who died for all.
>   For all my Lord was crucified,
>   For all, for all, my Saviour died.'

Every man of them, from Bishop Asbury down, was an organized missionary society in himself, and filled with the spirit of an intense evangelism. Under men of God thus equipped, armed with weapons not shaped by mortal skill, strong-souled, earnest men, knights of the true order of Jesus leagued in solemn covenant, American Methodism grew mightily and prevailed.

" The Christmas Conference in Lovely Lane Chapel, one hundred years ago, sent out the first missionary from America to foreign lands. The soul of Bishop Coke was inspired by the earnest appeal of William Black, who had made a long and perilous journey to be present at the conference, and there plead that the newly-established Methodist Church should send men and money to the then far-away region of Nova Scotia. Two missionaries were solemnly set apart from the scanty list at Lovely Lane to accompany William Black to Halifax, and the grace of God, bestowed on the members of the conference as upon the churches of Macedonia, so inspired the preachers that the ' abundance of their joy and their deep poverty abounded unto the riches of their liberality,' and the first missionary collection of the Methodist Episcopal Church was taken up in Lovely Lane. Two hundred and fifty dollars, in the depreciated currency of 1784, was the initial offering of our church for the spread of the Gospel in other lands. That sum was transferred into thirty pounds sterling for use in the dominion of George the Third. Thus were inaugurated the Foreign Missions of the Methodist Episcopal Church in the first week of its history, and one of its choicest spirits was spared from the imperative demands of the Home Work to bear Gospel tidings to the regions beyond. Freeborn Garretson, the brave and brotherly soul, distressingly self diffident yet full of fiery heroism, and of whom Asbury said, ' he will let no person escape a lecture that comes in his way,' and whose wise, rare gifts of grace and culture made him a fit leader of men—who had in the six weeks immediately preceding the opening of the Christmas Conference travelled twelve hundred miles, traversing the forests, swimming the rivers, preaching, shouting, and singing on his way to summon the preachers from their circuits to the conference—was the first volunteer to go out as a missionary to a foreign field, saying then in his heart, to the Mother Land from whom the colonies had been wrested by the bloody arbitrament of war, what we now, after a century's lapse, most heartily say, as we contemplate the relations of amity between these two great English-speaking peoples, and which every interest of mankind imperatively demands shall continue forever.

" The cause of missions was not new to the saintly men who sat in Lovely Lane Chapel. They had all been students of the sure word of prophecy. They knew it was as old as the hour when the Master led the wondering disciples out as far as to Bethany. They had heard the divine commission, as it came thundering down the roll of the centuries, speaking into existence the first Missionary Society, in the words : ' Go ye into all the world and preach the Gospel to every creature.' The steadfast mortals, beholding His ascension to the right hand of God the Father Almighty were with us, and all who believe in that Name above every name, summoned as witnesses for Him in Jerusalem, in all Judea, in Samaria, in gloomy and gorgeous India, in Ethiopia, with its dark nations, among the teeming millions in China, in populous Japan, and everywhere to the uttermost parts of the earth. ' That commandment of our ascended Saviour,' says James Montgomery, is ' the Magna Charta of salvation to all the fallen race of man.' It has never been restricted or repealed, and it never will be until all things are fulfilled which are written in the law of Moses and in the prophets and in the psalms concerning Christ. The hopes of the world and the everlasting destinies of the human family are involved in the measure of the church's obedience to the great commission.

"The prayerful counsels, the sacramental solemnities, the liberal devisings, the harmony of thought and speech, the merging and absorption of all distinctions in the immortal gathering we celebrate, was like to that rare and sacred fellowship of the disciples, in the 'Jerusalem chamber,' who were all of one heart and one mind as they there believed and prayed and waited the pentecostal hour with one accord in prayer and supplication until the tongues of fire appeared. They believed that no church could be a successful missionary church, that no man could be a successful missionary, till clothed with power from on high, and made fit to be co-workers with Him. They believed and taught that the real test of Christian Church and Christian character is the proclamation aggressively of the Gospel to the entire world. 'The Gospel for all mankind' was early inscribed on the banners of American Methodism, and its colors have never been furled. We this day lift our voices in glad acclaim with the Psalmist's outburst of song : 'Thou hast given a banner to them that fear Thee, that it may be displayed because of the truth.'

"Let us glance for a moment at the outcome of missionary work among the constituent Methodisms of this centennial commemoration. All Methodists on the American Continent ought to be represented on this glad occasion, in this great family gathering, as we sit down at the centennial Thanksgiving feast and talk over 'old times.' Here we are not a divided host—as for me I am simply a Methodist, and I greet you as Methodists, pure and simple, with no qualifying adjective thereto belonging or in any wise appertaining—*Methodism without a handle.* Let every partition wall be here broken down, each rejoicing in the progress of the other, and shouting over victories won for the Master under our common banner—forgetful of minor differences in the one grand brotherhood of faith in Christ. We give heed to the apostle as he implores us as he did those of Corinth. 'Now, I beseech you brethren by the name of our Lord Jesus Christ, that ye all speak the same thing, and that there be no division among you, but that ye be perfectly joined together in the same mind and in the same judgment,' and no discordant note disturb the harmony of soul and song as we lift our grateful voices and sing,

> "'Blest be the tie that binds
> Our hearts in Christian love.'

"When our organized Methodism entered upon its new and magnificent destiny at the adjournment of the Christmas Conference, it stepped over the threshold of its first century with a membership of about 15,000, and an itinerant ministry numbering 84.   As the silent footfalls of that century are passing out into eternity, the roll of our living membership records more than 4,000,000, our itinerant ministry 27,500 and local preachers 36,500.   We have no figures to express ' The army of the ransomed saints ' who have gone thronging up the steps of light from Methodist homes as the hundred years have rolled away, and are with that multitude that no man can number.   They are to-night among the great cloud of witnesses.   A very large percentage of those results has been attained through the domestic missions of the Methodists.

    " The total sums of money gathered into our missionary treasuries for home and foreign work aggregate about $30,000,000.   This sum has been disbursed in nearly equal proportions in these two depart ments of Christian endeavor.   Methodism on this continent has suc cessful missions the wide world around.   Its missionaries, male and female, and native helpers, supplemented by those serving on its medi- cal and educational staff, rank among the first in aggressive, evan gelistic force.

    " Its churches, hospitals, asylums, and schools are in every and all lands on the globe.   The aggregate disbursements on account of missions, under Methodist management, in the year 1884, will be about $1,500,000.

    " While with profound gratitude we study these statistics of Meth- odist Missions, and the first impulse is to say, ' Well done,' on a re- view of the exhibit, and a glance outward upon the great world, with its imperative demands, and inward upon the vast resources of the church withheld from Him whose right it is to possess them, we are led to ask, How do they appear as tests of Christian character? As illustrating the measure of our love for God and our fellow-men? As exhibits of the church's loyalty to Christ?   As we step over the threshold of the new century let us ask ourselves if we are quite ready to have this exhibit abide as our permanent record?   Shall we not rather say, This is but a beginning?   In the ordering of Provi- dence and of grace, upon this meeting-place of the ages, as upon no other era since John fell asleep under the purple skies of Ephesus, is placed the sublime duty of the world's evangelization.   The per- manent kingdom of our Lord Jesus Christ is waiting to be brought in.   It waits the completeness of the church's consecration.   Con- secrated men and consecrated money, humanly speaking, are all that is needed to give the Gospel to all mankind in the near future.   The world has opened every door to the coming of the Christian mis- sionary ; and the voice of Providence, like the trumpet of destiny, summons us to the great duty of entering in and in the name of the Master set up our banners.

" The conquest of the world for Christ need not be a ' far off divine event, if the great host of Christian believers in this and other lands would believe with greater faith, and rally the forces that wait their command for the final march and fight and victory. Christian America's corps in that grand army falls into line where ' Messiah's hosts are marshalling.' American Methodism, with its flying troops, always on the skirmish line, makes hot the hand-to-hand conflict with the forces of evil always in battle array and to our feeble sense a phalanx never to be broken. At the battle of Trafalgar, Lord Nelson divided his fleet into two portions, himself leading one and the brave Collingwood the other. Collingwood was in the ship ' Royal Sovereign,' the fastest ship in the fleet, and spreading all sail, he soon placed himself a mile or two in advance of Nelson, but instead of waiting until he came up, he dashed forthwith into the fray and alone challenged the combined fleets of France and Spain. Nelson, watching his trusted lieutenant, exclaimed to those about him, ' See that gallant fellow, how eagerly he takes his ship into action.' Collingwood, as the smoke and flame of battle surrounded him, said, ' What would Nelson give to be here, the first to break the line?' Our Methodism must eagerly take the front and lead on to victory. ' Forward !' rings along the line, and

> " ' With lifted sword and waving crest
> Our Captain leads to conquering.'

Not to a possible triumph. Possible is not the word. The Father hath said to the Son : ' He shall have the heathen for His inheritance and the uttermost parts of the earth for His possessions.' When the design for the first crusade to recover the holy sepulchre by force of arms was unfolded, the assembled multitudes of many nations simultaneously exclaimed, ' God wills it,' and the leader of the crusade, seizing upon the word, responded, Let that be the battle-cry ; let the army of the Lord, as it rushes upon its enemies, shout but that one rallying cry, ' God wills it.'

" The evangelization of the heathen is the great work devolving upon the Church of Christ. Eight hundred millions of our race are this hour bowing down to idols and dishonoring the Most High by rites and ceremonies which are a smoke in His nostrils. Our lamented Bishop Pierce, upon whose new-made grave, under the sunshine of Georgia, the earth is yet fresh, the music of whose voice we had fondly hoped to hear this day speaking to us the words of

life, and who was welcomed on the shining shore by our Bishop
Simpson, the loved and honored and trusted ; these two great bishops,
leaders of God's sacramental hosts, for whom there is the ceaseless
longing

> " ' Oh for a touch of a vanished hand,
> And the sound of a voice that is still,'

we enthrone them in our hearts with double honor ; *they* sowed the
seed of which the harvest waveth now.

> " ' They taught us how to live, and oh, too high
> A price for knowledge, taught us how to die.'

From the glory-illumed battlements of immortality do they look
down and enjoy the feast of vision ? Bishop Pierce, in one of his
masterly appeals in behalf of missions, said, with burning eloquence :
' The question is not whether the heathen can be saved without our
help, but whether we will be saved unless we help the heathen to a
knowledge of the true God.'

" Oh for a missionary revival, beginning from this centennial love-
feast, that shall sweep throughout our continental Methodism, leading to thorough missionary consecration that will subsoil our ability
to work and to give ! Oh for a divine spiritual anointing, in measure
abundant and overflowing, descending upon bishops and pastors and
churches ; upon the missionaries who stand in the regions beyond,
preaching Jesus and the resurrection—upon all who teach—upon the
noble Christian women of Methodism, who labor so efficiently in the
Gospel of the Kingdom—upon our Sunday-schools, that they may
give us a generation of loyal, hearty, generous, and cheerful givers to
this supreme cause.

" Not less than five millions of dollars per annum should be cheer-
fully cast into the treasury of the Lord for disbursement through our
Methodist Missionary Societies, a paltry sum for four millions of
Methodists, whose are the abundance of the seas, the forces of the
Gentiles, the flocks of Kedar, the glory of Lebanon, and the gold of
Sheba, and in our hands to be blent in one tribute and cast at the
feet of the Master.

" Brightly breaks the morning of the new century. Already we
hear ' a sound of going in the tops of the mulberry trees,' and
we must bestir ourselves. That glad crisis in the world's history
when its kingdom shall become the kingdom of our Lord and His
Church, is not far off, if the resources of the church, rich in men and
means, in brain power, heart power, hand power, and money power,
quickened by the life force from heaven, shall be consecrated to God.

"The century closing has in its last decades witnessed the forward movement of man toward the complete mastery of the material world. He is harnessing the forces of nature to the chariot in which shall ride the Son of Man with the millennial escort. How measureless are the triumphs of steam and electricity! The fiery steed of steam, whose breath is flame, whose sinews are brass and steel, whose neck is clothed with thunder, whose 'eyes are as the eyelids of the morning,' whose hoofs are iron—in speed outracing the wind as he goes storming through valleys, through and over the mountains, leaping rivers, onward rushing across whole continents, whose every whistle is a hallelujah to Him who by the mouth of the prophet hath said that every valley should be exalted, every mountain be brought low, and the crooked places be made straight. The very floods clap their hands as the leviathan steamships, without sail or oar, 'despite wind, darkness, tide, or tempest, straight as the arrow in its flight, seek the other side of the world on errands of commerce and civilization.' That marvellous combination of mind and metal, the steam printing-press, with its myriad-tongued utterances and mission of thought to the world with every rising sun and at the going down thereof! The electric telegraph, connecting land and sea, the great globe around, into a wondrous whispering gallery! The telephone, which with the speed of thought carries the living voice leagues of miles away! The photograph, painting pictures with light and 'enabling all the world to see all the world!' The photophone, vocalizing light! The megaphone, realizing the conceit of the old Norse legend of ability to hear the grass grow! The lightning of heaven, subsidized to illumine our cities and haul our carriages! The spectroscope, with which we are almost enabled to loose the bands of Orion and bind the sweet influences of the Pleiades! All these, born in the century now closing, as so well said by good Dr. Post, of St. Louis, are ministrant to the advancing kingdom of God—'This is the Lord's doings, and it is marvellous in our eyes.'

"The new century is before us, with its grander work, with its nobler heroism and its assured conquests. The chaste, sweet singer of Cambridge, whose 'Psalm of Life' made him immortal, with prophetic sweep of vision, as the morning eternal was dawning upon him, discerned the coming glory, when, seizing his pen for the last time, he wrote his final words of inspiration :

> "'Out of the shadows of night
> The world rolls into light,
> It is daybreak everywhere.'

We may not be among those who on earth shall be permitted to shout 'Hallelujah, the Lord God Omnipotent reigneth!' in that rejoicing day when He who for the salvation of a lost world stooped to the unutterable sacrifice of Bethlehem and Calvary, and who will not fail nor be discouraged until He hath set judgment in the midst of the earth and the thronging isles of this world are waiting in submission for His law ; but by the word of our testimony, in consecrated lives and gifts, and by the blood of the Lamb, we may be numbered with those who helped to overcome the dragon, and the accuser of our brethren, and other somebodies will send up from earth that glad acclaim. It is for us and our children to work, and believe, and pray, and give, until every coast shall be peopled by sincere worshippers and lovers of our Lord Jesus Christ ; until every mountain barrier shall be overcome, until every abyss shall be spanned, for the uninterrupted progress of the King's highway of holiness, and the people of the earth shall flow together as in the prophetic vision to the mountain of the Lord's house ; until the fires of sin are everywhere extinguished, and the pure light of holiness shall be everywhere enkindled ; until every idol is abolished, until every father becomes a high priest in his own household, offering the daily sacrifice of prayer and praise, and every mother shall teach her infant charge to lisp the name of Jesus ; until religion, pure and undefiled, shall conserve all people as virtue conserves the soul ; until the infinite power of the Holy Spirit to renew and sanctify shall be verified by the experience of every dweller on this earth. Until the world shall be full of the knowledge of the glory of the Lord as the waters cover the sea ; until there shall be but one story that every child shall lisp, one memory that every nation shall cherish, one Name that shall be above every name ! Let it be the covenant work of our Methodism to hasten that glad day ! and may the entire church, in all its revolving cycles of history, unceasingly have for its inspiration that blessed assurance which gave to our dying founder such consolation, when the everlasting sunrise burst in upon failing heart and flesh--' The best of all is, *God is with us.'* "

CHAPTER XXV.

IT has been seen that General Fisk's early political pre-dilections were all of the old-fashioned abolitionist sort. The first Presidential ticket he could vote for was nominated in 1852, and he then had rather more sympathy with the Democrats than with the Whigs. On the subject of slavery there seemed little reason for choice between them at that time. The Democrats had nominated Pierce and King, and were pledged to the Compromise of 1850, to the Fugitive Slave Law, and against all anti-slavery agitation. The Whigs had also indorsed the Compromise and the Fugitive Slave Law, and had nominated Scott and Graham. The only party opposed to slavery, in positive terms and purpose, was the Free Soil Democratic.

Locally, the Democrats in Southern Michigan were nearer right than any others. They stood straight up for temperance, and voted solid for the " Maine Law." General Fisk usually acted with them, but often voted for the best man, regardless of his party nomination, always making abolition sentiments the final test of a nominee. When he ran for Justice of the Peace on a " Maine Law " ticket, as has heretofore been related, his opponent was George A. Coe, who had been a Whig Lieutenant-Governor of Michigan.

In 1856 General Fisk cast his ballot for John C. Frémont. In 1860 his political surroundings were all Democratic, but of a divided faith. The Douglas

Democracy and the Breckinridge Democracy were contending for rulership, the latter Pro-Slavery to the core, the former seeking to evade all responsibility on that issue. Many Northern people in Missouri sided with Douglas, and were inclined to support him and Herschel V. Johnson ; but, as the campaign went forward radical feeling deepened, and they came into full Republican alliance. Mr. Fisk was one of the earliest to come out boldly for Abraham Lincoln, for whom he wrote, and spoke, and voted ; and from that year till 1884 he was known as a faithful Republican adherent, bearing its banner with as much enthusiasm as he had felt when a boy bearing the Birney flag.

It was no light matter for General Fisk to leave the Republican ranks, or to think of leaving them. Republicanism had meant for him, as for the country at large, liberty and union, national perpetuity, and the progress of civilization. The living chiefs of the Republican party were his personal friends, as had been the great ones gone—Lincoln, Seward, Stanton, and the rest. His nearest church friendships were among those who cherished Republican memories, and held the success of that party only less dear than the upbuilding of Christ's kingdom in the earth. As a matter of fact, scores whom he honored, and who honored and trusted him— bishops, and teachers, and preachers, widely influential, and conscientious as himself—regarded the steady domination of Republican power essential to religious growth, to national safety, and to the permanence of freedom for those once enslaved. Grave problems of race relation still confronted statesmanship and must be wrought out. The struggle for equal rights was not yet ended. And who should solve the problems, and finish the struggle as God might will, but the Republican Party ?

So queried thousands of the purest patriots our country knew, through years and months preceding the Presidential campaign of 1884. So queried General Fisk. But he and they were deeply concerned about one other and more vital question, which the Republican Party had not taken up in a national way, and which was growing to be, if, indeed, it had not already become, a national question. The organized liquor traffic was bullying Congress, shaping the national revenue policy, preventing a Commission of Inquiry to investigate its national effects, electing candidates for highest office, overriding State boundaries of Prohibition, compelling Government officials to bow to its behests; and this organized liquor traffic, lacking conscience, lacking patriotism, loyal only to greed, caring not for Christianity, heedless of home and happiness and human weal, had forced the issue of its Prohibition into national politics, and had made the final settlement thereof possible there alone. In the minds of many this final settlement must be entered upon, in that broad domain, without further delay.

But what a sundering it meant of old ties, dear even as the love of one's own kin! And how men paused, and wondered if to forsake the old party were not unwise —even wicked! How partisanship bound the best and truest souls to association grown hateful through liquor compromise and indifference to the enforcement of law!

The marvel, when one ponders it a little, is that men can come to love so much a thing so intangible and unresponsive as a political party. Precisely what they love, and upon which they bestow such unsparing devotion, no chemical or logical analysis can find out. Sans a creed, that is fixed and final; sans an organic form, that takes fixed and final mould; sans a local habitation, where it can be found, and in which there is something actual and tangible to find ; the political party quite eludes that analysis which would reveal an object of love or hate, and shows at most but an adjective, around which men have rallied with varying motive—some to defend a principle they believe represented by it ; some to secure honors and emoluments through it ; the major number, if their party be of long existence, to preserve their inherited or acquired political prejudice, and to demonstrate their unswerving political fidelity.   A party is not a church, nor a standing army ; yet men will love it as they do the one, and fear it as they would the other, and sacrifice principle for its maintenance when there is nothing to maintain, crucify conscience in support of it when there is nothing to support, and abuse other men for abandoning it when there was nothing to forsake — nothing but the adjective.   Bury all parties to-day and you shall miss nothing to-morrow.   No mourner could even find the burial-place of one, that he might weep over it.   The world would wag right on, undisturbed, and with no one the wiser or the worse.   Next week, or next year, as occasion should require, men would assemble and vote, and nominate, and elect ; and their principles would find declaration and official embodiment ; and no tears would be shed except over some dear adjective departed, with speedy resurrection possible in the dictionary.

General Fisk was not one of the first to espouse National Prohibition through party alliance. A few others had been out on the skirmish line of that reform several years, when he joined them with a small part of the main fighting corps. But all along his sympathies had been with them, and for a considerable time previous to 1884, he felt like singing, as often the " Fisk Jubilees " had sung in his hearing—

" I am troubled in my mind."

Over and over, before vast audiences, in the church and on secular platforms, he had spoken for temperance ; and his heart said " Amen " to every effort for the saving of society from drink and its universal curse. He believed in Prohibition, though he would welcome any application of law which, while it should not traverse right principles, might promise curtailment of the growing wrong. With Rev. Dr. Cuyler, in the National Temperance Society and out of it, he stood for any progressive measures that should throttle the power of rum, while confident that there could be only one logical and ultimate policy to make temperance reform a lasting success. That policy, he realized, must be political, and as inclusive as the curse it should seek to remove. It must be partisan, because to achieve political results men vote together for their achievement, and, banded so to vote, they are called by a party name and act in a partisan way. The partisanship must be national in scope, because a national policy had become necessary to meet and overmatch a national curse. With others, General Fisk had hopes that such a policy would be adopted by the Republican Party ; and he tarried in its affiliation a good while after mentally accepting the logic above briefly set forth. In the early summer of 1884 he held the same party attitude held by ex-Governor John P. St. John, of Kansas, who had trained loyally in the Republican ranks two years after being beaten for a third term as Governor of that State. Both, with Frances E. Willard and a host more of devoted women and patriotic men, were suppliants before the National Republican Party for some policy of opposition to the saloon. General Fisk and Governor St. John were yet loyal to the party they had loved so long and well. Both hated to leave it, and were willing to accept the most conservative utterances of anti-liquor purpose, rather than sever party bonds and step out with a few so-called fanatics for separate political action.

The Republicans met in National Convention at Chicago, on June 22d, that memorable year, and before their Committee on Resolutions went Miss Willard, representing the National Woman's Christian Temperance Union ; John B. Finch, representing the great order of Good Templars ; and others, bearing influential petitions that temperance be recognized and indorsed. Their prayers were denied. Miss Willard's pathetic plea brought tears to the eyes of some who listened, but her memorial, after she retired, was thrust from the table and spat upon. The Republican platform had not a word for the home as against the saloon. Previous platforms were reaffirmed—Raster Resolution of 1872 and all—but no new declaration, in favor of a new and worthy opposition to the liquor traffic, could be found in the new platform, to make glad the hope of those who had hoped so much.

Then Governor St. John swung out of Republican line, and so did General Fisk. The former was nominated for President by the Prohibitionists, at Pittsburg, July 23d, and the latter gave him hearty and helpful support. General Fisk attended the Pittsburg Convention, and had part in St. John's nomination. His name was only less familiar to temperance ears than Governor St. John's, and some talk was heard of putting him upon the ticket for first place, but he had not been so intensely

radical of utterance as Governor St. John, he had in
slight fashion committed himself to the policy of high
license a year or two earlier, though repentant of even
the mild commitment made, and he escaped sacrifice as
a leader at that time. His name was brought forward
in convention, however, for Vice-President, and had
warm reception ; and the speech in which he declined
the honor rang so strong and eloquent for prohibition
against license, and for the party there by representation assembled—it was so happy in temper, so uncompromising of spirit, and so admirable every way—that it
gave him instant national prestige, and was prophetic of
his future leadership.

The campaign which followed was a severe test of the
stamina in both General Fisk and Governor St. John.
Persistent efforts were made to induce the latter's retirement, and to win the support of the former for Mr.
Blaine, his personal friend. Every line of honorable
influence was tried with him, and he was even followed
from city to city, on his private business errands, by
men supposedly in such close relation as would give
special weight to their appeals. The boast was made,
even, that General Fisk had already abandoned the Prohibition candidate, or would soon forsake him ; but Mr.
J. B. Cornell heard it, and said :

" I would venture my whole iron business [and it was
worth millions] that he will not go back to the Republican Party ; and," he added, " I've not talked an hour
with him about it either."

The pressure grew heavy upon him, but at last General Fisk ended it all. He had not been able to take the
stump for St. John, and did not do it to any extent
throughout the campaign, but he was present at a great
mass-meeting in Newark, where that gentleman ap-

peared, and there he made a speech. It left no doubt
of his purpose, and his fixed principle, in anybody's
mind. It settled his party attitude beyond the peradventure of Republican needs or the wish of Republican
leaders. It cost him the friendship of some, genial and
full of charity as it was ; but it saved him further an-
noyance and importunity. Old associates conceded his
new political association final, after that.

In 1886 the Prohibitionists of New Jersey determined
on making their cause felt in the politics of that State.
Prohibition sentiment had been steadily increasing since
the Presidential campaign ended, and its promoters grew
sanguine. With active preliminary effort, a large convention, and a popular candidate for governor, they saw
it possible to push their issue squarely forward in public
recognition, and compel respect. They decided on all
these conditions, and achieved them. One, indeed—
that of candidate—was already settled quite to their
hand, by common party opinion, widely expressed. The
large convention came naturally from general interest
and the preliminary efforts put forth. It was the largest
ever held, and of overflowing enthusiasm.

Six hundred delegates came together in the Grand
Opera House at Newark, May 27th, forming such a
gathering, politically, as New Jersey never before saw.
They chose General Fisk permanent chairman, and proceeded to routine business, after a reception of the general, which lasted several minutes, and was tempestuous
beyond anything he had ever seen, perhaps, in all his
varied public experience. There were other wild demonstrations of popular regard for General Fisk as the
day wore on ; and when, during some informal speeches
by visitors, in the afternoon, pending committee reports,
his name was mentioned as that of the coming candidate,

enthusiasm boiled over, and spent itself in a regular riot of good feeling, party fervor, and superheated zeal.

They came to nominations next day. With intense desire to avoid political leadership, General Fisk had privately sought to turn the tide another way. It could not be turned. Its currents all set toward the one man who had been spontaneously selected, in the minds of those present, for service as their chief. Other names had been mentioned, it is true, but of gentlemen who insisted that General Fisk should be chosen instead, and who would not yield to his repeated assurances that he must be excused.

He was nominated by acclamation. This biographer sat near him on the stage, and saw how his frame shook with emotion as the test-hour struck. The platform had been adopted, and a whirlwind of applause had greeted that. A motion to proceed with raising a campaign fund had been made. Then somebody said :

"We of South Jersey will be able to give with a great deal better grace when we know that Clinton B. Fisk is our candidate."

The cheers rang out again at that.

"Mr. Chairman," said the Hon. Chauncey Shaffer, "I move as an amendment that we do now nominate General Clinton B. Fisk for Governor of New Jersey."

Never before was an amendment seconded and carried in such fashion. Delegates rose and swung their hats, their handkerchiefs, their umbrellas ; they stood upon the chairs, and waved banners, and shouted ; they subsided only to break out afresh more riotously; and the scene lasted several minutes. The *acclaim* of that nomination was wonderful, and never to be forgotten by those who heard it.

When General Fisk rose to speak they would not let

him, and again and again swelled the tremendous volume of applause as he sought to secure silence and their attention.   At length, when the storm had fairly spent itself, in the calm, masterful manner so habitual with him before an audience, though his whole form trembled with the feeling repressed, he said :

" *Gentlemen of the Convention :*

" I once was very near the track of a cyclone in the West, but fortunately not near enough for it to have any effect upon me.   This time I am in the very current, and find myself swept in.   Of course I did not anticipate until yesterday any such possibility as this result.   Many of you have my letters in your pockets containing the expressions of my unalterable decision never to be a candidate for public office.   When I was a boy I ran for a little place on a temperance ticket in Michigan and was defeated.   I have never tried my running powers since.

" I have had a wonderful time thinking about this proffered nomination and what I ought to do, since so many of my friends have come to me and so kindly urged me to give the matter consideration.   I had hoped until this morning that I might persuade another to be your candidate—another to whom your eyes have been turned.   None of you can doubt my adhesion to this grand triumphing Prohibition Party.   If I have entertained misgivings on my own score, it has not been because of want of confidence in the party or of devotion to it.

" I need not more than thank you for this very cordial and flattering tender of your nomination.   Only, gentlemen, I did not want it to come exactly in the way that it has come.   It has been painful, indeed, to sit here and listen to what you have compelled me to hear.   But, gentlemen, I am going to serve for you."

At this point the wildest demonstrations again burst forth, and were some time continued, until a delegate began to sing—

" Praise God from whom all blessings flow."

Suddenly, and with swift transition, the enthusiasm melted into song, which softened the hearts of all.   At least one present recalled that marvellous scene at Pittsburg, in 1884, when the nomination of Governor St. John had excited like approval, and when, in the very midst of it, a voice struck up—

' In the beauty of the lilies Christ was born across the sea."

And now, as then, there fell a solemn hush upon the tumultuous throng, till tears filled many eyes, and such devout tenderness stirred every heart as differentiated this from the nominating convention of any other party.

Their candidate was nearly broken down by the tense strain of feeling which these six hundred men had caused, and his voice trembled, even as did he, when he proceeded to say :

" I understand that before me is much hard work, and I will to the best of my ability do it. There will be no child's play the next five months in New Jersey. Things are going to be hot. All sorts of representations and misrepresentations will be made about us, and we must expect that. All sorts of calumny will be rained upon us by the rum-sellers and their parties—we can stand that. A word or two was said yesterday about the Trenton Conference. (The Republican Anti-Saloon Conference.) This morning I looked over that body's proceedings for the first time, and I found much in what they did and said which I can heartily approve. Hear what they say about the rum-seller ; see if we can say anything better:

" ' Intemperance is the conspicuous, the colossal curse of society ; it is the prolific source of poverty and pauperism, the breeder of and stimulant to crime, the waster and devourer of individual and national wealth, the blight of honest industry, the disorganizer and destroyer of the peace and purity of home, the antagonist of religion, the foe of law and order, and the enemy of good government.' "

Here a delegate asked—
" What are they going to do about it ?"
" Why," said the general, " they will have to come with us," and, as often during his speech, ringing applause came in as punctuation. Resuming, he said :

" When I read over the list of those who attended that conference, I found some most excellent names. There are men in that movement

who mean business—men who will have to change position soon.
There are men whose hearts will bleed as mine has bled when after
twenty years of faithfulness I had to leave the old party behind me
—the old party that had been behind me in quite another sense in
the smoke of the conflict. It will not be easy for them to change.
But if it is possible let us smooth the way, and prepare a new home
for them without making their poor hearts bleed too much. Let me
tell you it took courage for those sixty, seventy, or eighty to do what
they did.

" This cause is as sure as that the stars shine. Truth always con-
quers, always swells on, as resistless as the tides of yonder sea. 'Tis
weary watching, but remember :

> " ' Where the vanguard rests to-day,
> The rear shall tent to-morrow.'

Let us keep going forward with our first great party. Now, after
what has been said, I need not detain you with a formal speech. I
give you again my thanks for this nomination, and my promise to try
to make the most of it for you and for the cause."

CHAPTER XXVI.

THAT New Jersey campaign of 1886 was the most notable yet carried on for Prohibition in any State. "Things are going to be hot," General Fisk had said, in his address of acceptance ; and he made them so. He bore the banner of his young and aggressive party from one end of Jersey to the other, and always with a smile on his face, and words of kindly good-nature on his tongue. No asperities of speech could be charged to him. He was genial as a June day throughout the whole five months, during which he made one hundred and twenty-five speaking engagements and filled them all, travelling five thousand miles to do it. Nothing moved him from a serenity which impressed every one he met. There seemed always about him an atmosphere purer and sweeter than that in which political candidates usually walk ; he breathed forth a spirit of lofty patriotism that was uplifting and ennobling.

Yet the chicanery of old party methods tried to hedge him in. His nomination had changed the whole political aspect of New Jersey for some men. The most popular Republican that State held was planning to be its next governor, and had hopes of success till General Fisk took the field. Then he knew, and his friends, that no chance remained for him, unless the general would retire ; and plans to secure his retirement were contemplated, if not laid. One of these involved the election, by the Legislature, of General Fisk as United States Senator ; and for some days the press teemed with talk about it. A favorite popular scheme was the reverse of this, and meant the indorsement of General Fisk for Governor, by the Republicans, and his support and election by them, in return for which the Prohibitionists were to make no legislative nominations, and so insure a Republican Legislature that should return a Republican Senator to Washington.

On these two opposing plans rested the hopes of certain opposing Republican factions ; while the fears of both were excited lest Prohibitionists should develop sufficient strength, in some counties, to elect legislative candidates there, who should in turn make a deadlock possible in the Legislature, and give the senatorship to General Fisk anyhow.

The opportunity was ripe for some well-managed political " deals," and in a State, too, where " deals " have been common, if common report be true. But General Fisk scorned them all.

" We are not political Swiss Guards," he said ; " we are fighting to do away with the alcoholic liquor traffic, and propose to elect men to represent our principles. We have no ' deals ' to make."

He made none. He could have been elected governor by a turn of his hand, but he stood true to the white banner of Prohibition and would carry it unsoiled till November came. Meanwhile, all around him were uncertainty and ferment.

" The only thing certain at present about the New Jersey campaign," said a reporter for the Chicago *News*, under date of July 12th, " is that Fisk is making a brilliant canvass, and that he has the church forces largely at his back."

Yet another certainty did obtain. General Fisk himself stated it to a reporter for one of the Newark papers :

"The friends of temperance saw that if their ideas
were to be made dominant they must form a new party,
with lines as distinct as either of the old. This idea was
never thoroughly grasped until the State Convention
was held in Newark this year. When we agreed there
never to allow our candidates to enter the caucuses of the
old parties, a true political party was born, and not till
then. Its growth since has been like the spreading of
wild fire in a pine forest."

It was certain then that the Prohibitionists were not
political traders, and that their party was on the gain,
and gaining in the most purely independent fashion.

"If the Republican Party expects to indorse the Prohibition Party," frankly asserted General Fisk, "it will
have to come over into our camp body and soul."

Which did not so much imply belief that any party
has a soul, as that the sole purpose of the Prohibitionists
was to win for Prohibition, outside all entangling alliances, and with transparent candor and loyal single-
heartedness.

The general's campaign, as taken part in by himself,
was composed of a well-arranged series of county mass-
meetings, and something of their spirit and effect may
be gathered from this description, by Colonel R. S.
Cheves, an eloquent Southern lecturer, given in the
New York *Voice :*

"In my fifteen or twenty years of active political experience I
have never seen a mass of people so stirred in behalf of a political
idea, so enthusiastic in behalf of a popular leader, and so determined
to make their cause and their favorite triumphant, as the Prohibitionists of New Jersey are now for General Fisk and the things that
General Fisk represents. The weather is blazing hot, the farmers
are busy with their crops, and the general interest in politics has no

yet been duly pitched, since neither the Democrats nor Republicans are in the fight ; but every one of the general's meetings is an ovation.

" Why, the farmers drive to these county meetings by the hundreds ; and the proportion of those who come a distance of fifteen, eighteen, and twenty miles is not inconsiderable. They bring their families with them, arriving early in the morning ; and most of them remain until the night meeting is over. The interest that they manifest in the speeches is simply astonishing ; they will remain four and five hours at a stretch without leaving their seats.

" General Fisk, as a candidate and as a campaigner, deserves to be called peerless. The effect of his personal magnetism in this fight is going to be one of the greatest factors in it. There are incidents at these meetings that are profoundly affecting. At Belvidere, the other day (and indeed at most places where I have had the good fortune to be present with him) in introducing me to the audience he took my hand, stood up with me before the people, and in a most eloquent manner spoke of the war in which we fought to shed each other's blood—he on the Union side and I on the Confederate—and told how this temperance question is now wiping out sectional hates and jealousies and giving old enemies the burning desire to struggle unselfishly for the common good. The effect was remarkable. The contrast and the appeal went straight to the hearts of the listeners. I have seen whole crowds of men and women burst out crying and sobbing."

At each of these large county meetings, where two, and often three, sessions were held, General Fisk had the assistance of other speakers of large repute, that the labor might not fall so severely upon him alone. Mrs. Mary T. Lathrap, President of the Michigan W. C. T. U., and known all over the nation for her rare platform power, spoke at several places, and has written down her impressions of that campaign for these pages :

" One sure token of decay and weakness in the old political parties," Mrs. Lathrap says, " is the fact that much of their discussion has shifted from principles and issues to personalities and slanders.

" Great masses of our people leave their political thinking to party leaders, orators, and writers, so any campaign lifts or lowers the standards of patriotism, loyalty, and integrity, according as the ideals and arguments are high and worthy or the reverse.

" The time was when such months of discussion quickened brain and conscience, making the people worthy of their mighty trust ; the time is when the streams of political debate run thick with the slime of evil speech, and blacken the name and record of the man soon to be lifted to the highest honor.

" The campaign of 1884, with its coarse, low scandal, which crowded out all better thinking, left the country with patriotic enthusiasm slain and moral sense paralyzed.

" The pity of it lies in the fact that the man chosen by the people to a position higher than any other ruler in the world, limps to place with a wound in his manhood which all the show of office cannot hide.

" Political parties that pave the way to success by such methods are too corrupt for anything but swift burial. One mission of the Prohibition Party and its leaders is already proven, in lifting public thought once more from this low level of strife for spoils, to the high realm of principle, thus compelling public attention along patriotic channels.

" A most remarkable illustration was the campaign of General Fisk in New Jersey. Never was a worthier name put before a commonwealth for its highest office, and never a nobler contest was waged in the forum of open discussion. It was like the old days, when the princes of statesmanship went out to great convocations of the people with *a reason why* for the choices soon to be made.

" A series of county meetings was arranged, to be addressed by General Fisk and a corps of workers that assisted him. For the most part these gatherings were in the open air, and held through an entire day.

" The people rallied from afar, drawn by the novelty and interest of such discussion of the most pressing public question, and listened often by the thousands, helped always to pure and just conclusions, and inspired to better things. General Fisk was the grand magnetic centre. Party leaders feared and opposed him, but he made them ashamed of anything save manly opposition. Enemies sought to defame, but his patience and gentleness put ' coals of fire on their heads.'

" He never uttered a word too harsh for a parlor, or used an illustration unfit for the most sensitive ear. He took sharp issue with the positions of the old parties, by which evil was legalized and the price of life taken for revenue, yet he was ever fair to his opponents. His *reason why* was not the growth and power of his own party, but the sorrow and desolation in the homes of the people, and indignation at the wrong.

" In presence of his example all other speakers felt harshness out of place, and the entire atmosphere of the campaign was high, intellectual, even spiritual. General Fisk's speeches were not alone remarkable for the absence of what makes up the average political tirade, but for the presence of all that brings manhood to its best, in the interest of home and country. Story, argument, poetry, history, were all woven like cloth of gold into the rare fabric of his speech.

" He was a typical American, an ideal statesman, a pure patriot, conducting a model campaign.

" One scene will never be forgotten by those who took part in it. A great meeting was held in one of the southern counties. The grove was fitted up with seats made of railroad ties ; tables were set under the trees by the ladies of a village church near at hand ; and trains and carriages brought the people.

" The afternoon was rare as a summer day could be, but at evening a fog came up from the ocean, and clung around the world like a garment of gray gauze. Hundreds of men and boys came from the cranberry fields, for the evening meeting, representing the common toilers of the State and nation. The lamps and camp-fires gleamed dimly through the mist, and it seemed that with the strange concourse of people there might be failure to secure kindly and attentive hearing.

" What a gem was the address of Clinton B. Fisk that night ! He made no effort to catch the crowd by considering them at a distance from himself, and descending from his own high level of thought and speech, but found swift access to the hearts of men by way of his own, while he pleaded for home and country, and the best for every man's child.

" When pleading for the home against the saloon, and the whole people against the liquor-dealers, he often repeated, with touching pathos of voice and manner :

> " ' Through all the long dark night of years
>   The people's cry ascended ;
> The earth was wet with blood and tears,
>   But her meek sufferance ended ;
> This wrong shall not forever sway,
>   The many toil in sorrow ;
> The bars of hell are strong to-day,
>   But Christ shall reign to-morrow.'

" Life's slight distinctions seemed to melt away, as he lifted all men in common brotherhood to the sunlit regions of his own princely soul. It was reversing the usual political method, which drags politician and party down to the lowest while principle must be left behind.

" He went out to those who had less of moral chances, struck with master hand the highest chords, lifted all hearts, and discovered the manhood of men.

" That citizen is worthy of highest honor who has shown in the public debates of a great campaign patriotism for country, tolerance tor political opponents, and reverence for every human right. The Republic waits for such statesmen to build its new prophetic future."

CHAPTER XXVII.

FEW of General Fisk's addresses during that campaign found preservation in any way. They were not "set" efforts, elaborately prepared, but timely, familiar, conversational, bringing his hearers at once into full sympathy with himself. At Woodside Park, July 13th, before a grand open-air gathering, among other things, he said :

"A great cause, second only to that of the divine Master, brings the people of Essex County here to-day. A clergyman said to me not long ago that he believed in the justice and righteousness of our cause, but that he felt hardly prepared to enter into the conflict. In Heaven's name don't come until you are fully prepared ! This clergyman thought it was a moral question. I say 'Amen' to that ! He thought the Christian Church should take hold of it. Again, I say 'Amen !' Every pulpit in the land should thunder against the iniquitous liquor traffic.

"To-day the Prohibition Party of New Jersey is pitching its tents within the very picket-line of the enemy. Newark, with her 150,000 people, is the headquarters of the enemy in New Jersey, and no man of them is in doubt what he is to do. But we shall establish our headquarters there among them within three days. Mr. Cator says there are four thousand saloons near us. I am glad the Goddess of Liberty will have her nose out toward the sea. A Christian minister doubting for a moment as to his duty toward the cause of such a stench, is a matter of astonishment to me. It was hard work for me to turn back upon my old party. There are good people enough in that party who are hesitating to-day as to their course, who, if they would come with us, would smother rum with the ballot next November.

"How I did plead with the politicians of that old party last spring to give us Local Option. But it was no use. One of them said to

me, ' General, if I should vote for this bill it would lay me in my
political grave.' ' Vote for it and die, then,' said I, ' and I will write
on your tombstone, "Blessed are the dead that die in the Lord."'
A politician can always afford to do right. It is a short-sighted policy
to hesitate, as the Christian people of New Jersey will demonstrate
at the ballot-box this fall.

" Young men of the Prohibition Party, you are beginning right.
You have made no mistake in coming out to fight this curse, which
is above all others in strength. Not content with thrusting its grizzly
performance in the faces of decent citizens, it has the unparalleled
audacity to tax them, in order that it may keep up the hideous display, and parades its procession of idiots and maniacs before us with
the confident assurance of a legalized traffic. Respectable men,
bound by the political ties of the old parties, look on in seeming indifference until ' my boy ' is touched by the plague. Then they
awake. They do not know that every boy is ' my boy.' Brave Christian women who demand protection for ' my boy,' and for their suffering sisters, are denounced as fanatical. The Prohibition Party alone
is organized to destroy this curse. We are going to stamp Prohibition on every State, and weld it into the organic law of the nation.

" As a woman's inspiration depicted the great wrong of slavery,
till men could endure the hideous sight no longer, but swept it away,
so in the fight against this gigantic evil we know that the ballots cast
for its destruction will many of them come first through woman's
hands. The growing sentiment of Prohibition is not fashioned in
halls of Congress, in the stately courts or grand salons of the nation,
but it comes from the homes of the humble people. From the pulpit,
too, of many a God-fearing minister it is taught. It takes courage to
preach truth to the distillery which subscribes liberally and occupies
a prominent pew—but it is done.

" With the party of Prohibition we will restore a grand and purified Union. All other interests of our country will be well taken care
of when Prohibition prevails. We work for party purity and for
national honesty, for the upbuilding of a party founded upon the
:ternal principle of right."

At Hamilton Square, a quiet, hid-away hamlet in
Mercer County, remote from railroad stir and rush, the
Prohibitionists gathered with their friends for a campaign Harvest Home. It was a day of liberal neighborhood good cheer, of the pure cold-water type, and en-

joyed by many hundreds with uncommon zest. Their
welcome to General Fisk could not have been warmer
and more enthusiastic.   After gratefully acknowledging
it, he said :

"God's gracious hand have we seen in the waving meadow and
the bending grain ; our wagons have creaked under the accumulated
weight of His abundance ; our barns are bursting with fulness.   The
maturing corn in regiments tosses nodding plumes in welcome to the
approach of autumn.   It is befitting that we gather from field and
forest, from happy homes in smiling villages and in the city full,
with shout and song and praise to Him who sits in the circle of the
heavens, and is mindful of His children on the earth.   All hail the
Harvest Home at Hamilton Square !   May joy and gladness fill all its
happy hours !   What a blessed thing it would be for all mankind if
all the people of the world possessed the contentment and happiness
impressed upon the faces before me.   Then, indeed,

> " ' The beautiful and good would reign,
>   The smiling Eden bloom again.'

" Alas ! how many homes there are that celebrate no harvest save
that of wrath and sorrow and death.   In a myriad of such the arch
fiend of rum gloats over ruin wrought by its poison, homes where
men, transformed into beasts by the saloon, bring naught but darkness and woe to sorrowing wife and wretched children.   It is in
behalf of such homes that we this day come to plead for your sympathy, your prayers, and your activity in securing measures by your
suffrages which shall overthrow the greatest enemy of mankind-- the
liquor traffic.   There is no citizen who thoughtfully studies the monstrous wrong but knows that the chief destructive force in American
society to day is the American saloon.   Judges and juries, law officers
and overburdened taxpayers, ministers of the Gospel and philan-
thropists, ruined homes, destroyed hopes, pleading, sorrowing women
and suffering orphans, are all in harmony in their testimony to this
fact.

" How shall this destructive force be arrested ?   Manifestly by the
combined strength of moral and legal forces.   The Christian Church,
so largely represented here, without distinction of creed, should bear
aloft the pure white banner of Prohibition, for Christianity has no
such other foe in its highway toward the millennium as the saloon.
Let no pulpit voice be silent or equivocal on this booming question,
but rather with instructive entreaty and warning sound clear and

strong and afar ! But the State must also marshal its forces along-
side all Christian agencies, and with moral and political forces combined we will remove from the fair face of our civilization that cancer
and blistering shame—the American saloon. Prohibition will be
written in our statutes and stamped on our organic laws.

*   *   *   *   *   *   *   *   *

" All temporizing processes are a failure.

" The saloon is too enormous and atrocious to be hid, too cyclonic
and destructive to be regulated, and too insolent to be longer endured. Let us bring all the wandering and separate rays of protest
and remonstrance, repression and restriction, to a focus, and kindle
a flame that shall burn the citadel of wrong and wrath to ashes. Not
until then will the despoiler of innocence cease to bring sorrow to
New Jersey homes. Not until then will politicians and political
parties be delivered from the Satanic sorceries of the arch fiend. Let
us all, as we retire from the joys of this magnificent Harvest Home,
bear with us the high resolve that this supreme cause shall have the
most active support of our brains and hearts, until our beautiful State
shall be a citadel of sobriety and temperance and the saloon no more
hurt and destroy in all our borders."

During the great camp-meeting of the National Temperance Society, held at Ocean Grove, he spoke to an
audience crowding the Tabernacle, and uttered these
words :

" Of course defeat will come to a great many of us. Calumny will
be as plenty as the sunshine at Ocean Grove. But we will go on
steadily. *He who leans on God's arm cannot suffer harm.*"

Calumny was not quite so abundant concerning him as
he thus prophesied, but the campaign did not end without
it. So open had been his daily life, so clean and unsoiled his entire record, that even the most bitter editorial
partisans, wrathful as they grew over the new party's
progress in public esteem and support, hesitated to assail
him ; and his canvass was half spent before any tongue
of slander wagged malicious words. Then the charge
appeared in a Freehold paper, the Monmouth *Inquirer*,
that General Fisk was part owner and " reputed head "

of the Seabright Inn, in which liquors were or had been regularly sold under license, or in violation of law, with his full knowledge and consent. It was promptly taken up and spread abroad with varying comment ; and the liquor men of New Jersey, and thousands of old-party lovers, manifested great joy over an accusation which, if true, must sadly injure him and the party whose leadership he had assumed. This attack came out September 2d. On the 4th General Fisk addressed the following frank reply :

" To the Editor of the ' Inquirer ':

"In response to the attack made upon me by yourself in the *Inquirer* of September 2d, will you permit me to say in your columns that I am not an ' hotel owner ;' neither am I ' the reputed head of the Seabright Inn.' Personally, I have not a dollar's interest in the Seabright Improvement Company. One tenth interest in said company is owned by an estate I represent ; an investment originally made because it was represented that the property was being purchased by an association of gentlemen to prevent it from falling into the hands of the saloonists. I do not know that liquor has been sold at the Seabright Inn ; but I have not the slightest doubt of the truth of the charge that it has been, with and without license. It was leased to a party who, I am told, was not a Prohibitionist. I am not, and never have been an officer of the Seabright Improvement Company. Had I been, no whiskey-seller or whiskey-drinker could have leased the Seabright Inn. I have steadily and persistently opposed, and used all my influence to prevent, the issue of licenses to any hotel or saloon in Seabright or elsewhere. A majority of the shareholders in the Seabright Improvement Company, ten in number, instead of three, as stated by yourself, are not of my way of thinking on the license question ; I wish they were. The one tenth interest represented by myself as guardian is for sale, and has been for a long time, at a very low price.

"I cannot but believe that the liquor traffic is just what the Anti-Saloon Republicans emphatically declared it to be at their late conference in Trenton, to wit : ' The conspicuous, the colossal curse of society ; the prolific source of poverty and pauperism, the breeder of and stimulant to crime, the waster and devourer of individual and national wealth, the blight of honest industry, the disorganizer and destroyer of the peace and purity of home, the antagonist of religion, the foe of law and order, the enemy of good government.' For the overthrow of an evil thus truthfully characterized I shall continue to do my utmost, regardless of any and all attacks you intimate will be made upon me ' later in the campaign.'

      " Very respectfully yours,

                        "Clinton B. Fisk.

" Seabright, September 4th."

The *Inquirer* did not drop its personal assaults here, but published a second statement, more virulent still, and asserted that, according to official records, General Fisk was the owner in person of fifty shares of the Sea-bright Improvement Company's stock, and gravely implied that there was no " estate " represented by him in such ownership. This imputation was met as promptly as the original slander, and these facts were established : That the estate having interest in said Improvement Company was that of Miss Louisa V. Swayne (granddaughter of William Smith, the second husband of General Fisk's mother) ; that the investment was originally made by General Fisk as guardian, for the double reason of obtaining a profitable security and of preventing the inn's control by saloon purchasers ; that it had stood in his name at the instance of the company's president, and by advice of the estate's attorneys ; that it was legally assigned to the estate, though no transfer had been made on the company's books ; that Probate Court records of Wayne County, Mich., certified to this ; that the original understanding of shareholders was that no liquor should be sold on the premises ; that General Fisk called and presided at the largest meeting ever convened in Seabright, to oppose the granting of licenses to any hotel or saloon, and especially to that ; and that the managers denied all charges of liquor-selling and had not conducted a bar there at any time, openly or otherwise.

So conclusive was this final showing that papers of the opposition published it, absolved General Fisk from every accusation, and heartily indorsed him as a man while regretting his attitude as a Prohibition candidate. In his own town of Seabright there was deep indignation expressed at an attack so ill-based and unjustifiable, and the opposition paper there made plain condemnation of the petty spite and partisan malice which alone could be held responsible for the attack.

There were hints of other calumnies to be set afloat, as the campaign should come near its close—calumnies founded upon the blackmailing scheme referred to in a previous chapter ; and it has been said that these were actually in type in the offices of eminently respectable Republican newspapers of Jersey City and New York, to be disseminated at the most opportune hour for serving their party ends ; but, if this be so, better wisdom counselled to a wiser course, and the mud-throwing ceased with the *Inquirer's* puny attempt, of which even its own best friends were heartily ashamed, and which leading Republican managers openly rebuked.

The campaign had its pleasantries.   One of these General Fisk saw, in spite of the solemn setting of it, in a prayer made by an aged preacher at the outset of one meeting.

"O Lord," said the fervent veteran, lifting his hands toward heaven, "O Lord, Thou who didst see the Son of Man hanging on the cross between two thieves, look now in mercy upon this little State of New Jersey, *with New York upon one side and Philadelphia on the other*, and grant us Thy deliverance through Prohibition."

Riding homeward one day, in a Long Branch train from New York, General Fisk shared his seat with a

Newark brewer, and their conversation drifted upon politics. General Fisk facetiously asked the man of beer if he was not going to vote for him.

"No," said the brewer, with emphasis; "I had rather vote for the devil."

"Well," the general answered, serenely, "if your party don't take up the devil, perhaps I can then count on your vote;" and the crowd around had a hearty laugh at this brewer's expense.

On another occasion General Fisk was homeward bound upon the Pennsylvania road at an hour when few passengers who knew him were aboard. A talkative commercial traveller shared the same seat, and maintained a running fire of question and comment as they rode along. At length the political situation came up, and the commercial traveller asked:

"The Prohibition candidate for governor lives in this part of the State, doesn't he?"

"Yes," the general answered, "over here on the coast, at Seabright."

"Do you happen to know him?" was the next query.

"Oh, yes," came the answer; "I happen to know him quite well."

"What kind of a man do you take him to be?"

"Well," said General Fisk, musingly, "I've always been inclined to think more highly of him than perhaps I should. There's a good deal about him that's not exactly as it ought to be."

"Seems to have a pretty decent sort of reputation, don't he?" said his interrogator.

"Oh, yes," the general answered, as if in doubt, "but reputations don't amount to much; it's character that counts."

After more talk of this rather discriminating kind, the commercial traveller inquired :

" How is it that you know so much about the man as you seem to ?   Are you a neighbor of his ?"

" Not exactly," said the general ; " but you see his wife is a near friend of my family, and she has told me a great many things that the public never hears of.   It would be a great deal better for the general if he'd always do as she says."

Just then a brakeman shouted " Little Silver !" and the train pulled up at that modest station, where stood a handsome turn-out waiting for some one to come—thoroughbred horses, fine carriage, colored coachman, and a happy-faced lady sitting on the back seat.   The general rose, bade his questioner good-day, and left the car. As he made his way briskly from it, the commercial traveller stepped also to the platform, and seeing the conductor, asked :

" Whose carriage is that ?"

" General Fisk's."

" And who is the lady in it ?"

" Mrs. Fisk."

" Who is that man ?" more eagerly yet.

" That is General Fisk himself," the conductor said, smiling a little.

" That is General Fisk !" echoed the commercial traveller.   " And he's been selling me for the last twenty miles !" he added, with a mixture of chagrin and amusement ; while General Fisk, whose quick ears had caught the dialogue, entered his carriage laughing, and merrily recounted the incident to Mrs. Fisk as they rode the three miles from Little Silver home.

CHAPTER XXVIII.

It has been said that calumny was not so abundant while his canvass went forward as General Fisk prophesied. There would have been no dearth of it, if some men had but realized their wishes and carried out their will. One letter may illustrate this fact, and serve also to show up the scandalous methods of campaign politics, as conducted in these days of degenerate party character and unhallowed partisan zeal :

" SOMERVILLE, N. J., October 16, 1886.

" SENECA N. TAYLOR, Esq. :

" DEAR SIR : I learn you are President of the Lincoln Club of St. Louis. As you probably know, General Clinton B. Fisk is the candidate on the Prohibition ticket for Governor of our State. I am a straight Republican, and, if possible, desire the defeat of the third party. I learn some bad things of General Fisk, which, if true, should be published during this campaign, and should leave him at home and reduce his power of injuring our candidate (B. F. Howey). I learn that through the efforts of General Fisk and others a military organization was raised in St. Louis ; that General Fisk was given command ; one who had assisted the general to his office, with a promise of the favor of the general afterward, asked to be made quartermaster ; the general exacted $500 from him for the appointment, which was paid, and a complaint afterward made to the authorities against General Fisk, who was called upon to answer, when he ingloriously left ; also, that during the service he was a coward, crawled under a haystack upon one occasion, upon the appearance of the enemy. The person who informed me says these things are well known at the former home of General Fisk, which, I understand, was your city. I wish to know if you can give me any information

on the subject ; if so it will be very thankfully received. Awaiting
your early reply, I remain,

"Yours truly,

"H. F. GALPIN."

The early reply wanted was promptly sent. It ran
thus :

"St. Louis, October 18, 1886.

"H. F. GALPIN, Esq. :

"DEAR SIR : Yours of the 16th inst. is at hand, and contents noted.
I heard rumors, years ago, of what is indicated in your letter, but
personally did not think them true. General Fisk stands well in
this community. No intelligent person believes him guilty of these
charges. I will not be a party to circulating scandalous reports to
defeat or elect any one. I differ with General Fisk as to the proper
method of remedying the evil of intemperance, for it is an evil.
Think it should be done through the Republican Party. This, however, is no reason for slandering General Fisk. I hope the Republican ticket may be elected in your State, which means the defeat of
the third party ; yet it should be done fairly, else not at all. Raking
up threadbare scandals that the community in which they were circulated denounced as untrue, is not meeting the issue squarely.

"Yours respectfully,

"S. N. TAYLOR."

A copy of this reply was mailed by Mr. Taylor to Rev.
Dr. C. P. Masden, General Fisk's old St. Louis pastor,
then in New York, together with the original letter
which called it forth. Through Dr. Masden the general
soon received it, and against his desire it was made public. Replying, some days afterward, to a letter of grateful acknowledgment from General Fisk, Mr. Taylor
said :

" The gentleman whose letter you refer to, blames me
for allowing his to pass out of my hands, but I care not
for his blame. Sending it, as I did, was in keeping with
the golden rule. For I owed him no duty to keep it a
secret, but owed it as a duty to repel, and to enable you
to refute, the wicked slanders about to be circulated to

injure your reputation. I am entitled to neither praise nor blame in this matter, since I simply performed duty."

"I never heard of the rumors to which reference was made," General Fisk said afterward ; "my quartermaster was my warm personal friend."

The intimation of cowardice amused him very much, and he has often laughed over the alleged incident of hiding under a haystack.

It was impossible, according to political logic, that such a campaign as the Prohibitionists ran that year in New Jersey should end without some startling announcement. The very nomination of General Fisk had thrown Republican leaders into confusion ; his vigorous canvass had stirred public sympathy all over the State ; the Prohibition cause was moving onward with cumulative power day by day. In sheer desperation the Republican Party had been compelled to declare for submission of a Prohibitory Amendment to the Constitution, and for a Local Option Law, in hopes that so they might win chance of success ; but even this did not weaken the efforts of General Fisk and his aggressive followers. Clergymen were everywhere coming over to him ; the temperance women were actively supporting him, through their various organizations ; representative citizens, like Dr. McCosh, President of Princeton College, were forsaking old party lines and rallying under the new party's flag ; and Republican defeat was inevitable unless a change could be secured in the drift of things.

This, too, when General Fisk had deprecated any special attack upon that party of his former love, and had himself spoken of it, and of its leaders, in terms of kind regard.

"We make no war," he said to one interviewer,

"upon any party, or any persons connected with either party. We exalt Prohibition, and mass all our force against the liquor traffic. '*Down with the saloon!*' is our battle-cry.

"I am not in sympathy," he further declared, "with the utterances of some of our friends who indulge in bitter denunciation of other parties and party leaders, but you must remember that the provocation to do so is very great. We are bitterly denounced on many platforms, and in the columns of many newspapers, and it is no wonder that payment in kind is often made. If others have anything to say in advocacy of the saloon, by far the most destructive force in American society, and the controlling force in our politics, let them rise and say it, and not waste time and talent in denunciation of a party pledged to the overthrow of the saloon, and the promotion of whatever in politics shall advance the cause of party purity, national honesty, the protection of our industries, the proper adjustment of labor and capital, and the upbuilding of our people in all things that will make them better and happier. These are the fundamental doctrines of Prohibition, and in all charity we will give them vigorous advocacy until every home in this land is made to rejoice in the downfall of every dram-shop."

All the same it was a recognized and admitted fact that to advocate these doctrines, even in this way, meant for both of the old parties decrease, and for one of them defeat. That one Republicans believed was their own.

On October 20th there appeared in the *Mail and Express*, of New York, a telegraphic despatch from Trenton, announcing the rumored early withdrawal of General Fisk in favor of Mr. Howey, the Republican candidate for governor, and adding that anti-Sewell Republicans were pledged, in return for this action of General Fisk, to vote for him for United States Senator at the next legislative session.   This despatch made some local stir, but failed wholly of its purpose.   Other metropolitan papers contradicted it, the same day and the next ; the *Daily Voice* nailed it as a campaign canard within one hour after it saw print.   It did not send the converted Democrats back from Prohibition to their old faith, as was expected ; it did not stampede the growing Prohibition ranks.

"I will be a candidate until the polls close on election day," said General Fisk ; and all who knew him knew he would.

His final speech of the campaign was made October 29th, at Bordentown.   For weeks he had traversed New Jersey, and been met with enthusiastic welcome by men of all parties and creeds, who delighted thus to honor him as a man though they might not all support him as a candidate.   He had grown familiar with great crowds gathered to see and hear him.   But his last reception showed no falling off in public interest, no lapse in the enthusiasm of Prohibition workers, though stormy weather accompanied.   As he stepped from the Philadelphia train, at 6.30 P.M., he was greeted by Winkler's full Seventh Regiment band, the uniformed cadets from the Bordentown Military Academy, the city Prohibition Club, and hundreds of citizens, who joined in saluting him with music, and fireworks, and ringing cheers.

At eight o'clock the opera-house was densely thronged, and on its platform were the leading men of Bordentown —Professor Longen, President of the Military Academy ; Professor McFarland, Principal of Public Schools, and others of like local eminence.   The applause as General

Fisk entered was tremendous, and he received an ovation when he came forward to speak. Despite his long canvass, and the steady strain upon him, he showed little wear, and his rich, mellow voice was well preserved. Among other things, he said :

" Five months ago, at that most remarkable political convention ever held in New Jersey, the Prohibitionists of our commonwealth began their campaign for 1886. The utterances of our convention on all great questions of governmental policy, State and national, were clear and forcible. We acknowledged Almighty God as the rightful Sovereign of all men ; that from Him the great powers of government are derived, and that to His laws all human enactments should conform as an absolute condition of peace, prosperity, and happiness. We declared that the liquor traffic, sanctioned and protected by law, was the gigantic crime of crimes, the chief source of sorrow, the arch enemy of labor, the foe of industry, the destroyer of private and public virtue, the great fountain of political corruption, the parent of sedition, anarchy, vice, and social and industrial disorder. We declared that the suppression of the liquor traffic has become the supreme political as well as moral issue of these times. We reaffirmed our allegiance to the National Prohibition Party. We declared ourselves for both State and national Prohibition of the importation, manufacture, and sale of all alcoholic beverages, and for the enforcement thereof by appropriate legislation, administered by officials thoroughly in sympathy with the same. We expressed our hearty sympathy with every proper effort of the wage-earner to improve his moral, social, and financial condition, yet declared that total abstinence for the individual and the prohibition of the liquor traffic by the State lie at the threshold of labor reform.

" We demanded the enactment of laws requiring that our children be instructed in the public schools on the evils wrought on the system by stimulants and narcotics. We pledged ourselves that by precept and example we would do our utmost to preserve the sanctity of the Sabbath. That convention, with one heart and voice, called upon every good man and woman in New Jersey to rise up and go forth to battle against the unparalleled crime of Christendom, the fruitful mother of evils multiplied and monstrous. Five months have been given to educational forces. Our large mass-meetings held in every county, the smaller meetings in nearly every hamlet of the State, the voice of the press, and the dissemination of literature have aroused thousands of our citizens, and startled them into comprehension of the increasing enormities of the liquor traffic. The best men of both the old parties are flocking to our standard all over the State.

" We are in the closing hours of the campaign. At Bordentown is my last engagement to speak for our cause. Our forces are in battle array for the conflict on Tuesday next. We will on that day by our votes declare for sobriety and temperance, social order, virtue, peace, prosperity, and happiness for home and country, or the weight of our influence as citizens will be thrown for the perpetuation of the American saloon with all its barbarism and crime. Shall we for a moment hesitate to stand for truth and righteousness? Falter not, but rally as one man to the polls on Tuesday morning. See that our every vote is cast and counted.

" Our great chieftain, General Grant, with lifted sword and waving crest, rode along the lines at Cold Harbor and gave the command : ' Rally on the centre ! Forward, and open fire with every gun ! ' The Union forces, in obedience to that command, moved like an avalanche upon the enemy, carrying destruction, defeat, total rout and death into the ranks of the rebel forces, and victory rang through the air. The centre upon which we are to rally and rely is the ballot-box. The occasion for public address will for the time have ended, but every man and woman pledged to our good cause can secure an audience of one voter, and by invitation, persuasion, and entreaty secure that one more ballot for the redemption of our land from the domination of the grog-shop. Let our increased vote in New Jersey be an inspiration to our friends throughout the land. God speed the day of victory !''

The " increased vote " was " an inspiration " to Prohibitionists the country over. It showed the largest proportion of party Prohibition ballots cast up to that time in any State—nearly nine per cent. In 1883 the Prohibition candidate for governor had a trifle over four thousand votes ; in 1884 the St. John vote was about six thousand ; General Fisk's total, as counted and returned, was 19,808. He ran ahead of his ticket uniformly, and in some counties largely. By his character, and his canvass, he had lifted the Prohibition cause of New Jersey breast-high in public consideration, and compelled for it henceforward the respect of all candid men.

In his own county of Monmouth, always Democratic, he drew so heavily from that party that a Republican plurality resulted ; and in eight other counties the Republicans won by pluralities smaller than the Prohibition vote. In three counties this was true of the Democrats ; making twelves counties out of twenty-one in which Prohibitionists held the balance of power, while the State at large gave them the balance of power by over eleven thousand. Said one paper :

"The Prohibition Party owes a debt of gratitude to General Fisk which it can never pay. He gave to it the service of the most magnificent canvass ever made in the State, and the party has been put upon its feet to stay by the grand work of General Fisk."

To a reporter for the New York *Voice*, who called on him a day or two after election, General Fisk said :

"The result is simply magnificent. The foundations are now permanently laid on which to build a conquering party. . . . Never were men more true than those in the rank and file of New Jersey's Prohibition host. Our friends were more than willing to stand and be counted, in a minority large or small, that they might build sure foundations on which to stand as a majority in the not far-distant future. We have every reason to rejoice at the outlook, to thank God, take courage, and go forward.

"The result in my own town is very gratifying. Here, where last year we polled only twenty-eight votes this year I received three hundred. We could easily have elected three or four legislators in the State had we been willing to bargain, but our people stood squarely on the issue of Prohibition, and refused all offers of 'deals.' In one county we drew so heavily from the Democrats that two Republican legislators were elected. More Democrats than Republicans voted with us in this county of Monmouth.

"The outlook was never so hopeful and inspiring as now. Indications all point to a vote of at least five hundred thousand for a Prohibition President in 1888, with possibility of many more."

Who the next Presidential candidate of the Prohibition Party should be, that New Jersey campaign fairly well established.

"If we discern the signs of the times," one editor soon declared, "General Fisk is the coming man. He developed great strength in his recent canvass in New Jersey as Prohibition candidate for governor. He has made a fine record, and he commands the confidence and affection of the people. He has silenced the tongue of political slander, and established his title clear to the distinction of a *Christian gentleman.* He went through the New Jersey campaign with flying colors. He held aloft the Prohibition banner throughout the contest, never faltering for an instant. He has come out of the fight without even the smell of fire upon his garments. We lay no claim to the gift of prophecy, but we have no hesitation in predicting that General Fisk will be the Prohibition candidate for the Presidency in 1888."

This editorial utterance seems to have been suggested by an interview with Rev. A. B. Leonard, D.D., whose canvass in Ohio the year previous had approximated General Fisk's, and who had become nationally conspicuous on account of it. That interview was given in the *Evening Post,* and accredited to Dr. Leonard this remark :

"Clinton B. Fisk, of New Jersey, is my candidate

for President in 1888. He is the strongest man in the country—is widely known, is popular, is able, is clean. Nothing could be said against him in his campaign but that was immediately proven false. He is more popular with the colored people of the South than any other living man. He will, beyond a doubt, be our candidate for President, with a Southern man for Vice-President ; and he will get a big vote too !"

Similar expressions became frequent in the Prohibition Party press, and from the lips of other trusted Prohibition leaders. The voice of twenty thousand New Jersey homes had been heard across the continent.

CHAPTER XXIX.

The spring of 1887 saw a mightier contest than had before been waged for State Prohibition by Constitutional Amendment. It was fought between the moral and the immoral forces of Michigan, and the respective allies on both sides. Similar contests had been successful in Kansas, in Iowa, in Maine, and Rhode Island, and another had well-nigh won in Ohio ; but neither of those brought into full activity all the fighting hosts of the liquor traffic, and all the reserves which it could command, as did the Michigan campaign.

At its beginning General Fisk wrote a public letter, to his friends in that State, urging earnest effort for the Prohibitory Amendment. He did not feel sure that he could take part himself ; for his own late campaign had told severely upon him, and he did not rally as he wished from the reaction which had ensued. But his heart went out warmly to those who had inaugurated the battle, and were pressing it on as best they could—to the noble men and women who stood up bravely for home, and commonwealth, and God. They were a royal legion, led by Professor Samuel Dickie, of Albion College—that institution so linked with all General Fisk's memories of his young manhood—and by Mrs. Mary T. Lathrap, President of the Michigan W. C. T. U., who had rendered signal service in New Jersey the season previous. Reasons of personal regard and association alone would have made the general eager to assist ; added to these were the love he still bore the State where so much was at issue, and the greater love he felt for a great and holy cause.

And every able-bodied man was needed—he knew that. The liquor traffic of other States was pouring money without stint into Michigan. Potent political influences were being brought to bear to maintain the saloon. Party necessities were invoked, professional ambitions were appealed to, the greed of gain was aroused, the varied forms of human selfishness were played upon—all, that Prohibition might be beaten at the focal point of government ; that the purest concerns of society might be smitten down, while the brothel, the gambling hell, and the saloon should continue and multiply. Such desperation on the part of organized evil had not previously been seen, nor, it may be said, such open success in the efforts of evil to ally itself with good, and to seek respectability through such alliance. Had it been a conflict simply between moral forces and immoral, nobody would have doubted the result ; but immorality won to its help the selfishness of moral men, the partisanship of political managers, the business interests of a great multitude, the organized cupidity of State and nation, and facing this array the friends of Prohibition might well fear defeat, and appeal for reinforcements.

These latter came from many States ; not in vast sums of money, as contributed by the liquor trade in opposition, but in literature adapted to the time, and in platform talent consecrated unselfishly to this great reform. The month of March witnessed " Amendment " meetings all over Michigan, from Detroit to Marquette, where with prayer, and song, and speech, the lovers of God and home persuasively sought to win adherents for

the .right. Every night the watchfires of truth blazed
in a thousand places between Lakes Huron, Michigan,
and Superior, and around them able advocates reasoned
of temperance, righteousness, and a fearful judgment
to come if these were not henceforth to prevail.

With other able helpers, the Silver Lake Quartette
went to Michigan from New York, a group of singers
and speakers since become well known throughout the
country. To spare himself undue expenditure of vital
energy, and because he so realized the power of music
along reformative moral and political lines, General Fisk
volunteered a series of appointments in company with
this quartette, and filled them with but a single break.
So familiar was his name all over the State, and so universally was he respected by men of all political creeds,
that great numbers came to every meeting ; and his addresses were always in happy mood, with no harsh ar-
raignment of any one, though severely condemning the
saloon.

He joined the quartette at Adrian, in his old home
county of Lenawee, where an afternoon and an evening
meeting were held, at each of which he spoke. Monroe
enjoyed his presence next day, and, as at Adrian, the
hall was filled to suffocation. Other notable gatherings
were at Detroit, Ann Arbor, Albion, Coldwater, and
Hillsdale ; and everywhere his persuasive manner, his
Christian courtesy, his noble bearing, won friends for
the cause. Afternoon and evening, throngs came to
listen, many driving long distances, and went away
thrilled by the sentiments uttered in speech and song.

The general's keen zest for music made those days less
wearing upon him than otherwise they might have been ;
and he often recalled that first quartette he ever heard,
when as a Birney boy in Clinton he bore the Birney flag.

One song he daily called for, written by the quartette for this campaign, and it never failed to stir the audience to responsive enthusiasm. The words ran thus :

" Come, ye Christian fathers who've been praying for the right,
For God, and home, and native land now make a gallant fight.
Stand for Prohibition till the foe is put to flight, —
Surely we're marching to victory.

CHORUS.

" Hurrah ! hurrah ! we'll shout the jubilee ;
Hurrah ! hurrah ! from rum we will be free ;
So we'll sing the chorus from Detroit to Manistee, —
Surely we're marching to victory.

" Come, ye manly brothers who have sisters to protect,
Rally to the ranks of those with home's blue ribbon decked ;
Swear that lives no more shall be by law's permission wrecked, —
Surely we're marching to victory.

" Come, ye tipsy topers from the bars that we would ban,
Cease to paint your noses on the danger-signal plan,
Wear the temperance colors each, and vote to be a man, —
Surely we're marching to victory.

" Don't you hear the word of cheer go ringing down the lines ?
Don't you catch the music in the whisper of your pines ?
Listen to the echo from your busy northern mines, —
Surely we're marching to victory."

The most important appointments of General Fisk, in some respects, were at Detroit, on Saturday and Sunday, March 26th and 27th. Saturday night's meeting was an immense affair—though hastily arranged to counteract the influences resulting from one conducted by the liquor side, a few nights earlier, in that city, and addressed by two eminently respectable gentlemen—Mr. D. Bethune Duffield and Professor Kent. It was held in Beecher's Hall, which overflowed with people, so intense had public interest become. The chief address, and a most masterly one, was made by Mr. John B. Finch, whose incisive logic left no shred of argument for Messrs. Kent and Duffield to stand upon. General Fisk followed Mr. Finch—always a difficult thing for any one to do, and more than ever difficult that night—and admirably sustained the tone and temper of a meeting never to be forgotten by any man present. His good-natured thrusts at Messrs. Duffield and Kent were almost as cutting as the stabs of the javelin hurled by Mr. Finch.

With sweeping effect he reminded them how in January, 1861, when treason was rampant in the land, he listened eagerly for some word of cheer from his old State ; how a great meeting was held then in Detroit, where loyal men gathered for counsel ; and how one voice, in tones of conservative fear, urged that the country should keep hands off the question of slavery, because of slavery's great power and our national inability to put it away. "That voice," he declared, "was D. Bethune Duffield's, who now comes before a vast audience to insist that the liquor traffic must be maintained through a tax system, because Prohibition, as he affirms, cannot be enforced."

Next day, at an afternoon meeting in the Detroit Opera House, General Fisk was the leading speaker, and his address rang clear and powerful with Christian patriotism. Through a bleak March storm of snow and sleet more than two thousand people had come to hear him, and they were not disappointed. He was serene yet severe, and his denunciation of those church members, and even clergymen, who proposed to stand by the saloon, was not less scathing because uttered in such calm, unimpassioned language ; and it made a deep impression on all. With sweet charity, but uncompromising condemnation, he assailed that moral blindness which would permit moral men to advocate an immorality for the revenue it might yield ; and there, as elsewhere, he declared against the sin and crime of a license system, and fastened home upon Christian men the awful responsibility of its maintenance.

"High License," he said, "is the white flag of truce sent out by the alcoholic hosts to obtain a halt until they can get their demoralized forces marshalled once again ;" and he attacked the tax policy of Michigan as altogether wrong, unjust, and criminal, and utterly unworthy a great Christian commonwealth.

So convincing were the addresses of General Fisk, here and elsewhere, and so widespread was his influence against liquor, that anti-Prohibition managers felt the necessity of discounting his work in every possible way. The character of their cause would permit, if not justify, any depth of malice, of falsehood, of indecency. And as the campaign drew near its close, with Prohibition sentiment gaining every hour and Prohibition success grown almost certain, their desperation snatched at whatever means vile ingenuity could invent and unblushing audacity employ, to serve their unrighteous ends. Through certain unprincipled newspaper columns in Detroit, they disseminated, with considerable circumstantiality of statement, a story of drinking indulgence by General Fisk, on a former visit there, which no one who knew him would for a moment believe, but which, as they foresaw, might gain brief credence among the great voting mass to whom he was personally unknown.

It was met by instant telegraphic denial from the general, and by him stamped as "a most infamous lie, worthy of the saloon advocates and their associates, indicated in Revelation 22 : 15."

The passage referred to reads :

"For without are dogs, and sorcerers, and whoremongers, and murderers, and idolaters, and whosoever loveth and maketh a lie."

This vigorous Bible delineation of their true character enraged the enemy still more, and they repeated their attack, with added virulence and wrath, and refused to print the final message of explanation and denial sent them in answer by General Fisk. In this message, forwarded from Albion, April 2d, the general told precisely how and why he once paid for a night lunch eaten by four newspaper men of Detroit, of which he did not remain to partake, and added :

"The statement that I ordered champagne for any one, that I drank that or any other kind of liquor, is untrue. No liquors were ordered and drank by any of the party to my knowledge. I have been much abused and misrepresented since I entered the fight against the saloon, but have never been called a fool. If I could have said and done what Mr. Ireland states, then, indeed, I would have been both foolish and wicked."

Though this denial was not allowed publication in the same columns which had called it forth, other papers published it, and the slander fell flat at once.

Then one Thompson, referred to by a Detroit daily as "one of the gentlemen who arranged with Messrs. Duffield and Kent for the efficient work which they have done," after predicting the defeat of Prohibition by from fifteen to twenty thousand votes, made statements which found widespread repetition in this despatch to the New York *Tribune*, April 3d :

"A sensation was created this evening by the publication of an interview with W. G. Thompson, a Democratic politician, in which he asserts that General Clinton B. Fisk, who is the chief campaigner of the Prohibitionists, stumped the State of New York in 1884 for St. John in the pay of the Democratic Party. Mr. Thompson avers that he possesses personal knowledge of the truth of his statement."

To which despatch General Fisk made the following pithy reply, published in the *Tribune* of April 7th :

"The hotly-contested Michigan campaign for the Prohibition Amendment brought to the surface a large number of the tribe of Ananias. This man Thompson, the leader of the Rum Democracy in Detroit, does special credit to his ancestor. I did not make a speech in the State of New York in the St. John campaign of 1884. No Democrat, no Republican, no Prohibitionist, ever paid me a cent for making a speech in the State of New York or any other State."

The more decent friends of Mr. Thompson felt like subscribing in his behalf to the truth of Josh Billings's affirmation—"It's a great deal better not to know so much, than to know so many things that ain't so."

If the Michigan campaign had continued a week longer, there's no telling what further lies General Fisk would have had promulgated about him. But it ended April 4th, with two splendid meetings at Hillsdale, following two of like size and spirit at Coldwater. And at each of these places, as at Albion, on the 2d, former neighbors and friends of the general turned out *en masse* to greet him, while an overflow meeting became necessary at his old home, because the large Methodist church there could not accommodate all who came. At Albion, and at Hillsdale, the college faculties honored him by their presence and their welcoming words.

At these Amendment meetings, to illustrate the fixed and fearless attitude which ministers of Christ should maintain toward the liquor traffic, and the unyielding Christian courage requisite thereto, General Fisk several times related this incident :

"I came across a young man last year up near the Delaware Water Gap who had just such courage. Up there near the Water Gap, in the side of the mountain, is a beautiful village, where many people from New York, Newark, and Jersey City, have their summer homes. Just in the side of the mountain are two little churches, a Presby-

terian church and a Methodist church. The young man had been
sent over from the Philadelphia Conference to preach in the Methodist church, and the official brethren had the usual meeting to esti-
mate his salary. A good many of you, brethren, have sat in such
councils. They fixed his salary at a thousand dollars, a large compensation, he thought. And then they began to post him about the
peculiarities of the church ; and about this family and that family,
so that he might know just how to manage affairs and go along
smoothly. Then they further said to him :

" ' Now, in the summer-time a good many foreigners—people from
the city—come to our little church. One of the richest brewers of
Newark sits here in the summer-time in one of our best pews, and
pays fifty dollars a year toward the salary. He drives the finest
carriage that comes up to our little village. His wife dresses beauti-
fully, his daughters more so, and his sons are perfect patterns.
Now, then, while he is in the church, we would like to have you go a
little slow on the temperance question. Don't say anything about
the liquor traffic. Preach about the Mormons or the Lost Tribes—
anything but that, or we shall lose his presence among us and his
fifty dollars, and we rather like to have him drive his carriage to our
little church—monogram on the carriage-door, footman and groom
on the carriage, harness beautiful—nothing that goes to the Presbyterian church is anything like it, and we want to keep it.'

" The young man scratched his head a little. He had been educated at the Drew Theological Seminary, where they teach that to
preach against intemperance is one of the things to do everywhere and
anywhere. He rose to his feet, and the presiding elder told me that
as he began to straighten up, he looked to be about eleven feet high.

" ' Now,' he said, ' brethren, what did you fix this salary at ?'

" ' A thousand dollars.'

" ' You just take fifty dollars off. I must have a shot at that party
the first thing.'

" And they could not persuade him out of it. Just think of the
stubborn fellow ! By and by the beautiful June days came, and
among those who stopped at the little Methodist church on the hill-
side came the brewer, with a brand-new carriage, everything better
and brighter than ever before. He and his family filed into the pew.
What should this young man do but open the Bible, and for about
an hour he poured out on that audience all the woes that God had
pronounced against the men that put the bottle to their neighbors'
lips. One of the stewards told me that the ceiling of the little church
was fairly blistered before noon. Well, now, what was the result ?

Why, at the close of the sermon this brewer came forward to the altar and took this young man by the hand, and said, ' Do you know me?' ' Yes, sir.' ' Did you know my business?' ' Yes.' ' Did you know I was a brewer?' ' Yes.' ' Did you preach that sermon for me ' ' ' For you only.' ' Well, now,' said he, ' I like the courage of a man that will do that.' Says he, ' Give us your hand. I have been in the habit of giving fifty dollars a year to this church. I will give you a hundred dollars.' You see the brewer was a man of common sense. The official brethren had looked upon him as a man only of dollars and cents."

The Michigan campaign ended, but prayer, and song, and speech did not prevail. The work of godly women, the efforts of loyal Christian men, could not withstand partisan trickery, organized appetite, banded agencies of disorder, the indifference of the church, and the selfishness of sin. And having given nearly a month of his time, as freely of his means, and with unchecked liberality of his energies, to the sacred cause of a commonwealth very dear to him, General Fisk returned home regretful that once again right was defeated, and wrong triumphant, but conscious that his own duty had been fully done. And with brave Gerald Massey he could sing :

> " Our hearts brood o'er the past ; our eyes
>   With shining futures glisten ;
> Lo ! now the dawn bursts up the skies—
>   Lean out your souls and listen !
> The earth rolls Freedom's radiant way,
>   And ripens with our sorrow,
> And 'tis the martyrdom to-day
>   Brings victory to-morrow !

> " 'Tis weary watching wave on wave,
>   And yet the tide heaves onward ;
> We climb like corals grave on grave,
>   And build a path that's sunward.
> We're beaten back in many a fray,
>   Yet newer strength we borrow,
> And where our vanguard camps to-day
>   Our rear shall rest to-morrow."

CHAPTER XXX.

IF any further proof were needed of the necessity for a National Prohibition Party, and of his wisdom in allying himself therewith, General Fisk found it in that Michigan campaign, " non-partisan " as it was averred to be, and in similar results following similar campaigns later on the same year, in Texas, Tennessee, and Oregon. Had he never realized before, he must surely have realized then, how a power so dominant in politics as the liquor traffic can never be politically assailed, even by non-partisan ballots, or the purpose to cast them, without invoking and commanding the open or secret aid of party machines, and making for itself common cause with party leaders, party conditions, and party success. And he must have seen that the moral elements of a single State, contending with the liquor forces not alone of that State but of the entire nation, were contending also against the imperative needs of a great national party, dependent upon the liquor forces for control, in several States, and inevitably beaten in the next national campaign if these liquor forces were alienated in any State. He must have seen—he did see—that a State party's action, through its leaders and its legislative or administrative policy, will be dominated by the national party's needs, and that the final logic of politics, when reasoned from the mere party standpoint, will compel such legislation, or administration, or policy, within the narrower limits of a State, as may and will insure the national party's victory.

In the Michigan campaign General Fisk had spoken no word of partisan reference, made no plea that meant his party's gain. With the long list of Amendment advocates in that State, and their followers in other States that season, he kept the faith, as a non-partisan, upon the platform, every day. Yet nevertheless he knew, as did many beside, that non-partisanship was but a party sham, in all the four States which carried on Amendment campaigns during 1887; that influential party leaders were conniving at the Amendment's defeat, while claiming party credit for submitting it; that its defeat was counted by them a party necessity, in view of national conditions logically to be met the next year.

He knew, and he did not hesitate to say, that the National Republican Party, by its recognized leadership, and because of its composite liquor-and-temperance elements, defeated the Prohibition Amendment in Michigan and in Oregon; just as a like Amendment was defeated by the National Democratic Party, for exactly parallel reasons, in Texas and in Tennessee. He did not marvel that this was so. He only wondered that thousands of other men did not and could not see the truth of it, and the partisan excuses which could be urged in defence of such a course. And he grieved that men would any longer insist upon non-partisan methods, in settlement of a great wrong upheld by two great parties for party ends, when every such method must begin in legislative action of a party sort, and end in the administration of law by party officials; he marvelled that party action against the saloon could be expected from any party winning State or national victory through the saloon, and indebted directly to the saloon for dominant party life.

But he did not grow bitter. His patience was abundant, and his faith unfailing. The year before, referring to Maine's Amendment campaign, he had said :

"When Mr. Blaine turned away from the ballot-box in Augusta without discharging his whole duty as a citizen, he dropped his own flag to half-mast, and from that day began his melancholy march in his own political funeral procession."

So, now, he felt that any man, any party, stopping short of entire duty on this line of moral and political reform, was but joining a solemn funeral procession, and he might be grieved but he would not *bitterly* condemn. To man or party he would allow every excuse which necessity could frame, and let the procession go on, himself a mourner by the wayside of political progress and national achievement, but not a participant in the obsequies, or a part of the deceased.

He was not unmindful that the thought of many Prohibitionists turned steadily toward him as their next national standard-bearer. Certain papers of that party deliberately heralded him as their first choice, and some of the party's official managers declared for him without reserve. He was gratified by such tokens of confidence and esteem, as well he might be, coming from such sources ; but he grew sorely troubled over the embarrassments they brought, and sought in every way which modestly he might to divert serious purposes from himself. He wrote letters to near party friends, disavowing all desire for political honor, even refusing all consent to be mentioned in relation thereto. He insisted that as a private in the ranks of Prohibition he could fight better, and better serve the cause, than as captain of the host. He pleaded his varied church and philanthropic relationships, his overworked condition, his need of rest. He

as nearly declined possible nomination as any man feels
at liberty to refuse what has not been proffered, and
what he knows may be subject to circumstances over
which no one has or can have positive control.   And the
months went by.

On the night of November 30th, he stood before a
vast audience in Battery D., at Chicago, and said tender,
heart-warm words *in memoriam* of John B. Finch, for
whom the world's end came so suddenly not many weeks
before, and whose loss the world's greatest reform must
forevermore lament.   A National Conference of Prohibitionists had gathered there, that day, and that evening's tribute was but their due to one whose faithful,
fearless leadership they had all recognized.   And on the
night succeeding, in the same place, over five thousand
people gathered to hear General Fisk, Governor St. John,
and Mrs. Lathrap discuss National Prohibition.   It
was a monster assemblage—the largest of its party kind,
perhaps, ever till then seen in this country.   Enthusiasm
ran up to fever heat.   The pulses of men leaped like
flame.   The Silver Lake Quartette sang—

" We're not so lonesome as we used to be,"

and thunders of applause swept from floor to ceiling.

Delivering the main address of that occasion, General
Fisk stirred the hearts of all as mountain breezes move
the shallow depths of mountain lakes.   Men and women
laughed when he willed it, or, when he would, grew
sober unto tears.   He surprised even those who knew
him best with his oratorical powers, his versatility of expression, his exceptional aptness, and humor, and
strength.   And before he sat down he surprised everybody by persuading the audience to contribute six thousand dollars to a national campaign fund, wherewith

Prohibitionists were to begin their national campaign of 1888.

Mrs. Lathrap, as many will remember, followed him that night, in the strong, womanly manner which is her wont, mellowed often by pathetic tenderness ; and after her came Governor St. John, whose speech set thousands of lips and hands to eager cheering, and made that great military hall one tempest of enthusiasm. For the governor, as authoritatively as any one man could at that time, and with an inherent right, because of his own sacrifice, which every one tacitly confessed, nominated General Fisk as the next Prohibition candidate for the Presidency. The nomination had indorsement swift and strong enough to render anybody proud and glad, but mainly it made General Fisk sober and regretful, as those well knew who stood nearest his heart.

From that hour he faced the inevitable. He must bear the national banner of Prohibition in 1888, as he had borne the State banner in New Jersey in 1886—even as he had borne that despised Birney " rag " in " Log Cabin " days—must bear it, though contempt smite him, and prejudice assail him, and friendship falter and fail —must bear it, because duty so commanded, and manhood would not let him refuse. Yet he did not accept the inevitable, then, or soon. So much did he shrink from it, that he caught at any hope of relief, and would publicly have announced his refusal but for keen sense of possible duty, and the often earnest petition of friends who loved both him and the cause.

Wherever he appeared in a gathering of Prohibitionists, he was welcomed with demonstrations of personal esteem and recognition of leadership both flattering and embarrassing. On February 2d, 1888, he took part in a public debate upon " High License, and the Need of a

Prohibition Party," in the Brooklyn Academy of Music, and was there magnificently received. His opponent that night was Dr. H. K. Carroll, of the *Independent*, who followed able debaters upon high license, himself taking up the second theme assigned—" Does Temperance Reform Demand a Prohibition Party ?" Dr. Carroll read a carefully-prepared argument, the ablest ever made upon the negative side, and General Fisk read an affirmative address in return. Not having seen or heard the paper of Dr. Carroll, the general could not meet all the points made therein, but dealt with broad principles and specific facts. Among other true and unanswerable statements which he put forth were these :

" We are all agreed touching one thing—that the liquor traffic is the one great overshadowing evil of these times. The New York *Tribune* says it is ' the heaviest clog on the progress of our country. Sooner or later it will be necessary for the intelligent and progressive elements of society to drop all lesser enterprises and combine in one determined assault upon it.' The intelligent and progressive elements of society are more and more believing that a successful assault upon the great evil can be made only by massing in a National Prohibition Party. The liquor traffic is intrenched in national politics. The nation is the senior partner in the manufacture of liquors. Neither old party will grapple with the monstrous evil which says to each, ' Keep your hands off of me or I will rend the one more hostile to me by defeat, and give success to the more friendly organization.'

" The liquor traffic entered national politics in 1851. The distillers and bar-tenders held their first national convention and declared their purpose ' to be the organization of a political party to resist the enforcement, secure the repeal, and resist the enactment of all temperance and Sunday laws.' The leaders in both the old Whig and Democratic parties said, with great promptness : ' What do you want of a new party? We are both with you, and the party to which you will give the most votes will do the best by you.' Two years later, when the liquor convention at Cleveland declared, that ' liquor men could vote for no candidate who is not pledged to oppose in earnest and with decision the enactment of prohibitory laws,' the

Democratic Party hastened to place itself on record as the friend and protector of the saloon, and has ever since kept its word.

" In 1872 the Republican national platform was so constructed as to place the party in hostility to all ' so-called temperance and Sunday laws,' and the President of the Liquor Association said, in contemplating this action : ' I believe that it is only a question of time, and our entire nation, Government, and people will bow with affection and respect to the genial and beneficent reign of King Gambrinus.'

" The liquor interest established its headquarters in Washington, placing there one of the ablest men their money could buy, with instructions to defeat all national legislation prejudicial to the liquor traffic. We of the National Temperance Society can testify with what fidelity Louis Schade has discharged his duty. It has been impossible, as yet, with all the efforts we could concentrate, to secure the appointment of a non-partisan commission to inquire into the effects of alcoholic drinks upon our people. When some indiscreet, conscientious Republican had spoken out in meeting against this tyranny and arrogance of the liquor traffic, their famous orator said : ' Should separation from a polluted Republican Party become necessary, even if only for the especial purpose to crush prohibitory laws and procure condemnation at the seat of the Federal Government of all compulsory measures, it becomes important to consider where we can look either for new political connections with an existing party, or for the material for the organization of a new one.' The dominant party to this insolence replied simply, ' Don't think of moving out of the family mansion ; take the best rooms for yourselves.' Further, speaking of the political affiliations of the liquordealers, Mr. Schade said : ' Three fourths of them are Republicans. We can count upon their protection to the industry which contributes so largely toward sustaining the Government, and I assure you in general that the bonds of good-will between the Government and ourselves are more solid than ever.'"

While the Methodist General Conference was in session at New York, in the great Metropolitan Opera House, the Prohibitionists of New York County arranged a mass-meeting to be held there, and it came off as per announcement on May 20th, 1888. The vast auditorium was packed from parquet to dome, in despite of a drenching rain. Hundreds of clergymen were present, and doctors of divinity were liberally scattered among the four or five thousand people assembled there. Scores occupied the broad platform, and three of them made speeches. It was a concourse remarkable for its high character, for its extended church influence, for its average of intellectual ability. No political meeting of any party, it may be assumed, had ever before matched it in these particulars. And its enthusiasm grew electric.

Late in the evening General Fisk was seen quietly to enter a box upon the right of the stage, and calls for him from the audience soon put the chairman's programme quite one side. The calls did not cease, but swelled to a chorus, and swept from gallery to gallery with increasing power till they would not be denied ; and when the general was led forward upon the stage, that whole mighty assemblage rose and gave him salutation such as few private citizens have ever received, hundreds of white hands waving white handkerchiefs, and thousands of voices shouting forth their hearty cheers. It was a most emphatic echo of the Chicago nomination made six months before. Through it, and by it, the metropolis of the East said " Amen " to the choice named in the metropolis of the West ; and there could be no doubt of the inevitable after that.

To a close friend, substantially, he said :

" I do not want this nomination ; I shrink from it. It can mean for me only toil and sacrifice, calumny and contempt. I have no political ambitions ; all I crave is the rest which I so little can command, and the chance for private service in this cause as I am able to render it. But I must not shirk a clear duty, and there is no objection in my own mind against accepting the burden, and bearing it, which I am not ready to waive if that be the call of my Master and my fellow-men. Only we must

be very sure, and those nearest me must be well satisfied
to have it so."

He thought first of the cause, and of the home-circle
which he held so dear; last of himself, and the comforts, the domestic joys, he must forego. His chief
dread was that unhappiness might come to those he
loved; and some anxious hours were his on this account,
before the final decision came.

CHAPTER XXXI.

FORMAL choice of the Prohibitionists was made in their National Convention, at Indianapolis, the evening of May 31st.

That convention must be historic in the politics of this country. It was composed of more than one thousand regular delegates, about half as many alternates, and from two to three thousand visitors in active sympathy, who crowded Tomlinson Hall morning, afternoon, and evening for two entire days, beginning Wednesday, May 30th. They represented every State in the Union save two, several Territories, and the District of Columbia. They included scores of men and women whose names have become nationally identified with moral and political reform. They made up an assemblage of immense size, of magnificent character, of lofty patriotism, of masterful Christian faith. Their chief thought was—national suppression of the liquor traffic, through a national party to suppress it; and allied with this was another, not less pervasive, if rather less dominant—national unity through such a national party. These thoughts were varyingly but constantly expressed in the speeches made, in the prayers offered, in the songs sung, and in the mottoes liberally displayed about the hall. Among the latter were these:

" National Prohibition by a Party whose Supremacy depends upon its Enforcement will Win."

" No Evil can be Exterminated by Selling it the Right to Exist."

" No License ' for revenue only ' ; no Protection, no Free Trade, for the Liquor Traffic."

" Local Option is too Local and too Optional."

" Prohibition will obliterate the Sectional and Color-line in Politics."

" The Prohibition Army of the Blue and the Gray is coming, five hundred thousand strong, to Conquer Rum."

The spirit of non-sectionalism, of patriotic fraternity, from the opening till the closing hour, was deep, suffusive, hallowed, and tender. It gave tone and color to the whole proceedings. It lent beautiful emphasis to the fact that Prohibition, as a new national issue, can overcome old sectional prejudice, render past feuds but a present sorrowful memory, sweeten the bitterness of bygone strife, and blend the best impulses of all in one grand purpose for the common good. It had very sacred accentuation on the first evening, when a Memorial Day service was held by the convention, in which " Blue" and " Gray" bore equal part, and paid equally touching tribute to

" The thousands true and brave,
Who fought for the Right with a zealous might
That won for them only a grave ;"

and where delegates from the South and from the North, in the full sincerity of a new political brotherhood, their pulses throbbing with equal patriotism, together could sit and sing :

" Under the Flag they were flying,
Freedom forbids us be sad ;
Love, amid sorrowful sighing,
Even can smile and be glad.
One, in the Right that divided ;
One, in the courage both knew ;
One, by one flag ever guided —
Brothers, the Gray and the Blue.

" Here clasping hand within hand,
    Mourn we the brave and the true ;
Whether they sleep in the Blue or Gray,
Waiting the dawn of the Judgment Day,
    Brothers, the Gray and the Blue.

" Glad in the glory of freedom,
    Brothers, to-night, we embrace ;
Past are the trials of Edom,
    Bright is the Future's fair face ;
Heart beats with heart, in communion
    Tender, and trustful, and true ;
Love seals again a glad Union,
    Binding the Gray and the Blue."

In this pathetic service, the like of which had no previous record, and which may never be matched, in all our political annals—participated in by Colonel George W. Bain, Colonel R. S. Cheves, and Mrs. Lide Merriwether, as representing the South ; by Captain J. F. Cleghorn and Miss Frances E. Willard, representing the North, and by Rev. J. H. Hector, representing the colored race—General Fisk was to have taken leading place, but he could not attend.   As head of the Local Committee having in charge the Methodist General Conference, at New York, he felt that duty required him there, and so the convention missed his magnetic presence, while he lost the opportunity he would have enjoyed in superlative degree of speaking for the dead heroes and the living Union—for the fellowship of North and South, the obliteration of sectional lines, the uplifting by Northern and Southern hands of one banner against the entire nation's deadliest foe.

Lament was heard upon every hand that he was kept away ; his absence appeared the one cause for regret which that splendid gathering saw.   It was not a convention of hero-worshippers, yet it would gladly have paid honor to the man selected already for standard-bearer, just as it did royally honor John P. St. John, the standard-bearer of 1884, by making him permanent chairman, and by frequent demonstrations of esteem ; not a convention of hero-worshippers, because exceptionally made up of thinking men and women, swift to criticise, not slow to condemn, sure-set of opinion, fixed in ideas, and utterly impossible to be misled by crafty leadership, or to be stampeded for mere political ends.

No, not hero-worshippers—far from that—neither sentimentalists, nor idealists, nor fanatics ; but a body of clear-headed, brave-hearted, practical, brainy believers in God and man ; willing to work for truth, without reward, or hope of reward ; willing to give time, and energy, and reputation, and hard cash, to secure their country's redemption from the disloyal curse of drink ; willing to stand as a forlorn hope, in the mightiest contest of human history, between the hosts of right and the swelling legions of wrong.

They went about practical business on the morning of Thursday, by contributing over twenty-five thousand dollars for campaign expenditure, amid demonstrations of generous enthusiasm amazing. Rich men vied with each other in giving their thousands ; poor men became rivals in sacrifice for a needy cause ; a Catholic priest pledged one fifth of his modest salary ; women gave with an impulse like that which contributed the widow's mite centuries ago. And hundreds of unsympathetic spectators marvelled at the sight.

They framed their platform Thursday afternoon, with no difference of thought or desire save on the Suffrage Question. Debate upon that was keen enough to show the convention's mental quality, but not to impugn the Christian temper of those who took part ; and the plat-

form itself stands as witness that the convention knew
what it cared to say, and dared to say it, and cared and
dared to say it in direct, unmistakable terms. It is fit
and proper that these pages record the actual basis upon
which that convention placed its candidates for a campaign sure to form one of the vital chapters in political
history :

NATIONAL PROHIBITION PLATFORM.

The Prohibition Party, in national convention assembled, acknowledging Almighty God as the source of all power in government, and
believing that all human enactments should be framed in harmony
with His law, do hereby declare :

First. That the manufacture, importation, exportation, transportation, and sale of alcoholic beverages shall be made public crimes,
and prohibited and punished as such.

Second. That such prohibition must be secured through amendments of our national and State constitutions, enforced by adequate
laws, adequately supported by administrative authority ; and to this
end the organization of the Prohibition Party is imperatively demanded in State and nation.

Third. That any form of license, taxation, or regulation of the
liquor traffic is contrary to good government ; that any party which
supports regulation, license, or tax, enters into alliance with such
traffic, and becomes the actual foe of the State's welfare ; and that we
arraign the Republican and Democratic parties for their persistent
attitude in favor of the license iniquity, whereby they oppose the
demand of the people for prohibition, and, through open complicity
with the liquor crime, defeat the enforcement of law.

Fourth. For the immediate abolition of the internal revenue system, whereby our national Government is deriving support from our
greatest national vice.

Fifth. That an adequate public revenue being necessary, it may be
properly raised by impost duties ; but impost duties should be so
reduced that no surplus shall be accumulated in the Treasury, and
that the burdens of taxation shall be removed from foods, clothing
and other comforts and necessaries of life, and imposed on such
articles of import as will give protection both to the manufacturing
employer and producing laborer against the competition of the
world.

Sixth. That civil service appointments for all civil offices, chiefly clerical in their duties, should be based upon moral, intellectual, and physical qualifications, and not upon party service or party necessity.

Seventh. That the right of suffrage rests on no mere circumstance of race, color, sex, or nationality, and that where, from any cause, it has been withheld from citizens who are of suitable age and mentally and morally qualified for the exercise of an intelligent ballot, it should be restored by the people, through the Legislatures of the several States, on such educational basis as they may deem wise.

Eighth. For the abolition of polygamy, and the establishment of uniform laws governing marriage and divorce.

Ninth. For prohibiting all combinations of capital to control, and to increase the cost of, products for popular consumption.

Tenth. For the preservation and defence of the Sabbath as a civil institution, without oppressing any who religiously observe the same on any other than the first day of the week.

Eleventh. That arbitration is the Christian, wise, and economic method of settling national differences, and the same method should by judicious legislation be applied to the settlement of disputes between large bodies of employés and employers ; that the abolition of the saloon would remove the burdens, moral, physical, pecuniary, and social, which now oppress labor and rob it of its earnings, and would prove to be the wise and successful way of promoting labor reform, and we invite labor and capital to unite with us for the accomplishment thereof ; that monopoly in land is a wrong to the people, and the public land should be reserved to actual settlers ; and that men and women should receive equal wages for equal work.

Twelfth. That our immigration laws should be so enforced as to prevent the introduction into our country of all convicts, inmates of dependent institutions, and all others physically incapacitated for self-support, and that no person should have the ballot in any State who is not a citizen of the United States.

Recognizing and declaring that prohibition of the liquor traffic has become the dominant issue in national politics, we invite to full party fellowship all those who on this one dominant issue are with us agreed, in the full belief that this party can and will remove sectional differences, promote national unity, and insure the best welfare of our entire land.

Jubilant over the day's financial deeds, and elated over a platform unanimously adopted, which gave signal satisfaction—a platform so broad as to refute the charge of one-ideaism, while yet so single that upon it men might rally in true fellowship, if agreed upon the single issue of Prohibition—glowing with fraternal good-will, and glad in the prospect of large party gains because of the work so well accomplished and the greater things yet to be done, the convention reassembled Thursday evening to complete its task.

Between four and five thousand people densely crowded the hall. As much interest was manifest as if the nomination for first place were in doubt, and half a dozen aspirants had active support in their efforts to secure it. But it was not the interest of self-seeking ambition, of desire for political spoils. It was a hallowed, unselfish interest, throbbing with humanity's hope—an interest prayerful and consecrated, which found voice in the opening prayer, by Rev. W. R. Goodwin, of Illinois, as follows :

" O God, our Father, we come to Thee to-night with thanksgiving and with prayer. We rejoice in what our eyes have seen and in what our ears have heard, and we rejoice in the promise of a better day not far off when our homes shall be free from this evil curse, when this nation shall belong to God. We thank Thee, our Father, for the movement toward the right, and we pray Thee to bless us in all our efforts to bring Thy kingdom here, and may that time soon come when there shall be a school-house on every hill and a church in every valley, but saloons nowhere. We pray Thee to hasten the day when there shall be no smoke from any brewery or distillery to curse God's free atmosphere, and when this nation shall be a free nation—a nation of gallant men and of happy women. To this end we pray Thee, our Father, to help us by our prayers and lead us by our ballots to save our homes and to save our country. And we pray Thee, O God, that the time may soon come when every distillery, and every brewery, and every saloon shall be closed ; and if men will not forsake the evil of their ways in any other manner, we pray Thee to break up financially, root and branch, the entire system of liquor, until all our people everywhere shall learn the right and do it, and when God shall be honored and glorified, and when Heaven shall look down and see a country purified and in the enjoyment of God's blessing. Let Thy blessing rest upon the labors of this convention. We pray Thee to help us to-night in the selection of our standard-bearers who may lead us forward to victory, and may all things be done toward Thy glory and the welfare of this great cause, and give us victory in all our efforts in all our States, until this party of ours shall be the dominant party, and our Congress shall be pure, and our legislators pure, and our judges pure, and all over this land peace and righteousness shall prevail and God Himself shall rule. Hear us and bless us and save us for the Redeemer's sake. Amen."

There was no carefully-arranged programme planned for climacteric effect, as there might have been. Rev. Dr. I. K. Funk, of New York, moved that the convention proceed to the nomination of candidates for President and Vice-President; and the motion prevailed. Pending the ordered roll-call by States, some miscellaneous resolutions were entertained and adopted. When roll-call finally began, Alabama was first to respond, through Colonel John T. Tanner, with the name of Clinton B. Fisk; but Colonel Tanner's voice was weak, and what he said could not be heard far from where he stood. Professor Samuel Dickie, Chairman of the National Committee, suggested that States having no candidate of their own to present, should pass the call; and no further responses came until Kentucky was reached, when Colonel George W. Bain mounted his chair and was rapturously cheered. In those mellow silver tones which have delighted and fascinated so many audiences, in so many States, and with that charm of manner which makes him the crown prince of temperance orators, Colonel Bain said :

" *Mr. Chairman, and Ladies and Gentlemen :*
" Having the instructions of my State, I feel I must occupy your time for about a minute and a half. When the Kentucky Convention was held on the 20th of April last, it was the unanimous vote of the convention that the name of General Green Clay Smith should be presented as the first choice of Kentucky, and Clinton B. Fisk as her second. When they made that vote I believe it was especially meant

as a compliment to Green Clay Smith. I believe they knew that Green Clay Smith did not expect any nomination ; but they wished to honor him for his long service, to express the love Kentucky had for him—for the man who, though he knew he was fighting for the freedom of his own slaves, went into the war, and when the war was over and he was appointed Minister to Spain, with its salary, emoluments and honors of office before him, was converted to God, turned his back on political honors and went back to his own community, and in the little Baptist Church there went to preaching the Gospel. I received a letter from him day before yesterday, in which he says : ' I cannot attend the convention. I never expected its nomination. I deeply appreciate the compliment of Kentucky. I ask you to go before the committee, and also that you go before the National Convention, not to present my name, but to withdraw it, and to give my hearty support to General Clinton B. Fisk for President of the United States."

Everybody heard this nomination, and there went up at once a mighty shout of indorsement that set the blood bounding in every breast. General Green Clay Smith had borne the standard in 1876, and would have been a popular choice for 1888 had not the hearts of all become so fixed upon another.

Michigan gracefully waived her turn, that she might second the formal presentation which another State had prior claim to make, and, speaking through Hon. William H. Morrow, New Jersey thus declared :

" *Mr. Chairman, and Ladies and Gentlemen of this Convention :*

" It used to be urged against the Prohibition Party that it had but a single idea. Heretofore we may have been justly subject to the charge, but I venture to say had any one come into this convention at any time during the past two days, who had said that the Prohibition Party has only one idea, he would have seen that it has all the grand ideas of 1888, and means to hold on to them until victory comes. I will not linger ; but from all I have heard for the last six months, and from what I have heard in this convention, and from what I have seen upon your badges, and your banners, and your flags, I conclude you all have at this moment but a single idea. I don't know that the work that my New Jersey delegation has put upon me is more than needless, for why should I present the name of one who is known all over the United States? Why need I tell you of the patriot, why need I tell you of the statesman, and why, above all, need I tell you of the Christian man, whose conscience drove him out of the political party in which he was rocked in his babyhood by his sainted mother and father? Why need I say more in behalf of the son of Michigan, adopted by the State of New Jersey, than what you already know, more than to ask you by your votes next November, in pursuance of what I see written upon every face, to nominate and elect the grandest man of the day, General Clinton B. Fisk, of New Jersey."

It was not an elaborately composed speech ; it did not quite rise to the occasion in its rhetoric, perhaps, and the subject might fairly have called forth a more extended and more studied eulogy ; but never did rhetorician's florid art or eulogist's flowing praise invoke a grander climax. The scene that followed was one of magnificent disorder. Men sprang to their feet, and stood upon the chairs, and swung their hats, brandished their canes, flourished their umbrellas, and cheered till they became hoarse. Women waved their handkerchiefs and joined their clear treble to the baritone cries which grew and swelled to pulsing thunders of sound. Rhythmic huzzas rang out and died away, only to be repeated over and over again, with growing fervor and volume. And there, where but a night previous the Blue and the Gray had mingled their tender memorial tributes, and some had sung

> " Hushed are the roar and the riot ;
>   Spent are the furies of wrath ;
> Calm as an angel of Quiet,
>   Peace walks her beautiful path,"

ears once familiar with it, under other conditions and inspiration, could catch the short, sharp, ringing percussion of " the rebel yell," no longer up-leaping in wrath but in fraternal jubilee.

And so General Fisk was nominated. But Michigan lost her chance to second, for after some minutes of this tempestuous demonstration, in a momentary lull between the whirlwind gusts of it, Colonel Cheves, an ex-Confederate officer of Kentucky, secured the chairman's attention, and said :

"I move that General Clinton B. Fisk be made the unanimous choice of this convention for President of the United States."

The motion was put upon a rising vote, and the whole convention stood, at once.

Then said the chairman :

"I declare General Clinton B. Fisk to be unanimously the choice of this convention for President of the United States."

And once more delegates and visitors thundered their applause, while banners waved, and the band played, and handkerchiefs fluttered, and a huge wooden crank was whirled about in the centre of the hall, and above the stage unseen agencies lifted a large portrait of the general, beneath which was depicted a snake coiled into the word *saloon*, while the candidate's left hand grasped the reptile's throat, and below all floated in mid-air yet another device, on which, in evergreen letters, could be read, "Hail to the Chief—Fisk."

The names of several gentlemen were presented for the Vice-Presidency, but choice fell at length upon Rev. John A. Brooks, D.D., of Missouri, and after a speech from that gentleman, and some further miscellaneous business, the convention adjourned *sine die*.

CHAPTER XXXII.

CHAIRMAN ST. JOHN telegraphed General Fisk, as follows :

" INDIANAPOLIS, IND., May 31, 1888.

"The National Prohibition Convention, of over one thousand delegates, with the greatest enthusiasm has just nominated you by acclamation as its candidate for President. Accept my heartiest congratulation. May God bless you !   JOHN P. ST. JOHN."

One who desired the general's nomination as much as any others of the thousand, for sake of the cause, but who, in hope of saving him and his from burden and sacrifice, had agreed not to favor it, and had sat silent through all the turbulent enthusiasm of that flood-tide hour, sent over the wire this brief testimony :

" I was an atom before an avalanche.   You are called."

Judge Robert C. Pitman, of Massachusetts, author of " Alcohol and the State," wired greeting :

"Accept my congratulation upon your hearty and unanimous nomination as our leader .in the Presidential campaign. It is an honor unsought by you, but one that will last and grow brighter with the lapse of time."

These, and scores of other congratulatory messages, were not delivered to General Fisk that night. The Methodist General Conference had but just closed its labors, and, worn out with the incessant cares incident to his service in connection therewith, he had gone to his

New York City apartments and retired early for needed rest. His family would not disturb him, and the news of his nomination met him first on Friday morning of June 1st.

He was too troubled by it, and too exhausted by the month's Conference attendance and duties, for hourly interview and interruption, and at once forsook the city and sought the quiet of his lovely Seabright home on the Jersey coast.

A *Voice* reporter found him there next day.

"And so you have come to talk with me about the nomination?" he asked. "Well, you see how I am. I am completely worn out, and have come down here for a little rest."

Rumson Hill, his summer residence, and his only permanent abode, is a restful place. It is two miles, nearly, from Seabright Station on the New Jersey Southern Road, and overlooks the little Shrewsbury River, while beyond that, southward, and about four miles removed, is famous Long Branch, half-hidden by the timber growths between. The neighborhood abounds in palatial villas, surrounded by superb grounds, wherein and whereon wealth has lavished its adornments without stint. Nowhere else, it is said, in all that region so noted for its display of architectural and landscape art, can you find such an array of costly establishments as in the ten square miles of which Rumson Hill is a natural centre.

The Hill is not a mountain, but a gently-sloping, irregular eminence, and upon the sides of it are several residences owned by the money kings of New York. General Fisk's home is the most modest of all, and looks much, from the rather remote highway, like a liberal, well-kept country farmhouse, set amid some rural gentleman's wide acres, and generous of unpretentious enjoy-

ment for all who enter there. Such, indeed, it is. The
farm has eighty acres, and is carefully equipped with all
the appointments of a first-class agricultural "plant,"
including fine blooded horses and cows, and ample ap-
purtenances for their breeding and care. The general
bought it ten years ago, and has vastly improved it
since. Now, its lawns are as velvety as those of England ; its open grove is like an English park or a Kentucky blue-grass pasture ; its wide piazzas invite to the
leisure an overworked man so needs ; its extended southern outlook has the cool sweep of green fields, near-by
sparkling waters, and farther-away church spires point-
ing to the sky's own calm.

The library betokens excellent literary taste, its
crowded bookcases representing by their contents every
field of letters, and showing frequent familiar use. In
the broad hall a fine portrait of Bishop Simpson is conspicuous ; and near it may be seen, time-stained and
bullet-riddled, the battle-flag of the Thirty-third Missouri Regiment, presented to their colonel in 1862 by
the Union Methodist Episcopal Church of St. Louis.
In a fireplace in the parlor is an old-fashioned crane,
hammered into shape at his Clinton forge by General
Fisk's father, over half a century gone by ; and on the
south wall of that handsome room hang the portraits of
two beautiful children, whose faces haunt the beholder
long after he turns away, and upon which the general
cannot look without quivering lips and humid eyes.
They were his pets, those pretty immortals, and they
died long years ago.

Over this comfortable home, in the midst of such at-
tractive surroundings, Mrs. Fisk presides with as much
genius for administration as her husband has shown in a
wider sphere, and to her efforts are due for him in large

measure the restful possibilities of the place. She has
been his willing and invaluable coadjutor all his manhood through.   During part of his army service she was
with him, and when not with him she was usually at the
front, doing duty as a nurse.   With Mrs. General Frémont she organized the first Soldiers' Relief Society this
country knew ; and she stripped their St. Louis home
almost bare of beds and bedding, and everything else
that might serve, for the comfort of those first Missouri
regiments organized, notably that of General Frank
Blair.   From the summer of 1861 till the close of the
war she was well-nigh constantly active in attentions to
the sick and wounded, both Union and Confederate, and
came as near being a Florence Nightingale as any woman
of America.   Twice she visited the bloody battle-ground
of Shiloh, and tramped over it with special details of
surgeons and soldiers, gathering up the wounded, whom
she had carried to steamboats in waiting, and then accompanied them to St. Louis.

Dr. Douglass tells an amusing incident of one of these
visits to the Shiloh battle-field—the Dr. Douglass who
had charge of General Grant during that officer's last
days.   He was at Shiloh with Grant as an army surgeon.
In the first day's engagement he lost all his wardrobe and
medical supplies.   When Mrs. Fisk arrived from St.
Louis, with a steamer to carry the sick and wounded
back there, Dr. Douglass accompanied her over the
field, and gave needed assistance.   At night, as they
were tramping around searching for poor unfortunates
who required care, seeing but dimly through the darkness by their feeble lantern-lights, and guided chiefly by
the moans of stricken men, while they scanned the uneven
ground, the doctor stepped upon some brush and tore
his pantaloons nearly off him.

"What *shall* I do?" he asked of Mrs. Fisk; and, with real distress, he added, "These are all the clothes I have!"

Looking sharply about, Mrs. Fisk saw a rebel tent, left standing on the field, with its top burned off by the flame of battle.

"You go in there," she said, with woman's ready resource, "take off your pantaloons, throw them over to me, and I will mend them and throw them back to you." Dr. Douglass obeyed without delay; and he has often said that he saw no other scene through all the war so weird as that of Mrs. Fisk, sitting on a log, upon the bloody field of Shiloh, by the dim light of her lantern sewing up the awful rent in his unfortunate pantaloons.

To the reporter General Fisk talked freely of the convention and its work. Of his own nomination, he said:

"I have always had the conviction that I could be of greater service in the ranks than as a leader of the party. But it does seem as though the party wants me. Of course nothing but a strong sense of duty would induce me to accept. It does look almost like a call from God. I must have time to think about it, and will do what I think is best for the party, and just to my family and myself. You know what bitter calumny was heaped upon St. John, and if I enter this conflict I must expect the same kind of treatment. Any man would receive it. As for myself I don't care a particle for that. I was a resident of a border State, and I went through the war, and I know what this sort of thing means. I can stand it, but it won't be a pleasant thing for my family."

Shall we ever bring party politics to so high a plane in this country, will the standard of editorial ethics ever be so exalted, that those to whom a public man is nearest and dearest will not shrink from his accepting nomination to high office because of calumny waiting ahead? Are parties and press to be always the willing calumniators of good men which in recent years they have become? Must those who accept the full responsibilities of citizenship, and stand for the suffrage of their fellows, forever do so knowing that our boasted freedom of speech and of print means cruel license for party malice, for personal vindictiveness, for political hatred, and for wanton outrage?

Assuming that General Fisk must and would bring his thoughtful and prayerful consideration of this matter to an affirmative decision, despite any sensitiveness which might lead both himself and his family to decide otherwise, the Prohibition managers arranged for another great mass-meeting to be held in the Metropolitan Opera House, at New York, June 22d, and for the formal notice of nomination to be given their candidates there.

Once more the immense auditorium was crowded with Prohibitionists, till hundreds could get no seats, when this occasion came round. There was no storm now, but a torrid wave had swept across the land and whelmed the metropolis by the sea; yet the enthusiasm which floods could not quench in May could not be melted in June. Tier upon tier, the boxes and the galleries, one dense mass of people, looked down on the wide parquet, thronged to suffocation, and on the great stage whereon sat hundreds of well-known Prohibition believers and advocates; and over and about all glowed the many hundreds of gas-jets, giving brilliancy and more torridity to the scene. It was a wonderfully inspiring picture to look out upon from the platform, when at eight o'clock the meeting was called to order. Bishop J. N. Fitzgerald offered prayer, and Mr. W. T. Wardwell, Chairman of the Prohibition County Committee of New York, made these introductory remarks :

"This vast audience, this sea of upturned faces, this enthusiasm evinced, reminds one that Prohibition is a living issue, and that it has come to stay. [Cheers.] It means that we have come here to listen to two of the most illustrious men in all this land, and it means victory. [Cheers.] I would like to tell you what something else means, too. The failure of the Chicago Convention to touch this question of the liquor traffic means an additional hundred thousand votes for Fisk and Brooks. [Loud and continued applause.] We are here to-night not as any balance-of-power party. We make no deals. We are an advancing and increasing army, and we are in the field until we win the fight. In the name of all we represent, we welcome you here to-night at this grand gathering."

Rev. Sam Small, of Georgia, was to have made the address of notification to General Fisk, but became train-bound and did not arrive in time. His place was well filled by Chairman Samuel Dickie, of the National Committee, who closed with this utterance :

"We come to say to you, General Fisk, that among Prohibitionists you are the best-loved man in this entire Union. In behalf of the Indianapolis Convention we tender to you the nomination for President of the United States."

As General Fisk stepped forward to respond, the whole vast audience rose as one man—from floor to high fifth gallery—and gave him royal greeting. Cheer after cheer ascended ; handkerchiefs fluttered from the boxes, a cloud of waving white ; the band struck up "America," and scores of American flags waved rhythmic unison with its majestic measures ; the ovation of a month before was repeated and magnified in a fashion wonderful to hear and to behold.

After many minutes of this magnificent and persistent demonstration, when General Fisk was able to command silence, he spoke as follows :

"Mr. Chairman: This thronging multitude of noble men and women; this vast assemblage, representative of the best life in the Republic, crowding every part of this vast temple; this group of strong, earnest, resolute man- and womanhood on this platform, in which Georgia and Illinois, Missouri and Michigan, New York and New Jersey, clasp hands in one of the holiest covenants ever made; these eloquent and soul-stirring utterances of speech and song; these waving banners and waves of enthusiasm—all these give inspiration and help to one whose heart, throbbing with grateful emotion for honors undeserved—for partiality which ought to have been bestowed on another—would with imperfect utterance respond to the message borne to him from that most wonderful gathering at Indianapolis,

"'Beneath whose banners, proud to stand,
Looked up the noblest in the land'—

that convention which commanded the respect, the wonder and the admiration of the country. What it said has received the hearty commendation of the friends of true and Christian government all over the land, without distinction of race, color, sex, or previous condition of political servitude. What it did in its closing hour has seriously disturbed the peace of at least one household, which in its home by the sea has these many days been inquiring, 'What are the wild waves from Indianapolis saying?' The response comes to us this evening by the way of Evanston and Atlanta.

"Let us see for a moment where we stand. On the Indianapolis platform, of course, which, after solemnly acknowledging Almighty God as the source of all power in government, has for its Alpha and Omega the prohibition of the liquor traffic. First and last that is the dominant, the all-controlling issue in our national politics. Differing judgments there may be on other issues, but on the utter destruction of the American saloon we are of one mind, and heartily invite to full party fellowship with us all who are with us on that point agreed.

"We believe that a host of good men will come thronging into our camp in the immediate future. Men of thought and conscience, who have been waiting the weary years away, hoping that the political party with which they have had alliance, would say some emphatic words, do some brave deed on the side of this great reform, and declare that the saloon should not sit supreme in caucus convention and canvas. The campaign for 1888 has opened. Its banners and bandannas have been thrown to the breeze. Platform utterances have been read in every hamlet, and carefully studied in a million American homes to ascertain what was said in Indianapolis,

St. Louis, and Chicago on the greatest question now being debated among the people of this country. Home protection stands at the head of the list. Home protected against the saloon will be the greatest factor in protecting the honest industries of our people.

"Indianapolis plainly declared ' That the manufacture, importation, exportation, transportation, and sale of alcoholic beverages shall be made public crimes and prohibited as such ; that such prohibition must be secured through amendment to our national and State constitutions, that any form of license, taxation, or regulation of the liquor traffic is contrary to good government ; that any party which supports regulation, license, or tax, enters into alliance with such traffic and becomes the actual foe of the State's welfare.' It declares ' for the immediate abolition of the internal revenue system which now gluts our national Treasury with revenue from the blood and tears of American homes.' There's no ambiguity or want of clearness in these utterances.

"Let us turn over a leaf and see what St. Louis said on this all-absorbing question. Not a word do we find. There was a repetition of the same old story—1884 was reaffirmed—' We must not vex the citizen with sumptuary laws.' In the gray of the world's morning the original chairman of the committee on sumptuary laws said the same thing in a discussion with Mother Eve on the subject of prohibition. No word of hope from St. Louis.

"Surely from Chicago on the wings of the lightning there will come deliverances on this question that will gladden the hearts of thousands who in all sincerity believed and waited with patient faith and prayer for the words that did not come. The Anti-Saloon maiden, never very robust, after a lingering illness, during which kindly hands had ministered to her, and sleepless eyes had watched over her, finally found rest, ' after life's fitful fever,' in Chicago. Death stole in so gently upon the suffering one. We know the faithful-to-the-last friends who, with breaking hearts and tearful eyes, sang at the funeral obsequies in the great convention auditorium the touching lines of Tom Hood :

" ' We watched her breathing through the night,
  Her breathing soft and low,
  As in her breast the wave of life
  Kept heaving to and fro.

*   *   *   *   *   *

" ' Our very hopes belied our fears,
  Our fears our hopes belied ;
  We thought her dying when she slept,
  And sleeping when she died.'

"Dear friends, the problem of the liquor traffic will be solved only by a national political party making Prohibition the corner-stone of its creed. No party can successfully combat the monstrous evil that does not make such declarations as shall alienate from its ranks every rum-seller. There are a host of good men in this land who in these June days of 1888 are reaching that conclusion for the first time. They, like many of us, hoped against hope. They are coming into our camp. Public opinion, the mightiest advocate of any cause, is gathering force day by day and is marshalling that force a mighty host in our ranks. The day is not far distant when the nation will rise as one man and demand that the liquor traffic shall cease throughout our land. We stand on the threshold of a great national campaign for the right. Our watchword is not the destruction of any party, but the destruction of the American saloon. Let our camp fires gleam from every summit and illume every valley in the land. The combined forces of Christian home, Christian Church, and Christian commonwealth must be put in battle array against the infamous wrong.

"In response to the command of the chosen thousand at Indianapolis who bade me go to the front of this sharp conflict, I have now to say, God helping me, I will carry your flag in this contest. I know well what will be the cost to me and those whom I hold as dear as life itself ; I also know that God thrones the right at last in kinglier royalty because its coronation is delayed, and that neither earth nor hell can permanently harm those who are 'followers of that which is good.'

"We uplift a national banner under which sectionalism and sectional strife shall be forever buried—North and South, East and West, all join hands in our good cause.

"There will be those who will be 'exceedingly mad against us,' and who will persecute us even to strange cities. Let me exhort our friends everywhere to give our enemies a monopoly of personal scandalous methods of conducting political campaigns. Let us exalt our holy cause, and trusting in Him, in whose hands are the destinies of individuals and nations, go forward with courage, faith, and hope until victory, certain to come, shall be ours."

This speech was frequently interrupted by applause, and when General Fisk said, with deep feeling yet ringing utterance, "I will carry your flag," there came another mighty outbreak of enthusiasm, which had to spend itself before he could proceed.

In graceful and appropriate sentences Hon. W. J.
Groo tendered the Vice-Presidency to Rev. Dr. Brooks,
whose address of response kept the enthusiastic demonstrations in frequent repetition, while his opening words
excited another wild scene like those climaxes which had
preceded.   At the outset, he said :

"I believe in governmental progress.   The policy of the Government should at least keep abreast of our advancing civilization.
Amid the onward march of financial, educational, and moral interests, we cannot hope to draw our inspiration as statesmen from the
resolutions of '98, or the dead issues of the sixties.

" As an old slave-holder, I am here to-night to attest my joyful acceptance of the result, and I speak for nine tenths of my section.
General Fisk, whom for the first time I meet to-night, helped to form
the party that was mainly instrumental in the accomplishment of
this result.   I, on the other hand, stood with the party committed
against the principle, and did all in my power to prevent it.   I come
to-day, across half the continent, to say to him that he was right and
I was wrong, and now, over the bloody chasm of that dreary past,
will clasp his hand and say, Let there be no further animosity between us.   To-night let us send forth the cry, with clasped hand,
' No more sectionalism in American politics !   No more solid South
or solid North ! ' "

As the two candidates clasped hands before that vast
multitude, tears of patriotic joy overflowed thousands of
cheeks, and the cheers which resounded were prophetic
of the new national unity which a new political dispensation should bring.

An eloquent address followed by Miss Frances E.
Willard, and the opening formalities of the Prohibition
campaign of 1888 were ended, the campaign was formally begun, with General Fisk duly commissioned as
commander-in-chief of the moral forces that should wage
it, and bearing in his faithful hands the white flag that
shall be never a flag of truce with national sin, but always a signal of aggressive warfare and of ultimate victory, " For God, and home, and native land."

CHAPTER XXXIII.

THE platform demands for General Fisk, always numerous, and calling, even when but infrequently accepted, for much travel and sacrifice of time, became constant and importunate right after his nomination for the
Presidency, and would have made him a speedy martyr
to the cause. He wisely decided to meet, during the
months of July and August, only those engagements, for
camp and other special occasions, which antedated the
new pressure upon him. Among these was one at Roseland Park, Woodstock, Conn., where, every Fourth of
July, Mr. Henry C. Bowen, publisher of the *Independent*, groups a few great orators, and celebrates with them
and his chosen friends, and a large concourse from the
country round, our national anniversary. Upon this
occasion General Fisk represented the temperance idea,
as a year previous Senator Windom, of Minnesota, had
represented it, and his reception was very cordial. One
of the speakers preceding him was Senator Frye, of
Maine, who argued for Protection from the standpoint
of the Republican Party, and who made a vigorous appeal to General Fisk that he retire from his leadership
of the Prohibitionists and stand with his old associates
for their defence of American industry and American
interests. The General happily turned Mr. Frye's allu-
sions back upon him, and scored a strong point for the
Prohibition Party as being far more in favor of protect-

ing honest labor and all true American interests than any party can be which leaves the saloon untouched. He said :

" *Mr. President, Friends, and Fellow-Citizens :*

"I am sure, my friends, it was no doleful announcement that I was to be the last speaker of this occasion. On some festival day where Job was interested and many friends came, and the day was passed in orations, you remember that just before sunset some one said, ' Is there to be no end of words this day ? ' Of course, heretofore, the words have been such that you have not been inclined to make any suggestion. I shall not detain you very long, although I notice this, that all people that speak from a platform or a pulpit, if they say they are going to speak short, always make a long speech of it ; but I for one am going to make a short speech of it.

"I count it no light honor that my father and mother were born in Windham County ; that but a few miles from here on the Five Mile River, the village blacksmith in the first decades of this century was my father ; that in the little church at Killingly my mother was one of the sweetest singers in the choir. So that I feel very much at home in Windham County, although, like the Irishman, I wasn't born in my native State. I couldn't help that. I was born out West, and not here, as Brother Lounsbury has stated ; and, as a good Methodist, I shall not keep you all night on probation.

"If my friend Erye were here (he had stepped from the platform) I should be inclined to pitch into him for a moment or two ; for the people I represent are the genuine protectionists of this country. We begin at first principles ; we protect the home, and we would have a protection equal to anything he preached, and all ours beyond that. Why, he said, in building his factory in Woodstock, that ninety per cent of the $400,000 would go to working-people. Well, now, we will build in the same way. But according to Mr. Powderly's careful estimate, of that $360,000 paid to the working-people in Woodstock, $110,000 would be dropped into the tills of the dramshops, if you have them there. Now, we would save all that. We would save this vast sum that the working-people of this country pay for liquor all over the country, in order that it might be used in progress out of poverty ; in order that it might be used by these working-people that are paid good wages (and I wouldn't have them paid a dollar less), in greater comforts for the home, in better civilization throughout all the land.

"Now, I have in my hands, I suppose, the most able speech ever prepared. I am not going to give it all to you ; it is too good ; you couldn't bear it. I shall give you some of it, and for that which I don't read to you or speak to you I refer you to the *Independent*, that newspaper which should be in every man's family in this broad land. My family, they say, are remarkable for their culture and attainments ; they have always read the *Independent*.

" My friend Frye here to-day, in turning to me so gracefully, intimated that I stood in the way of a great triumph. It is not so at all. Why, if my friend Frye and all his people instead of throwing away their votes on somebody else next November—if they would only vote for me [loud laughter], how quickly we would turn those wicked Democrats out of office. [Laughter.]

" Again we celebrate the anniversary of the day on which American liberty was born and placed in her iron cradle. The country pauses to remember and rejoice, and with reverent heart lifts its voice in praise and thanksgiving to Him who hath ' made and preserved us a nation.'

" It was one hundred and twelve years ago last Monday when the Continental Congress declared that the United Colonies were, and of right ought to be, free and independent States. John Adams said that they were that day considering the greatest question ever debated on the continent, and that no greater question would ever be debated among men. ' I am apt to believe,' said Mr. Adams, ' that it will be celebrated by succeeding generations as the great anniversary festival.' In writing Mrs. Adams, he said : ' The day ought to be commemorated as the day of deliverance by solemn acts of devotion to Almighty God. Let it be solemnized with pomp and parade, with guns, bells, and illuminations from one end of this continent to the other from this time forward forevermore.'

" In the mighty march of time, in the procession of great events, that Declaration of Independence Day in Philadelphia took its place by the side of the great exodus from the land of the Pharaohs when Moses stretched his hand across the gulf of the centuries and rocked the cradle of American liberty. It took step with that bright day in June of the thirteenth century when in the long meadow of Runnymede the English barons met King John, and amid the splendor of that impressive and brilliant scene demanded and received from that cruel and perfidious king, under the frowning towers of Windsor Castle, the foundations of England's liberty in *Magna Charta*.

" Independence was born on July the second ; its baptism was on the fourth by that great apostle of freedom Thomas Jefferson, the beginning of whose enduring fame was the immortal State paper which promulgated the Bill of Rights and assigned the new Republic a place among the powers of the world. Adams and Jefferson, Franklin and Witherspoon were the towers of strength which stood foursquare to all the winds that blew ; grand, iron-sided, lion-hearted John Witherspoon, of New Jersey, that sturdy patriotic Gospel minister, that eloquent preacher of the Christian faith in whom combined rare scholarship and broad statesmanship, a worthy successor of Jonathan Edwards at Princeton. John Witherspoon's prayer for God's blessing in wisdom, righteousness, and guidance was answered with a baptism of power, and faith, and courage that had its glad fruitage when he in the last hour of that great debate rose, and said : ' The time for decided, firm action has come. The country is not only ripe for independence, but if its declaration is longer delayed, we are in danger of becoming rotten for want of it.' To that eloquent utterance came a responsive patriotic ' Amen ' from Franklin, Jefferson, and Adams, and ' freedom from tyranny ' rang through Independence Hall.

"It was just a sweep of a century from the hour that James Otis, in 1761, became the first torch-bearer in the old Revolution, to that day in 1861 when out of dark and portentous clouds came the thunder and lightning of civil strife and ' States dissevered, discordant, and belligerent, a land rent with civil feud and drenched with fraternal blood,' burst upon the vision of a startled world. In 1620 there sailed upon the ocean two ships whose prows were turned toward the western shores of the Atlantic ; one, a Dutch slave-ship, landed its cargo of living freight as slaves upon the coast of Virginia. In the cabin of the ' Mayflower,' the other ship, were the Pilgrim Fathers, who, on the rocky coasts of New England, planted the seeds of liberty. Slavery and freedom grew together on our soil, an irrepressible conflict from the beginning. We pause not to tell the story of the great strife out of which the nation had a new birth of freedom. The end came, and the immortal words of Mr. Lincoln at Gettysburg that this ' Government of the people by the people and for the people ' would not perish from the earth were a fulfilled prophecy. The Declaration of Independence, which had been a promise spoken in the ear of prophecy but belied by the facts all around it, became true in right, true in fact all over this broad land. From the darkness and gloom, from the smoke and flame of battle, 'mid the music of the breaking of the fetters of human bondage, we came forth to victory, our love of justice increased, the foundation of our institutions more firmly cemented, the blessings of peace secured to all the inhabitants of the land, and the pulse of the nation throbbed with a new life.

"True and Christian government rests upon great truths and immortal principles. Adherence to fundamentals that underlie a genuine Christian civilization is the only guarantee of national stability. It is wise to pause on this day of gratulation and joy and consider the perils of our national life ; and while we have just pride in the possession of constitutional liberty and statutes framed for its defence and perpetuation, let us remember that human constitutions, human enactment, and human government are manifestly vital only as subordinate to the eternal constitution, the eternal enactment, the eternal government of God. The Latin lyrist said to ancient Rome : ' While you bear yourselves subordinate to the gods you hold empire.' Our rapid growth in population and wealth, our National Treasury bursting with fulness, peace and unity within our borders —all these cannot perpetuate national life and glory if there be the breath of the pestilence upon us, and a gigantic wrong permitted to sit in all the places of political power in municipality, county, city, State, and nation.

"A heavier yoke than that the British king placed upon the neck of our Revolutionary fathers is upon us and our children. A bondage more abject than that which lifted its destroying hand against the Union a score and more of years ago is forging its fetters for the enslavement of the Republic. By a long train of abuses and usurpations King Alcohol, through the liquor traffic in this goodly land, openly declares his ability to reduce us to his despotic rule by his control of the dominant political organizations of the country. From a mount of patient sufferance let us on this Fourth of July in Roseland Park make a new Declaration of Independence. Let us resolve to throw off the Government of the American saloon. Almost a score of years ago, in the capital of the State within whose boundaries there comes to us the generous hospitality out of which springs this festival occasion, one of Connecticut's honored sons, now representing your State in the Senate of the United States, and whose voice this morning summoned us to a conscientious consideration of personal temperance, Hon. O. H. Platt, with prophetic soul, startled his fellow-citizens with his burning words, eloquently spoken on the great theme we now consider. Mr. Platt said : ' I do most firmly believe that *unless the sale and use of intoxicating drinks in this country shall cease, or be materially diminished, the result will be the complete overthrow of our Republican Government.*' While Mr. Platt was speaking so earnestly this morning—and he said such great truths, and he did it admirably—I could not help thinking how many men there are moderate drinkers, that would not be drunkards at all if there were no open saloon doors in this country. Let us slam that door to. I hold up before you *rum-selling and rum-drinking as the foes of national existence.* The danger of the Republic is that men do not realize the truth of this. I wish I could make all men who love their Government see this great peril of the nation. Let us not shut our eyes to the danger. The Republic must triumph over rum, or rum will triumph over the Republic. All history teaches this ; observation and reason confirm it. The sale and use have not ceased, nor ' materially diminished,' but, on the contrary, largely increased, and Senator Platt's words should find lodgment in the minds and hearts of his countrymen. There yet echoes through these matchless, charming grounds, on yonder height, and over yon beautiful lake, the eloquent words spoken on this platform one year ago to-day in the indictment found against the monstrous monarch. Let us recall some of the sentences then uttered. Their repetition ought to inspire us to rise up, and with one heart and one mouth make our new declaration. The presiding officer here one year ago was that genial gentleman, ex-Governor Long, of Massachusetts, whose happy thoughts so happily expressed on Independence Day caused your hearts to throb with joy and filled your souls with patriotic fervor. Governor Long, in introducing ex-United States Senator Windom, one of the best men the marvellous Northwest ever contributed to the Senate or Cabinet, said : ' We have kept until the last the most practically important subject that is to be discussed to-day on this platform ; the subject is " The Saloon in Politics," a subject that of late has begun to command the close and careful attention of all thinking people, and will command it more and more, and is to be a factor in our State and our national party. There ought to be no difference of opinion with regard to this great tyranny that is beginning to put its clutch upon the throat of American politics—the tyranny of the grog-shop.'

" Mr. Windom said : ' The discussion of this subject seems to me quite appropriate to the occasion. Perhaps the highest honor we can pay to the founders of our Government, is to accept with profound gratitude the blessings which, under God, they have transmitted to us, and to face with manly courage and patriotic determination whatever problems remain to be solved. Among those problems *none are so grave and pressing,* and none threaten consequences so disastrous to all that is most sacred in our institutions, as are involved in the American saloon system. In the wide sweep of its malign influence it touches and threatens the very warp and woof of our social, political, and industrial organisms.

" ' How to curtail and finally destroy this evil is the great problem of the hour. Its solution stands next on the world's calendar of progress. It has been called for trial, and cannot be dismissed or postponed. The saloon has boldly entered politics, and it has come to stay until vanquished or victorious.

" ' Briefly stated, the question is, Shall the liquor power, with its dire and deadly influences, rule and ruin, or shall it be utterly destroyed ?

" ' This malign power has organized and massed its mighty forces for the conflict. It has raised the black flag, and proclaimed that he who will not swear allegiance to it, and thereby become *particeps criminis* in its work of destruction and death, shall politically perish. It has even drawn the assassin's knife and lighted the torch of the incendiary, in order to inspire dismay in the ranks of its enemies. The time has, therefore, come when this issue must be met. Political parties can no longer dodge it if they would. Private citizens must take sides openly for or against the saloon, with its methods and its results. " Neutrality is henceforth impossible ; indifference is henceforth a betrayal of the trust involved in citizenship.' "

" ' The saloon creates a demand where none before existed, that it may profit by supplying that demand. It artificially stimulates an evil habit, that it may thrive by pandering to it. It methodically breeds debauchery, poverty, anarchy, and crime for pay. It purposely seeks to multiply the number of drinkers, and hence of drunkards. It invades every new community, demands tribute from every home, and lies in wait with fresh enticements for each new generation of youth. . . . Each one of our two hundred thousand drinking-places forms a distinct centre of aggressive forces and skilful devices for spreading the drink habit among men. Every plausible temptation and solicitation that trained talent can suggest are used to entrap the young, the ignorant, the toiling, and the homeless with the knowledge that a customer once secured is usually a customer for life. . . . Experience indicates that four fifths of American drinking and drunkenness is due in the first instance not to any natural appetite of our people, but to the presence and sleepless efforts of this gigantic enginery, working seven days a week and twenty-four hours a day, unrestrained by any scruple and everywhere contemptuous of public and private right.'

" This is by no means an overdrawn picture of a system which insists upon the right, untrammelled by law or conscience, to manufacture drunkards, paupers, and criminals. To maintain this right the saloon power has organized its vast forces, formed its political alliances, and now, conscious of its strength, bids open defiance to law and public sentiment. To maintain the right to get money by the wholesale destruction of life, health, and property, it corrupts the ballot, bribes Legislatures, tampers with juries, and seeks to intimidate the weak and cowardly by arson and assassination.

"In most of our cities the drinking saloon is the central power around which politics revolve, and which dictates candidates and party politics. Even in our national elections it sometimes exercises a controlling influence and decides Presidential contests.

"Not less than eighty thousand victims go annually to the drunkard's grave from the homes of this land. Pestilence and war combined do not, in this country, equal its destructive energy. The waste of human life wrought every five years by our two hundred thousand saloons is equal to the destruction of life by both armies, numbering millions of armed men, during the entire War of the Rebellion. In their hands strong drink is a weapon so fatal that the five hundred thousand drunkard-makers are able to accomplish more in the same period than four times their number could with shot and shell, fire and sword, and all the appliances of modern warfare. The cruelty of war is not measured by the number of those who fall in battle, but by the unutterable woe and bitter anguish of broken hearts and desolated homes. Most emphatically is it true that the mere destruction of eighty thousand lives every year affords no measure of the relentless cruelty of the liquor power in its war against society. To realize this you must go to the dishonored homes, question the broken hearts, read the voiceless misery in wan and haggard faces, hear helpless children cry for food, see them stricken down by drunken and infuriated fathers, and sometimes even by besotted mothers, witness the debauchery and ruin of youth, and the utter degradation, ignorance, poverty, and misery which everywhere and always accompany the victims of the saloon.

"Alas, how true and terrible is this indictment of the saloon! Oh, that from every hill-top and valley, from mountain and prairie, from city and hamlet, from Lakes to Gulf, and from sea to sea there might this day arise the united voice of our sixty millions of people in most solemn Declaration of Independence of this cruel king whose injuries and usurpations threaten the destruction of our free Government! As did our fathers when they resolved to throw off the absolute tyranny of a bad king, so let us give certain facts to a candid world.

"This monster, sitting supreme in the politics of this country, has enacted laws authorizing him to open in all our towns and cities slaughter-houses of men, women, and children, and of all virtue.

" He has enacted laws permitting him to transform men into beasts.

" He is the direct cause of nine tenths of the woes and sorrows which blight and curse our people.

" He, hiding his monstrous deformity under the forms of law enacted by his own vassals, over whose heads he cracks the slave-driver's lash in halls of legislation, maintains at our expense an army of miscreants, who at the very doors of our homes, and in the shadows of our sanctuaries, prosecute the work of murder and death.

" He has despoiled labor, burdened property with excessive taxation, impoverished whole communities, hindered education, corrupted morals, fostered crimes, aided all classes of vice and wrong, and plunged his unhappy victims into shame and degradation.

" He would have us transmit to our children a heritage of distilleries, breweries and saloons, and chain to the weary backs of society increasing burdens of paupers, criminals, idiots, and insane.

" He seizes and debauches innocent children, tears sons from the arms of sorrowing mothers, and bears them away to dishonored graves.

" He wrings hot tears from the eyes of widows whose husbands he has sacrificed at the shrine of the drunkards' Moloch.

" He sits supreme in the National Congress and makes laws in the country's capital.

" He governs courts of justice, and makes ministers of the law and legislatures his lackeys.

" He silences the preacher in his pulpit, and muzzles the editor at his desk.

" He wastes, directly and indirectly, in his revels, annually more than a thousand millions of our dollars, and marshals in his staggering procession to death and hell a half million of our people.

" He is a cold, heartless, cruel murderer and assassin of the deepest dye.

" He counts his victims by millions. His butcheries go on daily and nightly within sight of the portals of our homes. We can hear the shrieks of his victims and the wail of the bereaved.

" He is the howling, prowling, destroying wolf, with scorching, fierce breath, descending upon every fold, slaying and devouring our best loved. Let us rise in our united might as did our ancestors in Old Windham at the call of Israel Putnam on Pomfret Heights in the last century. *Let us hunt this wolf to his den and shoot him.*

"The time would fail me to tell the thousandth part of the evils, multiplying and destructive, that flow out of the infamous liquor traffic, and in all this vast throng the great evil has no friend. Dear friends, have we the courage this day to issue, and thereto affix our signatures in the pronounced handwriting of John Hancock, our new Declaration of Independence; and with a firm reliance on Divine Providence, pledge our lives, and fortune, and our sacred honor that from this day henceforth no word or act of ours may be construed into allegiance to this felon king? He must be driven from his places of power and utterly overthrown. The conflict is upon us. It is a life-and-death struggle. Oh, for an uprising of righteous indignation, for an aroused American conscience, for patriotic devotion to home and country like that which gave inspiration and faith to Jonas Parker and his neighbors when they reddened the village green of Lexington with their blood on that glorious morning a century and more ago, when the old Revolution burst into magnificent blossoms as the shot was fired that echoed round the world; for an enlightened public opinion, the mightiest advocate of any question, for the combined forces of Christian home, Christian Church, and Christian commonwealth in battle array against the traffic in theft and murder until it shall be thundered from every political Sinai, national and State, 'Thou shalt not,' and there shall be no legalized saloon where floats the starry flag of the free! Not until then will the infamous business cease; not until then will we be delivered from its Satanic sorceries. Temporizing policies are a failure.

"Under all systems of license, regulation or tax, the work of ruin and death goes on. Myriads of homes are poisoned, the prosperity of the nation is undermined, the strength of our race wasted, millions are hurried to early and dishonored graves, and a lurid shadow is cast upon the life beyond. The prohibition of the liquor traffic is the demand of the people, and politicians and statesmen who fail to heed it are treasuring up wrath against the day of wrath. Prohibition is in the air. The nation's heart is beginning to throb to its music. Its coming is whispered on every breeze. The rising tide breaks all along the shore, and each succeeding white-fringed billow washes farther up the strand.

"Nothing can resist the onward march of a genuine reform. Every such movement enters into and becomes a part of the Messianic purpose to set judgment in the earth. Agitation on this question is the duty of the hour. Let it go on from press, platform, and pulpit, in the prayer-meetings, and at the ballot-box, until every patriot who loves his country, every Christian who loves his God, every philanthropist who loves his race, every father who loves his child, every son of the Republic, will, a marshalled host, uplift the Constitution as a banner of reform, and under its folds march to the ballot-boxes of the land, and under an avalanche of freemen's ballots bury beyond resurrection the American saloon. Then shall our whole Union become the citadel of sobriety, the national name be purged of this great shame, and our glorious banner,

> " ' Whose hues are all of heaven,
> Its red the sunset's dye,
> The whiteness of the moonlit cloud,
> The blue of morning sky, ' "

shall be the flag of hope for all mankind as it floats over our sober, free, and happy people—

> " ' O'er the high and o'er the lowly
> Floats that banner bright and holy,
> In the rays of freedom's sun,
> In our nation's heart embedded,
> O'er our Union newly wedded,
> One in all, and all in one.

> " ' Let that banner float forever !
> May its lustrous stars pale never,
> Till the stars shall pale on high ;
> While there's right the wrong defeating,
> While there's faith in true hearts beating,
> Truth and freedom shall not die.

> " ' As it floated long before us,
> Be it ever floating o'er us,
> O'er our land from shore to shore !
> There are freemen yet to wave it,
> Millions who would die to save it,
> Wave it, save it, evermore.' "

One other formality remained for General Fisk, even though his speech at the Metropolitan Opera House had formally placed him before the country as its Prohibition candidate for President. According to custom, there must be a written acknowledgment of his nomination, and this he made in the following :

LETTER OF ACCEPTANCE.

SEABRIGHT, N. J., July 25, 1888.

HON. SAMUEL DICKIE, *Chairman :*

MY DEAR SIR : With a grateful sense of the honor conferred upon me by the Prohibition Party, at its late National Convention, and with equal appreciation of the responsibilities involved therein, I accept the nomination which I did not seek, and which I earnestly desired should pass me by, and with God's help will bear our standard of Prohibition as best I can through this Presidential campaign. And thus formally responding to the formal notification received at your hands, it is fit and proper that I add some further words.

Within a few years the temperance reform has altogether changed front. In the great conflict which has been and yet is waging, temperance forces no longer face human appetite and habit alone ; they oppose legislation, law, the purpose of political parties, the policy of State and nation. What law creates, law alone can kill. The creature of law, the saloon—the liquor traffic—can die only at law's hand, or the hand of law's executor. .Conceived in avaricious iniquity, born of sinful legislative wedlock, the licensed saloon, the legalized liquor traffic, bastard child of a civilization professing purity and virtue, must be strangled by the civilization which begat it, or that civilization must go forever branded with the scarlet letter of its own shame.

It is not enough that we reform the individual ; we must reform the State. The policy of great commonwealths, of a whole people, must be re-made and put in harmony with sound economic principles, the true cooperation of industrial effort, the essential conditions of national prosperity, and the genuine brotherhood of man.

So broad a demand as this can be met in but one way. It has been well said : " A political reform can become a fact in government only through a political party that administers government." A reform so vast as this we advocate, involving such radical changes in State and national policy, is utterly dependent, for its agitation and consummation, upon some party agent or force. To give it success, to make it indeed and indisputably a fact, that party force or agent must be in full accord with the reform, and must have in itself the power of successful achievement apart from those elements and influences alien to the reform. No party which is made public administrator by the enemies of temperance, or which owes the election of its candidates to saloon influences, can ever establish Prohibition as a binding fact in government anywhere.

It was with great reluctance that I accepted these conclusions and came to admit the imperative need of a new party, while yet the party of my old choice—the national Republican Party—maintained its organization. I had followed with pride and patriotic love that party's flag, while above it floated the Starry Banner for which so many brave patriots fell. I had seen that party establish as a fact in government one political reform dear to me from boyhood, a boon to millions in bondage and a glory to us all. A long, long time I waited, against conviction and the logic of political events, hoping that my old party would take up this old reform with changed front and new conditions, and make it also the fact so many millions craved, and for which they pleaded before men and God. It cost me the sacrifice of cherished associations, when, four years ago, I enrolled myself in the ranks of party Prohibitionists, under the flag of Prohibition bleached snowy white by the tears of smitten women and children through generations of sorrow and want.

I have seen no hour of regret. Every day since then has shown yet more clearly the logic of my course, and the inevitable truth of my conclusions. In Michigan, in Texas, in Tennessee and Oregon, so-called non-partisan efforts to establish Prohibition have failed through partisan necessity born of liquor elements in old-party composition. In Iowa, and Rhode Island, and Maine, the laws have been shamelessly defied for like reason. The entire trend of things, these last four years, has proven hopeless the broader range of Prohibition effort through non-partisan means, and equally futile, as a final consummation, the narrower methods of local option and high license ; while from the Supreme Court itself has come, with startling emphasis, a declaration so nationalizing this reform that it can never be made of local or State limitation again. No lines of territorial wish or will can hereafter bar the liquor traffic and its fearful brood, while by national policy that traffic is recognized as legitimate, and while under that policy the National Government derives revenue therefrom.

The National Democratic Party in its platform utters no word in condemnation of the greatest foe of the Republic—the liquor traffic. That party having steadfastly, in its utterances at national conventions, maintained its allegiance to the American saloon, it was no disappointment to any one that at St. Louis, in 1888, it reaffirmed its old position on this the greatest question now being debated among men.

" The first concern of good government," said the recent National Republican Convention at Chicago, " is the virtue and sobriety of the people, and the purity of the home."

Revenue, then, is not the Government's chief concern, whether coming from internal taxation or from a tariff on importations ; and any source of revenue which discounts "the virtue and sobriety of the people" and begets impurity in the home, should be the first object assailed by every party professing to seek good government ; while the revenue derived from such a source should be the first to be forsworn—not alternatively, for sake of a protective tariff, but positively, for sake of protection dearer and more vital than the tariff can ever yield. Had I not left the Republican party four years ago, I should be compelled to leave it now, when, after reading the words I have quoted, from a resolution supplemental to but not included in its platform, and finding in these words my own idea of government's "chief concern" set forth, I search the long platform through in vain to find condemnation of the saloon, or hint of purpose to assail it, or any sign of moral consciousness that the saloon is a curse, and its income too unholy for the nation to share.

If the "chief concern" has no place in a party's platform, and a party has no policy as to that "chief concern," that party does not deserve the support of men who love good government and would see it maintained.

The Republican Party knows to-day, and knew at Chicago, in June, that the public surplus, which in 1884 it declared *dangerous*, and then proposed to reduce, comes, about ninety per cent of it, from a source more dangerous than the surplus—the liquor traffic.

When the greatest Republican statesman declared, in 1883, that "it is better to tax whiskey than farms, and homesteads, and shops," he knew, as he and his colleagues know now, that to tax whiskey is to tax farms, and homesteads, and shops—since it is always these which pay the tax—that nine tenths of the surplus represents want in the home, impurity in the home-life, crime on the street, paralysis in the shop, and an impaired demand for the products of the farm. These men must know these things, for these things are plain as the multiplication-table. And they must realize that the swift way to reduce the surplus is to end the national policy of revenue from liquor; that the right way is to end it by declaring the manufacture, importation, transportation and sale thereof public crimes against good government, and by prohibiting and punishing them as such.

The Prohibition Party's " chief concern " is for the purity of the home and the virtue and sobriety of the people. It asserted this, in plain and unmistakable terms, at Indianapolis; and it further plainly said that " the burdens of taxation should be removed from food, clothing, and other necessaries of life." It is to-day the only avowed and consistent party ally which the home and labor have, for it would make the blessings of home cheap, and remove altogether its curses; it would bring labor to sobriety, and ensure employment; it would keep the factories busy to clothe labor, the farms active to feed it, and would give to our whole industrial system the impetus of a prosperity never yet known, and never possible till the saloons are put away.

That party is not labor's truest friend which would bar the importation of paupers from abroad, or close the tariff door of competition to pauperized foreign industry, and then by a liquor system perpetuate the manufacture of paupers and criminals in our own midst, with whom honest labor must compete, and whom largely honest labor must support.

I shall bear with glad heart and reverent hands the only party standard on which is inscribed—" For God, and Home, and Native Land ;" the standard of the only party which recognizes God as the source of government, and would defend His holy day from desecration ; which is the guardian of home's best interests and the defender of the nation through these ; and which, burying the dead past of sectional strife and bitterness, would build a living future on the sure basis of sober manhood, and pure womanhood, and untainted youth, for all our united country.

It was my privilege to aid in the good work of restoring peace and goodly fellowship, and in assisting to establish industrial relations under the new order of things, at the South, after war had swept bare so large an area of our national heritage ; and I hold no other service of my life of such account as that which brought order, and the return of property, and the rights of protected labor, to a large region prostrated by the arbitrament of arms. And now, when more than twenty years have passed, and the last sword of rebellion has been beaten into the ploughshare of loyal peace, and a new South, knowing no other than the Union flag, rejoices in the nation's " new birth of freedom," I count it the truest glory of patriotism to lead where men of the South and men of the North alike may follow, black as well as white, with equal faith in the national reform to be achieved, with equal fidelity to the Union we would protect from its only remaining foes. And I rejoice that, standing on the platform so well framed at Indianapolis, which so admirably recognizes other great principles than this of Prohibition—declaring, as we do declare, that citizenship " rests on no mere circumstance of race, color, sex, or nationality," and affirming, as we always shall affirm, the full rights of citizenship for all—standing ever, as we must, for the defence of the weak and the oppressed, we can and do assert that Prohibition is " the dominant issue in national politics," and we can and do " invite to full party fellowship all who on this one dominant issue are with us agreed," believing that, as we settle this broad question for the right so shall we best conserve the welfare of our entire nation and of every class within it, so shall we make certain the wise and speedy settlement of every lesser question involved and arising, so shall we prove ourselves Christian patriots, and ordain the perpetuity of this Christian Republic.

Faithfully yours,

CLINTON B. FISK.

JOHN A. BROOKS.

JOHN ANDERSON BROOKS.

LIFE OF JOHN ANDERSON BROOKS.

CHAPTER I.

BOYHOOD AND YOUTH.

JOHN ANDERSON BROOKS was born in Mason County, Ky., in 1836, on the farm which had been his grandfather's. His father, John T. Brooks, was born there in 1808, and was educated for and became some time a practitioner at the bar, but later devoted himself to the Christian ministry as a member of the Church of the Disciples. John T. Brooks married Elizabeth B. Anderson, daughter of Captain John W. Anderson, a wealthy planter and slave-owner of Mason County; and her mother, before marriage, was a Cook. The Andersons and Cooks were originally from Virginia, and related to the large and influential families of like nomenclature in that State.

Soon after Miss Anderson married Mr. Brooks, her father lost all his property, and died, leaving his heirs in destitute circumstances. Nor was Mr. Brooks in much better condition. The once large estate of his father had dwindled to a small holding, encumbered with debt, and a few slaves; and yet these must be made to support the widow and three daughters, while somehow the son should find support also for himself and wife. This was the problem of life with which John T. Brooks was wrestling when his boy's recollections begin, and which

occupied all that good man's earlier years.   Add to its
difficulties the conviction that he must preach the Gospel, and so subtract from his business opportunities and
results, and you reach the exact situation which obtained
in the Brooks household when John A. came to a boyhood
he can now recall.

His father, 'Squire Brooks, as commonly designated,
though a preacher, was not liberally educated, for the
sole school advantages enjoyed by him were those of the
log school-house in that neighborhood.   But he had the
quickness of intellect and tenacity of purpose born of
early mixed English, Irish, and Welsh blood, and he
largely made up for lack of outside educational advantages by private study and persistent application.   Hence
he read law, and was able to practice it, and studied the-
ology sufficiently to become a preacher, though striving
meanwhile to make the small farm and the few negroes
yield a living for those dependent upon these and him
for maintenance.   He became eminent in the church of
his faith for excellent judgment, the use of classical English, and strong presentation of truth.   He died in Missouri, in 1877, some years after removal there, and while
devoting himself partly to editorial duties on the Mexico
Ledger.   Of his worth, a leading contemporary said :

" He was an able minister of the Christian Church, and as an editorial writer one of the ablest in the State.   One of the earliest recollections of this writer was of the grave and dignified appearance, the
always neatly dressed form, and proud step of Esquire Brooks, as he
was called in all the country side of Mason County, Ky.   We say
proud, for he was : proud of his good name and stainless lineage ;
and he had reason to be proud, for the blood that coursed his veins
was blue as that of any kingly Stuart.   A better man or purer Christian never lived or died in any age or country, and the boy
whose waywardness he has often gently chided, now grown to
manhood, hastens to lay this votive garland upon his honored
tomb."

The early opportunities of John A. Brooks were
meagre. Comparative poverty surrounded him, and
forbade both the sports and the study common to young
lads. When very small he was set to field labor with
the negroes on the little farm. If he had shown less
ambition, perhaps, he might have been spared some toil,
but even at seven years of age he was eager to do the
work of a man, and home conditions made all effort
needful. At that time his father was one day ploughing
in oats with an old-fashioned shovel-plough, and the willing boy asked permission to try his hand. His father
consenting, he made a round or two, and succeeded so
well that he was left in possession of the field—to his
great regret, as he would afterward confess. Two years
later the double-breaking plough followed, with all the
severe labor which that implied ; and to this day he feels
a kind of pity for the boy he was, considering the work
he was set to do.

A white lad among black field-hands, with high spirit
and untamed will, he was ambitious to lead ; and lead
he would. In his father's absences as a preacher, the
master of all work was Simon, a lusty negro, who bossed
everything, and was the easy leader of those under him.
One command of 'Squire Brooks to John was that he
should never try to lead Simon, or to excel him ; that
Simon must remain the acknowledged first at every task.
It was a prohibition irksome to the boy destined one
day to become a leader of Prohibitionists, and he had for
a long time an unconquerable desire to violate paternal
law and put Simon in the shade. He did this, too, at
last. Having excelled all the others with the reap-hook,
and borne the taunts of old Simon several days, he determined to down that black overseer anyhow. Start-
ing in behind the gang, with Simon at the fore, he

272 LIFE OF JOHN ANDERSON BROOKS.

passed one by one till reaching Simon's side. Then there was a quiet race for some rods, when with a sudden spirit the fifteen-year-old boy went by the black man, and swept on exultant, while all but Simon shouted over his defeat. With Simon it did not end in "thumbs up." Simon was "down," indeed, and too much humiliated even for complaint to the boy's father, but many a time afterward John suffered at the old slave's hands for this deadly offence.

Tobacco was the principal crop in Mason County, and its care continued the better part of every year. It was only in "the betweens" of tobacco handling that the hard-worked lad could have school chances at all; and these "betweens" were brief. They came never while the crop was growing, and in winter, while its curing went on, they afforded but broken opportunities for study. Loving books, however, and quick to learn, and so athirst for knowledge that he would sacrifice anything to attain it, John's progress when at school kept easy pace with those about him, and held him abreast of his companions in every branch of study pursued. He had such resolute will that he could and often did work hard all day and then toil at his text-books half the night. Many a time his mother went to his room and robbed him of his light at a late hour, that he should be forced to abandon study and seek sleep. He read with avidity every volume on which he could place his hand; and it was during these years of growing, toiling boyhood that he gained his extensive knowledge of history and laid the foundation of his college course.

He was a great favorite at home and at school. Combative by nature, active in disposition, of a temperament high-wrought and impulsive, he yet made friends of young and old. He sought no encounters of any kind, save those of peaceful rivalry, but when assailed he was not slow to respond.

His controversial activities began at the age of twelve years. Hon. Elijah Currens then brought together the youth of that community in his own parlors, and organized them into a debating society, wherein John A. Brooks took eager part. Four years later the same gentleman, then Grand Worthy Patriarch of the Sons of Temperance, granted a special dispensation and admitted him to the local division, preliminary to taking him around the adjacent country for temperance talks. He had evinced such talent for public speaking, thus early, that Mr. Currens felt justified in this course ; and thus his temperance work began when he was yet but a stripling.

At seventeen he entered Bethany College as a Freshman, and pushed rapidly to the front. Here, as before, he would not let others lead. He was in haste to know and to do. He hungered for the severer contests of actual life. His ambition craved mastery, and a place where there were masterful chances. He crowded a four years' curriculum into three, and graduated with honors in 1856.

In college his mental tendencies were confirmed, and his moral convictions fixed. A wide reader, and deeply interested in current topics of debate, he became a partisan as naturally as young men of his type must. Bethany College, situated on the border-line between freedom and slavery, and receiving students from both sides of that line, was an active theatre of discussion and of partisanship, touching the great question that was as much up for settlement between 1852 and 1857 as is the liquor traffic now. There met in daily contact, the hot-blooded fire-eater of the South, the hot-headed Aboli-

tionist of the North, and the cooler conservative from
either section, who daily discussed the issue of those
times.

Young Brooks was radically Southern, in temper and
sympathy, and he took the extreme Southern side. Yet
with all his fire and vigor he stood for free speech. He
considered the black man inferior, and fit only to be a
slave ; but for the white man who held otherwise he
claimed the right of opinion, and the right to voice that
opinion when and where he would. Upon one occasion
an older fellow-student, of opposite political faith,
preached an Abolition sermon, and nearly all the slavery
advocates but Brooks left the church before it was
ended, and hastily prepared to mob the Northern offender
when he should come forth. Brooks and a few others
declared against the outrage, and said they would defend the young man with their lives. They formed a
cordon around him as he left the church, and saw him
safely home. Brooks hated the utterances of the Abolitionist, and despised him for making them, but insisted that freedom of speech must be preserved.

Up to the beginning of his college course Mr. Brooks
had intended to enter the legal profession, and, young as
he was, had commenced the elementary study of law
under his father's direction. But the teaching and
preaching of Alexander Campbell changed the whole
trend of his life. The conviction that he, too, must become a preacher of the Gospel, as his father had become,
grew upon him, and would not be put away. He struggled against it long and bitterly. His temperament inclined him with strong leanings to a career where com-
bativeness would tell most efficiently, and in which he
could exercise his controversial talents to the fullest extent. He rebelled against the milder and more serene

work of the ministry. Yet he accepted it in full and
final surrender of his own desire, and leaving Bethany
when but twenty years old, went about his Master's
work with prompt cheerfulness, as ambitious to push
forward in that as in his boyish labors gone by.

CHAPTER II.

Mr. Brooks began preaching in the same community where he was raised, and began with "a protracted meeting." He had but three sermons arranged, and probably did not apprehend the success which came. People rallied for miles around, and the movement grew in power from the start. The young preacher grew with it, and went forward successfully without the preparation usually deemed indispensable. The excitement spread beyond that locality ; his name became widely familiar ; and for five years he was occupied in Mason and the adjoining counties of Northern Kentucky, in pastoral, evangelical, and controversial effort, with results quite surprising. Thousands were brought into the Church of the Disciples, which received an impetus of growth and an accession of influence, through all that region, gratifying and lasting. There must have been strong magnetism in the young man, and unusual pulpit gifts, to yield such a harvest, even where the fields were white.

During his first year's ministry, he met in his native county Miss Sue E. Osborn, one of Kentucky's beautiful and accomplished young ladies, of a rare, refined nature, almost ethereal, and won her to himself. They were married on October 14th, 1857, and in three weeks, with heart near to breaking, the young husband laid her away—

> " But a cold, white silence, with sainted face,
> And a smile that an angel of God might grace."

He coveted release from service thereabouts, and wished greatly to go where memories would not be so abundant and powerful ; he made up his mind, in fact, to remove to Missouri, where already his parents had gone.   But Flemingsburg held him for a series of meetings there, and keeping this engagement fixed the after course of years.   The church at Flemingsburg invited him to remain as its pastor when the revival meetings were over.   He declined, still meaning to go West.   The presiding elder, a brother of Governor Bishop, of Ohio, asked him what salary would induce him to stay, and he named figures which were intended to overmatch any possible seriousness of consideration ; but Mr. Bishop accepted them at once, and concluded the contract on the spot.

He was not permitted, however, to settle down at ease in the pastoral care of one church.   He went about much, as has been intimated, in evangelistic ways, and erelong found himself drawn into religious controversy, to which, it may be assumed, he had no grave objection.   The Methodists and the Disciples came somehow into heated public debate, and it was natural, perhaps inevitable, that Mr. Brooks should stand as the defender of his Church.   He was called for from many places, and gladly met every call.   Popular feeling ran high. Men of all classes grew absorbed in the sectarian discussions going on, and the topics there considered were up for debate as well on every highway and at every country store.   For the pulpit contests the best talent was employed on both sides, and logic, wit, keen retort, and profound erudition had their frequent opportunity. One of Mr. Brooks's most notable debates, with Rev.

Dr. Fitch, in Winchester, Ky., had pamphlet publication and was widely scattered.

The encounter most happy for Mr. Brooks was at Bethel, Bath County, for during that discussion he met Miss Sue E. Robertson, to whom, after a brief courtship, he was married, in 1859. She possessed remarkable attractions, and was much sought after, but the brilliant and impetuous young Disciple cleared the field of all competitors, and has been supremely grateful for his good fortune ever since. To them have been born five children, one of whom lived but a few weeks. John T., the only son, is now married and in business at Kansas City; Lida, the oldest daughter, has been several years her father's private secretary, and is known and loved by the temperance workers of Missouri; Bessie is just blooming into womanhood, and five-years-old Susie is the pet and favorite of all. Dr. Brooks freely admits the helpful influence of his wife upon all his life these nearly thirty years. He needed, he concedes, the wise restraint of her gentleness, and her calm, equable disposition; and to her he credits his success in varied lines of being and doing, while she modestly disclaims any hand in his achievements, and confesses herself proud of his career.

While he remained at Flemingsburg the church there determined to establish a college to meet the demands of Northeastern Kentucky for an academical institution. Mr. Brooks raised the money wherewith to erect the necessary building, superintended the erection thereof, and turned it over to the Board of Curators. Then, not wishing to quit his chosen calling, he resigned the pastorate, that a distinguished educator might accept the pastorate and the college presidency together, marrying the salary of both places; but the infant college was a

failure the first year, though equipped with a full faculty.
Mr. Brooks was urged to take the presidency and controlling management, and consented, under stipulation
that he should retire so soon as the institution might
come to a self-sustaining basis. This end was achieved
in two years, when there were two hundred students in
attendance, an able corps of instructors, and prosperity
in each department. It was on account of his success
here that his Alma Mater gave him the honorary degree
of A.M.

It was during the first year of the war that Dr. Brooks
took charge of this school. And those were warm times
in that neighborhood, for Flemingsburg was on debatable ground, one day in the Union lines and the next,
perchance, in the Confederate. Both armies occupied
it, or contested for it, and worried its inhabitants with
their vacillations. The Southern Methodist Conference
met there on one occasion when a company of Union
soldiers held the town. Pickets were thrown out by
these, and all egress was denied, and rumor said that
each member of the conference would be required to
take the iron-clad oath then provided for all rebels,
such as most of those preachers were known to be.

On Sunday morning, as the bells rang out their tune-
ful call to church, pickets west of town reported a flag
of truce, borne by one Pete Everett, who said that
Humphrey Marshall's troops were just over the hill,
and who in his name demanded unconditional surrender
of the place. The Federal commander, though uneasy,
was brave, and gathered his little command in the court-
house to make fight. Everett, with a score of men,
waited on the hill, ostensibly to hear from Marshall's
force behind him, and then issued an order to clear the
town of women and children, as attack would begin in

thirty minutes. It was all a flimsy ruse, but effectual. Women and children left for the fields, and with them went those preachers who did not wish to take the hated oath. One of them was a guest of Dr. Brooks, who has never seen him since, and who sometimes wonders if he is fleeing yet.

An incident of the same period illustrates the grit in and firmness of Dr. Brooks's character. The Union Legislature of Kentucky had passed a law compelling all teachers to take an iron-clad oath of non-sympathy with the Rebellion. This oath Dr. Brooks had resolved never to accept, and yet it embarrassed him greatly. His Board of Curators was composed of both Unionists and rebels, all friendly to their president, and desirous that he continue in his position ; but because he was a known rebel sympathizer, and refused to swear otherwise, the Grand Jury, then in session, were about to indict him. One of the curators, himself a magistrate, visited the college, and informed Mr. Brooks of the proposed indictment and arrest, and urged him to take the oath and save trouble. Looking him steadily in the eye, Mr. Brooks said :

" My dear sir, you know me, and you know that I will never take that oath. I cannot swear to a lie ; I would go to prison first. My horse is now saddled, and in two minutes I will be on his back, and on my way to Marshall's army. I am not going to prison ; I will not take the oath.''

" But," said the curator, " it will ruin the college and the church.''

" So be it," said Brooks ; " I had rather ruin both than to perjure my soul. But if you are so anxious for me to stay, as you are a magistrate, I will take an oath such as I may prescribe ; and you can return to the

Grand Jury room and say that you have just come from the administration of that oath to me and thus stop proceedings. I will take this oath : ' I solemnly swear that I will support the Constitution of these United States and of the State of Kentucky as long as I am a citizen of this State.' '' And this oath, there and then taken, was the only one to which he ever subscribed during the war, though the experience referred to did not close all his difficulties growing out of secession sympathy.

In 1862 the Union authorities in Kentucky determined summarily to arrest certain leading ministers of his Church, and throw them into prison, as a wholesome lesson to all, hoping so to check rebellious tendencies and weaken the Confederate cause. The most distinguished minister in the Church of the Disciples at that time was Dr. Winthrop H. Hopkins, a warm personal friend of Mr. Brooks. Dr. Hopkins was arrested at Lexington, and sent to the military prison at Louisville. On his way there he passed through Eminence, where Mr. Brooks was then preaching, having left Flemingsburg, and shook hands with the latter from the car-window, whispering, as he did so,

" I am gone up, and you are second on the list."

Knowing what this meant, Mr. Brooks grew more wary, and set himself to avoid arrest. Influential friends were vigilant in his behalf, and arranged to warn him when danger came near. Warning came on one Sunday morning after his sermon's close. He was to be arrested and imprisoned next day. That night he slipped out of town, and sought the safeguard of some rebel forces then in Northeast Kentucky, with whom he remained awhile, until the excitement passed over. Then he returned and quietly resumed pastoral duty in his old field.

Mr. Brooks was never an enlisted soldier, though all

his sympathies and hopes lay with the rebel side. He did not hesitate to feed and clothe rebel soldiers at any time, to nurse them when wounded and to care for them whenever in his power ; and this, too, in the face of General Burnside's order making death the penalty for such aid. He believed they were fighting for the rights guaranteed him and others by the Constitution, and he was as loyal to them as he thought they were loyal to said rights. But it should be said also that he never refused to care for Federals in need, when call was made upon him in their extremity. His humanity was not less quick and responsive than was his sectional feeling and his love of State rights.

In 1865 Mr. Brooks left Eminence, where his pastorate was highly successful, and took charge of the church at Winchester. His Eminence people voted unanimously, save one man out of three hundred, to have him remain, but Winchester needed him. The church there was large, and all broken up by the war, having at one time both a Union and a rebel preacher. He remained there five years, and restored unity, church fellowship, and admirable religious feeling. He counts that pastorate the most fortunate and efficient in his experience. When he retired from it, in 1870, to take charge of the First Christian Church in St. Louis, every member of his congregation protested. The love between pastor and people was there something uncommon, and very beautiful to see. He had brought them all into the fruits of Gospel peace. They were loth to bid him good-by. Nothing but his long desire to make a residence in the West, and the opening there of wider fields of usefulness, induced him to sever the ties so dearly cherished and so binding, yet he has never regretted the change.

CHAPTER III.

In the eighteen years since his removal to Missouri,
Dr. Brooks has held successful pastorates in St. Louis,
Mexico, Warrensburg, and Belton, and now has charge
of the Independence Avenue Christian Church at Kansas
City. He has also done wide evangelistic work, bap-
tizing many thousand converts. For three successive
years he presided over the General Conference of his
Church in Missouri, and with entire satisfaction. It is
said, to-day, by those who should know, that no man in
the denomination of Disciples, in that whole State,
wields greater influence, or carries more weight than
he. His activities have been ever varied, and his energies always aggressive. He has not stood content with
moderate effort and average returns. His native desire
to push forward and achieve mastery has never left him.
He was born to keep in the front rank.

His inclination to reach out in many ways early identified him with organizations outside the Church. One
of these, and the one which he holds in warmest regard,
is known as the Ancient Order of United Workmen.
It is reputed the oldest benevolent institution, or order,
in the country, as it is numerically the largest. Its
geographical jurisdiction extends all over the United
States and Canada, and it disburses annually two millions of dollars to the widowed and fatherless. It is a
mighty brotherhood. Dr. Brooks has been a member

of the supreme body—the law-making power—several years, and has had much to do with shaping its polity and moulding its administration.

It does not exist for the ordinary purposes of a secret order, but is purely benevolent. As such it had a genuine "boom" in Missouri, beginning about the time of Dr. Brooks's early active connection with it. In 1877 there were but twenty lodges in the State; the next year these and their membership had doubled. He was chosen Grand Foreman in 1879, and Grand Master Workman in 1880, since which time he has attended every meeting of the Supreme Lodge. In 1886 he was unanimously elected Supreme Master Workman—the head of the entire order—and his administration was one of the most successful ever attained in the history of the organization. He regards his elevation to the Supreme Mastership as one of the greatest honors ever conferred upon him, and holds himself at the order's call for service and sacrifice whenever he is needed.

As has been said, his temperance efforts began when he was very young. After his early identification with the Sons of Temperance, he became a Good Templar, and was conspicuously active in that temperance order, often appearing on the floor of the Grand Lodge.

When "the Murphy movement" struck Missouri, in '78 and '79, Dr. Brooks threw himself into it with his accustomed zeal, and his appeals in behalf of total abstinence were most effective. Up to that time all his temperance activities had been along the old lines of moral suasion; he had never thought much about the legal side of this reform. But the more he labored to save men from their cups, the more futile appeared such labor with the saloon left unmolested, the more imperative did it become, in his opinion, to *prohibit* the liquor traffic. Thinking so, and feeling always intensely what he thought, he began talking his mind rather freely in the "Murphy meetings," much to the consternation of those mild-mannered temperance evangelists whose motto was, "With charity for all and malice toward none," and whose methods meant no harm to saloon-keepers. Naturally they came to disparage his utterances, and between him and them there has been no real fellowship since. Perhaps, like the craftsmen of Ephesus, they feared the ruin of their business if Prohibition doctrine should prevail.

But moral suasion talk led naturally to legal suasion endeavor. Months of agitation through Missouri resulted in the published call for a convention, to meet in Sedalia, July 4th, 1880 ; and to this convention, when held, came twenty-five delegates, who organized the Prohibition State Alliance, and chose Dr. Brooks President. With this organization began the real battle against liquor in Missouri, and it has not ceased a day since.

Preaching on Sundays to his charge at Mexico, Dr. Brooks travelled from one end of the State to the other, arguing for Prohibition from the time that alliance was formed ; and the first result was a Legislature elected under pledge to submit a Prohibitory Constitutional Amendment to the people. And submission would have followed, but for the management of party leaders, speaking from Washington by command of Mr. Schade, the brewers' attorney, kept there at national headquarters under large pay. The amendment was defeated for lack of a few votes in the Upper House, as has happened more than once in Legislatures not Democratic, at the North. The national party's necessity compelled submission's defeat ; and why those few votes were lacking in the Missouri Senate, some Democratic politicians and certain Republican brewers could tell, if so disposed.

There was increased Prohibition sentiment in the Democratic Party, as nobody could doubt; and this fact greatly encouraged Dr. Brooks, while it as greatly alarmed the liquor men. Earnestly believing that political leaders must respect the popular will, the alliance met in 1882, at Cameron, and resolved to push on agitation and the manufacture of Prohibition sentiment with greater zeal, determined to secure the next General Assembly, beyond any peradventure, and force their pet measure through. Of course the brewers took fresh alarm, and Senator Vest, in their interest, took the field to down Prohibition. So taking the field, he took open issue with his party; for the Democrats, in convention assembled that season, had resolved, "That we favor the largest liberty consistent with the public good." And this inoffensive utterance was regarded by Dr. Brooks and his coadjutors as a temperance plank; indeed, it was so regarded by the liquor side.

Three influences or agencies were employed to bring the Democratic Party back into line with the brewers:

1. High license, as a professed temperance measure.

2. Mr. Vest, as the eloquent advocate of the brewers.

3. Personal abuse of Dr. Brooks, as the wretch who, under the guise of temperance and morality, had turned the party over to the Republican theory of Prohibition.

These influences were expected to stop the Prohibition craze, to cool the heads of fanatical reformers, and to perpetuate the liquor system securely. They were worked for all they were worth, and the Missouri State campaign of 1882 went upon record as remarkable in many ways. Senator Vest and Dr. Brooks were squarely pitted against each other inside the Democratic Party ; for Mr. Vest planted himself on the national platform of that party, and Dr. Brooks put both feet on the State platform, as everywhere interpreted for temperance, and their long debate came to be ranked with that of Benton and Shannon, in Missouri, and of Lincoln and Douglas, in Illinois, on the earlier great reform. Mr. Vest was witty, sarcastic, fiery, and eloquent, but unacquainted with the history and philosophy of Prohibition ; while Dr. Brooks added to like platform gifts close familiarity with his theme, and the advantage of approaching it upon high moral and religious ground. It is probable that never, in his most combative earlier years, did Dr. Brooks covet a wider field for controversial exercise than was now afforded him, and he enjoyed it to the utmost. He blazed across the State like a hot cyclone. He amazed his opponent, who had made the serious mistake of underestimating his abilities ; and he never failed to down Mr. Vest before a fair audience.

Again, a submission Legislature was elected ; again, the people looked to their representatives for honest service in legislative halls ; again, the liquor powers forced party managers to do their will. High license was sprung upon them, as being, with the brewers, a choice between ills ; and members of the Legislature known to be temperance men, and chosen representatives as such on the distinct issue up, snatched at any excuse to serve party ends, voted for the sham, and made it Missouri's policy. Dr. Brooks opposed it with all his might, declared it a subterfuge and a cheat ; but the party decree had gone forth, Democracy must nowhere be committed to Prohibition, the people must not rule, the commands of the brewers must be obeyed.

It is true that some noble and influential Democrats

held with Dr. Brooks in this contest, and did most val-
iantly assail the saloon.   Among them were Mr. J. M.
McMichael, Colonel William F. Switzler, Governor
Charles P. Johnson, and Governor B. Gratz Brown.
And concurring in their judgment, loth to leave the
party they upheld, Dr. Brooks and his colleagues of the
State Alliance agreed to continue the fight along its old
lines, and pull true as Democrats yet another year.
The alliance met at Warrensburg that fall of 1883, and
was welcomed by Miss Lida Brooks.   Dr. Brooks, in
his annual address, reviewed the progress of Prohibition
effort in behalf of constitutional amendments wherever
proposed, citing Oregon, Maine, Ohio, Iowa, Texas,
Missouri, Indiana, and West Virginia, and briefly stat-
ing what causes led to the defeat of submission in some
States and the partial or complete failure of submission,
when before the people, in others, and speaking more
in detail of Missouri and of their late failure before the
Legislature, he declared :

"Two successive Legislatures had refused to submit the amendment to the voters of the State, and that, too, in the face of a demand
for submission such as had never been manifested before.   This repeated unwillingness to trust the people aroused an indignation which
made itself felt in every part of the State.   Under the influence of
this spirit the last Democratic Convention assembled in Jefferson
City.   The Republican brewers of St. Louis had entered into a contract with Democratic leaders to transfer their vote to the Democratic
Party, and to give it a solid Democratic delegation to Congress upon
condition that the Democracy of the State would antagonize submission and Prohibition ; they to furnish the sinews of war and the
leaders to arrange matters in the Democratic camp.   With this
understanding the Democratic delegation appeared at Jefferson City,
demanding an anti-Prohibition plank in the platform to be adopted.
This was refused by the decisive vote of 82 to 21.   While this vote
was not an absolute test of the submission strength in the convention, yet friend and foe recognized it as the triumph of submission-
ists in the party.   On the other hand, the Republican Convention

convening afterward in the same city, at the dictation of the same brewers, declared in favor of high license, the chair arbitrarily ruling out a motion to amend."

Then Dr. Brooks went on to show how, with the party overwhelmingly for submission, the brewers captured the party's executive, placed that and Mr. Vest upon the national platform, and made the State fight as shown, and how these brewers, failing before the people, were again successful in fixing things with the Legislature to their entire satisfaction. "Principle, honor, and country all went down," he declared, "in the eager contest for the vote of the saloon-keeper." He was evidently sick of the whole Democratic situation, as determined by Democratic leadership.

He grew sicker yet. For in a few months it became evident that acknowledged leaders were bound to commit the State party to its national saloon policy without reserve, and that General Marmaduke, a violent opposer of Prohibition in speech and personal habit, was to be made the party's candidate for governor, in open alignment with that policy. On behalf of the alliance, after no doubt could be entertained of the Democratic plan, Dr. Brooks interviewed leading Republicans, to see if they would not declare for Prohibition, and either nominate some Prohibition Democrat, like ex-Lieutenant-Governor Johnson or Governor Brown, or make no nomination and allow such a nominee to be put up by Prohibitionists and pledge him their support.

In accordance with this appeal, leading Republicans held a conference at St. Louis, where the Democratic Prohibition element had representation through Judge James Baker. The decision was to stand by the brewers. "We have little Republican strength outside St. Louis," said the leaders of that faith, "and here our strength lies with the brewing class. We should lose that were we to espouse temperance." Thus reasoning, they declined to accept the suggestions made ; and for Dr. Brooks, Judge Baker, Governor Johnson, and others who believed with them, there was left only the alternative of a new party relation, or open support of Marmaduke and the saloons. Against this latter course conscience and patriotism made revolt ; and they issued the call for a convention, to meet at Sedalia, August 19th, 1884.

Radical State Prohibitionists, in favor of the National Prohibition Party and its candidates, had already called a convention to meet in Sedalia that day, and both calls brought together a fine assemblage of men and women numbering nearly five hundred. Though they met in separate halls, they were in hearty accord on the matter of State action, and differed only as to endorsing a national ticket. A Committee of Conference was appointed by each body, and their proceedings went forward in close harmony. After much enthusiastic discussion, and encouraging reports from the entire State, both bodies nominated Dr. Brooks for governor, and the issue of Prohibition was fairly and permanently made in Democratic Missouri.

On September 6th Dr. Brooks formally accepted this nomination, in a letter which pungently told many truths. Among other things, he said :

" There can be no question in the mind of any intelligent citizen of the Republic, that the permanency and stability of our form of government depends upon the intelligence and morality of the voter."

And after further utterance like this, he asked :

" Shall the Church and school, or the saloon and beergarden, educate the future voters of the Republic ?"

The campaign which followed was hot and unsparing Dr. Brooks had burned his Democratic bridges behind him. He had fine opportunity to lash the opposition, for General Marmaduke, the Democratic candidate, was a known user of liquors, and Mr. Ford, the Republican nominee, was a wholesale whiskey-seller. But the Prohibition candidate held himself on the high plane of principle, and made his canvass tell mightily for clean politics, honest party methods, and the election of pure men. In forty days he spoke in forty counties, and from two to four hours a day. He was much assailed, but his record could not be impeached.

The election returns gave Mr. Cleveland 30,000 majority, while Marmaduke ran in, as by the skin of his teeth, on a pitiful margin of 420. Ford led his ticket by about 5000. By the count of returning boards Dr. Brooks was given 10,500 votes, but it was discovered afterward that in some counties the Prohibition vote was thrown out bodily, and some have believed that the vote so disallowed would have exceeded the vote returned. Clearly, the Republicans who had so professed temperance did not support Brooks ; indeed, their great organ, the *Globe-Democrat*, had advised them all to stand by Ford.

CHAPTER IV.

THE campaign of 1884 brought Dr. Brooks into conspicuous prominence, and the national leaders of Prohibition came to look upon him as the natural head of their forces through the Southwest. In 1886 he was appointed Southwestern District Agent for the National Prohibition Bureau, and as such he visited Arkansas, Texas, Mississippi, Alabama, and Tennessee, doing efficient service for the cause. A former slave-holder, and a life-long Democrat, he could appeal to Southern reason with less of prejudice against him than met the Northern Prohibitionist going there. He also visited the Eastern States during camp season, and appeared upon various platforms in New York, Pennsylvania, and Ohio.

At the great National Convention in Indianapolis, he was from the outset regarded as more certain than any other man to be nominated with General Fisk. When roll-call was progressing by States for a Vice-Presidential candidate, Mr. George C. Christian, an ex-Kentuckian of Illinois, eloquently presented his name, summarizing what these pages have shown about him, and referring to him as " the peer of any man in statesmanship, in loyalty, and in Christian character." His nomination was seconded by Mrs. Clara Hoffman, President of the Missouri State Woman's Christian Temperance Union, in these words :

" MR. PRESIDENT : I am glad and happy to be chosen to voice the unanimous sentiment of the delegation of Missouri for the candidate that has been brought forward—my brother, Dr. John A. Brooks. [Applause.] Having worked side by side with him for five years in the State of Missouri, one of the most difficult States that we have to work in ; one of the border States, you will remember ; having worked with him side by side to break down the aristocracy of rum, and to break down the prejudice that had been built up and maintained against Prohibition or anything looking toward Prohibition ; against the voice of woman being heard upon the platform or anywhere outside of her home, even though it were heard in entreaty for protection to her home—I say, having worked side by side with John A. Brooks during these years, I stand here prepared to speak of his worth, of his ability, of his loyalty, of his courage, of his matchless eloquence, which against all the odds that he had to meet in the State of Missouri he was able to overcome, taking a great Democratic majority, a great arrogant majority, a great aristocratic majority in that State, and reducing it to a mere pitiful plurality in one campaign, never rivalled since the matchless campaign made by Thomas Benton in that State. I come here to stand for and second the nomination of Dr. John A. Brooks, because I know of his Christian character, because I know of his loyalty to the Prohibition Party, because I know how he set the wheel in motion in that State by his earnest, constant work with the Legislature ; and I am proud to stand here before you to-night and say that no man, from ocean to ocean, nor from the Great Lakes to the Gulf, can be found worthier to bear our standard on to victory than this man. I come to second that nomination, because I know that here we shall truly have a union in our standard-bearers—a true union that shall unite North and South, and East and West—that shall be the union so touchingly spoken of here last night of the Blue and the Gray. And I trust that this nomination will receive the unanimous indorsement of this most magnificent convention." [Applause.]

New York's total vote of one hundred and thirteen was thrown for Dr. Brooks, and his nomination followed finally by acclamation. He was called on for a speech, and roused his hearers, if possible, to a higher pitch of enthusiasm than they had known since the outbreak over General Fisk's nomination ceased, an hour before. In part, he said :

"I wish it were in my power to-night to express to you my feelings upon this occasion. Having placed at the head of your ticket that peerless American statesman, the pride not only of New Jersey but of this country, and especially of my adopted State, of which he was so long a citizen, by your sufferance to-night and your partiality I shall believe, you have placed me with him upon this ticket. I confess to you to-night that but one man in all America has been honored more, or can be honored more on this continent, than he who speaks to you, and that man is Clinton B. Fisk. I had rather stand to-night indorsed by this body of my countrymen as its candidate, without the faintest semblance of a hope of election, than to be indorsed as the candidate of both the old parties put together. [Applause.] And as I stand, my countrymen, under that motto, I want to emphasize, with all the heart that I have, those precious truths which it enunciates. Standing as I do, looking back upon half a century gone, looking over the education and training of early life, the conditions that surrounded that life, the dark cloud of sectionalism that arose and the final baptism of blood and fire that swept over my section, I want to stand to-night in this presence in the hope before God that this sectionalism is buried, and buried forever. [Applause.]

" Cradled in the lap of human slavery, brought up under its fostering care, it is not strange that I, in the morning of life, felt, in common with my section, that I was not half so great a sinner as I now know myself to have been ; and if you think that is strange, you have only to look around upon these Republicans and Democrats who continue to be such awful sinners in the presence of the light of this day in which we live. [Applause.]

" When the war had closed and I had time to look around, I remembered one precious utterance from that Book of books which you and I love so much and revere, that no murderer can enter into the kingdom of God, and that he that hateth his brother is a murderer. I hated some of you with all the hatred that I had or was capable of, and when these clouds cleared away, I said : ' My God ! I want at last to enter the portals of the skies, and by the grace of God I will tear from my heart the sectionalism of the past.' But if I had not succeeded, before God and the Judgment I would not want to act as do these extremists North and South, and hand that hatred as a bloody heritage down to my posterity and close the gates of heaven against them.

" I remember, some years since, to have stood upon the Common of Boston in the presence of a bronze statue. There stood the great Commoner. At his feet a slave was chained, and in his hand was a hatchet or an axe that was falling to break the chain of the slave. I was all alone. I stopped and looked up into his face, and the memories of a lifetime flooded through my mind. I was back again in the arms of my old negro mammy in the South, playing with her children upon the green, romping with them and sharing with them their sorrows and joys, realizing that they would have died for me, if need be. I saw as I grew up in life the agitation that sprang up in this nation over that institution, and I saw the little speck of cloud as it gathered in its majesty and broke upon my section with all the fury of internecine war. I saw the battle and heard the groans of the dying, the whistle of the shell and the rattle of musketry, and I saw my country baptized in the blood of my section. But I looked into the face of Abraham Lincoln, and I said : ' Sir, on that question of slavery and the preservation of the Union, I want to say to you now, that while I was as honest and sincere as any man living, you were right and I was wrong.' [Great applause.]

" But I want to say to you another thing ; I do not want to deceive you, my countrymen. I want to say to you that there are sad memories among our people. We were whipped. Sam Jones says that you say you whipped us, but that is a mistake ; we simply wore ourselves out trying to whip you. But whether that be true or not, we were whipped, and we went back to our desolation and to our homes under such conditions, loyal, as Mr. Small said to-night, loyal throughout the South to the flag of our country and to the Union that is restored forever. But, my countrymen, there are sad memories that linger back in those days of trial. And when an old man—in his dotage now—like Jefferson Davis, who led a forlorn hope, goes out from home a few miles, and some old comrade that was with him upon the battlefield gets out an old rebel flag, and they fall upon it and kiss it, does that indicate, as some of our friends up North would seem to think, when they paw the earth like wild bulls from Bashan, that the South is in rebellion again? No, sir ! In God's name let these old men, as they think of their fallen comrades, shed a tear of sympathy at their graves ; but those who wore the ' Gray ' are with you upon the living issues of this hour, and would go into the battle-field and die for this Union and for its redemption from the hands of men who would injure it.''

At the immense meeting in the Metropolitan Opera House, June 22d, when the formal tender of his nomination was made by Hon. W. J. Groo, he delivered a powerful address of acceptance, and immediately set out upon his campaign.

www.ingramcontent.com/pod-product-compliance
Lightning Source LLC
Chambersburg PA
CBHW021034030726
47496CB00006B/1530